THE DRUID NEXT DOOR

FAE OUT OF WATER - BOOK TWO

E.J. RUSSELL

RIPTIDE
PUBLISHING

Riptide Publishing
PO Box 1537
Burnsville, NC 28714
www.riptidepublishing.com

The Druid Next Door

Cover art: Lou Harper, louharper.com/design.html
Editor: Rachel Haimowitz
Layout: L.C. Chase, lcchase.com/design.htm

ISBN: 978-1-62649-622-4

First edition
August, 2017

Also available in ebook:
ISBN: 978-1-62649-621-7

THE DRUID NEXT DOOR

FAE OUT OF WATER - BOOK TWO

E.J. RUSSELL

RIPTIDE
PUBLISHING

Dedicated to those of us who believe we've learned all there is to know about ourselves, only to realize (to our great astonishment) that it's never too late to uncover a new truth that changes everything.

TABLE OF CONTENTS

CHAPTER ❈ 1

A jar of pickles.

A fecking jar of fecking pickles, gods damn it to all the hells.

Mal Kendrick stood in the middle of his kitchen, the victorious pickle jar jammed in the crook of his right elbow, his thrice-blasted useless right hand flapping in the air. *Foil a coup to topple the Queen from her throne and this is my reward?*

Sod it, he was a bloody legend on both sides of the Faerie threshold: the never-defeated Enforcer of the Seelie Court, the designated muscle for every supe council from vampire to dragon shifter, the undisputed lord of Outer World bar hookups, who'd never failed to pull the hottest man in the place for his shag-du-jour.

Yet he was helpless against a jar of fecking pickles.

"It's not fair."

"Talking to yourself is a sign of mental instability, Mal." His brother-in-law swept into the kitchen, a grocery bag in one arm and a cardboard box tucked under the other.

At least David hadn't brought his infernal physical therapy machine this time.

"Don't you ever knock?" Mal set the pickles on the counter next to the bloody energy-efficient refrigerator.

"Why bother? You never answer."

"I could have been banging some guy over the counter for all you know," Mal grumbled, relieving David of the grocery bag with his left hand.

"In that case, I'd have discreetly withdrawn and done a happy dance all the way down the sidewalk."

"Spare the neighbors that sight—they hate me enough already."

David pouted, which was far more adorable than should be allowed. "Alun loves my dancing. He told me so just last night."

"He's your husband. He has to say shite like that. Besides, maybe he needed a good laugh." He peered into the bag. *Beer.* Thank the Goddess. He was running dangerously low. "The sight of you dancing would be enough for the covenant committee to fine me for violation of the eyesore ban. They might ask me to vacate the premises." He stopped, one six-pack of microbrews in his hand. "Although that might be a good thing. Go ahead, boyo. Dance away."

"I don't know why you don't like this place." David set the box on the fecking recycled glass countertop. "We thought you'd like it because you've got the whole wetlands preserve practically in your backyard."

Mal shrugged. "It tries too hard. Solar panels. Geothermal energy. Drought-resistant ground coverings. Feh. Besides, I never asked you to buy me a fragging house."

David's gray-blue eyes turned serious and so kind that Mal wanted to punch the refrigerator in its energy-efficient gut. "If you hadn't stopped Rodric's sword strike, Alun would be dead. I'd buy you fifty houses, a hundred, the whole freaking *subdivision*, and it still wouldn't be payment enough. Besides," he flipped open the box, "I'm the one with the dragon treasure. I can afford it, and we're family now, so you can just shut up and deal."

Although David's chin lifted with the stubborn pride that kept Mal's perfect big brother totally dick-whipped, he still looked like an apprentice brownie who'd spent hours on a feast for his master, only to have the bastard throw the beautifully prepared meal on the floor.

Ah, shite. I can be such a bloody arse sometimes. Most times, actually, but he used to be able to cover it up with something resembling charm. Seems he'd lost that ability along with his hand, his job, and his place in Faerie.

He pulled one bottle out of the six-pack and pried the cap off with the opener Alun had mounted on the underside of the counter. Shite, he wouldn't have been able to open his own damn beer without help from his brother. "Yes. Sure, Dafydd *bach*. It's great."

David smiled crookedly and turned away to poke about in the box, but not before Mal caught the hurt his lake-storm eyes. "You know, I'm still not used to your face without the scruff."

Mal rubbed his perfectly smooth chin. None of the highborn fae sported facial hair, although when he'd still commanded his fae powers, he'd manufactured a little magical stubble to make the club boys swoon. "What can I say? No connection to the One Tree—no *glamourie*. No *glamourie*—no scruff."

"Oh. Right. Well, um, I brought you some things."

"You brought me beer, so you've already qualified for sainthood."

"You don't believe in saints."

"Just because the fae don't have any doesn't mean I can't adapt to my new home." His permanent home. Away from Faerie. Away from the Seelie Court and everything he'd ever known. Away from the only work that gave him any satisfaction. He chugged half his beer. "Not like I have much choice."

"Mal, you can't lose hope. Alun says there's always a way to reverse a curse, that the end is always contained in the beginning." He took Mal's unresponsive right hand. "That night, the Queen said—"

"I have to make whole what I cost her. Not a chance." Mal pulled away and strode to the French doors that opened onto his patio—paved with recycled concrete, for shite's sake—and stared at the greensward that sloped to the edge of the wetlands. "Even if I could put that bastard Rodric's hand back on his arm, I wouldn't. That piece of shite deserved what he got and more."

David's footsteps whispered on the cork floor. "Believe me, no one is more on board with that than I am. I'm the one he planned to sacrifice, remember? You didn't only save Alun that night. You saved me. You saved the Queen. You saved every single Seelie fae from suffering under Rodric's rule. Trust me—I don't blame you. But there has to be a way to lift the curse. We just have to find out how."

"Can you . . ." Mal swallowed around a sudden lump in his throat. "Isn't there anything you can do?"

He immediately wished he could take back the words. David had recently discovered he was *achubydd*, the last known member of a meta-magical race who could heal with a touch, whose essence had the power to reverse catastrophic harm or effect extraordinary physical change. But the bigger the change, the higher the toll on the *achubydd*. Until now, Mal had resisted begging for help because— well, for one thing, he never begged. Why the hells should a jar of fecking pickles push him over the edge?

"I'd do anything for you or your brothers. But I'm still learning how this stuff works." He recaptured Mal's hand, stroking the palm, but Mal felt nothing. Not a touch. Not a tickle. Nothing. "With Alun's curse, I could see the lines of energy running through his body, the pain backed up in his veins. But with your hand . . ." He shook his head. "It's as if it's not there at all. Your energy patterns are perfectly normal. They simply stop at your wrist."

Mal tugged his hand away and tucked it under his left arm. "Maybe you should just amputate the useless thing. At least then I could get a prosthesis."

"Don't say that. We'll find a way." David sounded so fierce that Mal had to chuckle. His brother-in-law had more determination than any ten men, and he'd needed it to break through Alun's armor of guilt and self-recrimination. "But, in the meantime, come and see what I've got for you."

Mal groaned. "Goddess preserve me."

David grinned and smacked Mal's shoulder. "Don't be a jerk. Accept our help. It won't kill you."

"No. I'll just wish it had. At least you didn't bring that blasted physical therapy machine this time."

David caught his lower lip between his teeth, and his gaze skittered away from Mal's face. "Well . . . as a matter of fact . . ."

The front door creaked open, and something scraped and clattered against the slate tiles in the entryway.

"Dafydd *bach*?" *That sounded like . . . No, it couldn't be.* "Where the hells should I put this thing?" But even the obvious irritation in the tone couldn't mask the beauty of a true bard's voice.

Mal turned a stunned look on David. "Gareth? How did you . . .?"

David shrugged, sheepish. "Um . . . surprise?"

Mal set his beer on the table and bolted around the corner into the living room. Sure enough, his younger brother was standing inside the door, the cables of the PT machine draped over his shoulder, the sun backlighting his golden curls like some freaking halo.

Mal covered the distance between them in three strides and grabbed Gareth in a tight hug, pounding him on the back, one-handed. "Shite, man. I had no idea you were back from your tour."

Gareth returned the hug and the pounding with interest. *Little brothers. Always trying to one-up their elders.* "I'm not. Portland's one of our stops. We're playing the Aladdin tonight, so I decided to squeeze in a trip out here to the wilds of—what is this benighted place again? Oh right. *Hills*boro."

"Smart-arse." Mal pulled back and flicked Gareth's hair with his fingers. "Get a haircut. You look like a revenant from the Middle Ages. Or the seventies."

Gareth's expression locked down. "I like it this way."

Shite. It wasn't Gareth who liked the outdated hairdo. It was his lover, gone these two hundred years and more.

"Well. Come in and check out the house Alun and his husband have forced on me."

Gareth handed the machine off to David and strolled into the living room. "Seems like a nice enough place. Beats the hells out of that hut where you squatted in bleeding Faerie, right?"

"It wasn't a hut."

"A hut, Mal, face it." Gareth pointed to the flat-screen TV mounted on the wall. "You have anything like that in Faerie?" He waved a hand at the L-shaped sofa upholstered in slubbed natural fibers. "Furniture that doesn't numb your arse? Hells, indoor plumbing?"

"I didn't need it." Mal gritted his teeth. "I had magic."

Sorrow flickered across Gareth's face before he recovered his habitual sardonic half smile. "Nothing technology can't replace. Trust me—in another few days, a month at most, you won't miss Faerie at all." He wandered through the archway into the dining room. "Goddess knows, I never do."

Mal followed in time to catch David opening the insulated blinds in the kitchen, flooding the rooms with unwelcome sunshine.

"I don't know why you want to live in a cave, Mal, I really don't."

"Don't you know, Dafydd *bach*?" Gareth sauntered over to the table and dropped into one of the ladder-back chairs, his long legs stretched out in front of him "It's his natural habitat."

"Then sunlight will do him good. You too, since you spend most of your time in dark studios or concert halls."

Gareth snorted and got up to wander off down the hallway.

Mal waited until he was out of earshot. "He's spending time with you and Alun now?" he murmured. "They've made up?"

"They're . . . working on it. Gareth still gives us the side-eye sometimes because you know—" David gestured between the two of them. "Cross-species relationship. He's still not a fan. But at least he's not treating Alun like a monster anymore." He held out a strange wooden object: a hinged wooden rod, each arm bowed out in the middle into a padded half circle. He brought the ends together to form a full circle, about ten centimeters in diameter. "Here."

Mal took it, letting it fall open again. "What is it? Some kind of kinky sex toy?"

"No, doofus. It's a jar opener. Aunt Cassie asked Nola to make it for you."

Mal dropped it on the counter as if it were hot iron. "Druid crap? Not on your life. With druids, there's always a catch."

"It's not bespelled, if that's what you're worried about. You can buy something like it at Fred Meyer or Kitchen Kaboodle, but Nola's is prettier."

"No, thanks. I'll manage without."

"Honestly. You and your brothers. Does *y Tylwyth Teg* mean 'stubborn as a twenty-mule-team hangover'? Go club-hopping and find someone to bang over the counter, for pity's sake. Work off some of that temper with sex the way you used to."

"How many guys do you think would be interested in me now? I can't even jack myself properly, let alone live up to my reputation."

David propped his fists on his narrow hips and glared. "Listen up. You've sustained a traumatic injury, like many other soldiers, and you've got a disability—a *temporary* disability. Don't you think it's time to accept that and learn to take help when it's offered?" His expression softened. "From where I stand, you're a hero—but not even heroes can handle *everything* on their own."

Mal scooped up his beer bottle and drained it. Damn it, he'd never had to ask for help before. Goddess knew he didn't want to do it now. He'd had no trouble twisting people around to do his will before, when it was only a matter of taking the mickey out of Alun or Gareth or even David. But now? When he had no choice? It stuck in his craw like an enchanted fishbone. He couldn't do it.

"Where's Alun today? I'm surprised he didn't tag along to make it a full family funhouse."

"He's mediating the quarterly supe council executive meeting." David shot Mal a half-guilty glance as he jockeyed the PT machine into position next to the dining table. "I'm sure they'd have asked you, just like usual, but two of the werewolf packs had a territorial dispute and the council leaders thought Alun's psychologist chops would be necessary."

Mal's hand clenched around the empty bottle. Typical of David to try to spare his feelings, but Mal held no illusions about his usefulness to the council. He'd only been the stand-in, the understudy, the Queen's Enforcer.

Alun had been the Queen's *Champion*.

Once the Champion was back, the Enforcer had to retire from the lists, and Alun had been miraculously restored to his full status, rights, and abilities, thanks to David helping him overcome his curse. So the councils, the Queen, even the club boys could get along without Mal just fine now.

But if I hadn't cut Rodric Luchullain's hand off at the wrist, Alun would be dead now—David too, and maybe Gareth as well.

Some sacrifices were worth the cost.

"Mal?" David fidgeted with one of the machine's cables. "Is that—I mean, are you okay?"

He forced a smile for David's benefit. "Aye. Alun's a manipulative bastard. Much more suited to the job. He should be able to get them to toe the party line."

David chuckled, the anxiety fading from his expression. "It takes a manipulative bastard to know one, Mal."

Mal glanced around, checking for Gareth's whereabouts. Judging by the sounds emanating from the back of the house, Gareth found the place just as ridiculous as Mal. Not that Gareth, the last full bard in all of Faerie, ever sounded anything less than perfectly musical, even when snorting derisively at low-flow toilets, LED light fixtures, or whatever else had caught his fancy.

"Has Alun had a chance to talk to the Queen yet?" Mal kept his voice low. With Gareth's longstanding hatred of the Queen, he'd have a fit if he knew Mal was angling to get an audience with

Her coldhearted Majesty—even though it was to get his sentence commuted and his curse removed.

David didn't meet his eyes as he set up the PT machine and affixed the contacts on Mal's right arm and hand. "I told you. He's been tied up with the supe councils."

"They can't take all his time. He has a practice to run and a husband to shag. You'd be a damn sight less chipper if he'd been neglecting that particular duty."

David's cheeks pinked—adorable, really. No wonder Alun had fallen so hard, but it had made him even more self-righteous than usual, holding his relationship up as the way to true happiness.

True happiness would be the end of this fragging exile and a return to my rightful place in Faerie.

Mal knew why he'd earned his cursed hand—he'd broken one of the primal laws of Faerie when he'd maimed the Queen's Consort. But why had he been cursed with one brother who believed the process of redemption was a necessary part of recovery, and another who didn't care if he ever set foot in Faerie again?

Mal wanted his old life back. All of it.

David turned on the machine, fiddling with the dials. "Do you feel anything?"

"No. Come on, Dafydd *bach*. It'll be awkward for Alun, begging a favor of the Queen, but you can talk him into it. You can talk him into anything with a flutter of those eyelashes and a wiggle of that perfect arse."

Instead of rising to the bait, David took Mal's right hand in both of his, his brow furrowing and his eyes losing focus. Mal felt the bone-deep heat that signaled David's *achubydd* powers and jerked his arm away.

"Stop it. Alun would kill me if I let you waste your essence on me."

David grabbed his hand again. "I'm not wasting it. I'm not giving you any more than a boost." He opened Mal's crabbed hand and pressed the fingers wide and flat. "Push back."

"I told you, I—"

"Damn it, Mal. Push back. As much as you'd like to think there's a magic bullet for this, there's not. One way or another, you have to put in the effort, just like any other wounded veteran."

Heat burst under Mal's sternum at the unfairness of David's words, and he leaned forward. "I—"

"There! You did it. You pushed back."

Mal stared at his hand, the heat dissipating under a flare of hope. "I did?"

"Absolutely. See? Human PT, plus a little *achubydd* special sauce, and you can make progress. But you have to do the work."

This work is shite. I want my old work. A position backed by the full tradition of Faerie. Mayhem sanctioned by the Queen. Magic as full and easy as breathing. Men who fell to his charm as easily as his enemies fell to his sword. Why was it that the one time he'd done a selfless thing, he'd gotten everything stripped away from him?

Right, then. Lesson learned: screw self-sacrifice. And as for taking the high road to recovery? Bollocks to that. He'd find an easier way.

He always had.

"You know what? Never mind. I'll figure this out on my own." He jerked his right arm, dislodging the machine contacts, and surged out of the chair.

"Mal—"

"You two can let yourselves out. And take that infernal contraption with you. I never want to see it again."

Ignoring David's wide-eyed hurt, he threw open the gods-be-damned triple-glazed French doors and stalked across the fecking reclaimed concrete patio toward the wetlands, his empty beer bottle still clutched in his hand.

CHAPTER ❈ 2

Bryce MacLeod stoppered the last water sample and carefully settled the test tube into the rack in his satchel. He'd run the preliminary tests in his home lab before he shipped them off for official analysis, but they were bound to be perfect—all the beneficial microbes in place, water quality well within the standards he'd specified when the reclamation project began four years ago.

The preservation of the wetlands and the adjacent woods, named in his grandmother's honor, were the result of years of environmental activism and fundraising. He knew it was fanciful, not fitting an environmental studies professor, but he swore he could almost feel the fragile ecosystem knitting around him, the scents of plants in each appropriate stage of growth and decay, the buzz and whine of insects, the chirp and flutter of birds, the sunlight glinting off the water under the reeds.

He remembered how he'd cried as a boy when his grandmother had told him there were no wild honeybees in Oregon anymore, that they'd been killed off by a mite introduced by an illegal import of infected specimens. That, along with the love of the land she'd instilled in him before her death when he was barely twelve, had shaped his life, his career.

He sighed. His sabbatical had been ideal for finishing up this project, but it had sucked big time when it came to his social life—not that he had much of one anyway. Being a Myers-Briggs one hundred percent introvert pretty much guaranteed that. But at least when he was teaching, he spoke with other professors, interacted with his students, had a reason to get out and exercise his vocal chords and practice his minimal social skills. Now that the majority of the labor on the wetlands was completed and he was no longer managing work crews, he'd turned into a virtual hermit. It was rather disquieting how much that suited him.

"Probably start talking to myself next," he muttered to the Steller's jay perched on the branch of a nearby crabapple.

He made his way along the berm that cut a wandering path through the wetlands, carefully designed to allow access without disturbing any plants or habitat. He slowed when he rounded a clump of thimbleberry to see a blue heron standing in the shallows amid the cattails. He hunkered down in the shade, hardly daring to breathe as the bird dipped its bill into the water. *So beautiful.*

He'd been waiting for a moment like this since he'd begun lobbying for the project.

He caught a flash of motion out of the corner of his eye and turned to see an emaciated coyote approaching through the underbrush. Bryce didn't want to do anything to drive the heron from the area, but he didn't want it to fall victim to the coyote either. He straightened, hand reaching out to rattle the thimbleberry branches, when a beer bottle rocketed across the water and struck the coyote in its washboard ribs.

The heron flapped away, squawking its distress, as the coyote bolted for the woods. Bryce whirled in time to see his surly next door neighbor—*Kendrick, M.*, according to the tag on the mailbox—standing ankle-deep in the slough, laughing like a loon. Under Bryce's stunned gaze, the bastard actually fist-pumped the sky as if he'd thrown a winning touchdown pass.

Bryce considered himself an even-tempered guy, the quintessential mild-mannered professor, but anger at his irresponsible neighbor boiled up under his sternum. He stalked over to the spot where the bottle had struck the coyote. Luckily, it hadn't shattered, so he fished it out of elbow-deep water. If he hadn't been afraid of damaging the fragile biosphere, he'd have sloshed straight through the water, slashing the reeds out of his path. Instead, he continued along the berm, his fury building with each step.

Marching straight up to the idiot on the bank, who was grinning as if bashing a starving animal entitled him to a medal, Bryce brandished the bottle under *Kendrick, M.*'s nose.

"What the hell do you think you're doing? I could have you arrested for littering, let alone endangering the ecosystem. This is a protected site."

Kendrick blinked as if he hadn't even noticed Bryce's presence. He probably hadn't. Men this handsome never did. And this man was definitely in the top one percent of male beauty, with his square jaw, cleft chin, and model-worthy cheekbones. Stylishly overlong dark hair waved across his forehead and curled against the collar of his snug white T-shirt. At six three, Bryce wasn't short, but Kendrick topped him by a couple of inches, and his shoulder width and upper-body definition marked him as someone who wrestled with more than test tubes and sloppy undergraduate lab notebooks.

Kendrick's grin didn't falter. "Did you see that? I nailed him. I never thought—"

"Yes, I saw." *Shit.* The guy had a killer British accent too, a weakness of Bryce's that he blamed on too much *Masterpiece Theatre* as a kid. *Be strong.* "I saw you purposely flinging dangerous refuse at a starving animal. What if the bottle had broken? The glass could have injured dozens of fauna. The health of this whole area is very precarious. We've only just—"

"Whoa, whoa, whoa." Kendrick held up one hand, palm out, angling his body so that his other arm was hidden. "Sorry. I wasn't thinking."

"The rules about the wetlands and woods are clearly spelled out in the CCRs."

"'CCRs'?"

"Codes, covenants, and restrictions. The by-laws for the whole development." He tore off his hat, bunching it in his fist, and flipped up his clip-on sunglasses, the better to glare. "We've got a zero-tolerance policy for environmental negligence, let alone intentional pollution. It's in the papers you signed when you bought the house."

Kendrick shrugged his wide shoulders. "A little behind on my reading. Like I said. Sorry." His tone of voice belied the words.

"I suggest you catch up, because we also have a zero-tolerance policy for ignorance." Bryce pulled a notepad out of the pocket of his vest. "Since I'm on the board of the homeowners' association, I'm reporting you."

"Do your worst."

"There'll be a fine."

"Yeah?" Kendrick's grin was nearly feral. "Don't expect me to pay."

"Then we can put a lien on your house. Foreclose. And you'll be out before you can do irreparable damage."

"Flaming abyss, man, will you calm down? You've got a bigger stick up your arse than my self-righteous brother." He flicked a finger at Bryce's vest. "Fishing's forbidden in your holy wetlands. I do know that much. How do you justify that to your fellow inquisitors?"

Bryce's hands twitched, and he resisted the urge to pat his vest pockets. "It's not a fishing vest. It's a *tactical* vest."

Kendrick smirked. "I suppose those are *tactical* pants."

Bryce raised his chin. The pants with built-in kneepads (and more pockets) were practical, but not exactly man-magnet material. He looked like what he was—a science geek. "As a matter of fact, they are. Very useful in fieldwork."

"I'm sure. What's next? Tactical underdrawers?"

"I didn't buy any of those."

Kendrick barked a laugh. "Shite. You mean they actually make them?"

"Yes, but I don't need them for my purposes."

"If your purpose is being a nosy parker, you've got it nailed, mate." He yanked the dripping bottle out of Bryce's hand. "I'll put this in the bleeding recycling, shall I?"

"Glass," Bryce grumbled, wiping his hand on his pants.

"I know it's glass. I don't drink beer out of a flaming paper cup."

"I mean you have to recycle glass separately from other waste. You always throw everything in the same bin. I should have reported you for that infraction already."

"What are you, the bloody trash police? Why didn't you, then?"

Bryce didn't have a good answer for that, not one that he wanted to share with Kendrick anyway. He couldn't exactly say *I've been sorting it for you because I liked watching you walk out to the curb and bend over the bins.* It had seemed a fair trade. But now that he'd had a chance to talk to the man, the bloom was off that algae.

"Maybe I wanted to be neighborly. Unlike some."

Gwydion's bollocks, and I thought Alun was a prig. Mal's irate neighbor had him beat to flinders. Under the man's self-righteous glare, Mal's elation over discovering his left hand was good for something faded completely away. Shite, he'd done the bloke a favor—he'd *nailed* that Unseelie redcap who'd been about to piss in the water to paralyze the heron before it ate the stupid bird raw.

Still, Mal supposed he had to cut the guy some slack. The redcap was undoubtedly cloaked in *glamourie*. Before Mal had been deprived of most of his fae abilities, he could have easily perceived both the illusion and the reality. Now, since he could no more detect *glamourie* on others than he could cast one on himself, he had no idea how the blasted assassin had appeared to human eyes. Probably as something totally inoffensive, fluffy, and cute, so Mal looked like a sociopath.

Just fecking brilliant.

"Look. We've obviously got off on the wrong foot. I'm Mal. You are . . . ?"

The man crossed his arms over his chest. "Not amused."

"I got that. Thanks." The bloke wasn't bad looking, although he wasn't the sort Mal usually hooked up with. Taller, for one thing—and he'd never had a man other than his brothers frown at him that way. He offered the best grin he could conjure under the circumstances. "Another chance maybe?"

Neighbor-bloke's chest lifted in a sigh. "All right. Dr. MacLeod . . . er . . . that is, Bryce."

Without thinking, Mal held out his right hand. Bryce extended his, ready to shake, but then his eyes widened behind his black-framed glasses. Shite. Mal snatched his crabbed hand behind his back, the pity in Bryce's face making him want to bite something.

"Anyway. Sorry about the bottle and the . . . what was that thing I hit?"

The pity faded under a look of disbelief, bordering on contempt. Much better. Anything was better than pity.

"A coyote. Don't they have those in . . . England, is it?"

Oh, if only you knew, boyo. "Wales, actually, but it's been a long time." A very long time. He brandished the bottle. "Anyway, I'll take care of this, shall I? Nice to meet you, Bryce. Cheers."

He trudged up the hill and through the shady path between their houses to where his refuse containers stood outside the garage. Bryce was watching him from the corner of his patio, a scowl still bunching his eyebrows.

Mal held the bottle up between two fingers, placed it in the bin labeled *Glass*, then bowed in Bryce's direction. *Ha.* Just as he thought—a smile on those lips made all the difference.

Maybe I don't need to troll the bars for a little action after all.

CHAPTER ❈ 3

The next morning, Bryce had recovered from his less-than-pleasant introduction to *Kendrick, M.* Mal's curtains were drawn tight as Bryce passed by on his way into the wetlands, so there'd be no encounter with his surly neighbor to spoil his optimistic mood. If today's water samples were as clean as yesterday's, he could officially report the project ready to move to maintenance mode.

He took the alternate way through the slough this morning, past the succession pools that were part of the housing development's water conservation and reclamation infrastructure. The morning sun glinted off the water, turning the chevron wake of a trio of ducks peach against the dark water.

He loved this whole community, proof that environmentally sound building practices could be beautiful and functional as well as planet-friendly. His grandmother would be so proud of what her legacy had produced.

He took a detour off the berm and into the woods to check on the progress of a family of bluebirds that had moved into the nest box he'd mounted in a bitter cherry tree in the spring.

For a few minutes he paused, soothed by the bluebirds' song, the chirrup of chipmunks, and the hum of mason bees in the lupines. Yes, all the work had been worth it.

He turned back, ready to jump the stream that fed into the slough, when a glint of silver in the reeds caught his eye.

Damn it. Mal had better not have been tossing trash in here again.

Bryce crouched down, parting the knife-edged cattail fronds. A trout was floating belly-up at the edge of the water.

His breath sped up, heat shooting up his throat. *Calm down. This could be the heron's abandoned kill from yesterday. Doesn't have to be a setback—or evidence of Mal Kendrick's malice.* He edged along the berm, peering down through the reeds, and spotted a second dead fish, a third, a fourth.

This time, the blood rushed out of his head, and he had to sit down and hunch forward over his knees. *This cannot be happening.* Just yesterday, the water quality had been perfect. Had an unexpected source of pollution leached into the water? Something upstream in one of the feeder creeks or a failure in the reclamation fields?

Examining the dead fish at this point wouldn't tell him anything since their internal organs decayed so quickly after death. Pulling on a pair of disposable gloves from his satchel, he removed the pathetic little corpses from the reeds, dug a shallow trench in the soft ground under the thimbleberries, and buried them. He ought to search for a live affected fish to collect for a necropsy. *Later. Not now.*

Instead, he retrieved a water sample from the site, and another from further along, near where a creek emptied into the slough. He was about to head back into the woods to check further upstream when he saw Mal standing knee-deep in the water in the same spot where he'd tossed his bottle yesterday.

Bryce's temper boiled over again. Christ, hadn't the man promised to keep out of the wetlands? Well, maybe not in so many words, but he'd said he'd stop throwing bottles. Was he dumping something else in the water, something that was toxic to fish and possibly other species?

"Hey!" Bryce shouted.

Mal's head snapped up, but before Bryce could deliver a more articulate reprimand, Mal toppled face-first into the water.

"Oh, just fucking perfect. Is he already drunk at this time of day? Bad enough he throws his trash here, now he's decided to bathe in the . . ." *Why isn't he getting up?* Mal was floating on the water, bobbing in the wake from a passing duck.

Shit.

Bryce dropped his pack and raced down the path, wading into the water to flip Mal over. He pulled him to the bank and rolled him to his side. All his CPR training fled—*a fat lot of good it does if I can't remember it when I need it.*

Before he could descend into full-fledged panic, Mal choked and retched, bringing up at least a beer bottle's worth of slough water. Bryce kept a steadying hand on his shoulder until Mal had subsided to wheezing gasps. As he helped Mal sit up, he noticed that the man had a bloody lump the size of a golf ball on the back of his head.

"Where did it—" Mal coughed again. "Bloody hells, that water is foul."

"It's not intended for drinking, let alone breathing."

"I'll keep that in mind." Mal lifted his left hand to the back of his head, wincing when he came in contact with the lump. "Shite. Must have been more than one of the bastards. Did you see where they went?"

Bryce looked around, but the greensward leading up to the back of both their houses was empty, as was the bank of the slough. The only things in sight were a couple of raccoons and a well-fed nutria. "Nobody here but us." Mal shot a narrow glance at him, and Bryce raised his hands. "Hey. I promise. I didn't conk you on the head. Although I would like to know what you were doing down here today."

"I was . . ." Mal pinched the bridge of his nose and muttered something that sounded like *bloody curse.* "I saw some suspicious characters down here."

"Suspicious, huh? Were they perhaps wearing masks?" Bryce jerked his head at the raccoons peering at them from the underbrush.

Mal lurched to his feet, and the raccoons bolted toward the woods, the nutria waddling after them. "Bloody bastards. I'll—"

"Hold it, neighbor." Bryce grabbed him before he face-planted in the reeds again. Maybe the bump on the old noggin had done a little more damage than it appeared. "You can't slaughter the wildlife any more than you can use the slough for your personal trash bin."

"I didn't— They . . ." Mal grabbed a handful of his hair, nowhere close to the lump. "Ah, shite."

"Look. I think you should maybe go to the ER. Get your head checked out."

"No bloody chance of that, mate."

"Then at least come over to my place. Let me patch you up."

"I'll be fine." Mal turned, but before he could take two steps up the hill, he wobbled and nearly fell on his ass.

"Sure you will. *After* you're patched up." *And see a doctor, if I have anything to say about it.* Still, thanks to his grandmother's training, Bryce wasn't completely without resources. "Come on. I've got everything I need in my kitchen."

"Planning to grind my bones to make your bread?"

Grind? Bones? Wha . . .? Oh. Bryce pulled his thoughts out of the gutter and chuckled. "I'm not a giant, Jack. You're safe from me. Let's go."

He put a hand under Mal's elbow, supporting him up the hill and through the French doors so he could park him in a chair at the dining table.

"Your kitchen has the same bloody appliances as mine."

"Of course it does. They're part of the specs for the development." Bryce pulled his first aid kit out of the cupboard over the refrigerator. He'd inherited the wooden box from his grandmother, and he still regularly replaced the herbs and ointments with fresh preparations according to her instructions. He sorted through the pots of jars until he found the ones he wanted—the antiseptic soap paste and the antibiotic ointment. "You know, I still think you need to go to the—"

"No."

"Fine." He beckoned Mal over to the sink, pulling two tea towels out of the drawer. "Can you lean over the sink? You'll stay dryer than if I try to wash the wound while you're sitting in the chair."

"'Wound'? I wouldn't dignify it with the term." Mal stood up and walked around the breakfast bar into the kitchen. "It's not that bad." He touched the back of his head and seemed stunned when his fingers came away coated in blood. "All right, then. Bugger it." He crossed his arms and propped them on the edge of the counter, his head over the sink.

The way Mal's jeans fit over his ass as he shifted from foot to foot, the play of his back muscles under the wet cotton of his T-shirt, made Bryce swallow convulsively and edge away. Mal hadn't shown any overt signs of sexual preference, but he'd definitely shown signs of finding Bryce annoying. Not a recipe for a successful hookup, even if the man *was* gay. Besides, now was not the time, regardless of inclination.

Bryce cleared his throat as he unscrewed the lid of the soap, releasing the scent of mint and apple. He'd always been glad that his grandmother's remedies weren't overly floral, and he imagined Mal would appreciate not smelling like a nosegay while he healed as well. "Did you get hit anywhere else other than your head?"

"No. Didn't drown either, thanks to you."

"Well, I'm opposed to littering the slough, so didn't have much choice." Bryce filled his cupped hands with warm water and let it trickle over the back of Mal's head. He froze when Mal twitched and groaned. "Sorry. Does that hurt?"

"No. Feels bloody marvelous."

"Good." He smeared a fingertip of soap onto the wound, and Mal shot backward as if Bryce's touch had been red-hot.

"Shite, man. What in all the hells are you doing to me?"

"Just washing off blood."

"With what?"

Bryce held up the pot. "It's just a homemade herbal soap. Perfectly safe."

"Like bloody hells it is."

Mal strode to the table and pawed through the first aid box, tossing the contents onto the table, occasionally holding a packet or pot up to his nose. "Rosemary. Vervain. Rue. *Faugh*." He flung the packet across the kitchen and it burst against the refrigerator, scattering fine brownish-green powder across the floor.

For a moment, Bryce couldn't do anything more than goggle, his jaw sagging like a freshman non-major in his geomorphology class. But the destruction of hours' worth of painstaking work finally refired his motor neurons.

"What the devil do you think you're doing?" He took two giant steps across the kitchen and yanked the box out of Mal's reach. "If this is how you repay hospitality, no wonder you never leave your fucking house. Isn't polluting the wetlands enough for you? You have to destroy my property and vandalize my kitchen too?"

Mal swept a half-dozen pots off the table with his right forearm, the first time Bryce had seen him use his disabled arm for anything. One pot, an opaque white glass holding an insect repellent, shattered, sending blobs of yellow lotion in a blood-spatter spray against the cabinets. The others rolled across the floor as if they were fleeing Mal's temper. "Who sent you? Was it my brother-in-law? His busybody aunt? The others in her circle? Did one of *them* give you this shite?"

Anger curdled Bryce's belly and tightened his chest. He could count the times that he'd lost his temper in his thirty-two years on one hand, and three of them had been in the last twenty-four hours, the direct result of Mal Kendrick.

"For your information, this 'shite,' as you put it, is mine—made by my own hand from recipes I learned by the time I turned twelve."

Mal crowded up against Bryce, but Bryce refused to back away, putting them almost chest to chest, nose to nose. "Was it the Queen, then? Are you her spy, sent to make sure I'm working my cursed arse off to return her Consort to her in all his traitorous glory? Well, you can tell Her bloody Majesty—"

"I have no idea what you're talking about," Bryce ground out between clenched molars, "but I'm *trying* to help you. Although I'm beginning to think that's beyond my abilities. Or anyone's."

Mal sounded positively deranged. *And I was so blinded by a pretty face that I invited him into my home without knowing anything about him.* Brilliant, just brilliant. If his students ever found out, he'd never live it down.

Although perhaps living *through* this should be his immediate goal—he'd worry about living it *down* later.

A druid, damn it to all the bloody hells. He had a gods-forsaken *druid* for a neighbor. How likely a coincidence was that? Not one Mal was willing to believe.

But if the twisted magician wasn't part of Cassie's coven, and if he hadn't been sent to spy for the Queen . . . Gwydion's bloody bollocks, could his tree-hugging neighbor be in league with the Unseelie thugs who had attacked him this morning? An unaffiliated druid was worse than a dozen loose cannons.

Shite, he should have known the word of his helplessness would spread. He shouldn't have tipped his hand by winging that redcap yesterday. He should have remembered it would have pack mates.

Mal's vision dimmed around the edges, sharpening everything in his direct line of sight, a sure sign he was falling into battle-trance. Good. This bastard deserved it.

"Who's paying you?"

"I beg your pardon?"

"Come off it. No wonder you're arse-deep in this bloody green-construction shite. The recycled building materials—you use them to tap into the earth, don't you? Draining power from their old life as well as the new."

Bryce drew back, his eyebrows bunched over his glasses. "Listen, I'm willing to cut you some slack because of the head injury, but—"

"Stop evading! I'm not an imbecile."

"I never said you were. But your head. A possible concussion—"

Mal shouldered Bryce against the wall. "Shut. It. Did you cast a summoning? Blood magic? Something to lure my brother-in-law to buy that gods-be-damned house? I should have known he'd never have chosen it on his own."

Bryce shoved Mal's chest with respectable force, but Mal hadn't spent the last two hundred years swinging a broadsword for nothing. Druids might have unfair advantage with their theurgic charms and potions, but when it came to brute strength, Mal had the upper hand—even if only one of them worked.

His right forearm blocked Bryce's windpipe quite nicely though. Mal leaned in, but not with his full weight, not yet. He still needed answers, and for that Bryce needed his breath.

But not that much of it.

Mal bared his teeth in a battle grimace. "You have one more chance. Who." He jerked his arm against Bryce's throat and felt the man's Adam's apple spasm. "Paid." Another jerk, and Bryce's brown eyes widened and watered behind his glasses. "You?"

"Fuck you," Bryce croaked, and pain burst in Mal's bollocks as Bryce grabbed and *squeezed*.

Goddess. He dropped his arm, scrabbling at Bryce's wrist, attempting to loosen that deadly grip, but his fingers flopped uselessly against the corded muscles. *Left hand. Left hand.* He dug his fingers into the tendons at the base of Bryce's thumb, both of them sweating and grunting with pain and effort.

"Shite, man. Let go."

"I will if you will."

Mal nodded once, teeth clenched, and released Bryce's wrist. Immediately Bryce dropped the grip on Mal's balls.

"Flaming abyss, man. Did you have to try to neuter me?"

Bryce snorted and rubbed his throat. "Seeing as you were about to strangle me, yes." He moved to the other side of a heavy antique maple table, countering Mal's staggered movements so the table remained between them, blocking either of them from another assault. Probably a good idea.

"Air. Pfaugh. Not as necessary as bollocks."

"Listen. I'll forgo pressing assault charges this time, but only if you agree to go to the hospital. Get checked out. Because I have to tell you . . ." He shook his head and pulled the wooden potion box across the table, laying a protective hand on its lid. "You sound fucking insane."

"I told you. No hospitals. But if it makes you stop hovering like a ministering angel with a homicidal streak, I'll give my brother-in-law a call. He's a nurse. Or almost."

"Nope. You get *official* help. If you don't, I'm reporting you to the police and the homeowners' association as a danger to both the public and the community."

"I—"

"No negotiation. Show me the discharge orders tomorrow or it's the police." He rubbed his throat again. "No doubt I'll sport a very nice bruise that'll match your handprint to help them with their case. Now get out."

"No fear. The less time I spend in your presence, the better I'll like it."

Mal managed to maintain his dignity—and a marginally steady gait—until he exited the blasted druid den. Then he gave in to the pain and limped across the grass and through his own door.

Shite, what a disaster. Unseelie thugs stalking him with intent to kill. A fragging unaffiliated druid living next door. Bollocks that felt as if they were on fire.

At least he could do something about the last one. He minced his way to the refrigerator and pulled a flexible ice pack out of the freezer.

Since David had outfitted the place, it had every first aid supply in his nurse's bag of tricks, and despite being the adopted nephew of the local arch-druid, David always stocked human remedies, not magical ones.

He didn't need them, after all. As an *achubydd*, he was a walking first aid station all by himself.

Come to think of it, he could use David's healing touch right about now—on his skull, not his bollocks. If Alun found out Mal had asked David to touch him there—even if the touch was metaphysical, not hands-on—his brother would finish the castration Bryce had started. Besides, Alun would consider the pain Mal's own damn fault.

Mal settled on his sofa and eased the ice pack over his crotch. *Shite, Bryce has a grip on him.* He pulled his cell phone out of his pocket and speed-dialed David, who answered on the first ring.

"It's a good thing you called," David said, no hint of his usual cheerful teasing tone, "or Alun was going to take steps."

"He doesn't scare me."

"He should."

"Fine. He scares me, but only because I never know what self-righteous stunt he'll pull on me next. I'm surprised he doesn't make me wear a chastity belt in your presence."

"You'd look hot in one, especially if it was all you were wearing."

"Thanks, love, but don't let Alun hear you say that." He winced and rearranged the ice pack. "Although I'm not sure any sex restraints will be necessary for at least a while. My bollocks are in recovery from a run-in with my neighbor's fist."

"What? He punched you?"

"That would have been too easy. No. I think he mistook them for a stone and was trying to extract a little blood."

"Oh my god, Mal. Do you need me to come over?"

"I do, but not for that."

"There's something else?"

"I got hit in the head."

"He hit you in the head too?"

"Not him. An Unseelie redcap ambushed me in the wetlands and his cronies nailed me in the back of the head with a sling full of elf-shot."

"I'll be right there."

"Wait, David. There's more."

"More? What else can there be?"

"I think my neighbor is a druid. An unaffiliated."

"Is that bad?"

"Ask your aunt. And be ready to duck."

"Oookaaay. I'll swing by to pick her up, then. Can you lure him to your house?"

Mal shifted on the sofa. "I don't think he'll be amenable to an invitation from me."

"Why not?"

"Well . . . I kind of tried to choke him."

Silence. He could imagine David's eyes narrowing and hear his foot tapping. "Was this before or after he crushed your balls?"

"Kind of during. Although I suppose my part came first."

"Mal . . ." The exasperation in David's voice carried clearly over the call.

"I know. I'm not the Enforcer anymore. I can't kill anyone with impunity, including the Unseelie swine lurking in the fragging swamp behind my house."

"It's not a swamp. It's a wetlands reclamation project."

"Considering I swallowed half of it this morning, I can tell you without a doubt—it's a swamp. I'll see you when I see you."

CHAPTER 4

After one of his grandmother's pain remedies, washed down by two tall glasses of ice water, Bryce could finally swallow without wincing. He swept up the spilled herbs from the kitchen floor. Useless, damn it, and his herb garden wouldn't be ready to harvest for at least another month. He'd have to hope he wouldn't need the rue before he had a chance to replenish his supply.

He should have known that Mal was unstable after the bottle-flinging event yesterday—although he'd never have imagined the guy would go so far as to attack *him*. And that rant about—well, whatever it was. The man was clearly paranoid and probably more than half-crazy.

Bryce paused, the paper of meadowsweet in his hands. Paranoia. Was that a symptom of subdural hematoma? Should he have allowed Mal to go home without ensuring that he'd go to the ER?

He wasn't even sure the man owned a car. He'd only ever seen an enormous Harley, which Mal had never actually ridden. He'd just let it idle in the open garage, polluting the air with exhaust.

Oh. His hand. He probably couldn't ride the bike anymore. His disability must be pretty recent if he hadn't figured out how to function with it yet. Maybe some of his anger was post-traumatic—and now Bryce had exacerbated it by adding borderline genital mutilation.

Fantastic.

He stalked to his own garage and checked the charge on his LEAF. It was ready to go, so if he had to, he'd drive Mal to the hospital himself. He unhooked his old Louisville Slugger from the pegboard over his workbench—although he'd approach Mal to insist on medical intervention, he wasn't stupid enough to do it without a little insurance.

He walked out the side door and across the strip of fescue between his house and Mal's, adjusting his grip on the bat so he didn't look quite so much like a basher. As he walked past the recycling bins, an emaciated coyote slunk around the front corner of the house and froze when it caught sight of Bryce and his bat.

Bryce froze too. Was it the same one that had stalked the heron yesterday? An animal that starved, that obviously unhealthy, was a wild card. Normally a single coyote wouldn't attack a human, but thanks to Mal, this one already had experience with human aggression. That, coupled with desperation, might alter its behavior.

The coyote crouched down, belly brushing the grass. Its eyes, even in the shadow under the wide eaves of Mal's house, glowed yellow, and its black pupils looked almost vertical, like a cat's. *That can't be normal—does it have issues other than starvation?*

It crept backward. Bryce frowned. He didn't know canines could do that, but then he was an environmentalist, not an animal behaviorist. He kept still, waiting for the beast to make its next move.

It continued its retreat. When it moved through a shaft of sunlight reflected off Bryce's study window, a trick of refraction wildly distorted its shadow on Mal's garage wall, making it look more like a squat, misshapen child than a cowering canine.

The crash of a door being thrown open startled the animal to its feet.

"Oi!" At Mal's bellow, the coyote took off, racing within inches of Bryce, and disappeared into the woods at the foot of the hill.

Mal barreled around the corner of the house, skidding to a stop when he saw Bryce.

"Oh. It's you."

"No projectile weapons this time? I doubt the animal was any real danger to either of us."

"That's what you think," Mal muttered. He nodded at the bat in Bryce's hand. "Looks like you thought it necessary to take up arms against it as well though."

"This old thing? This is for you." He swung the bat to his shoulder and grinned. "Think of it as anti-Malware."

Mal's eyes narrowed. "Is that supposed to be a joke?"

"Trust me, it would get a *huge* laugh in the IT bullpen at the college."

"So this is . . . what? A bit of persuasion to make sure I follow your instructions?"

"More like a precaution. I wanted to make sure you were okay, but didn't want to take the chance you'd try to throttle me again."

"Mmmphm."

"Seriously, you shouldn't be racing around in this heat, chasing inoffensive woodland creatures. You need to be resting or, ideally, on your way to the ER."

Mal scowled. "Do you always spend this much energy enforcing your agenda on your neighbors?"

"It depends on whether or not I think they're a danger to themselves or others. So how about it? Do you have a way to get to the hospital? I can give you a ride if you—"

"Save it. I called my brother-in-law, the nurse. He's coming over."

Bryce hesitated. He wasn't sure Mal was telling the truth—about his brother-in-law's arrival or his profession—but it wasn't as if he could wrestle Mal into the LEAF without being accused of attempted kidnapping. "All right, then. But remember, I'll expect to see a medical release." Bryce raised a hand in farewell. "Later."

Mal was clearly about to tell him to fuck off—Bryce could practically see the words forming in the tightening of his jaw, the inhale through flared nostrils. He braced himself for another onslaught of blistering profanity, but instead, Mal lifted a hand to his temple and clenched his eyes shut. Listed to one side.

Bryce tossed the bat to the ground and lurched forward, catching Mal before he could collapse into the mixed recycling.

Shite. Mal had almost buggered a perfect opportunity. Here he'd been worried about how to orchestrate a meeting between Bryce and Cassie, and the bloody man had waltzed right into it. As much as Mal wanted to tell him to take his druid arse on a flying leap into the swamp, if he wanted to get the man corralled and under the control of the local circle, he had to pretend he was a pansy-arse who couldn't take a piddling bump on the head.

Pissed him off, but all in a good cause.

He let Bryce catch him against his chest, warm and solid despite the miscellaneous lumps from those tactical pockets. He took a deep breath.

Mistake.

He got a good whiff of Bryce's skin. The astringent scents of that bloody herbal soap underlaid the earthy smell of clean male sweat. Goddess, he hadn't had a man in his arms since well before his curse. *Not a man. A druid.* His cock, not inclined to split that particular hair, stirred in his pants, and he decided he might as well enjoy it. Not like he'd be getting any further with Sir Druid, not if he valued his will or his sanity.

"Take it easy." Bryce's low voice rumbled in his ear, his breath warm on Mal's neck. Mal couldn't help it—he shivered.

Luckily, Bryce took it the wrong way.

"You've overdone it. I knew I should have kept a closer eye on you."

Mal let himself sag in Bryce's arms, which was not as much of a hardship as it should have been. He let his limp arms swing, brushing against Bryce's backside. Even without an actual grope, he could tell that arse was exactly as fine as it seemed, despite the camouflage of those ridiculous tactical pants.

"The sun . . . it's the heat. Could you help me back inside?"

"Absolutely. Here. Can you put your arm across my shoulders?"

Oh, I most certainly can. And did. Bryce tucked him against his side with an arm around Mal's waist, a hand the size of a hubcap splayed against his ribs. Mal groaned. Goddess, he loved big hands.

"Sorry." Bryce adjusted his grip. "Did you get hit on the back too? Your ribs?"

"No. Just a little light-headed. Lead on."

Mal dragged his feet as much as he could to prolong the unsteady shuffle into his house, leaning against Bryce in a brazen—yet perfectly forgivable under the circumstances—effort to feel him up with as much body contact as he could manage.

When Bryce lowered Mal onto his sofa, Mal was tempted to pull him off-balance and force a full-frontal encounter, but that would be pushing his luck beyond the limit of reason.

You were almost feeling up a druid—reason has clearly abandoned ship already.

Bryce stood and tugged on the hem of his vest. "You okay? Can I get you some water? You really should stay hydrated."

"Yeah. Water would be good."

"Right. Back in a sec."

Mal lay back on the oversoft cushions and grinned at the ceiling fan—solar-powered, of course—rotating in the diffuse light. As much as he loathed being helpless in truth, faking it was damned fun, especially when he could use it to cop a feel.

Bryce's footsteps clipped against the bamboo living room floor, and Mal wiped the grin off his face, attempting to look wan and wounded. He rolled his head to smile bravely at Bryce, whose eyes widened in shock as if Mal truly were wan and wounded.

Fuck that.

He frowned and tried to sit up, only to have his head swim sickeningly.

"Hey." Bryce sat down next to him and steadied him with an arm across his back. "Take it easy. You're bleeding again."

"I'm—" Mal glanced behind him. Sure enough, the pristine oatmeal upholstery of his sofa cushion sported a lopsided crimson splotch. "Shite."

"Drink this." Bryce held the glass to his lips.

He jerked the glass out of Bryce's hand, splashing water across his thigh. "I'm not a bloody invalid."

"Well," Bryce drawled, "maybe not an invalid, but evidence suggest that you are, in fact, bloody."

"If you—"

The front door burst open and David rushed in, all twink indignation. He marched across the living room and planted himself next to the coffee table—made from wood salvaged from a water-damaged high school gymnasium, Goddess help him. Every damn thing in this house had an ecologically approved pedigree.

"You *said* you were fine. You *said* this was nothing. You *said* I shouldn't worry."

While Bryce was distracted by David's tirade, Mal took the opportunity to jerk his head toward him and mouth *druid* at David, but it didn't deflect his brother-in-law's death glare. *Have to use my words, I guess.*

"Bryce. This is my brother-in-law, David Evans-Kendrick." He leaned closer to Bryce, the better to stage-whisper into his ear. "He's pissed."

"I gathered." Bryce's tone was as dry as his damned druid herbs. Nevertheless he stood up, offering his hand to David. "I'm Bryce MacLeod. I live next door."

David reached out to take Bryce's hand, but he was pushed aside, revealing a tiny, wizened woman with bird-bright black eyes, a rainbow headscarf, and an oak cane the size of a horse's leg. Mal blinked. Was he really so out of it that he hadn't noticed David's aunt until that moment, or had the blasted woman appeared out of thin air? *She's an arch-druid. Maybe she did.*

She thrust the cane at David so she could take Bryce's outstretched hand in both of hers. "Young man, what in bloody blue blazes do you think you're about?"

Bryce tugged his hand, to no avail. "I—"

"This is my aunt, Cassie Bowen," David said. "Resistance is futile."

Mal settled back to enjoy the show. "You think he's kidding."

Bryce shot a panicked glance at him, still trying to pull his hand from Cassie's grasp without injuring a frail elderly woman.

Mal shared a grin with David. The only way Bryce could escape from Cassie now was if he brought the full force of his unaffiliated druid powers down on her, and regardless of what Mal might think of druids in general and ones that hid behind fragging tactical vests specifically, he knew Bryce would never ever hurt someone who appeared so obviously weaker than himself.

More fool him.

"Davey, take Lord Maldwyn into the other room and see to his hurts."

Mal winced at Cassie's use of his full name and title. "And miss the fun?"

She skewered him with her midnight gaze. *Right, then.* He'd better move before she broke out the power voice, because that shite was . . . well . . . best avoided to say the least.

He held out a hand and batted his eyelashes at David. "Give me a hand up, boyo? I'm feeling suddenly faint."

David snorted and shook his head, his shaggy brown hair rivaling the shine of any elf-maid's tresses. Damn, his brother had all the luck. *Assuming you ignore the massacre of his first lover and two hundred years cursed with the face of a beast.*

"Your lines never worked on me when I *didn't* know you. Why do you think you'll have better luck now?" Nevertheless, David pulled Mal to his feet, steadying him with a hand on his shoulder when he swayed. David's hand tightened. "Mal? You all right?"

"Yes. Just a little . . ." His vision swam. "Light-headed. Must be your proximity. Never could resist your—"

"That will be enough, Lord Maldwyn. Davey, the kitchen."

Mal attempted to put a little swagger in his stride for Bryce's benefit, even if he'd never fool Cassie or David, but the way his head continued to swim made it look more like a stagger. David's hand on his elbow was the only thing that kept him from colliding with the doorjamb.

"For pity's sake, Mal, stop trying to pretend nothing's wrong. I can see the lines of pain in your head. Sit."

"'S nothing." He sat though, because for some reason his knees didn't want to support him anymore.

"I thought you said Bryce administered first aid."

"He tried." Mal kept his voice low. There might be a wall between them, but the open archway between the living room and dining room didn't exactly block sound. "But it was druid shite. No way would I let him lather that stuff on me. You know what that potion did to Alun."

"Well, you should have manned up. If you hadn't called me when you did . . . here." He handed Mal a glass of water. "Drink that and give me your hand."

"You know better than that, boyo. I can't give you my hand if I'm using it to hold the bloody glass."

"You still have two hands, Mal. Give me your right hand. It will do fine for my purposes."

Mal surrendered his useless paw and studied David's face over the rim of the glass as he gulped down the water. As much as he hated to admit it, the water in this house tasted wonderful, nearly as pure as the stream outside his cottage in Faerie.

David's forehead wrinkled in concentration, and healing *achubydd* heat traveled up Mal's arm and across his shoulders, winding around muscle and vein and tendon until it found the spot on the back of his head—although it started at his wrist, gods blast it. He still felt nothing in his hand.

"Alun will have my hide if he finds out you're using *achubydd* juice on me."

"Shush. I've told him, I've told you, I've told everyone—aid freely given is its own reward. I don't lose anything that I don't get back." David frowned, and the heat at the back of Mal's skull increased, then ebbed, taking the pain and wooziness along with it. "There. Feel better?"

Mal set down the glass and probed the back of his head with tentative fingers. No pain. And the borderline double vision was gone as well. "You're a wonder, Dafydd. My brother is one lucky son of a bitch."

"And you're lucky you called me. Even a high lord of the fae can slip into an inconvenient coma with a skull fracture and a subdural hematoma."

"A what? It was just a bump on the head."

David smirked at him. "Guess your head's not as hard as you thought. Now. How about a little eavesdropping?"

CHAPTER ❈ 5

With his hand imprisoned in Cassie Bowen's astonishingly firm grip, Bryce had to fight the urge to apologize—although for what, he couldn't imagine. He'd done nothing but try to get Mal treatment for his injury, but he felt like he had when he'd been a boy and had to admit a transgression to his grandmother.

"MacLeod," she said, turning his hand palm up to peer at it closely. "A Scot."

"Actually, I'm from Connecticut." He wanted to close his fist under her scrutiny. Not because he was ashamed of the calluses at the base of his fingers from all the digging in his garden—Gran had always told him to be proud of that—but because her scrutiny harked back to the days when Gran had inspected his hands for proper washing before supper.

What was it about this woman that called his grandmother so irresistibly to mind?

She flicked his wrist with one finger, just as Gran had when he'd said something she felt was ill-considered. "The geography doesn't matter, boy. You're a Scot. I'd have preferred a Welshman. Scots are so independent. And there's always a danger of that Highland temper."

"You'd have preferred a Welshman for what, ma'am?"

"An apprentice, of course."

"I may be on sabbatical now, but I'm a tenured professor at the Pacific Northwest College of Arts and Sciences. I think I'm past apprenticing for anything."

She raised one sparse eyebrow. "Best think again, then. I don't know what your people fancied they were about."

"See here." He tugged his hand, still hesitant to put his full strength behind it because she looked as if the bones in her frail fingers would snap like so many dry twigs at the least pressure. "I appreciate you and your nephew coming to take care of Mal, but since you're here, I'd best be getting home."

"Oh, Lord Maldwyn didn't call us for himself. He called us for you."

Lord Maldwyn? No wonder the man was so arrogant, particularly if he'd decided Bryce wasn't behaving in an appropriately serf-like manner. "But I'm not injured." *Barring a little bruising around the throat.* "And I really must go."

"You'll go nowhere, Bryce MacLeod, not without my leave." Her eyes seemed to burn like black coals, and her voice deepened and thrummed in his bones. He tried to pull away in earnest now, but found he couldn't move no matter how he strained.

"What the hell is going on?"

"You, my lad, are a druid born, and it's past time for you to take up your birthright." She studied him, head tilted to one side. "You can start by minding your language when you speak to me."

"A druid?" He would have laughed if he could draw breath into his frozen lungs. "I'm a second-generation college professor. A scientist."

"What of the generations before? Your grandfather. Your MacLeod grandfather. What was his occupation?"

"He—he owned a bookshop. But he died before I was born."

"And your grandmother? What was her name before they wed?"

"Bruce. I was sort of named for her."

She rocked back on her heels, and the bands around his chest loosened, allowing him to take a deep breath at last.

"Bruce? Of the line of Robert the Bruce?"

"No. Different branch."

"Ach. Just as well. He was a papist, after all. The blood wouldn't have run as strong."

"What blood?"

"The druid blood, of course."

"But druidry as a religion died out with the coming of Christianity."

"Religion. Bah." She finally dropped his hand, and he retreated a few steps, although he could go no farther. "You hear the song of the earth, don't you? You crave the feel of it in your hands, just as you seek the cool wash of a stream, or the warmth of the sun on your back."

"I . . ." He swallowed. Wanted to deny it, but how could he? His devotion to environmentalism had been born of the respect for nature and its bounty Gran had modeled for him every day in the garden, the kitchen, the woods. But that was just passion and aptitude. It couldn't be anything else. But as he tried—and failed—to move farther away, he had to admit that empirical evidence was piling up for a different conclusion altogether.

"Think of the perfect design of a honeycomb or the certainty that if you plant a morning glory seed, a thistle will not grow in its stead. Call it science if you will, but in truth, it is magic as old as the earth itself." She leaned forward and patted his hand. "Your grandmother—she taught you of these things, did she not? To tend, to transform, to heal?"

"She did." He throat tightened, and not because of Mal's manhandling. He hadn't spoken to anyone about his grandmother since she died. His aunts, his mother's sisters, hadn't wanted to discuss her. They'd found her acerbic wit uncomfortable, and no wonder. She'd held them, and their obsession with social position, in total contempt.

Perhaps he should have denied it all, though, because Cassie peppered him with questions on everything from first aid remedies to his gardening methods. Bryce tried to remain calm and respectful, but he was beginning to think he'd be better off avoiding Mal and his crazy friends and sticking to his solitary life until his sabbatical ended and he went back to work in January.

"Well, you've a grounding, then, in some of the craft. But in all else you're woefully ignorant."

Bryce bristled. Ignorant? He had a bachelor's degree in chemistry. A master's in plant biology. A PhD in environmental science. Ignorant?

A low chuckle from behind him prevented Bryce from retorting. "A pisser, isn't it?" Mal lounged against the dining room arch. "You thought you were so bloody smart, but Granny Two-Shoes says you don't belong out of short pants."

Bryce glared at him. "'Short pants'? You've been watching too many costume dramas."

Mal sauntered into the living room, no hint of his earlier instability. "No need to watch them, mate. I lived them."

David bustled in from the kitchen, throwing Mal an exasperated look on his way past. "Don't expect a straight answer from him, ever. Both his brothers are just as bad. I think it's a fae thing."

What? "'Fey'? You mean gay? Not exactly politically correct anymore, is it?" Or maybe it was. He'd be the first to admit his street smarts were lacking.

David chuckled. "As it happens, all three of them are gay—at least I've only ever heard about male partners—but I don't mean f-e-y. I mean f-a-e."

"Right. Delusional. All of you."

Cassie clapped her hands, one sharp crack. "We've wasted time enough." She pulled a small pot out of her handbag. "Come here, boy."

"I don't think—"

David patted his arm. "I know you think you still have a choice, but you really don't. You might as well give in and get on with it."

Bryce glanced between him and Cassie, avoiding Mal's amused gaze. "Get on with what?"

"Your new life, boyo. Or maybe it's the old one you mislaid for a decade or two."

Bryce sighed and approached Cassie. Anything to escape these people and get back to his house and water samples and his statistics and his— God, he was boring.

She pointed imperiously to the floor at her feet until he got the picture and knelt, ignoring Mal's evil grin. She unscrewed the lid on the little pot, and immediately he was back in Gran's kitchen, stirring the pot on the stove while she added a pinch of this and a paper of that, telling him as she did so what each herb was for. What it would do. How it would work with the others in the concoction.

"This is your destiny. You clearly have the Gift, though not all do, regardless of heritage. Your grandmother must have seen it, since she chose you as her apprentice. She would have done this for you when you crossed the first threshold of manhood, had she been alive to do it. Close your eyes."

He glanced at David and Mal. "Uh . . ."

"Just do it," David said. "You'll feel terrific after."

Mal draped an arm across his brother-in-law's shoulders. "I think that's my line."

Part of Bryce, the part that craved the stability of logic and predictable results, argued that there was nothing beyond the observable, measurable world. But the other part, the part that had been astonished by the way a pea sprout uncurled from warmed soil, or awed by how a flock of starlings in flight folded like silk through the air—that part whispered, *What if?*

He closed his eyes.

She smoothed the salve on his eyelids and it tingled, but not with the burn of a muscle balm. More . . . effervescent, as if it were the medicinal equivalent of champagne. He touched his eyelids, but felt nothing other than his skin. *No residue. I wonder how she managed that.*

"Open your eyes." Cassie's voice had lost its resonance, but he felt compelled to obey nonetheless, and when he did—

"*Oh.*"

Cassie was no longer a frail old woman—or rather, she was still an old woman, but frail? Hardly. A brilliant aura surrounded her, easily twice her size, seething with what Bryce recognized as sheer power. Beneath her sternum, the place Gran called *the wee center*, a flame burned bright and gold.

He turned to David. His aura wasn't as spectacular, but another sort of power curled around his glowing blue center, like a dragon of amber and amethyst. He took a deep breath and turned to Mal.

Who looked exactly the same.

"Why do you look so different but Mal is the same?"

Cassie smiled and gave a decisive nod. "Excellent. You've passed the first test."

"The first?"

"The first of many," she said with mock severity. "You're bound as *my* apprentice now."

"But I never agreed to that."

"If you didn't want this in your heart, you would see me as no different than I was before. Your heart knows what your head denies. For your first task, you must bring heart and head into alignment."

Bryce eyed her warily. "How exactly do I do that?"

"You learn." She held out her hand. "My walking stick, Davey." After David passed her the cane, she stumped to the patio doors and glared at Bryce. "Well? Give me your arm, boy. Show me what you've labored on these four years and more."

Bryce exchanged a glance with Mal, who raised an eyebrow. However, he offered his arm to Cassie and stepped outside.

And nearly fell on his ass.

The landscape he thought he'd known so well was transformed. Greens more vibrant, yellows and whites nearly luminous, the blue of the sky almost artificial in its intensity.

"What is this?"

She cackled like a contented hen. "Your druid sight. Don't worry. You'll grow used to it."

"Do I have to? It's not just sight though—it's everything." Without looking, he was conscious of Mal and David crossing the patio, of the difference between Mal's firm tread and David's lighter step.

He led Cassie forward, drawn to the edge of the slough by a sound like silver striking glass. *It's the creek, tumbling over the rocks.* And the birds—he could make out the voices of each one as they flitted from tree to tree. The rustle of small animals in the underbrush, the secret swish of fish under the water. *Hell, if I concentrate, I bet I could understand the wind soughing through the cattails.*

He grinned, joy threatening to lift him off the ground. "It's like a glorious synesthesia. I can hear the scent of the pines. Smell the color of the water. I—"

Wait. There, near the reeds where he'd spotted the dead fish earlier—Christ, had it been this morning? Underneath the glitter of sun on the water's surface crept a bilious yellow current.

"Do you see that? What is it?"

Cassie looked at the spot where he pointed. "Something that doesn't belong, not in this world." She turned and pointed imperiously at Mal. "Lord Maldwyn. Tell me of your injury."

"Unseelie redcaps. At least three. Two got me from the back when yon baby druid distracted me."

She tsked. "You are losing your touch, sulking out here on your own."

"It's not my choice. I'd be back at court if I could."

"Pfaugh. You could find a way if you put your mind to it."

Bryce tore his gaze from the creeping blight as another fish went belly up in the reeds. "What are you talking about? And what can we do about that—that *thing*?"

"We are talking of that thing now, you impatient boy, if only you would listen with your eyes open."

What? "That makes no sense. What's 'Unseelie'? Is it some kind of poison that someone's dropped into the water?"

"Poison." Mal snorted. "That's one way to put it."

Cassie rounded on him. "Lord Maldwyn, you are not helping, and if you are not part of the remedy, you are part of the ailment." She studied him, glancing between him and Bryce. "Hmmm. Perhaps that is the answer."

"Shite," he muttered. "When a druid gets *that* look in their eye, best run like bloody hell."

Mal wanted to back away before it was too late, torn between self-preservation and acting like a coward in front of David and Bryce. Cassie—hells, she already had his measure. *Bloody druid.*

"You, Lord Maldwyn, shall be Mr. MacLeod's tutor in all things supernatural. If he is to be an asset and not a liability, he must learn of our ways, and quickly. We must discover how far the blight has already encroached on this place."

"Not bloody likely. It's not in my job description to cater to druids. Why would I want to increase the druid population? There are already too many, in my opinion."

"All due respect, ma'am, but I've worked on my own for years." Bryce shot Mal an irritated glance. "I don't need a study buddy, let alone an involuntary one. I've got this."

She jabbed her cane into the ground. "You do not. If you had served your apprenticeship when you ought, between your thirteenth and eighteenth year, you would have no need of . . . a remedial tutor. But as it is?"

She bent and plucked a blade of fescue from the edge of the pool. With remarkable dexterity for someone with fingers like knobby twigs, she tied a tiny knot in each end, then held it in the palm of her hand and blew on it. The little twist of grass rose, higher and higher, until it was snatched out of the air by a passing sparrow.

"What was that in aid of?" Mal growled.

Cassie laced her fingers on the head of her cane, her druid-black gaze spearing first him and then Bryce. "The two of you have much to learn."

"I know everything I want to know, thank you," Mal said. "Chief among them: never get involved with druids. There's always a catch."

"You are a man of action, Lord Maldwyn, not a man of thought and contemplation. This cripples you far more than the lack of your sword hand." She turned to Bryce. "And you, Bryce MacLeod. You deny your instincts, depending instead on the results of this *data* you collect. Neither of you will succeed in your quests unless you learn what the other has to offer. So. You will now learn. Whether you will it or no."

She held out an imperious hand. "Davey, I'm ready to go."

"So am I," muttered Mal, and took off up the slope toward his patio. He got barely ten feet when a tug in his middle, as if a hook were embedded behind his navel, startled him to a stop. *What the—* He glanced behind him: at Cassie, who was leaning on her cane, her expression too bland to be innocent; at Bryce, whose hand was pressed against his own midsection. *Bugger this.* He took another step, and the pull turned insistent, uncomfortable. Two, and it flared into a burn so sharp that his knees gave out. *Shite.*

He levered himself to his feet, set his jaw, and broke toward his house again, but he managed only a few more feet before the pain in his belly erupted as if he'd been impaled by a poisoned lance. Bryce's gasp and moan told Mal he wasn't the only one afflicted.

Bugger this. I won't dance to a druid's piping. He gritted his teeth, the pain nearly whiting out his vision, and leaped. Bryce cried out and fell forward onto his knees as Mal was yanked backward onto his ass as if he'd been landed like a bloody sturgeon. For a moment, he lay blinking at the sky, chest heaving with his labored breath. Then he crawled down the hill until the pain receded enough to allow him to stand.

Bryce struggled to his feet as well, still far enough down the slope that his every move tweaked the invisible hook in Mal's belly, although the sensation wavered between *tug* and *burn* rather than *skewer* and *eviscerate*, thanks be to the Goddess.

"Gwydion's bollocks, woman." Mal staggered forward until the discomfort vanished completely. "What have you done?"

"Merely made certain that neither of you will shirk your responsibilities."

Bryce pushed his hair off his forehead with a hand that wasn't entirely steady. "I take my responsibilities very seriously, and because of that, I can't agree to this."

"You accepted the ointment of sight."

"Yes, but—"

"Then you've entered the apprentice contract. Now it's time to learn what that means." She pointed her cane at Mal. "You are tasked with teaching Bryce about the hidden worlds. It will be good for you. Give you some purpose until you accept the conditions of your exile."

"Accept it? Not bloody likely."

"You must accept it before you can resolve it." She turned to Bryce. "I'll send you some recipes for remedies that your grandmother might not have shared with you."

Bryce brushed at the grass stains on his ridiculous tactical pants. "I really don't think—"

"Then you should. Come, Davey."

She marched up the slope, leaning on David's arm, spearing the ground with her cane on every other step.

"Wait just a bloody minute." Mal charged after her and once again got pulled up short by whatever evil spell she'd used to shackle him to his proto-druid neighbor. "Shite."

"If you don't mind, Mal, I'd prefer not to have my guts yanked out by an invisible harpoon. Could you please, by anything you hold holy, stop trying?"

Mal grimaced, running his hand through his hair. "A point. Sorry."

Bryce stumbled up the slope until he was level with Mal. He waved his hand between their bodies as if he were testing for hidden wires. "There's nothing there, nothing in the air, but there's clearly some kind of tether connecting us."

"Druid magic. Lesson one, mate."

"So we're prisoners in some kind of magical chain gang?"

Mal barked a laugh. "Something like that."

A look of hurt flickered across Bryce's face. "I thought . . . she seemed so nice at first."

"Lesson two—druids are never nice. There's always a fecking catch." He gestured to Bryce's midsection. "And as catches go, the old witch has outdone herself this time."

He headed toward his back door, but since Bryce stayed rooted in place, Mal was forced to stop after he reached the end of their metaphysical leash—about ten feet, give or take. He sighed and turned around. "I don't know about you, mate, but I could use a drink. You can join me, or you can brood while you watch me down a pint or two, but either road, you need to come with me unless you enjoy the feeling of being eviscerated."

"Why do I have to come with you? Why don't you come with me?"

"I told you. I want a drink."

"Well, I want to check out that poisoned area in the wetlands. I need to run some tests, take some measurements. Hell . . ." He tore off his glasses and pressed the heel of his hands against his eyes. "Just looking at it with these freakish new perceptions could give me information I'd never dreamed of before."

"Thrilling as that sounds, I'm opting for the beer."

His eyes narrowed. "I thought you were supposed to tutor me."

"We can start with what kind of beer I prefer."

"I don't think that's what she had in mind."

"I don't bloody care what she had in mind. She's a druid." Mal kicked at a tuft of grass, which sprang back immediately. Fecking stuff was as annoyingly tenacious as Bryce. "Their minds are twistier than the road to the underworld."

For a moment, the only sound was the cry of an angry jay. "Did you just insult me?"

"I wasn't talking about you."

"No? But aren't I a druid now?"

Mal sighed. "Look on the bright side. If I refuse to tutor you, maybe she'll declare your apprentice contract null because you're too ignorant for her purposes."

"You're trying to weasel out of this, aren't you?"

"Hells yes. Aren't you?"

Bryce turned and gazed out over the wetlands. Mal could just imagine what he was seeing now—his first true glimpse of the etheric energy that bound everything in nature. Until Mal's exile from Faerie had deadened his own sight, he hadn't realized how much he'd taken that sight for granted. Not only had he lost the ability to detect *glamourie*, but he could no longer perceive the etheric sparkle that imbued the landscape.

"You know, I don't think I am. My grandmother was the most important person in my life. I worshipped her as a child, maybe because she was the only person in my family who seemed to give a damn about me. If this is what she was—if this is who *I* am—I want to find out everything I can about it. And if I have a . . . a birthright, a legacy from her? There's nobody else I'd rather be heir to."

"Touching. Now about that beer . . ."

"It'll still be there later. Come on." Bryce took off down the hill.

"Damn it man, hold up." If Mal didn't want to engage in an undignified—and painful—tug-of-war on the back lawn, he had no choice but to follow. "You'll pay for this, boyo," he muttered, struggling to keep the distance between them to under ten feet. He had no desire to get dunked in the swamp because Bryce decided to take an unexpected sharp turn.

When Bryce halted suddenly, Mal nearly plowed into his backside.

"What the hell is *that*?" Bryce's voice broke on the last word.

Mal peered past him. A small figure with pebbled brown skin and hair like a tuft of moss was watching them with wide yellow eyes. "*That* is an Unseelie bauchan. A sort of hobgoblin, as you might say."

"Don't tell me." Bryce turned his head, and the lift of his eyebrows, the quiver of his lips reassured Mal that he was facing this latest shock with his usual mixture of aplomb and curiosity rather than abject terror. "Lesson three?"

"You could say that, since if you hadn't been initiated into the Sight, you'd probably see the little bugger as some kind of animal you'd expect to find hereabouts."

"Wait. You mean when you threw that bottle yesterday, it was—"

"Yes. An Unseelie redcap, stalking a heron and about to piss in your precious swamp."

"And this morning?"

"Ambushed by the bastard and his mates."

Bryce frowned, his gaze darting between Mal and the bauchan. "Why are they after you?"

"My position in the Seelie Court—"

"'Seelie Court'?"

"Don't interrupt. This is lesson four, and it's all about me."

"Well then," Bryce said, his tone dry, "do carry on."

"Some call the Seelie Court light, and Unseelie dark. But it's not that . . . that . . ."

"Binary?"

"I was going to say simple, but that will do. Faerie itself is a magical construct, created by the elder gods in the time before."

"The time before what?"

Mal gave Bryce a look of disgust. "The time before Faerie, of course. It's essentially the result of an extremely powerful spell, and it's based on immutable rules. Each court has four basic tenets, and if you violate them, you can't be part of that court. If you violate *enough* rules, you can't be part of Faerie at all."

"Is that what happened to you?"

"More or less. Although I'm appealing the decision."

"How's that working for you?"

"Not well so far, however—"

"Hey! You! Stop that!" Bryce grabbed Mal's arm. "Did you see that? That thing just was about to toss something in the slough. I'll bet it's what poisoned the water in the first place."

"Could be. Although I'm not sure why—"

The bauchan turned and disappeared into the woods. Bryce bolted after it, splashing through a shallow inlet and showering Mal with malodorous water as the tug in his belly warned him to join the chase before the distance between them reached the disemboweling point.

"Goddess bless, man, hold up."

Bryce slowed but didn't stop. "I want to catch that thing. Ask it what it did and how to fix it."

"You really think if you catch it that you'll be able to talk to it?"

"Why wouldn't I?"

"It's a bauchan, boyo. A lesser Scottish fae. It probably only speaks Gaelic."

Bryce came to an abrupt halt, wildly scanning the trees and underbrush. "Where did it go? No way it could have gotten through that blackberry thicket without leaving a trace."

"You've been leaving plenty of traces your own self, crashing along like a battalion of trolls. I thought you wanted to preserve this place, not trample it into the ground."

"Shut up and be useful. Where could it have gone?"

Fair question. Too bad Mal didn't have an answer that made any sense.

CHAPTER ⌘ 6

With the energy of the woods sparkling in his peripheral vision, Bryce could barely contain his urge to bounce on his toes, or failing that, to shake Mal until he gave up some information. "Well?"

Mal rubbed his left hand along his jawline. "The only way it could escape was if there were a threshold into Faerie along here."

"Is there?"

"No. At least there shouldn't be. The thresholds are all known, and nobody mentioned one here. The nearest one is in Forest Park."

Bryce blinked, his anger at the desecration of the wetlands warring with the sheer delight of discovering a whole alternate reality. "There's a gateway into Faerie in Forest Park?"

"Yes. It leads to the bottom of the tor where the Seelie Court holds its revels."

"If Seelie and Unseelie are so inimical, why would one small lone Unseelie risk venturing so close to a large population of Seelie, especially if they're your size? Maybe it's using an Unseelie entrance."

An expression of almost comical perplexity skated over Mal's features. "Shite. Why didn't I think of that?"

"You mean that never crossed your mind? In however many years you've been alive?"

"We don't measure time the way you do in the Outer World, but no. It never did. As a Seelie fae, maybe I was only ever able to perceive the Seelie gates. Damn it all to Arawn's hells. How bloody stupid could I be? I assumed those were the only ways in or out, that the Unseelie would be using them too. No wonder I could never catch one going through a gate. They use a different bloody network."

Mal paced under the trees, far enough to strain the invisible whatever that linked them, but he turned before forcing Bryce to move or be disemboweled. Would that happen? If something, some external agent were to separate them forcibly, would that sleeping weight in his abdomen rip him open? It certainly felt that way, but he didn't think Cassie intended him to die, or Mal either.

He hoped.

Clearly he needed to do some research on druids. *A prerequisite for my own destiny. How typical of my life.*

He let Mal mutter for a few more passes before stepping into his path. "Now that you admit the possibility of an unknown entrance, how can we find it?"

"We can't." The force of Mal's voice startled a curious chipmunk into a scolding retreat. "That's my bloody point. I know where the Seelie gates are because I've always known, but I can't detect them anymore. My link to the One Tree was severed when I was exiled."

"There's only one tree in Faerie?" That seemed so wrong.

"Of course not, you twit. *The* One Tree, the one at the heart of Faerie, the one the elder gods hung their whole bloody construct on. It's the core of our magic."

Bryce frowned and sat down on a flat-topped boulder. "Is there a Seelie tree and an Unseelie tree?"

"If there were, it wouldn't be called the One Tree, now, would it?"

"Don't take your ill temper out on me." Bryce kept his tone mild. "I'm not the one who's spent however many hundreds of years—"

"Thousands of years."

"Thousands of years without bothering to test his assumptions."

Mal whirled, his face contorted in fury. "It's not like that. The fae aren't— We don't *question* things, not like humans. We can't. Our whole bloody society is based on an immutable spell. It can't change, unless you happen to have an elder god in your pocket and could convince her to pay attention to anything as insignificant as yourself."

Bryce's chest tightened as his habitual barriers snapped into place. He'd developed a standard defense strategy after Gran's death, coping mechanisms to deal with hostility and contempt. Ordinarily, he'd retreat into the safe isolation of his house, but he didn't have that option, did he? *Isolation just isn't the same when you have to share it with someone who despises you.*

"We can't all be lords, I suppose." He couldn't keep the bitterness out of his tone. "But that doesn't mean those of us who aren't noble aren't worth common courtesy."

Mal clutched his hair with his good hand. "I didn't— You're not— Shite. You don't understand."

"That's because you won't tell me anything. Christ, Mal. Could you give me a fucking break? After all, I just clued you in on something that escaped your notice for your entire life. Maybe, just maybe, you could return the favor and bring me up to speed on whatever it is Cassie thinks you have to teach me. After all, the sooner we meet her requirements, the sooner she'll cut us loose, right?"

Mal stopped pacing, and his shoulders fell. "Who knows what she'll do, but you have a point. You have any beer at your place? Food?"

"No to the first. I was planning on throwing together a vegetable stir-fry tonight, but—"

"Don't tell me. You don't eat meat, right? Not only a tree hugger, but a bloody vegetarian."

"I'm pretty sure that one of the points of vegetarianism is the *lack* of blood, but yes. I'm an ovo-lacto pescaterian."

"A which?"

"I eat fish and dairy as well as eggs, but no land-based animal flesh."

"Charming. In that case, it's my place. If I have to put up with this shite, I need alcohol. I've got leftover Thai food from last night, and I'm pretty sure there's something free of offending flesh."

Bryce trailed behind Mal in the gathering dusk, the lap of water at the edge of the slough harmonizing with the cheep of tree peepers in the gathering dusk. *The wetlands—it's a symphony, but all I heard before was a lone kazoo.*

Following Mal into his shadowed living room, Bryce aimed for the couch to keep out of the way, but the tug in his belly reminded him why that wasn't an option. Although he'd been understandably distracted by the juxtaposition of pain with the wonder of new druid senses, he was still a scientist, trained to observe: at ten feet, he and Mal would feel the pull; at twelve, the cramps would hit; at fifteen, they'd be certain their entrails were being yanked out with a meat hook before they hit the you-shall-not-pass limit. He really didn't feel like testing it again, so he sighed and joined Mal in the kitchen.

Mal stood framed within the open refrigerator doors, bent over, rummaging through paper containers stacked on the shelves. Bryce's gaze snapped to the man's ass, hugged perfectly by his worn jeans.

Holy crap. I'm going to be trapped within ten feet of that ass for the foreseeable future.

How the hell did this work? Obviously, they had to share quarters. Given the layout of both houses, either of them could piss or shower without an audience, provided the other one stayed in the next room. But would the invisible cable pass through walls? Could they close doors between them? On one hand, the scenery wouldn't be a hardship. On the other hand, *hard* might be an all too apt adjective for parts of his anatomy that would be impossible to hide from someone in close proximity.

Mal swore as he fumbled one of the cartons that he'd tried to balance on his right forearm.

"Here. Let me."

Mal glared at him over his shoulder. "I'm not helpless."

"Didn't say you were. But from the label on the side of that carton, it's shrimp curry, and if that's the only thing in your fridge that I can eat, I'd rather not have it splattered all over the floor."

Mal's jaw tightened, and Bryce wondered if he'd gone too far, but then the man snorted and grinned. *Christ, those dimples.*

"Good point. As a matter of fact, I've always wanted a lackey. And if you're a novice druid, you'd better get used to the feeling."

Bryce rescued the containers and set them on the counter. "So, this druid thing. I take it not just anyone can sign on. There are . . . aptitude requirements?"

"A bit more than that." Mal opened the cabinet and retrieved a couple of plates. "It's an actual bloodline. An offshoot of homo sapiens back in the days before the elder gods created Faerie." He pulled a handful of spoons out of a drawer and tossed them onto the counter with a clatter. "Get used to it, boyo. You're not entirely human."

"But you're not human at all, right?"

"Maybe a little. The planet had a limited pool of DNA to build with, so the elder gods made use of the materials available. But you're closer to human than any of the fae, barring cross-breeds. *Achubyddion* are somewhere between druid and Fae."

"What's an *achubyddion*?"

"One *achubydd*, two *achubyddion*. Although as far as anybody knows for sure, there's only one *achubydd* left on earth—my brother-in-law, David." He pulled a bottle of Double Mountain IRA from the refrigerator. "Want one? Or are you a teetotaler as well as a tree hugger and a veggie-lacto whatever?"

"I'll take one. Thanks. I drink, I just don't drink alone, and since I wasn't expecting any company, I didn't stock up." He accepted the beer from Mal and set it on the table. "So *achubyddion* are essentially extinct? What happened?"

Mal plopped a spoonful of rice on his plate and dumped the contents of another carton on top of it while Bryce filled his own plate. "Ignorance, greed, and power lust. The usual. *Achubyddion* are healers—they use their magic, which is really their personal etheric force, to effect change in another. Rumor had it that they could journey to the Hidden Realms too—not just Faerie and the Outer World, but to any of the underworlds they chose."

"Why doesn't anyone know?" Bryce transferred their plates to the table. Mal quirked an eyebrow at him, but didn't otherwise comment on Bryce's presumption as they both sat.

"Because, like the druids, their traditions were all oral, and since they were nomadic, you never knew where to find them. Then two hundred years ago, the last known band of *achubyddion* was massacred by a power-hungry bastard who was trying to use their energy to elevate his status from noble to royal."

Cold snaked up Bryce's spine. He pushed his plate away, suddenly not hungry. "Genocide?"

"That's the way of it. My brother Alun got caught in the middle of it, the poor bugger. Blamed himself for two centuries until David popped up to help him pull his head out of his arse."

"Sounds like a story there."

"Aye." Mal took a swig of his beer, then smiled wryly. "You could say so."

Bryce laid his hand on Mal's right forearm and squeezed. "Tell me. Please."

Bryce's voice was low and gentle, and for some reason, Mal actually wanted to tell him, if only so he wouldn't judge Mal too harshly. He'd been a worthwhile person once, even if he was bloody useless now.

"The fae who engineered the massacre back then, Rodric Luchullain, was the Consort of the Seelie Queen. He wanted to depose her. Become King himself. But although he was of the highest rank, a Daoine Sidhe, he wasn't royal. He thought he could use the bloodbath to elevate himself, but it didn't work. Then, this past summer, he found out he hadn't eradicated the entire race, so he launched a more targeted attempt. He believed if he sacrificed an *achubydd* in—" Mal swallowed against bile when he remembered the way in which Rodric intended to murder David. "—in a particular way, he'd be able to use the death energy to make himself royal."

"Christ. Would that have worked?"

Mal shrugged. "Who knows? I doubt it, from what we've learned from David since then, but the point is that Rodric believed it, and that's what drove his actions. Then my brother intervened and bested Rodric in a duel, but didn't kill him."

"Having met David—and if your brother is anything like you— I'm shocked he restrained himself."

"He's nothing like me, the self-righteous arsehole, but stopping wasn't his idea. David begged him not to, and since Alun is completely dick-whipped, he threw down his sword. But then the bloody idiot actually turned his back on Rodric." He still couldn't believe Alun's stupidity. If he'd paid closer attention, at least kept eyes on the traitorous git, Mal wouldn't be in this predicament. "Rodric picked up the sword and was about to run Alun through. I objected."

"'Objected.'" Bryce's dry tone wasn't a question.

"Strongly. Cut the bastard's sword hand off at the wrist." He drained the rest of his beer and slammed the bottle down on the table.

"Christ," Bryce whispered. "Did he wound you too somehow?"

"Nah. Never saw me coming." He held up his crabbed right hand. "This is thanks to one of those damn rules of the Faerie construct.

The rules protecting Consorts, even when they're murdering traitors." Mal got up and fetched another two beers. "Until I make whole what I took, I'm barred from Faerie, and my hand might as well be missing too."

"So you're supposed to, what, magically reconnect this guy's hand? Can fae magic do that?" Bryce accepted the second beer, although he hadn't finished his first yet, his eyes lighting with excitement. "Can *druid* magic do that?"

"Sorry. No. An *achubydd* probably could do it, but David's the only one around, and he wouldn't heal Rodric if the man were his last hope of a handjob. The boyo could forgive the whole kidnap-rape-sacrifice plot against himself, but Rodric tried to kill Alun. That, he'll never forgive."

"But . . . isn't David still at risk? Couldn't he be attacked? Kidnapped again?" Bryce leaned forward, the light from the fecking LED wall sconce sliding over his skin and catching on the dusting of brown hair on his forearms.

Mal's cock stirred in his pants. Shite. The man might be a gods-forsaken druid, but he was still bloody fine. "Nah. David is Alun's Consort now, so he's protected by the same rule. And he's got other protections in the Outer World. If Rodric could get by Alun—which is highly unlikely—he'd still have to run the gauntlet of the shifter and vampire communities. They've kind of claimed David as a mascot."

Bryce froze with his beer bottle halfway to his mouth. "'Vampire'?" He set the bottle down. "'Shifter'? As in werewolves?"

"Well, the dragons are the ones who're most invested, but where the dragons go, the rest of the shifters follow."

"Exactly . . ." Bryce swallowed. "Exactly how many kinds of shifters are there?"

Mal grinned. "Get out your notepad, tree hugger. You're about to get a crash course in Supe 101."

Several hours—and rather more beers—later, Mal peered blearily at Bryce across the table littered with empties. "Those are the basics."

"Incredible." Bryce slid down in his chair and leaned his head against the backrest. "So your Queen unified all six branches of the Celtic Fae?"

"Yup." Mal suppressed a belch. "Scots, Irish, Manx, Bretons, Cornish, and of course," he bowed his head, "the Welsh."

"How long ago?"

"Not long as the crow flies."

Bryce squinted at him, obviously trying to focus. "The crow doesn't fly across time."

Mal snorted. "That's all you know."

"And everyone was okay with that?"

"Define *okay*." He held up his right hand. "Let's not forget the foiled coup attempt by Rodric bloody Luchullain, ex-Consort, traitor to Queen and realm. Or, as we now call him . . ." he grinned and mocked the royal wave, "Lefty."

"So why are the Seelie and Unseelie still at odds?"

"She unified across nationalities, not affiliation. You need another beer?"

Struggling upright, Bryce frowned at the bottle in his hand. "Is this one empty already? No wonder I—" The bottle dropped from his fingers and rolled across the table, caroming off several others before it spun to a halt. He head fell forward onto the table with a clunk.

"You can't be that drunk, can you?" *Or am I that boring?*

Suddenly, the pressure in the house fluctuated, flattening the blinds against the windows and popping Mal's ears with the kind of displacement that signaled a major working.

With his only ally passed out and drooling on the table, Mal regretted the last three beers. Only a high mage—or fae royalty—could cross the boundary without a fixed gate, and given that Mal had no weapon—and no way to wield it if he did—he was at a distinct disadvantage.

Ah, bugger it. He had no defenses; he was either dead or he wasn't, so no point cowering here, waiting for his doom to fall. He thrust his chair backward and staggered to his feet. With the hair on his arms standing on end, he edged past Bryce and peered into the living room.

The caped figure standing in the shadows by the fireplace had to be at least seven and a half feet tall. Its deep hood completely hid its face, although the uneven silhouette suggested that the skull underneath the heavy black fabric might rival Alun's old beast-face.

"Didn't hear you knock." Mal kept his voice casual. *Yeah, a half-dozen beers'll chill anybody out.*

"I didn't." The being, whatever the hells it was, had a voice like a brass gong.

"Ah. That would be why. Mind telling me what you're doing in my house—uninvited, I might add?"

"I believe we have an opportunity to benefit one another, Lord Maldwyn."

"I never bargain with anyone if I can't look them in the eye. Are you willing to drop the disguise?"

"That would be . . . inadvisable."

Damn it, he should have pulled that twelve-inch blade out of the knife block. If he was about to get snuffed, at least he'd do some damage on his way down. At this point, he'd almost welcome the release.

Except Bryce was passed out and vulnerable not five feet away, possible collateral damage if Mal pissed the intruder off. Despite being a druid, Bryce didn't deserve to be slaughtered in his sleep by something he hadn't known existed until two hours ago.

"Can I offer you a beer? Some Thai curry?" A blade through the eye?

"I'm not here for conviviality."

Clearly, because this guy could make a circus sound like a funeral. Mal propped himself against the wall between the dining room and living room. "Could you spare me your name? Or didn't you come here for that either?"

A rumble in the massive chest could have been a growl, a suppressed laugh, or simply gas. "You may call me . . . Steve."

"Steve." *And I'm bloody queen of the May.* "Right, Steve. What's your proposition?"

"We've something in common, you and I." Steve paced from the fireplace to the front door, his cloak swirling around his massive booted feet. "We both suffer under a curse."

Mal shifted so his left shoulder was toward Steve. "Mine is as good as handled."

Silence, except for Steve's stentorian breathing. "We both know that is a lie. If you had any hope of lifting your curse, you'd not cower here in this Outer World hovel."

"Hey. It's not a hovel. It's state-of-the-art passive house construction." Or so the brochures claimed.

"Yet you make no secret of your disdain for it."

"I haven't . . ." Well, maybe he had, but that Steve knew about it sent a bolt of alarm down Mal's spine. *I'm being watched—by beings more powerful than redcaps.* "Your point?"

"We can aid one another. You assist me in lifting my curse, and I will assist you with yours."

"Promises are easy. How do I know you can deliver?"

Steve raised one enormous gloved hand and pointed. Magic crackled in the room like captive lightning, lifting the hair on Mal's scalp.

The fingers of his right hand tingled and twitched. Mal sucked in a breath. He extended his arm and, for the first time in two months, made a fist. And he could feel it—nails biting into his palms, the stretch of long-frozen tendons.

Relief shot through his chest. *I'm whole again. I can—*

Then, just as suddenly, the magic bled from the air, his hand once more a dead weight on his wrist.

"As you see, I've the means to aid you. My abilities are limited by my curse, you understand, so I can only loosen your bindings for a brief moment, but when I am returned to my true form, my power will be likewise restored."

Mal closed his left hand over his right, forming it into a fist again. *Goddess, it had felt so good to* feel *again.* And if Steve was true to his word, Mal could be free of his curse without giving anything back to Rodric bloody Luchullain. But with high mages, just as with druids, there was always a catch. *Now I* really *wish I hadn't had those last three beers.* If he were slightly more sober, he'd stand a better chance of reasoning his way past Steve's evasions.

Nah. Cassie was right—thinking had never been his strong suit.

"You've told me how you'll help me. How do I help you?"

"By performing three tasks."

Three. Why was it always three? *Bleeding Welsh triads.* "Let me guess. Bring you the Spear of Lugh? The Stone of Fál? Hells, why not the head of Bran the Blessed while we're about it?"

Steve rumbled. "Nothing so difficult. At least, not difficult for one such as you—someone with a degree of natural cunning and a certain disregard for . . . tradition, shall we say?"

"I'm not sure whether to be flattered or insulted."

"Flattered, to be sure. You're a man known for getting the job done, and results are all that matter here. My bane lifted as well as your curse, and both of us restored to our full rights and responsibilities."

Mal squinted in the dim wash of light from the dining room. He was missing something in his beer-induced haze, but damned if he could figure it out. At least Steve had said *responsibilities* and not *privileges*. He grinned. Look at him, paying attention to words. Alun would be so proud.

"All right. I'm in. But—"

White hot pain seared the palm of his left hand. He doubled over, his hand clutched to his chest.

"What the bloody hells, man?" Eyes watering, he uncurled his fingers and peered at his palm. A Celtic knot glowed in the flesh, fading to the reddish black of a tattoo as the burn receded.

Steve removed the glove from his left hand and held his palm up. The same knot glowed there, and in this light, his flesh looked blue. "Lest you think you alone suffer, we share the geas brand."

"I'd have appreciated a little warning."

"Would it have rendered the pain any less?" Steve pulled his glove on. "We're now bound by the contract."

"Wonderful." The pain had cleared some of the alcohol haze from Mal's brain, and it struck him that perhaps he should have asked for a little more detail about the nature of these alleged tasks. Bloody hells, he couldn't even open a jar of fecking pickles.

As he stalked toward the liquor cabinet next to the fireplace, a tug in his belly halted him, reminding him of his other disability.

"Ah, shite." Mal might be willing to endure a little—all right, a lot—of discomfort for the sake of another drink, but Bryce didn't deserve the added torment. The poor blighter was already the victim of a supernatural Mickey Finn. He stopped, stretching his arm toward the brandy bottle, but couldn't quite reach.

Steve plucked it off the cabinet with one long arm and held it out.

"Thanks." Mal snatched it and took a swig directly from the bottle. "You may not know this, but I've got an unscheduled sidecar."

"If you mean the druid, yes, I'm aware. That's why I rendered him unconscious before our discussion."

Mal peered through the archway at Bryce, still out cold with his head amongst the empties. "You did that?"

"It seemed prudent." Steve strode to the archway in an operatic swirl of cape. "I can increase the play of your bindings while you're in Faerie, but I cannot remove them. You must simply convince him to accompany you."

"Right. I'll tell him I'm about to engage in a little supernatural espionage for a mysterious—"

"No." Steve's voice rang, vibrating the bones behind Mal's ears. "You cannot tell him—or anyone—about our agreement, nor anything about me."

"Considering I don't bloody know anything about you, that's no hardship, but how am I supposed to—"

"I'm confident of your powers of persuasion."

That makes one of us. Mal leaned against the wall across the archway from Steve and crossed his arms. "Let's cut to the chase, then. What's this famous first task?" No harm in finding out what Steve had in mind. If it sounded impossible, he could back out now by calling Alun and telling him some jacked-up mage was trying to convince him to go on the take.

"Retrieve the Seat of Power from under the throne of the Unseelie King."

Mal blinked. "Say what?"

"Retrieve the—"

"Yes. I heard that, but what the bleeding fuck, man? Even when I wasn't an exile, I couldn't enter the Unseelie Court, let alone the throne room. I didn't know there were separate gates for the blighters until today. If the Queen finds out—"

"As long as you keep to the Unseelie lands, avoiding the common sites, I can guarantee you'll remain undetected."

"Great, but that still doesn't explain how I find my way in, or how I can waltz into the King's presence and ask him to move his arse so I can steal the Seat of Power, whatever the bloody hells it is."

"Here." Steve reached under his cloak and pulled out something that glinted gold in the lamplight. With a flick of his thumb, he sent it flipping through the air.

By reflex, Mal tried to catch it with his right hand, only to have the thing drop to the floor when it hit the deadened flesh. He retrieved it, and the light from the dining room sconce revealed a hand-hammered gold disc etched with the same Celtic knot as the geas brand.

"What's the purpose of the shiny?"

"The token will grant you access to the Unseelie sphere for the next twenty-four hours, as well as the ability to find the needed threshold."

"Twenty-four hours? Are you mental? I've never been to the Unseelie sphere, and you expect me to plan and execute a heist inside the throne room?"

"Twenty-four hours is all you'll need. The King has decreed a mandatory gathering at the Stone Circle at midday, so the Keep will be deserted. That will give you the necessary window of opportunity."

As intelligence went, it left a lot to be desired, but it was better than nothing. Mal pocketed the coin. "I'm not exactly up to my old fighting trim. What if we run into some hungover lordling playing hooky from the King's little jamboree?"

"You won't. A mandatory decree is magically enforced. But if you suffer from an excess of sensibility, this—" he flashed the brand on his palm "—is the same spell used to lock the Keep, protecting it when it's unmanned. If it's activated, your mark will allow you to pass. Does that soothe your troubled nerves?"

"I don't have excess sensibility or bloody troubled nerves, you blasted—" Mal crossed his arms, tucking his right hand against his rib cage. "Fine. What exactly is the Seat of Power?"

Steve hesitated. "I cannot describe it. But you'll know it when you see it."

Steve's certainty of Mal's ability to navigate unfamiliar terrain and recognize previously unseen objects was touching but alarming. "Can you give me a ballpark idea of size? Is it bigger than a bread box? Able to dance on the head of a pin?"

Rumble rumble. "Small enough to fit under the throne. Large enough to be visible, even with eyes less keen than Balor's." He reached under his cloak again and pulled out a carved wooden box, about the size of his two massive fists. *Shite, where does he keep this stuff?* "When you've secured it, place it in this casket, and I will retrieve it."

Mal took the box. He tried to open the lid, but it was locked. "How am I supposed to put anything in it? You plan to give me the key?"

"It will open in the presence of that which it seeks."

"Of course it will." He gestured to the mantelpiece. "Is this an acceptable location for it, or do I have to bury it under an oak tree by the light of the full moon?"

"The mantel will do."

"Grand." Mal set the box on the narrow shelf next to a blown-glass vase (courtesy of David). "Especially since the moon won't be full for another week and a half. Shame for you to have to twiddle your thumbs for so long to get your prize."

"As you say." Steve turned in a billow of black velvet. *And he accuses me of drama?* "One last thing. If you think to violate our contract in any way, the geas brand will render your left hand as lifeless as your right. You'll do well not to betray me, Lord Maldwyn."

Bloody fecking hells.

CHAPTER ❈ 7

S omeone was playing a timpani inside his head. Bryce moaned and rolled over, only to fetch up against . . . was that skin?

He cracked an eye open. *Yes, definitely skin.* His scalp prickled with alarm. *Oh God, am I—* But no. He was still wearing his Henley, and as he patted down his body with one cautious hand, he found boxer briefs still in place, thank the powers that be, but no pants.

What? How? And perhaps more to the point, where? He drew back cautiously, blinking at what appeared to be a veritable cliff of golden-skinned flesh, decorated by two copper disks that must be—

He scrambled backward, which only served to expose his bare legs to the breeze wafting in through the open window. Clutching the sheet to his groin, he knelt on the mattress. Without his glasses, he could make out dark hair and delphinium blue eyes. Christ. He was in bed with Mal Kendrick.

Why can't I remember?

A chuckle vibrated the bed. "Good morning."

"Uh . . ."

"Looking for these?" Mal held out Bryce's glasses.

Bryce snatched them and jammed them on. Faced with Mal's knowing smirk, he was tempted to yank them off again. Sometimes soft-focus was your friend, especially when humiliation threatened to swallow you up in a full-body blush.

"What am I doing here?"

Mal sighed hugely, resulting in a truly astonishing expansion of his already formidable chest. "You don't remember? Those deep secrets, those tender avowals . . ." He waggled his eyebrows. "Those dirty promises. I'm hurt."

"We didn't— You— I wouldn't— Did I?"

Rolling onto his back, Mal flung one arm across the bed and hid his eyes with the other. "You don't remember our special, special night. I may go into a decline."

"Now I know you're full of shit." Screw it. Bryce threw off the sheet and scuttled the eight feet to the bathroom, keeping his back toward his infuriating neighbor to hide the fact that his dick was attempting a daring escape from his underwear.

Closing the door on Mal's laughter, Bryce checked his reflection in the mirror over the sink. No beard burn. Taking a fortifying breath, he peered down at himself. His shirt looked as if it had been slept in, of course, but on first glance, he wasn't sporting the residue of any embarrassing bodily fluids, nor was he sore in any telltale locations. That tightness in his chest was relief, surely, not disappointment. He didn't fuck arrogant men—especially arrogant men so far out of his league.

He staggered forward, but a muffled curse from Mal coincided with a pull in his belly. *Those damned supernatural shackles. I'd forgotten.*

"Do you mind getting out of bed so I can make it to the toilet?" he called. "I need to pee, and being doubled over with cramps plays hell with my aim."

Judging by the stream of unintelligible words, Mal took as little pleasure in their predicament as Bryce, but at least the pressure eased and he was able to make it across the bathroom. He supposed he should be grateful—at least he could close the door. And what if the length of the invisible chain had been shorter?

Didn't bear thinking of.

After finishing at the toilet, he washed his hands, splashed cold water on his face, and used a fingertip of Mal's toothpaste to clean his mouth out, since it tasted like the floor of a brewery. How many beers had he drunk last night? Whatever the count, it was that many more than he usually drank.

He pressed his fingers to his forehead and winced. *Hangovers don't hurt on the* outside. He pushed his hair back and peered at himself in the mirror, where a bruise purpled his forehead. Had Mal frustrated him so much he'd finally given in and beaten his head against the wall?

I need answers, and to do that, I'll have to face him. So what if the man was the hottest thing this side of a solar flare? Bryce was a scientist, damn it. He could be dispassionate and analytical. *But I still don't want to have the conversation wearing no pants.*

He rummaged in the cabinet under the sink and located a towel to wrap around his hips, to give himself a little more coverage than his briefs. Then, taking a deep breath, he opened the door.

Mal was standing on the other side, leaning one hand against the doorjamb, wearing nothing but a smile. "You know, if the old biddy doesn't give over soon, we'll have to install a recliner in the middle of the bedroom. The wall is rubbish for comfortable waiting."

Mouth suddenly dry, dick attempting to emulate a compass needle to Mal's true north, Bryce turned sideways and scooted past, ass brushing Mal's hip. "Bathroom's all yours."

"Yes. Glad you remembered that."

He scanned the room for the rest of his clothes while Mal continued to lounge in the doorway. As Bryce's gaze skittered from the top of the dresser to the floor to the bed, he still managed to collect enough data about Mal's body to know (a) he sported no tan lines, (b) he was uncut, and (c) Bryce was in so far over his head that he might as well be at the bottom of the Mariana Trench.

For lack of anything better to do with his hands, and to keep his obvious interest out of Mal's line of sight, he turned his back and fussed with the bed, pulling the sheets straight and mitering the corners like Gran had taught him.

"Don't know why you're in such a pelter, Dr. MacLeod. You've got nothing to be ashamed of. It happens to the best of us. Or so I'm told."

Bryce's anger trumped his libido for a change, and he faced the god in the bathroom doorway. "Listen, Kendrick. You can't have it both ways. Either we fucked like randy teenagers, which given the dearth of physical evidence, I seriously doubt, or nothing happened at all." Mal opened his mouth, but Bryce forestalled him with an open palm. "And if nothing happened, it was not because of erectile dysfunction."

Mal winced. "Shite, man, watch your language."

"Will you tell me what happened?"

"First you declared your undying devotion to—"

"Enough. At least tell me how I got this." Bryce shoved his hair off his forehead and pointed to the bruise.

"Shite." Mal took a step forward, but retreated when Bryce pulled back. "Look. All jesting aside, we have to talk, so I'll try to be quick in there." He grinned. "Unless you'd like to shower with me? You being such a devoted conservationist and all."

"Thank you, but no."

"Suit yourself." He stepped into the bathroom.

"Wait. Do you mind telling me what you did with my clothes?"

"They're strewn around the living room. You got a bit enthusiastic with your striptease."

"Kendrick."

"Sorry, mate. They're in the other room. I thought we'd have to camp out on the sofa at first, and your tactical costume was a wee bit lumpy for comfort, so I, er, helped you out of it. Then I managed to wrestle you down the hallway after all." He nodded at the bureau. "Since you won't be able to reach them until I come out, help yourself to shorts and a fresh T-shirt. I shouldn't be more than a half an hour or so."

"Wonderful."

He paused, doorknob in hand, and grinned. "By the way, nice legs."

Despite his taunts about taking his time, Mal didn't linger in the bathroom. Bryce had barely pulled on a T-shirt and a pair of sweat shorts before he was out again. Still naked. Still tempting. Still totally out of Bryce's league.

"Listen, mate. Sorry about your forehead. You went facedown amongst the dead soldiers before I knew you'd had one too many."

"Dead soldiers?"

"Empties."

"Oh. Right."

Mal bent over (ass!) and pulled a pair of faded jeans out of the bottom (don't think about *bottom*) dresser drawer. He stood up and stared at them dangling from his left hand for a moment.

"Shite," he muttered. "You mind sashaying over to the bed? Don't worry. I won't try to have my wicked way with you. It's just . . ." He brandished the jeans, not meeting Bryce's gaze, a faint pink staining the crests of his perfect cheekbones. "Can't pull them on while standing. Haven't quite got the way of the one-hand, one-leg action."

"Of course." Bryce matched Mal's pace across the room to the bed, but when Mal sat on the foot, Bryce edged around to the other side so he wasn't sitting smack in the middle of the man's personal space while he wrestled his jeans over his legs. "How long ago did it happen? Your curse?"

Mal huffed. "Remember that much about last night, do you? Couple of months. Right after the summer solstice."

"Not long, then."

"No? Seems like for-fragging-ever."

"I suppose it would. I'm sorry."

"Not your concern, is it? Except—" Mal stood and pulled his jeans over his hips, commando, tucking his penis inside but leaving the button fly open to display a thatch of curly black hair. "I need your help."

"To button your fly? I don't think so."

He smirked. "Not that that doesn't raise some interesting images, mate, but this is something else again. Not as entertaining for us both, perhaps, but it might tempt you nonetheless."

This *persuasion* shite had been a damn sight easier when Mal had been in possession of his fae powers. For most of his life, he'd only had to lean a little heavier on the *glamourie*, and no man could say no to him. Even without the *glamourie*, he'd managed to get his way with a suggestive charm that had failed him only once—with David, who had a jaundiced, club-wise ability to identify a player at fifty paces.

Just his luck that his tree-hugger neighbor would be the second man in history to be able to resist him.

With Bryce, however, it seemed more like a shy nobility—he refused temptation precisely because he *wanted* to give in to it. Mal hadn't missed the obvious evidence, despite the man's clumsy—and rather endearing—attempts to conceal it. He was like one of Arthur's more virtuous knights. Bors, perhaps, or Peredur—never as self-righteous as that bloody prig Galahad.

But Galahad himself couldn't have been more restrained than Mal last night when Mal had hauled Bryce into the bedroom so they wouldn't have to sleep on the dining room floor. One-handed, removal of clothing had been a frustrating thirty minutes, during which he couldn't enjoy any of the scenery. He hadn't even copped a single feel—at least not on purpose.

Despite David's claims of Mal's hero status, though, he wasn't so much of a bloody saint that he hadn't *looked* once Bryce was stretched out on the bed.

The man was beautiful. Long and lean, and although his chest was hidden by his shirt now, its proportions were obvious, tapering in a neat V to narrow hips. His legs were dusted with hair that glinted copper in the light, and when he'd rolled over? *Goddess have mercy.* That arse in tight cotton was a bloody work of art.

But although Mal was no saint, he was not so much of a sinner that he'd take advantage of an unconscious, nonconsenting man, no matter how tempting the target or how long it had been since his last hookup. He'd virtuously covered that delectable arse with the sheet and lain down on his side of the bed.

But with Bryce awake and looking ready to bolt, Mal needed a plan. He had twenty-four hours before he'd be in default of Steve's first task. If he failed, would that mean he'd forfeit the whole bargain, depriving him of the hand he had left? Shite, he wished he'd been more sober last night. He'd have asked for more bloody details.

As Mal watched Bryce fidgeting about the room, he realized Bryce reminded him of those prissy knights for a reason other than his virtue. He had a cause, just like they did. A quest. His wetlands and this ridiculous "green" community were his obsession as much as the Grail ever was for Arthur's goons.

Seduction—it's all about the right lure.

"You know that bauchan we chased yesterday?"

Bryce stopped faffing about with the insulated blinds and turned around. "The one who was contaminating the creek? The one we lost in the woods?"

"The very same. What if I told you we have a chance to track it into Faerie?"

"I thought you said you couldn't—"

"Normally, no, I can't. But while you were so fetchingly asleep"—Mal grinned at the wash of pink that stained Bryce's face—"I received some information and a . . . a talisman that changes things up a bit."

Bryce's eyes narrowed. "Changes things how?"

"What do you say we discuss this over coffee and a nosh?" He patted his belly and realized he'd left his fly hanging open. No wonder Bryce's gaze kept drifting to points south. Maybe button-fly jeans were the wrong choice. He could unbutton with one hand—he'd had plenty of practice in clubs and alleys—but the reverse? He had no desire to share that awkward process with Bryce. He'd just have to spill some judicious hot sauce on his pants to give him an excuse to change. "Don't know about you, but I'm feeling a bit peckish."

"Right. I . . . uh . . . Sure." Bryce bolted from the room, and Mal followed before the invisible leash could yank him down the hallway.

In the kitchen, Bryce frowned at the refrigerator, the cabinets, the pantry, as if his glasses granted him x-ray vision into Mal's pathetic food stores.

"What do you normally eat for breakfast?"

"Whatever's left over from last night's takeaway."

Bryce lifted his eyebrows and peered at Mal over the top of his glasses, his lips tipped in a lopsided smile.

A surge of lust tightened Mal's balls, and his cock pulsed inside his inconveniently open pants. *Holy shite. That mouth. Those eyes.* He broke the gaze and opened the pantry. "Or . . . you know . . . cereal. Toast. Whatever."

"Do you have such a thing as a vegetable in this place?"

Mal poked his head out from behind the pantry door, keeping the rest of his body safely hidden. Why hadn't he thought to put on a shirt? Shite, even his nipples were hard, and it wasn't all that cold in here.

"Might have heard a rumor of one once or twice. David stocks the fridge and cooks for me sometimes. Have a look."

Bryce opened the refrigerator and bent over to dig in the produce bins, giving Mal an outstanding view of the way those soft terry shorts hugged that admirable arse. *Gahh!*

He grabbed the coffee and scooted past Bryce's tempting backside to sling grounds into the coffee maker.

"So tell me about this change-up." Bryce emerged from his refrigerator reconnaissance with a carton of eggs and a handful of green things of various shapes. "Rather overly convenient, don't you think?"

Mal dumped water into the coffee maker and switched it on, then retreated to a safe distance, putting the breakfast bar between him and Bryce. "Not necessarily. One of the things you'll learn about the supernatural worlds, Faerie in particular, is that everything—people, places, events—are more closely woven than you might think."

"So a coincidence isn't really a coincidence?"

Mal grinned, able to relax now that his weakness wasn't on literal display. "Never. Think of life, of all levels of reality, as a giant tapestry. Pull a thread in one place and you can change the fabric in places you don't imagine."

"So you're saying the bauchan pulled a thread."

"Or maybe its action was the result of a pulled thread. We can't know. That's the problem with fecking synergy."

"Listen to you. So scientific." Bryce cracked an egg into a bowl with one hand.

Huh. Maybe I could learn to do that.

"Not science. Nature."

"Nature *is* science. Applied science. Science in its natural habitat, if you like."

"Your grandmother teach you that?"

Bryce shrugged and selected the largest knife from the block. "To begin with. But it's also an argument I've had many times over the years with colleagues. Whether science should force synthetic processes on a natural environment. Whether the very nature of the synthetic contaminates the natural biosphere."

"Well, however you want to account for it, we've got an opportunity. But it's not open-ended."

Bryce chopped a zucchini faster than Mal used to parry sword thrusts. "Tell me."

"Midday today. That's our target to be in place in the Unseelie sphere."

Bryce paused with a double handful of zucchini suspended over a hot skillet, a smile transforming his face. "You're kidding. We're actually going into Faerie? For real?"

"Don't set your hands on fire."

Bryce colored and dropped the vegetables into the pan. "Sorry. But another whole world? To someone who's spent his whole life in one country—most of it in one city—this is a huge deal."

"We won't be there to sightsee. We've got a mission."

"Right. We'll track the poisoner."

Mal briefly wondered whether he'd be struck dead for deceiving Bryce the instant they crossed the gate into Faerie. However, considering one of the tenets of the Unseelie Court was *Honor is a lie*, for all he knew, he'd be hailed as one of their own.

"We'll *look*. But we may not be able to find it. You should know, however, that bauchan aren't independent thinkers. We're looking for a bigger fish."

Bryce's brows knit together as he tossed the zucchini with a deft flip of the sauté pan. "Do we know who the alleged big fish is?"

"No."

"Do we know where the alleged big fish swims?"

"No."

"Do we have any idea if the alleged big fish even exists?"

"Again no. But they must. Fae are captives to their nature. Some of the lesser orders have nothing resembling free will—only instinct and a desire for approval. The bauchan couldn't have come up with the idea on its own. It had to be following orders."

"So what's the plan?"

Mal rubbed the back of his head. "Well . . ."

Bryce pointed a fork at him. "Don't tell me. We don't have a plan." He attacked the eggs in the bowl, beating them into submission before pouring them into a second skillet. Mal hadn't even known he had two skillets. "Isn't there something we could do to prepare?"

"Look. My informant claims the Unseelie masses will all be occupied from midday for at least a while, and the Keep will be deserted. We have this narrow window to get there and retrieve an artifact from the throne room."

"Will this artifact help us find who's responsible for the pollution?"

"It's the best lead we've got." Mal forbore mentioning it was a lead that had nothing whatsoever to do with the Unseelie incursions into the wetlands, but Bryce accepted the evasion at face value.

Gwydion's bollocks. The man should not be let out alone.

"All right, then." Bryce divided the eggs between two plates, topped them with fragrant vegetables, and pushed one serving across the bar to Mal, along with a fork. "Eat up. I'm not walking into an unknown world with no field gear, let alone in your shorts and yesterday's underwear. We've got to prepare."

CHAPTER 8

By midmorning, Bryce was so antsy he was surprised Mal hadn't clocked him on the head just to keep him from fidgeting. But he couldn't help it—he was about to enter another *realm*. How freaking cool was that?

For a brief time when he was a kid, he'd dreamed of being an astronaut, of being the first man to set foot on another planet. He'd been obsessed with the stars and astronomy. Then he'd realized that the level of technology necessary for extraterrestrial exploration had no chance of materializing during his lifetime, and he'd focused on his own planet instead.

But this was nearly as good. Maybe even better, because it had the possibility to transcend science. To give him a glimpse into that *other*, the flip-side of science.

Magic.

He glanced at Mal standing in the doorway of the bedroom. Why did he look so much bigger here in Bryce's house than he did in his own? Architecturally, the buildings were identical, but reversed. Both had muted natural tones on the walls and floors. Maybe the juxtaposition of the larger-than-life man—no, *fae*—with the furniture Bryce had owned for years threw the perspective off.

Not to mention that the sheer raw beauty of the man—damn it, *fae*—caused everything within range of him to look shabby, dull, and paltry.

Bryce patted the pockets of his vest and pants, assuring himself that all his gear was in place. "Are you sure you don't want to borrow a pair of pants?"

Mal glanced down at the leather pants he'd changed into after breakfast. "Something wrong with the ones I've got on?"

"No." *God, no.* The leather hugged Mal's anatomy in almost pornographic detail. "Just, you know, some extra pockets could come in handy." Bryce winced. Poor word choice, given Mal's sensitivity about his disability. "I mean, you said yourself we don't know exactly what we're up against."

"These have always served in the past." He slapped his hip, his hand lingering over a welt pocket. "I'm willing to risk it. Besides . . ." He waggled his eyebrows. "I'm sure you're tactical enough for the both of us. You're kitted up like we're off on a month-long trip down the Nile."

Bryce ducked his head, the heat spreading up his throat and over his cheeks. "It only makes sense. It's a place I've never been—a place I never even *imagined*. Who knows what we'll run into."

Mal pushed himself off the doorjamb with one shoulder. "You're building this up too much, mate. It's bound to be anticlimactic."

"You don't know that. You've never been to this part either."

"True enough. But Seelie or Unseelie, it's all bloody Faerie. Can't imagine it'll be that different. Shall we?"

Mal led the way out the French doors onto Bryce's patio and strode off down the slope toward the wetlands. Bryce followed, the instruments in his pockets clacking and clinking against one another, noises he'd never noticed before. When they got to the shoreline, Mal stopped and gestured for Bryce to precede him.

"This is your territory. Lead on."

Bryce skirted the water along the path and entered the woods following the same route they'd used yesterday. When they reached the edge of the clearing, he halted, appalled.

The leaves of the crabapple that yesterday had been healthy and green, if dusty from the seasonal lack of rain, had curled in on themselves like Mal's cursed hand. He touched one of the shriveled leaves with the tips of his fingers, but flinched back when *something* skittered along his skin, raising the hair on his arms. He touched the leaf again. *Pain. A burn like acid as the tainted water was carried inexorably from root to leaf.*

Plants weren't like people. They couldn't refuse to drink. He laid a tentative hand on the tree's trunk—and could swear he heard it weeping.

Tears pricked his own eyes. "Damn them. Why are they doing this?"

"Your guess is— Shite." Mal's voice dropped to a ragged whisper.

"What?"

He nodded past the tree to a mossy boulder. "The threshold."

Bryce stroked the tree trunk again. "We'll fix this," he whispered. "I promise." He turned to Mal. "Why are we standing here? Let's go."

Mal cocked his head, mocking again. "I should warn you, tree hugger—"

"Yeah, yeah." Bryce tugged on the hem of his vest and settled his hat more firmly on his head. "Once we're through the gate, you're the boss. I know."

"Glad to hear it. What I was going to say, though, is you need to mind how you go." He elbowed Bryce in the ribs. "Because, in Faerie, the trees might hug back."

While Bryce was still blinking, attempting to assimilate this latest bombshell, Mal urged him forward, past the boulder, and they were . . .

Exactly where they'd started.

Bryce whirled, his misery at the state of the wetlands and his anticipation at the otherworld journey morphing into fury. "Is this your idea of a joke? Taunting the science geek? Baiting the druid's apprentice? Aren't we past that by now?"

"You see me laughing?" Mal didn't avoid Bryce's gaze, but was that guilt flickering across those perfect features? "Not like I've come this way before, now, is it?" He squinted, studying the woods around them. "Faerie is always bounded by water. Maybe we have to cross the stream." He gripped Bryce's shoulder, his fingers tightening to the point of pain. "Think you can stand down while we try again? Wouldn't do to burst into an unfamiliar destination in the middle of a bloody row, right?"

Bryce swallowed his fury. Mal had attitude to spare, but he wasn't petty, small-minded, or cruel. He had a purpose, and he actually needed Bryce's help. "Okay."

"Good man. I've got to keep hold of you as we cross, all right?"

Bryce nodded and took a deep breath. "Let's go."

They splashed into the stream, and midway across, everything changed.

The flow of the water, the angle of light, the very *air* felt different. Older, as if he were standing in the same river, under the same sun that had shone on the ancient Celts when the Romans first set foot on British soil. Instead of the ever-present smell of fossil fuels, the air held the tang of wood smoke and ozone, as if lightning had just struck and ignited a fire nearby.

And the trees—Jesus Christ, they towered overhead. "Old growth," he murmured, peering up through the heavy canopy. He reached out to touch the trunk of an oak larger around than his LEAF, but then remembered Mal's comment about trees hugging back and hesitated. Even so, a grin split his face. "It's real."

Mal chuckled. "Got it in one, boyo."

Elation bubbled up in Bryce's chest like a cauldron of joy boiling over, spilling into his veins. He turned to look back the way they'd come, and plants from a whole different ecosystem had replaced the native Oregon plants in the preserve.

He frowned and took a step forward. That beech just across the stream . . . It was taller, broader, older by far than the crabapple in the same spot in the Hillsboro woods, but it was clearly suffering from the same wasting disease. On a tree that old, that majestic, it wasn't just heartbreaking; it was a tragedy.

"Mal. Look at that. The blight isn't only on our side of the gate."

"Guess that answers part of the question. Whatever's going on, it's not only an Outer World attack. It's happening here too."

"Is that why your informant sent us here? Because he knew there was a connection? Some kind of symbiosis between Faerie and the human world?"

Mal turned and picked his way through a heavy blackberry thicket. "Could be."

Bryce followed, pulling the Felco pruners out of his vest pocket. He tapped Mal on the shoulder. "Can I clear a path? I won't be . . . you know . . . dismembering anything sentient?"

"Even in Faerie, brambles are just brambles." He stood aside. "Have at it, mate."

Bryce clipped runners out of the way, careful not to take too much or disturb any more than he had to. After about ten feet, they emerged onto a dirt path almost wide enough to be called a road.

Bryce paused to tie a yellow flag onto a branch close to where they'd emerged. "Where to now?"

Mal didn't answer. Instead he stood in the middle of the road, his left fist propped on his hip, peering around as if he'd never seen the place.

"Shite. I don't know. The bastard said I'd know it when I saw it, but I don't see anything but—"

"Mal." Bryce gripped Mal's elbow, his voice low. "Look."

Cowering under an elm on the opposite side of the road was a creature with the same mottled brown skin and green hair as the one they'd seen in the wetlands. Its back was to the two men, and its shoulders shook, a low keening sound drifting on the breeze.

No wonder. The poor thing's back looked as if someone had scooped chunks out of its flesh. Its bright-red blood was startling amid the soothing browns and greens of the forest.

As if it could detect their scrutiny, the creature peered over its shoulder with enormous vertical-pupilled golden eyes. It bleated in distress and scrambled into the undergrowth to disappear from their view.

"Shite," Mal muttered. "So much for going undetected."

"What was that?"

"Our bauchan. You ought to recognize it by now."

"But . . . when we saw it, it didn't look as if it had been attacked by a saw-toothed ice cream scoop."

"No."

"So what—"

"It's been tortured in the worst possible way for its kind." Mal's voice was troubled. "Those divots on its back? That's where its kits should be. Someone's ripped them away before they were ready to be weaned, hurting the parent and possibly killing the young. There's no reason for that, unless whoever's giving the orders enjoys inflicting pain."

"Is that kind of thing—" Bryce fought a surge of dismay "—common in Faerie?"

"Unseelie are driven by self-interest, so if the means justified the ends, I doubt they'd be squeamish. Seelie? I'd like to think we're above torture." He stared at the spot where the creature had vanished. "But I've been wrong before."

Running into the bauchan had been a stroke of unbelievably bad luck, not that Mal should have expected anything more from this life these days. Mal had no love for Unseelie, but it was incumbent on the higher orders of both courts to care for the lesser, especially if they were bound in service. If the condition of the poor thing's back meant what he suspected, then its master was beyond cruel—and had failed in his covenant with Faerie. *Let's hope the bastard isn't my new pal, Steve.*

He glanced at Bryce, who still looked as if he were trying to decide whether he'd gotten the world's best birthday gift or had stepped into the hells' grimmest anteroom.

"Do you think it's okay?" Bryce took a half step toward the bauchan's bolt-hole. "I've got some salve in my pocket that—"

Mal caught Bryce's arm. "Even if we could catch it, which I doubt, since it knows this realm and we don't, we don't have the time." He pointed to the sun, nearly overhead. "Narrow window of opportunity, remember?" Mal had his doubts about whether the same talisman that granted them access would keep them safe after its expiration date. The last thing he needed was for the Queen to discover he'd been mucking about in Unseelie lands.

Shading his eyes with his hand, Bryce peered up at the sky, and his jaw dropped. "Christ. It's yellow. And the sun looks twice as big as it does at home. Are we even on the same planet anymore?"

"Same old, same old. But Faerie's a construct, remember? Here, size can be relative to importance. The elder gods were fiends for solar and lunar cycles, so this is their idea of a joke."

"Or a warning." Bryce tugged the bill of his cap lower. "Right, then. Which way?"

"I . . ." Shite, maybe they should have followed the bauchan after all. Maybe it was supposed to be their guide. Bloody Steve and his *you'll know it when you see it.*

Bryce snorted. "If your old job was tracking down fugitives, how did you find them? Stand in the middle of a road and hope they drove by and hit you with their cars?"

"Oi. Watch the disrespect. Magic, remember?" He would have felt it, even here in the Unseelie sphere, filling him with the peace, the rightness, the belonging that was the birthright of all fae.

But the void under his heart where his link to the One Tree used to root gaped wide, leaving him hollow, yearning for something to fill him again and give him a reason to breathe.

"Do you even have a plan?"

"I told you everything I know about the maneuver." Well, not exactly everything, but anything that related to navigation.

"Maybe you should have demanded more information."

Mal slapped his forehead. "Why didn't I think of that? The man is bloody brilliant."

"You don't have to be sarcastic." Bryce scowled and fussed with the zip on a vest pocket. "If someone gives you a project, it's reasonable to expect a complete rundown of its parameters."

"Welcome to the world of espionage, boyo."

"Espionage?" He stopped faffing about with his vest and stared at Mal with wide eyes. "We're . . . spies?"

"We didn't knock on the bloody front door, now, did we? But there's no point in moaning about what we don't have. If we don't find the Keep within the next half hour, we might as well go home now." A frisson of fear shot up Mal's spine at the idea. If he gave up now, would he wake up tomorrow with no functional hands at all?

"The Keep. Got it." Bryce strode off down the road, dust puffing out from under his thick-soled boots.

"Hold up. Where you going?"

"Since the Keep clearly isn't hanging in a tree or hiding under a convenient boulder, I'm going to that curve in the road to reconnoiter."

"Big words from a tree hugger." But the man had a point. Mal checked in the other direction. The road fell away, disappearing under the canopy of the woods, but beyond it, with mist circling it like a tattered crown, was the green sweep of the hill where the Stone Circle lay, already crawling with Unseelie.

Right, then. Not that way.

He turned around, but Bryce had disappeared. Shite. Had he gone after the bauchan? Gotten snatched by a roving band of duergar? Why hadn't Mal felt the tug on their blasted druid tether?

Steve. He'd said he could increase the play of the binding. Why hadn't Mal thought to test it before now? Bryce could be anywhere.

He took off down the road at a run, looking for signs that Bryce had left the path to venture into the woods to commune with some random tree. He rounded the first curve in the road. Still no Bryce, although a scatter of boulders, ranging from man-sized to troll-sized, lay partially blocking the way, leading into the woods.

Mal skidded to a stop, raising a cloud of dust level with his knees, and approached the stones cautiously. It never paid to make assumptions about rocks in Faerie. He checked behind each one, but couldn't find any sign of Bryce.

"Shite. Last time I go walkabout with a bloody druid."

"If you have something to say, by all means, don't hold back."

Bryce's voice echoed oddly among the rocks, almost as if he were . . . Mal looked up in time to see Bryce drop from a tree branch and climb down the nearest rock. He dusted off his hands.

The burst of relief at finding Bryce unharmed lasted five seconds before it turned into outrage.

"What the bloody hells were you doing?"

"Looking for this alleged Keep of yours." He jerked his thumb down the road. "Thataway. Just around the next bend."

"Are you out of your bloody mind?"

"What? Because I decided that *finding* the Keep would require *looking* for the Keep? Are you angry because you didn't think of it?"

"No, you sodding idiot. I warned you about the trees in Faerie, and you go climbing one before you've been in the place for five minutes. Do you have any idea what could have happened to you?"

"Be careful, Mal." Although Bryce's tone was dry, it held a bit of an edge. "I might almost think you care."

CHAPTER ❈ 9

Bryce waited, arms crossed, while Mal spluttered. *Yeah, I know it's not me you care about.* "What's gotten up your ass anyway? You're the one who keeps stressing our timeline. I'd think you'd be glad I've discovered at least a general direction to go, given our lack of a plan."

Mal flung his right hand out, cursed, then pointed with his left. "Do you see these rocks?"

"Yeah. They were convenient for scaling the tree."

"Look closer."

Bryce, still on a rush from his first steps into a new world and getting a leg up on Mal for a change, strolled over to the largest stone, docking his nose against a large protuberance. "Looking. This close enough?"

"That boulder used to be a troll, and you're nose to prick with him right now."

Bryce reared back. "Wha—"

"Who knows? Maybe a druid blowjob is all the poor sod needs to re-animate. Think of it as a public service."

"Screw you." Bryce marched down the road, not much caring whether Mal caught up to him or not. At least their spectral chain didn't seem to be present on this side of the gate.

"Oi. How do you know that's the right way?"

"I told you. I looked."

"Why is it that you can see it but I can't?"

Bryce slowed his headlong pace, and Mal pulled up level with him. "I didn't exactly *see* it with my eyes." It was more like a game of hot-cold. When he faced in one direction, he felt a warmth under his sternum. Turn away—warmth fades; turn back—warmth blooms. "I just know this is the way to go."

"No doubt it's another damned druid thing," Mal grumbled.

"Don't knock it. At the moment, it's all we've got."

As they continued on the path—Mal stomping along with his trademark scowl firmly in place—they didn't see any other Faerie denizens. At one point, they heard a low roar from somewhere behind them, like the sound of the crowd at a football game. Since Mal ignored it, Bryce assumed it was nothing to worry about.

Then, out of nowhere, a vast gate blocked the road, as if the entire Keep had been dropped there like Dorothy's house on top of the Wicked Witch of the East.

Bryce hoped it wasn't a portent.

Nevertheless, he couldn't help feeling vindicated—and a little smug. "Voilà. The Keep."

"Don't get cocky, boyo. It's not like you built the bloody thing."

Exasperated, Bryce stepped in front of Mal. "I realize that, but do you suppose you could at least acknowledge that I helped get us here? If I depended on you for my self-esteem, I'd be ready to hang myself from the tree, not climb it."

Mal rubbed his good hand on the back of his neck. "Right. Sorry. Not at my best lately."

"I hope not, because if this is you at your best—"

"Stow it. Let's move on, shall we?"

Bryce tilted his head back and surveyed the door. It had to be at least double the height of his house, solid oak, and hinged with heavy blackened iron. A faint image, like a hologram of a Celtic knot, glimmered in the air above the lintel. *That's not ominous at all.* "Are you sure it's deserted?"

Mal studied the hologram for a moment, head tilted to one side, then glanced at his hand for some reason. "Absolutely."

At least one of us is confident. Still, there didn't seem to be anyone around. "Do we knock?"

"Hells no. If the place is deserted, who'd answer?"

"How do we get inside, then? I have no idea how to pick a lock." Especially one that size. The key that fit that thing must be as long as his arm.

Mal cocked an eyebrow. "Aren't you supposed to be the brains of this outfit?" He set his palm against the door, shoved, and it creaked open. "Before you overengineer a break-in, it pays to try the door."

Bryce's mouth dropped open. "Doesn't leaving a fortress unguarded and unlocked sort of defeat the whole point of a fortress?"

"Magic, boyo. Works a treat." Mal grinned wolfishly. "Unless the other bloke's got a better spell."

He slipped inside, and Bryce followed him into a vast vaulted hall. Long narrow windows pierced the stone walls up near the rafters, but most of the light came from torches set in iron wall-sconces. Their footsteps echoed on the flagged floor.

"All right, bloodhound. Which way do you reckon?"

Bryce was about to disclaim any knowledge of castle architecture, but the warmth in his chest had other notions. "There. Through that arch and down the corridor."

"Useful trait, that. Do you suppose you can find my missing spanner when we get home?"

"Shut up," Bryce muttered, and led the way across the room.

The corridor opened out into another room wider than the entry hall, but just as long and high. This one was brighter, the windows wider to allow the oddly close sun to shine fully into the room. Bryce frowned. *Wait a minute.* The sunlight spilled through the windows on all three sides of the room. How could that be?

He didn't bother to ask Mal. He knew what the answer would be: *magic.*

The room was empty of furniture except for a high-backed wooden throne, intricately carved and set with jewels. It sat on a raised dais midway down the long side of the room, backed by a huge tapestry depicting a single enormous tree.

The One Tree, I presume. A tall fae stood under the tree, a midnight-blue cloak trimmed with ermine across his shoulders and one of those ornate Tudor-type crowns on his dark hair.

As Bryce faced the throne, the warmth in his chest began to pulse like a second heart. "It's there. The thing we're looking for."

"The Seat of Power." Mal strode across the room, his gaze fixed on an enormous ruby mounted at the apex of the throne's back. "He said I'd know it when I saw it. That's got to be it. It's the most obvious thing in the room."

Bryce trailed after him, rubbing his chest. "I don't know. It doesn't feel right."

Mal rounded on him. "If you're so bloody informed, you tell me what it is."

Bryce circled the throne, studying its sides, although its rear was covered by the tapestry. The One Tree was as detailed and perfect on the back as it was on the front, but the rear-facing figure was a woman in a green gown, her hip-length red hair bound by a thin gold circlet.

He finished his circuit and stopped at the foot of the dais, trying to interpret his newfound senses. *Where is it?* What *is it?* Mal shifted from foot to foot next to him in the first sign of nerves he'd ever shown.

Bryce shook his head. "It's not the ruby. Too obvious."

"That's the point. It's meant to show who's got the goods, right?"

"No. If it really is something that confers power, you wouldn't want to flaunt it like that or it would encourage thieves." He inclined his head at Mal. "Our presence being a case in point. In fact, you probably wouldn't want to advertise it at all. You'd— No." Bryce burst into laughter. "It couldn't be. Could it?"

Mal glanced over his shoulder again. "Look, mate, I'm all for a good joke, but we need to move things along."

"Don't worry. I've got this."

Bryce lay on his back at the foot of the throne and slid underneath until his head and shoulders were between the massive claw-footed front legs. *There.* The woodcarver had made an attempt to camouflage the tiny compartment amid the whorls of Celtic knot-work, but it was as obvious to Bryce as if were outlined in neon. His laugh burbled up again at the pure joy of these new senses, at the proof that he could be more, that he *was* more, than the nerdy college professor.

"What the bloody hells are you doing down there?"

"I need your hand."

Mal's face appeared upside down next to his shoulder. "Now is not the time for a handjob."

"Don't be an ass. Here." Bryce grabbed Mal's left hand and held it under the compartment. For some reason, he didn't want whatever was inside it to fall to the floor. He worked his fingernail into the nearly invisible seam and popped it open.

The contents dropped into Mal's waiting hand, although Bryce couldn't see what it was from his angle underneath. He closed Mal's fingers over it. "Don't drop that."

He scooted out from under the throne and scrambled to his feet as Mal uncurled his fingers. "This? This is the Seat of Power?"

Holding his breath, Bryce cupped his hand under Mal's and gazed down at the tiny object: an agate, striped in all the colors of the forest. The stone pulsed in time with the warmth in Bryce's chest. "Absolutely."

"Doesn't look like much."

"Are you kidding? You don't see it?"

"See what?"

"Its . . . its energy. Its aura. Its . . . I don't know, its essence."

"Just seems like it should be more impressive, is all, with a name like 'the Seat of Power.'"

"Look at it, though. It has all the layers of the world. Brown for earth. Green for plants. Gold for sun. Quartz for water. Pyrite for fire. It's the whole world contained in a single stone. It's perfect."

"Right, then. You take it." Mal dumped the stone into Bryce's hand. "Stow it in your tactical whatevers."

Bryce cradled the stone against his chest. "You sure?"

"It'll be safer that way." Mal glanced over his shoulder at the archway that led to the front door. "But we need to move."

"All right." He tucked the little stone into the inner pocket of his vest, the one that rested over his heart, and its pulse aligned with its own.

Mal's nerves blazed as if they'd been ignited like a *Calan Mai* bonfire. He'd been on edge since they'd passed the threshold—who wouldn't be with a possible death sentence hanging over his head—but this was beyond ordinary caution. It didn't help that the geas brand had started to burn the instant that bloody stone had hit his palm.

Sweat broke out on his forehead and the back of his neck, and his shirt clung to him as if he'd just gone three rounds with his longsword.

Then the talisman in his pocket shot a burst of heat straight through the leather and onto his hip.

"Shite!" The bloody thing might leave a brand of its own. "Bryce. Give me one of your gloves. Quick."

The druid moved fast, Mal gave him that. He unhooked one of the canvas gloves from his ludicrous pants and slapped it in Mal's left hand—at which point Mal simply stared at it stupidly. He couldn't put the damn thing on. Meanwhile, the talisman was burning like a bitch. He'd probably have a Celtic knot etched on his arse for the rest of his life.

Bryce grabbed his shoulder. "Either let me help you with the glove or tell me what the problem is."

"It's . . . ah, oak and bloody thorn." Mal gritted his teeth. "My hip pocket. A . . . a coin. Hot."

Bryce didn't bother with the glove. He shoved his hand into Mal's pocket and drew out the talisman. "Got it."

"Damn it, man. You shouldn't have . . . at least the glove . . ." Mal struggled to put a sentence together. What was wrong with him? A sense of doom loomed over him like a wyvern inches from clamping its teeth on the back of his neck. Mal grabbed Bryce's hand, ready to knock the bloody talisman into next week before it could harm those long elegant fingers.

"Hey." Bryce closed his hand over Mal's wrist and held the coin up, pinched between the thumb and index finger of his other hand. "It's okay. It's cool. To the touch, I mean, not as in copacetic. Although it's that too." Bryce grinned. "Mission accomplished, eh?"

"Don't say that. Don't ever say that." Not when they were in the throne room of the Unseelie Court. "We still have to get home, and something tells me we'd better—"

A boom echoed down the hall, and the tapestry behind the throne rippled in a sudden gust of wind.

Bryce's eyes grew huge behind his glasses. "Was that . . ."

"Front doors. We're about to have company." Judging by the hurried tread of booted feet, they'd either been discovered, or someone else had clandestine business in the throne room while the King was playing his power games in the Stone Circle. "At least four. Warriors, by the jangle of metal."

Which meant swords—while he and Bryce were armed with nothing but a pair of bloody pruning shears and a magic rock.

Bryce pointed at a half-sized door in a shadowy corner behind the throne dais. "Could that be a way out?"

"Probably leads to the kitchens, or the mews. Those are usually staffed by lesser fae."

"Let's go, then."

The booted footsteps were closer, in the corridor between the hall and throne room. "The point of the wee door is to keep big bastards like me out."

"Have you got another option?"

The first of the warriors reached the archway and shouted a hoarse battle cry. "Not a bloody one. Go."

They raced to the door, and Bryce flung it open. "You go first."

"Not likely." Mal glanced over his shoulder at the group advancing toward them. The fact that they were in no hurry was troubling. Did that mean this exit was a trap? A dead end? Did the passageway get smaller before it reached the kitchen? The notion of getting wedged with a sword at his backside had his breath sawing in his lungs. Shite, he hated small places.

Bryce grabbed a handful of Mal's shirt. "Can you drop the alpha jerk crap? We don't have time for it. You know where you're going. I don't. I can shut the door. You can't. Not if the hall is the same size as the door. If—"

"Maldwyn Kendrick. Stand down."

Mal whipped his head around at the sound of that voice. Gwydion's bloody bollocks—*Rodric Luchullain*. An evil grin plastered on his perfect Daoine Sidhe face, the bastard slowed to a swagger. The trio of warriors at his back shuffled in confusion, which meant Rodric had them in thrall.

Leaning closer, Bryce murmured, "I'm guessing that since that guy knows you, we're screwed."

"You're a bloody genius. Get on. Now."

Bryce ducked through the door, and Rodric's grin morphed into a grimace. "Stop him, you fools."

Mal took a deep breath, doubled over, and dove through the door, the slap of size twenty-two boots and the *zhing* of unsheathed swords spurring him on.

He landed on his knees on a stone floor worn smooth by the feet of lesser fae. He tried to catch himself, but his reflexes hadn't yet twigged to the absence of his right hand. He hit the floor with knees, left hand, and right shoulder, but caught himself before braining himself on the stone.

The door slammed behind him, followed by the thud of a bar dropping into place.

"Come on." Bryce gripped his arm. "The ceiling's high enough. You can stand." He helped Mal to his feet, teeth glinting in a manic grin and eyes sparkling behind his glasses. "Guess it's bigger on the inside than it is on the outside."

Mal stared at the ceiling, nearly as high as the one in the entry hall. The hallway should have been dark, but instead it was flooded with light from knee-high windows along one wall—a wall that should have had nothing but more Keep behind it.

The other wall was far enough away that it should have been smack in the middle of the throne room, and above the tiny door, it was splashed with murals depicting all manner of lesser fae wielding weapons twice their size, slaughtering a battlefield full of greater fae.

"Bloody hells," Mal breathed. "The little buggers have been holding out on us."

"Don't tell me. None of the ruling fae ever bothered to look in here."

"How would I know? I've never been to this gods-forsaken realm before."

"What about in your own realm? Ever checked on how the other half lives?" Bryce studied a spot in the mural where a brownie in an apron stood victorious on the chest of a fallen—and headless—body in the armor of a Daoine Sidhe. "Might be time for a little labor negotiation. Seems they've got a few issues with management."

A boom thudded against the door. Mal grabbed Bryce's arm. "Save the egalitarian shite for later. In the meantime—"

"Right. Haul ass. I get it."

They raced down the hall, past more scenes of mayhem, until they fetched up against another half-height door. Mal yanked on the handle, but the door didn't budge.

"Shite. Do you suppose it's barred on the other side?"

"Let me see." Bryce peered along the edge of the door. "I don't see anything. Maybe if we—" He leaned against the door, and it swung open without a creak. He lifted his eyebrows with a cheeky smile. "Push, not pull."

Mal scowled at him. "The hinges are on this side, damn you."

"Magic. Gotta love it."

"I don't—"

"Look, you want to argue, or do you want to escape? I don't know why those goons haven't made it into the hall yet, but I suggest we take advantage of it, yeah?"

"Right." Mal shouldered past Bryce into the empty kitchen, under braided swags of onions and sheaves of dried thyme and rosemary, down three broad stone steps into the scullery. He tried the door between two enormous sandstone sinks. It didn't budge with either a push *or* a pull, damn it.

He thought of the murals in the hall and what kind of punishment might rain down on the lesser fae if any of the nobles suspected what direction their art took. *They'd never risk it.* "It's spelled. All the doors are spelled against greater fae." He turned to Bryce. "You try."

Bryce grinned evilly, the prick, and hooked one finger under the carved wooden handle. The door opened without protest. Mal suspected it would have opened without any touch at all if Bryce had simply asked it to.

Bloody druid.

How twisted was it that he found the man totally fecking hot?

CHAPTER ❧ 10

The kitchen door opened into a small graveled courtyard. Bryce followed Mal across it into the trees, still gloating over his unexpected ability to—to what? Open tiny doors? Detect magic rocks? Chill cursed metal? Maybe it was trivial and stupid, but *damn*. Just . . . damn. It was so *cool*, even if it was nothing compared to whatever magic or battle skills or whatever-the-hell-else Mal and his ilk could do.

He'd always been so ordinary. Workmanlike. Brown in a world that valued bright colors. But this. This was something he could do that even Mal couldn't. For the first time in his life, he felt special.

As he pounded down the path under the trees in Mal's wake, he should have been terrified. He was in a place that he'd never dreamed existed. Several really big guys with really big weapons could be chasing them right now. But he didn't care. If he didn't need all his breath for running like a maniac, he'd laugh until his belly ached.

He settled for a grin so wide it practically met his ears.

He stopped grinning pretty damn quick, though, when Mal skidded to a halt next to an ancient oak at the edge of the road.

"What is it? Are those guys already out there?"

"They're not yet, but they will be. Shite." Mal ran his hand through his hair, squinting through the trees at the way they'd come. "This is not the same bloody path. I have no notion where the gate is."

"I—"

A ululating cry echoed in the woods, startling a flock of starlings out of the trees.

"Shite. They're on our trail. Now what?"

Bryce's hot-cold sense kicked in again, aiming him toward a moss-stippled boulder. "Over there." He led the way past it, then across a rivulet that cut a deep groove in the hillside.

The cry repeated, accompanied by a thunderous crack, underlaid with a sound that lifted the hair on the back of his neck—a sustained keening at the high edge of his hearing. Another crash, like the sound of an ax hitting wood, and the keening increased.

"*Augh*." Bryce stumbled, pressing his fingers to his mastoid bones. "Christ. What is that sound?"

Mal stopped next to him, chest heaving. "Most likely the sound of our impending doom. If we don't find our way out of here, those battleaxes will land on our skulls next."

"Not that. It's something . . ." He staggered against the trunk of the nearest beech. "It's— Oh." He circled the tree with both arms, Mal's taunts about tree-hugging be damned. The vibration under his hands felt like the quiver of a plucked violin string. He pressed his ear against the bark, and the sound got louder, lower, more desperate. "The trees. They're crying."

"That'll be us in a brace of minutes if we don't move our arses."

A shout echoed through the woods along with another thud of an ax against wood.

"I can't let them keep that up. I can't let them hurt the trees." Bryce pushed himself off and spun around. The road. They'd walked up the road to the Keep. It was—he consulted his new senses, and they didn't fail him—that way. He took off.

"Shite," Mal growled, but thudded along in Bryce's wake.

They broke out of the trees and onto the dusty path. Bryce whirled, waving his arms overhead. "Hey! Over here!"

Mal grabbed him by the front of his vest. "Are you out of your bloody druid mind? You want them to find us?"

"Better us than the trees. We can run. They can't." He cupped his hands around his mouth. "Yo! Bozos! This way!"

"'Bozos'?"

"You wouldn't understand." The first of the giant guards crashed through the underbrush onto the path, and the keening retreated to a manageable thrum in his skull. "Now we run." He sprinted down the road, Mal at his heels.

"Running's fine, mate," he panted, "but we need a bloody destination."

"Don't worry about that. I've got it." And he did too. Somehow the sound of the trees changed, herding him in the right direction. Like a glow stick in the dark of a cave, he spied the flag he'd tied around the blackberry cane, pulling him toward the gate.

He grabbed Mal's wrist and towed him between the trunks of two alders, dodging rocks that might or might not be former trolls.

There. That poor withered beech marked the spot. "Can they follow us across?"

"I don't know. Depends on what their orders were and whether the bloody conclave on the hill has them locked inside." Mal was breathless, his right arm clenched against his ribs, his crabbed hand flopping at his waist. His skin had turned from its normal healthy bronze to almost gray.

"Mal. You look like shit. Are you okay?"

"I—" Mal stumbled, and Bryce caught him against his side. "Shite. This bloody place. It's not friendly to the likes of me."

"Lean on me, then. We're almost home."

A shout behind them, far too close for comfort, spurred Bryce across the stream. One instant, the keening of the trees was vibrating his bones, and the next it was gone, replaced by the familiar sounds of the slough.

But he didn't stop. He wanted to lure any potential followers as far as possible from the fragile wetlands ecosystem as he could. He hauled Mal along the berm toward the slope of the lawn behind their houses, an odd sizzle in his blood.

Whoa. This must be what adrenaline feels like. No wonder people became addicted to extreme sports. *Although running for your life from an alternate realm isn't exactly something that's likely to catch on.*

Finally, they stumbled up the bank. Around them, everything seemed normal. Birds called cheerfully from the trees; insects hummed; frogs croaked. That damned evil blight hadn't disappeared, but it hadn't grown too much either.

"I think we're okay. Nobody's following."

"Yet." Mal sank down on the grass. "Don't get cocky."

Bryce kneeled in front of him. "Are you okay?"

"Yeah." He took a deep breath and blew it out. "The Unseelie sphere. It's— Shite, how do those people live like that?"

"It bothered you? Really?" Bryce rubbed his hands up and down his thighs. "I've never felt anything like it. The sky, the earth, the trees. They could nearly talk. It was incredible."

A dimple quivered in Mal's cheek. "Sometimes they do. In fact, sometimes they *walk*. And when that happens, running like the *Cwn Annwn* are on our arses won't help for shite."

Bryce stared into those eyes, bluer than the wild iris that dotted the shoreline in spring. *God. He's gorgeous.*

Bryce blamed the adrenaline still coursing through him for what he did next. He knee-walked forward until Mal had to lean back or tacitly agree to their proximity.

Mal's smile widened. "Got something on your mind, mate?"

"Maybe."

"Don't hold back, then. Let's hear about it."

Bryce advanced further until his mouth was a breath away from Mal's. "How about this?"

"I'm listening." Mal's voice was a suggestive growl, and Bryce's cock responded as if it were a customized mating call.

"I'm done talking."

"There's a wonder. I thought—"

Bryce closed the last half inch, shutting off Mal's sarcasm by the simple expedient of fusing their mouths together.

Goddess preserve me, but that mouth is a wonder. Mal threaded his good hand through Bryce's hair so Bryce wouldn't get any ideas about backing off. The weakness that had hit him all of a sudden in the Unseelie sphere ebbed as if Bryce were feeding energy back into him with every touch of his tongue. If this was what kissing a druid was like, Mal had been wasting his time in human clubs.

Not that many druids were as hot as Bryce.

Mal sank back on the grass, and Bryce followed until he was stretched out above Mal, the kiss going on and on as if they were vying for the tongue-jousting championship of the whole Seelie Court.

Mal had been without sex for so long, longer than he'd gone since he'd first learned to wield the sword at his groin with the same skill as the sword in his hand. Whatever it was, his cock was on board with any plan Bryce had. Although . . .

He tugged Bryce's hair, pulling him back from the kiss—a crime if ever there was one. "You know, boyo, I suspect sex in public violates your precious neighborhood CCRs. Besides, we might traumatize the wildlife."

Bryce grinned, wolfish, his eyes sparkling behind his glasses. "The wildlife has less shame than you do—they copulate in public all the time. However, you have a point. My place or yours?"

"Mine. I've got supplies."

"You think I don't?"

"Do you?"

Bryce huffed a laugh. "No. At least not anything you'd let near your genitals, considering your reaction to the first aid soap."

"Right, then. Mine it is."

Bryce stood. "Give me your hand."

Ordinarily, Mal would have spurned the offer—he wasn't completely helpless, and the inexplicable weakness that had overcome him in the Unseelie woods had dissipated. In fact, he felt better than he had in months.

But he craved Bryce's skin against his, so he clasped the offered hand and stood, stealing one last, heated kiss before leading Bryce up the hill and into his living room. He closed the doors, his back against the glass, and studied the man in front of him.

"Take off the tactical gear, man. I don't want those pruners anywhere near my bollocks when I take your arse."

Bryce raised one eyebrow. "What makes you think it's my ass that'll get taken?"

The thread of confidence in Bryce's voice made Mal's cock throb in his pants. *But I never bottom.* Why did the idea of Bryce buried in his arse excite him to the point of coming like a stripling? Still, he'd learned never to tip his hand too soon. "No expectations. No strings. No—"

"No clothes."

Bryce stripped off his vest and flung it across the room, where it caught on the mantelpiece. When he pulled his T-shirt off as well, Mal's breath caught in his throat, for no reason that he could fathom. Bryce wasn't his usual type. He went for club boys with a bit more spice than his brother-in-law: men with attitude but who appreciated his size and swordsman's physique. Occasionally, he'd sparred with one of the other warriors in the bedroom as well as the practice ring, so he could admit appreciation for the kind of chest he sported himself.

But Bryce was neither of those things. His muscles weren't overdeveloped by centuries of sword practice and fae genetics, but they were there. Defined subtly under the smooth skin, across the taut stomach and in the chest like Roman marble. Beneath his navel, a trail of dark hair led down, pointing the way to where Mal was determined to go.

He stepped forward, unthinking, reaching out with his right hand.

"Shite." He snatched his arm back, but before he could turn away, Bryce closed his long fingers over his wrist.

"Stop. It's okay."

"How can it be okay? You see this pathetic thing? How can you want it near you? I want to feel you with both hands. I can't even strip you out of those gods-be-damned tactical pants."

"You don't need to." Bryce drew him forward, grip firm yet gentle on his right wrist, and laced the fingers of their other hands together. "We've got three working hands. Surely we can manage to get the job done."

Mal tried to muster up some of his standard bravado. "The handjob, you mean?"

"I'm hoping for a little more, but we can start there. However . . ." His brown eyes held a wicked glint. "Who says hands have to be involved at all?"

He released his hold, although his gaze stayed locked with Mal's as if the arch-druid witch had tethered them there as well. He flicked the button on his own fly, teased down the zipper, barely a tooth at a time.

Mal's mouth watered, and his dick leaked in his pants. "Shite, man. Are you trying to kill me?" He reached out with his left hand and yanked the zipper all the way down.

Bryce chuckled. "See? No problem here." He tucked his fingers under the waistband, under his nontactical briefs (which were doing a piss-poor job of hiding an impressive bulge), and shucked them all the way down to his ankles. "Uh . . . here's a problem. I forgot about the damn boots."

"Remember them later." Mal dropped to his knees, because the sight of that cock—long, cut, leaking, *gorgeous*—was more than he could take. He'd thought the man's chest was spectacular? His cock should be in a gods-be-damned shrine. And Mal would be first in line to be an acolyte.

He engulfed the head in one gulp, moaning when Bryce's flavor hit his tongue. Goddess, how he'd missed this. He'd forgotten. In his years—decades, centuries, millennia—as the prize being pursued by other men, he'd given blowjobs aplenty, but never like this. Never as the supplicant. Never with the desperation to feel the weight of Bryce's cock on his tongue, in his throat, pinning him, *owning* him.

What was that about?

Who cared? He'd think about it later.

Now he had other priorities. Namely drawing that groan out of Bryce again, the one that shivered all the way down his torso, vibrating Mal's fingers where they grasped one of Bryce's indecently cut hips.

He hollowed his cheeks, keeping the suction perfect as he drew his mouth up the shaft, swirled his tongue around the bell, teased the slit until Bryce's hands clenched in Mal's hair, the tug just past the point of pain. *Yes.*

"Wait." Bryce was breathless, his voice strained. "Not yet."

Truly? If the man wanted to wait, Mal couldn't be doing this properly. He sucked all the way down the shaft until the head lodged in his throat. His eyes watered with the unaccustomed sensation, his breath trapped by Bryce's very presence as well as by his cock.

Inconceivably, Bryce pulled Mal's head away, sliding that delicious dick out of his mouth. *Goddess, did I just whimper?* What in all the hells was the matter with him? And why didn't he care?

"Mal." Bryce hunkered down awkwardly, his ankles still trapped by his pants. "As great as this is, I don't want it to be over too quickly."

Mal eyed Bryce's cock, straining, weeping, and nearly purple. "Your dick might disagree, mate. And I'm on its side."

Bryce chuckled. "Maybe. But I've learned never to listen when that head tries to argue logic with me. Let's go to bed, yeah?"

Mal stared Bryce's cock in its single eye, then looked up into his face. His brow was bunched as if in pain—and judging by the way his balls were tucked against his body, Mal knew exactly where that pain was centered.

But even with that pinch-browed grimace, his eyes were kind—too kind for anyone with Mal's baggage. But, flaming abyss, he needed this. He'd save the man from himself later.

"Yeah. Let's."

CHAPTER ❈ 11

Despite his aching cock and balls, Bryce found room in his brain for shame. How stupid not to take off his boots before trying to shed his pants. Served him right for trying to be sexy when he wasn't—not like the man on his knees in front of him, lips still swollen from taking Bryce's cock to the back of his throat.

He bent down to unlace his boots, only to find that Mal had gotten there before him.

"Brace your hands on my shoulders and lift your feet."

"Uh . . . right." Problem with that position was that it put his cock right in Mal's face again, and the damn thing was hard as granite. When Mal's breath gusted across the head, Bryce had to grit his teeth to keep from thrusting his hips forward.

Somehow, he managed to get his feet out of his boots without coming all over Mal's face. Someday he'd have to write a paper on the effects of reciting the byproducts of animal decomposition as an abstinence tool.

Mal chuckled. "Let me guess. Tactical socks?"

"I—"

"Never mind. Let's just strip the gods-be-damned things off, shall we?"

"Right." Bryce kicked off his pants and briefs, while Mal, still on his knees and fully clothed, smirked at him. He managed to get his socks off with only one or two awkward hops, bracing himself on the mantelpiece and nearly knocking a heavy wooden box off onto his toes when his hand tangled in his vest.

"Steady there, mate." Mal rose with a controlled grace the exact inverse of Bryce's awkwardness. "Don't want you to hurt yourself." He pushed the box back and slung the vest on top. "You still game?"

Bryce glanced down at his cock, which seemed determined to bridge the distance between the two of them. "What do you think?"

"Right, then. You remember where the bed is. Lead the way."

Bryce narrowed his eyes. "You're the one who's still dressed. You lead."

"What fun is that? You've nothing to hide from me now. Might as well let me enjoy the view."

Well, it was his funeral. Bryce marched down the short hallway, forcing his chin high as if parading naked through neighboring houses was standard operating procedure, Mal nearly on his heels. The bedroom was cool and dim, the blinds belling outward in the breeze, and the bed—

The bed. This isn't the first time you've been in that bed. With him. Naked.

And therein lay the problem. He remembered exactly what Mal looked like naked: the sheer perfection of his body, nearly hairless except for a nest of dark curls at the base of his cock; chest broad and sculpted; biceps bulging and defined. He remembered the uncut cock too, and heat washed through his chest. He'd see it erect this time. What would it taste like? What would it feel like if Mal fucked him? His sexual experience was laughably small and had rarely extended that far, either top or bottom.

Christ. Where was the damn adrenaline when he needed it? The least it could do was hang around long enough to make sure Bryce didn't immolate himself with his own ineptitude.

He hunched his shoulders, his knees pressed against the mattress, wondering how the hell he could escape before he embarrassed himself even further.

Except he couldn't escape, at least no farther than ten fucking feet away. Had his new mentor—master—whatever—known how she'd doomed him when she'd shackled him to the most gorgeous man to walk the earth or Faerie?

"I can hear your mind whirring from here, boyo." Mal's hand stole across Bryce's stomach, his bare chest warm against Bryce's back. Shit. While he'd been freaking out over his own nakedness, he'd missed Mal removing his shirt.

"I—I'm sorry."

"The only reason to be sorry is if you don't plan on getting on that bed."

"You didn't ask for this. I shouldn't have jumped you outside."

"I didn't fight you off. And, trust me, mate, even one-handed, I can still hold my own in a clinch."

"I know. You're strong. And gorgeous. And incredible. And I'm completely devoid of any superlatives whatsoever."

"Are you now? I'd call you brave."

Bryce snorted, but then Mal kissed the back of his neck, and he nearly choked sucking in his breath. "I'm not."

"No? How about crazy, then, for drawing those berserker guards after us. On purpose."

"That was— I couldn't let them hurt the trees."

"Crazy, definitely. Too soft-hearted for your own good, for someone forced to endure my company. Smart too." He pressed a kiss between Bryce's shoulder blades.

"How can I be both crazy and smart?" His cock, which had started to flag, perked back up again.

"Don't know, but you manage. Besides, this is just a little sex, yeah? No need to get in a swivet." Mal didn't lift his lips from Bryce's skin, and Bryce shivered. "Now turn around and let me kiss you properly."

Well, he'd been warned. Plus, he had a point. It was sex, nothing more. Since they were bound together for as long as Cassie deemed necessary, this counted as a definite perk. Later, they could always claim no harm, no foul. *The druid made me do it—sure, that'll fly.* But if he were honest with himself, he needed no excuse other than that he wanted Mal so badly.

He turned.

His mouth dried because Mal was totally, gloriously naked. How had he peeled out of those leather pants without Bryce hearing? Who cared, not with all that skin on stellar display.

God. Mal's cock was every bit as incredible as Bryce had imagined. His knees buckled, and he reached for it, but Mal caught his elbow.

"Not so fast, boyo. Didn't you promise to plow my arse not ten minutes past?"

"I—" Bryce swallowed, trying to scare up some saliva. "That was … I didn't … You don't have to—"

"Oh, I know. But I want to." Mal kissed him, a brush of lips and the tickle of the tip of his tongue against Bryce's lower lip. "Don't you?"

God, yes. He nodded, and Mal sat on the edge of the bed, scooted back, and lay down, spreading his legs and drawing his knees up to expose himself fully.

Bryce nearly came just from the sight, but that truly would have been humiliating—not to mention a waste of the most incredible opportunity he'd had in his life.

"Supplies?" he croaked.

Mal grinned and jerked his head in the direction of the nightstand. "Help yourself."

Mal had no idea why he was going through with this, now that Bryce's little dom act had left the stage. He only knew he wanted it—not as much as getting his hand back, perhaps, but with a burn in his belly that made his multitude of past sexual encounters seem like nothing more than pissing in the wind.

Bryce fumbled the lube out of the drawer. "I— Damn it, where are the condoms?"

"Don't need them, mate. I'm fae. You're a druid. No human STDs for us."

Bryce's eyes widened, his pupils so blown his eyes looked black. "I've never—"

"But you like the idea."

Bryce's gaze locked on Mal's, and a slow grin spread over his face. Suddenly he looked less like a tree-hugging professor and more like what he was: a druid about to accept a sacrifice. "I *love* the idea."

Mal shivered in anticipation as Bryce tossed the lube onto the duvet and knee-walked across the bed, pushing Mal's legs down so he could straddle his waist. He leaned forward and captured Mal's face in those huge hands, and Mal closed his eyes, fighting a groan.

Bryce took Mal's mouth in a bruising kiss, a fierce passion in the crush of his lips, the thrust of his tongue, the sure grip of his hands on Mal's jaw. But Mal wanted more: to be taken, to be filled, to be *owned*.

His head spun, so he opened his eyes. Bryce's eyes were open too, black as a winter night, and Mal couldn't look away—wanted never to look away. He opened his mouth as wide as he could and let Bryce fuck him with his tongue. *Goddess, what I wouldn't give to have his cock down my throat now.* To swallow every bit of his essence. Take it into himself and keep it there, a part of him, forever.

Wait. What? Mal had always avoided any kind of permanence like the Black Death.

Later. Think about it later.

He heard the snick of the lube bottle. *Yes.* Another way to prove he could take anything that Bryce had to give. Then Bryce's fingers were there, circling his entrance, the lube cool and slick on his skin. One fingertip slipped in, then out again. In, then out, just the tip. Not enough. Not nearly enough.

He tore his mouth away from Bryce's intoxicating kiss. "More. I can take it."

Bryce's lips, wet and swollen from their kisses, spread in a predatory smile. "Are you begging?"

Mal swallowed against the surge of need that crested over him. "Yes," he whispered. "If that's what you want."

Bryce shook his head. "Not now." He kissed Mal again, hard and merciless. "But soon," he murmured against Mal's lips. And shoved two fingers in to the first knuckle.

Mal's back arched, and he gasped. "Goddess, yes. More."

"Mal—"

"You won't hurt me. I'm fae, damn it. Fuck me. Fuck me now. Fuck me hard. I need to feel you spill inside me before I go fecking insane."

Bryce's chest expanded on a huge breath, his nostrils flaring. Another squirt of the lube bottle, and his elbow pumped as he slicked his cock. Then he hooked Mal's knees over his shoulders.

"Let me in."

The broad head of Bryce's cock stretched Mal's hole, not meeting as much resistance as there should have been. Mal had an instant to wonder why before Bryce pushed.

All. The. Way. Inside.

Mal whimpered. "Bryce. Please."

An expression of surprised wonder flitted across Bryce's face, followed by pure unadulterated lust. He thrust again, nailing Mal's gland, and Mal nearly burst out of his skin. Bryce's fingers closed on Mal's shoulders—a welcome, grounding pressure. "Brace yourself."

Bryce pulled back nearly all the way and thrust home again. And again, his pace increasing until the rhythm matched Mal's racing heartbeat.

Goddess, it was too intense. He couldn't stand it, yet he wanted it to go on forever.

Above him, Bryce's gaze skewered him, night and fire and steel. His thrusts slowed to a standstill, and Mal nearly came off the bed. "*Now* you can beg."

"Goddess, Bryce, *please.*"

"For you, anything." With a glint of a smile, Bryce hammered home, where he belonged.

Mal's balls drew up, lightning gathering in his spine, and his vision whited out as he came on a howl, his spend painting his belly, his chest, his chin.

"So beautiful." Bryce's hands clenched tighter, his back arching, shouting wordlessly as he came.

Goddess, is it always like this? Mal's breath hitched on a near-sob as he was filled with tender fire, a blessed heat more welcome than his heart's blood.

Bryce kissed him again, softer this time, but to Mal it felt like another brand of possession.

"I'll be right back." Bryce got up and padded to the en suite, then returned with a warm washcloth while Mal was still blinking in the aftermath. "Good thing the sink is in range, eh?"

He wiped Mal down from face to groin, trailing kisses in the wake of the cloth, while Mal trembled and tried to realign his thoughts.

What just happened to me? I never bottom. But submitting had stroked his pleasure centers with unholy intensity until he would have done anything, abased himself in any way, to please Bryce—as if he'd suddenly taken on the personality of a lesser fae.

Maybe I should have tried bottoming before after all.

Because Goddess, it had felt so fecking good—as if he'd finally found what he'd been searching for his whole eons-long life.

He rolled over onto his side in a fetal curl, causing Bryce's hand to trail over his hip in a way that made him want to tuck himself under the man's arm and *snuggle*, for shite's sake.

Bryce chuckled and kissed the back of his neck. "Tired? Rest, then. You earned it."

Why did that praise make Mal want to turn over and spread himself again? Flaming abyss, he was a high lord of the Sidhe. Could this be a throwback to before the Unification? Was the ceremony that had elevated the greater of *y Tylwyth Teg* to the status of the Daoine Sidhe wearing off?

He'd never felt this way until after his visit to the Unseelie sphere. Maybe that's what this was—a side effect. It would wear off like that unexplained weakness. *It has to.* Because this wasn't who he was, and he'd have wagered his other hand that this wasn't who Bryce was either.

So who the fuck were they, and how had they put on someone else's skin?

A minuscule shift in the mattress and an almost impossible silence from the other side of the bed clued him in that Bryce was awake and trying his best to pretend to be asleep.

Was he as mortified by what had happened as Mal? How could he be? He wasn't the one who'd begged to be fucked—hells, begged to be fecking *subjugated*.

Wrong. So wrong. Mal had no idea how he'd let it happen, but it wouldn't happen again, no matter how talented Bryce's mouth. Shite, if his kiss could make Mal abandon every sane thought he'd ever had about sex, he shuddered to think what he'd be willing to offer if the man ever got his mouth on Mal's cock.

He shivered at the thought and stopped himself when he realized he'd edged closer to Bryce's seductive heat.

Fuck this shite.

Mal forced himself to roll up and sit on the edge of the mattress, his back to Bryce. The bedclothes rustled, signaling Bryce had finally decided to stop pretending to be asleep just as Mal had.

"So . . . um . . . sex."

"Yeah," Mal growled.

"I'm pretty sure I'd have remembered if we'd done *that* before." His voice was tentative, yet edged with teasing, and it pissed Mal off.

"That's because we didn't. I lied."

"I know."

Mal grunted. "Humoring me?"

"What? No. Just, you know, checking in." The mattress dipped as if Bryce were moving toward him, and Mal froze, his left hand clutching his knee, his useless right hand dangling in front of his cock as if he could hide the way it responded to Bryce's proximity.

Bloody traitor.

"Look." Bryce touched his shoulder, but withdrew his hand when Mal flinched. "We need to talk."

"Fine. Talk. Nothing's ever stopped you before."

"You seem . . . upset. Did I do something you didn't like? If I did, I'm sorry. I've never— That is, I don't have a lot of experience, but I've never *imagined* doing anything like that, and never in a million years with someone like you."

"Leave it, all right? It happened. But it won't happen again."

"Oh." Bryce swallowed audibly. "I see. Very well." More rustling bedclothes, and his distracting heat retreated. "Do you think now that we have the Seat of Power, the wetlands will heal on its own, or do we need to do something else?"

"About that." Mal half turned so he could see Bryce's face when he kicked him in the balls. A pissed-off Bryce would keep his distance, and Mal wouldn't be tempted to do . . . whatever the hells he'd done. "That had nothing to do with the blight. I lied."

Bryce's expressive face shut down completely. "You lied about that too? Why?"

Mal shrugged, his gaze sliding away. "I needed to get into Faerie. I couldn't go without you. Seemed like the best way."

"You could have tried asking."

No doubt about it—the man was royally pissed. Why did that make Mal's chest feel so hollow? "Funny. David tells my brother that all the time. Must be a family failing."

"Don't joke about this, Mal. We risked our necks with no plan and no backup—and we didn't even do what we needed?"

"We did what *I* needed."

"Fuck you." Bryce stood up. "Except we're not doing *that* again, are we?" He strode across the room. "I need to take a piss." Instead of going into the en suite, though, he stormed off down the hall.

"Wait! Use the— *Augh!*" The metaphysical hook in his midsection pulled Mal out of bed and onto the floor. He scrambled on all fours until he could stand and run down the hall with a very undignified bounce of his semi-erect cock.

Just bloody brilliant. He leaned against the wall next to the bathroom door and slid down to sit on his arse, his arms draped over his knees. He closed his eyes, cursing both himself and Bryce as he clenched his fists.

Wait—he clenched his *fists*? His eyes snapped open and he held his right hand up, inches from his face. Was it less crabbed? The fingers more extended? Could he feel a tingle in their tips? He frowned, concentrating fiercely. *Clench, damn you, clench.*

His fingers twitched. Not much, but they definitely twitched, and he could bloody well *feel* it.

He threw back his head and laughed. Even though he hadn't gotten around to stowing the Seat of Power in the sodding box, Steve must have picked up anyway. *Guess "close" is good enough for a mage with that kind of power.* If this was the result of the geas brand's spell— lessening the curse on Mal's hand as he completed each task—then whatever Mal had gone through, whatever had come over him in the Unseelie sphere, was worth it. Whatever he needed to do, he'd do it, humiliation be damned.

The toilet flushed in the bathroom.

Oi. Right. He'd have to convince the pissed-off druid to get with the program too—not promising at the moment, but fuck it. If he had to suck Bryce off twice an hour, he'd do it, if it meant he'd recover the use of his hand.

He refused to consider why the idea of sucking Bryce off twice an hour made him hard.

"Listen. Bryce. You're right, mate. We should talk."

No response. Fine. Mal probably deserved a little silent treatment after he'd played the arsehole card.

"Look. I get that you're pissed. I don't blame you, but—"

A massive *thunk* inside the bathroom cut him off, as if Bryce had kicked the side of the bathtub with one of those damn boots of his.

Except he wasn't wearing boots—or anything else, either.

"Bryce?"

CHAPTER ✤ 12

Mal's ears popped as a wind swept down the hallway. He scrambled to his feet, wishing he were wearing something other than original skin, because sure enough, Steve was looming in the doorway to the living room, the top of his hood brushing the lintel.

"Gwydion's bollocks, man. Did you just knock him out again?"

"It seemed prudent."

"'Prudent'? It sounds like you nearly dashed his brains out on the edge of the bloody bathtub." Mal rattled the door handle. "Can you at least unlock this so I can be sure he's all right?"

Steve raised one gloved finger, and the lock *snick*ed open. Goddess, what Mal wouldn't give to have his powers back. He pushed open the door until it lodged against Bryce's legs. Sure enough, he was splayed on the bathroom floor, a clear lump forming on his forehead.

Mal fought an almost overwhelming compulsion to drop to his knees and cradle Bryce's head in his lap. "If you expect me to finish your gods-be-damned tasks, you'd best make sure my unwilling partner stays ambulatory."

Steve rumbled. "A point. I shall make the spell less potent in future. And check for nearby obstacles."

"A real gentleman, you are." Mal took the opportunity to snatch a towel off the rack and wrap it around his waist. "So. First task accomplished. I'm guessing you're here to give me the next assignment."

Steve inclined his head. "As you say."

"Before we get into that, I need to know something." Mal licked his lips, glancing down at Bryce, gorgeously naked even if he was unconscious. "Something happened."

"Several things, I imagine, since you returned with the Seat."

"Yeah, well, some of those things were damned unsettling. If you expect me to finish this out, you need to share a little more with me."

"What I can share is limited by my own curse, but nothing prevents you from asking."

"So when I touched the Seat of Power—"

"Ah." Steve stilled for a second. "Of course you did."

"What? It's not like I could retrieve it without handling it. Is that a problem?"

"Not as such, although it was careless of me not to consider the ramifications. Exposure may make you sensitive to certain . . . conditions . . . but it is not of itself a danger."

"'Sensitive.' That's putting it mildly. After that, your talisman heated up so much it nearly branded my arse through a layer of leather."

Steve waved a negligent hand, the jewels in his cuff glinting in the uncertain light. "That was merely a failsafe. A warning, if you will, that your time was drawing short."

"We still had hours to go."

Steve rumbled. "Were you beset?"

Mal thought back to the throne room. The talisman had misbehaved right before Rodric and his goons had shown up. "Yeah."

"Time is measured by circumstance as well as the clock."

"You could have *told* me."

Steve rumbled and inclined his head again.

Not exactly a promise to mend his behavior, was it? "When we were nearly at the gate, I came over weak. Bryce had to practically carry me across the threshold."

"Did you still hold the talisman?"

"Shite no. The bloody thing nearly seared my arse off."

"That is why. It wasn't only a token of passage; it temporarily made you a part of the Unseelie sphere. The realm has its own ways of protecting itself from outside threats such as—" he inclined his head "—Seelie incursions. It was attempting to neutralize you."

"It nearly neutralized us both to death."

"Noted. Should you need to traverse the barrier again, I'll alter the warning spell to make it . . ."

"What? More precise? Less potent? Seems you've got a bit of a problem with overkill. Compensating for something, are you?"

"I forget how fragile others can be. My form deadens me to certain sensations, and everything else is so . . . small. Forgive me. I must remember to scale the spell to fit the target."

"Can't say your lack of finesse fills me with confidence." Unfortunately, the bloody *tynged* ensured that Mal had no other option for assistance or advice—and he was in dire need of both. Swallowing, he glanced down at Bryce again. Could he admit this? Sod it, he had to know if the Seat of Power and the damned Unseelie neutralization had affected him in other ways. And when it would wear off. Might as well ask. Couldn't be any more humiliating than what he'd done with Bryce, after all.

"There's another thing. When we got back, I . . . ah . . . acted in a . . . well . . . uncharacteristic way." He pointed to Bryce. "With him."

Steve studied them—or at least Mal assumed he did, since his hood was pointed first at him, and then at Bryce. "Did you lie with him?"

"Of course I lied to him. I *can't* tell him the truth, thanks to your geas."

"I don't mean did you prevaricate. Did you exchange fluids of the body?"

Mal's face heated at the memory of exactly how many and in what way the fluids were exchanged. "You mean like blood?"

Steve rumbled. "Blood. Saliva. Semen."

"Ah. Yeah." *Two out of three anyway.*

He nodded. "And did you copulate?"

Heat washed up Mal's chest, and shite, he started to get hard under the towel. "We did."

"That's why. Now, as to the next task—"

Mal took a step forward. "Hold on there, mate. You haven't answered the question. What do you mean, 'That's why'?"

"He is a druid. Now, the next task—"

"That doesn't answer the question either." He took another step forward, perversely gratified when Steve retreated into the living room. "What does him being a druid have to do with anything?"

"You know nothing of our origins, then?"

"The elder gods constructed Faerie. Blah, blah, blah."

"They also constructed Faerie's inhabitants. Such as yourself, Lord Maldwyn."

"And such as you?"

"More or less. But the druids came before. Their relationship to the elder gods predates Faerie. Just as the lesser fae were constructed to serve the greater, the greater fae were constructed to serve the druids."

"You mean what I did"—what he still wanted to do, damn it to all Arawn's hells—"is because of fecking fae genetics?"

"As you say. If a druid forces a fae to accept bonds of the body, that fae is essentially the druid's slave."

Mal spun and punched the wall. "Bloody druids! There's always a catch and this one beats them all." But had Bryce actually forced him? Not physically, perhaps, but with some mental juju? Would he be second-guessing his motivations from now until he was uncursed or Cassie relented and released their magical shackles?

"In these latter days, with druids dispersed and without central power, they're more civilized about it. Most of them feel as you do—that subjugating another race is wrong. I believe they have spells and potions to prevent the condition." Steve pointed his cowl at Bryce, and his rumble took on a definite note of disapproval. "In fact, I believe they censure those who practice the art."

"It wasn't his fault. He just found out about his heritage yesterday. The old biddy who apprenticed him hasn't told him squat yet." Mal turned away so he couldn't see Bryce sprawled in all his naked glory, and had an uncontrollable urge to block him from Steve's sight. "In fact . . ." Shame coiled in Mal's belly. "I'm supposed to be educating him on the ways of the supernatural worlds."

"Then you'd best get to that. Although," Steve's rumble turned sly, "all he need do now is ask, and you'll scramble to do his will and more."

"Yeah. Going to take care of that." He'd be placing a call to David as soon as Steve departed for whatever realm he lurked in between visits to Hillsboro. "So. The next task."

Mal tried to be subtle about closing the bathroom door, but by Steve's rumble, he wasn't fooling anyone, including himself. *Definitely calling David ASAP.*

"For the next task, you must acquire a scale from a molting dragon shifter."

Mal barked out a laugh. "You're joking."

"No. You see my dilemma? Adults would never part with something that will eventually increase their treasure. And as for children, who have not yet learned to hoard them, there've been none born this fifty years or more."

Mal blinked. There *had* been a dragon child born. Furthermore, Mal knew who it was. *How can* Steve *not know that?* Apparently Steve's unpredictable magical powers weren't his only limitation. *Not as omnipotent as you'd like me to believe, are you, boyo?* That knowledge was a bit of a double-edged blade. On one hand, Steve might have exaggerated his ability to lift Mal's curse. *Not that I can demand references from previous satisfied customers.* On the other hand, any weakness in an opponent—even if they were supposed to be an ally—was worth exploiting, and Mal needed all the advantages he could squeeze out of this predicament. "If this task is so impossible, why do you think I can handle it?"

"Not completely impossible, else I would lose hope. As you well know, the man without hope is a dangerous—and unpredictable—thing. Far better to give him a quest, be it ever so arduous." The sound emanating from Steve's chest could have been a mournful chuckle or a cheerful sob. Hard to tell. "It gives him something to occupy his time."

"Not very noble of you to sacrifice my time to your bloody arduous quest, especially since my time isn't all that's on the block. I can't forget that this," Mal held up his hand to display the geas brand, "will cripple me for good if I don't succeed."

Steve shrugged. "Desperation makes criminals of us all. You, Lord Maldwyn, should know that better than most, with your years as the Queen's Enforcer. How many of those you tracked and killed felt they had any choice?"

Shame scalded Mal's throat. He'd never asked, had he? He'd just gone about his duty, accepting the Queen's decree as absolute. Maybe he should have examined some of those pronouncements more closely. If he—or any fae, for that matter—had questioned the mandatory oath-taking at the Midsummer Revels, Rodric Luchullain wouldn't have been able to stage his coup and Mal would still have two functioning hands.

"So, a scale from a dragon shifter. What's our timeline?"

"The final task must occur on the equinox, and since it may require some . . . persuasion on your part, the sooner you accomplish this one, the better."

"In two days? Cutting it a bit close, aren't you, mate?"

Good thing Mal didn't need any time at all for this task—not that he'd let Steve know that little detail, not with the trust between them as thin as a pixie's wing. A simple call to his brother-in-law, and the deed would be done. *And David can bring his meddling aunt with him to take care of this ludicrous D/s bond between me and Bryce with her thrice-blasted druid "spells and potions."*

"Shall I help you get the druid situated more comfortably?"

"No!" Damn it. He knew from experience that wrestling Bryce into bed with only one functional hand was a chore, but the burn in his belly ordered him not to let anyone else touch his druid.

His druid. Shite. He was going to kill Cassie Bowen for this.

Bryce blinked bleary eyes, the percussion session in his head making it difficult to concentrate. *Something's off.* Why was the wall of the bedroom cream-colored? His bedroom walls were blue and green.

Mal's house. In Mal's *bed.* He turned his head on the pillow to meet those cornflower blue eyes. *With Mal.* Again. Why was waking up with Mal always accompanied by a screaming headache?

He groaned, clenching his eyes shut. "How did I get back in bed? I was in the bathroom. I remember that much." He cracked one eye open. "And don't try giving me that line about post-sex-induced amnesia, because I didn't fall for it before and I'm damn well not falling for it now."

"I— You— He— Shite!"

Bryce opened both eyes at the pain in Mal's voice. "That's not very descriptive."

Mal glared, the tendons in his neck standing out as if he were lifting a massive weight. "I'm trying. The— *Augh!*" He doubled over, his left hand fisted against his chest. "Damn it all to Arawn's hells."

"Also not helpful. But never mind. We've already determined that we won't repeat the sex."

"You got that right," Mal muttered.

Obviously the encounter hadn't been as transformative for Mal as it had been for Bryce. *But the unexpected way he'd responded— surely that means something.* Given his normal swagger and aggressive behavior, who'd have suspected he wanted to be dominated in bed?

Who'd have suspected Bryce would be the one doing the dominating?

Even now, something whispered in the recesses of his brain: *You could* make *him tell you. You could make him do* anything. He stared at Mal, willing him to break their eye-lock. Mal licked his lips, and his pupils dilated, his breath catching.

"Mal," Bryce murmured, "tell me what you really want. Don't lie to me. Tell me."

Mal leaned forward as if Bryce were reeling him in. "I—"

A brisk knock at the front door, followed by a double ring of the doorbell startled them both, and Mal jerked back as if he'd been burned. *Thank God—what the hell was I doing? I'd* never *coerce anyone.* Although he doubted he'd be tempted to try with anybody except Mal, who was currently struggling with his pants and cursing a blue streak.

"That's my brother-in-law at the door, mate, so you might want to put on some clothes. Who knows who he might have with him."

Bryce bolted upright. "His aunt?"

"Could be. I wouldn't put it past either of them."

"My clothes—they're still in the living room."

Mal yanked open a dresser drawer and tossed Bryce a pair of sweatpants and a T-shirt. "Here. You'll have to free-ball it. Sorry."

"I'll deal." No danger there. Any unfortunate reactions to Mal would be counteracted by Cassie's ball-shriveling intimidation.

The knock repeated, with four doorbell attacks.

"Shite. I better answer the door before he electrocutes himself. You ready?"

"Lead on, Macduff."

Mal snorted. "I'm not a bloody Scotsman, thanks."

"You're welcome."

Mal stalked down the hallway, and Bryce followed. Mal's sweats were too baggy to hug his ass. A pity, in a way. When he opened the door, David breezed in, thankfully alone, a messenger bag slung over his shoulder.

"Good morning, gentlemen." He pulled a small box out of the bag. He squinted at Mal, head tilted to one side, as he held out the box. "Is something wrong?"

"No," Mal barked and stalked over to the fireplace to set the box on the mantle. Bryce had an urge to peek inside.

"All right, then, Mr. Grumpypants. Have it your way." He turned to Bryce with a brilliant smile and offered him the bag. "I've brought you something from Aunt Cassie. Your first homework assignment." His smile dimmed a bit. "Are *you* okay? Your head—"

"I'm fine." Bryce took the bag as if it might turn sentient and bite his hand off. Considering some of the things he'd seen in the last twenty-four hours, it wasn't that much of a stretch. "Homework, you say?"

"You're an apprentice now, my friend, and they don't make druidry SparkNotes to give you any shortcuts. Apprentices traditionally learn by doing—usually all the boring grunt work, I'm sorry to say. By the way, Auntie says there'll be a test later."

"How much later?"

"Not for a few days, so don't stress. Instructions and supplies are all in the bag. My cell number too, in case you need anything else."

Bryce peered into the bag. It contained a Ziploc bag full of paper twists like Gran used to store her herb samples, a sheaf of computer printouts, and an old journal with a cracked leather binding and yellowed pages—with a bright-pink Post-it Note attached. "I'm sure I'll be fine." Couldn't be harder than his dissertation.

"Oh, you might need salt and water too. Maybe olive oil, so I'd suggest working in the kitchen. Even Mal has those on hand."

"Got it."

As he walked into the dining room, staying close to the living room wall to keep within the optimum tether comfort perimeter, he caught a significant glance between Mal and David. He shouldn't feel hurt that they needed a private chat, but he did. It brought home again that even though he was supposed to be a supernatural being—*were* druids supernatural? Semi-supernatural? Meta-supernatural? Whatever—he was still an outsider where the Kendricks were concerned.

The story of my life.

CHAPTER ✵ 13

David peered up at Mal, his gull-wing brows drawn together over his nose. "Are you sure you're okay? There's something wonky in your energy signature."

"No, I'm not okay." Mal adjusted his position, standing with his back to the wall so Bryce would be able to move freely in the kitchen. He kept his voice low, though, so Bryce wouldn't overhear. "I need to talk to your aunt."

David's eyebrows shot up. "Really? Oh. You mean without Bryce? Why? Did something happen?"

"Never mind that." Mal still hadn't recovered from the pain in his hand when he'd tried to tell Bryce about Steve's visit. Between that and the pain in his chest from defying Bryce's order, he'd have fallen on his own sword, assuming he still had it, just to get some relief. "Could you ask her how to neutralize the bond between druid and fae?"

"There are bonds? I didn't know that."

"Neither did I. Probably some kind of bloody druid trade secret."

"Wait. You mean you and Bryce have a bond now? Like some kind of connection besides the . . . you know . . ." He pointed at Mal's stomach. "Thingy?"

"Unfortunately."

David grinned. "But that could be fun, right? He's pretty dang cute, and you haven't gone clubbing since the unfortunate incident."

"It's not a fun kind of bond, Dafydd *bach*." How *would* he describe his simultaneous desires to repeat the experience yet never go near Bryce again? Devastating, yes. Life-altering, maybe. Humiliating—the jury was still out. "Apparently, the elder gods were bigger bastards than we ever knew. They engineered the fae to be subservient to the druids."

David's eyes grew round. "Subservient. You mean like a slave class?" Mal nodded, heat washing up his chest. "You mean you and Bryce—" Mal nodded again. "Holy cats. How powerful is the compulsion? I mean, you can resist it, right?"

"Barely. Right now, all I want to do is run into the kitchen and kneel at his feet. Goddess, I don't *do* shite like that!"

David rested his hand on Mal's shoulder. "I know you haven't before, but there's nothing *wrong* with wanting it. I mean, I'm ready to kneel at Alun's feet at the drop of a tiny white handkerchief, and considering how often he does the same to me—"

"Stop." Mal threw up a hand. "No sex details."

"I'm speaking *figuratively*, you dork. Although . . ." David squinted one eye and peered at the ceiling. "If you want to get *technical* . . . well, never mind. Haven't you ever had the teensiest desire to let someone else take the lead for a change?"

Mal shook David's hand off. "Never." But did he secretly want it? When had he ever had the opportunity to test it? Before the Unification, he and his brothers had led the fight to keep Annwn intact, and look how well that had turned out. After Unification, they couldn't have displayed anything less than full control or the Daoine Sidhe would have had them for lunch.

"It's nothing to be ashamed of, you know, as long as it's consensual." David blinked, his eyebrows rising. "It is, isn't it? I mean, I know you're not the biggest druid fan. Crap, Mal, did he *do* something, some druid thing, to *force* you? Because if he did, I'll tell Cassie and she'll come down on his head like a *ton* of druid bricks."

"No!" Panic tightened his chest at the thought of Bryce being hurt. Shite, was the fear real, or something born of his damned fae heritage? "He doesn't know anything about it either. But S—" Pain seared his hand, and he gritted his teeth. Clearly the geas wouldn't let him divulge anything about Steve, even if it had nothing to do with their bargain. "I've heard that it's against the current laws for druids to indulge, and that there are spells or potions or some other shite they use to make sure it doesn't happen. Can you ask her about that?"

"Of course. But I can't promise what she'll say or do. She has her own ideas of what might be good for people's souls." He pulled his cell phone out of his pocket. "I'll call her right now."

"Not yet. Wait until you're out of the house. I don't want Bryce to hear." Assuming he hadn't already. "Is the dragon scale in that box?"

"Yep."

"Thank you, boyo. I owe you."

"Oh this was no hardship. Benjy was thrilled—he got a Death Star Lego set out of the deal." One of David's friends was the dragon shifter prince, a six-year-old who shared David's obsession with science fiction action figures.

"He must be a prodigy if he's molting already at six."

"Oh, that's not Benjy's scale. It's his mom's."

"You brought me a scale from the dragon shifter *queen*? Shite, Dafydd, won't that create its own kind of bond? I don't want to—"

"Chill, BIL. When will you fae ever learn? If it's freely given, there is no debt." David's eyes twinkled, and given that he was the last known *achubydd* on the planet, the sparks probably came from inside. "As far as Benjy is concerned, the Death Star trumps emeralds and rubies every day of the week and twice on Sundays. And Teresa is ecstatic that he's hoarding like a champ. He may be the only kid on the planet who never leaves his Legos scattered on the floor." He dusted off his hands. "While I'm here, let's do a little PT."

"Let's not."

"At least let me look at your hand." David didn't wait for Mal to respond, just grabbed Mal's hand and cradled it in his own. "Mal, there's improvement." He pressed Mal's fingers apart and down. "I mean *real* improvement—the contraction is significantly reduced. Can you feel anything?"

"A little. Some tingling."

David rotated Mal's hand at the wrist, a frown wrinkling his forehead. "I don't understand. There shouldn't be this much difference from our last session." His eyes narrowed. "Is there anything you want to share with the class? You're not trying some sleazy fae shortcut, are you?"

The geas brand heated on his palm. "Not a thing."

David released Mal's hand. "All right. I guess."

"Stop borrowing my trouble, boyo. Go home and shag your husband. Take your mind off other people's business and improve his temper at the same time."

David sighed. "I wish I could. But Alun's kind of . . . well . . . missing."

"Missing?" Mal grabbed David's arm. Had the Unseelie attacks escalated beyond Mal to his family? "Why didn't you say so? What have you done to find him? Have you contacted Gareth? You need to be careful too. You may have the protection of the vampires, the shifters, and the Queen, but—"

"Hold on, cowboy." David patted Mal's hand, then gently disengaged it. "He told me he'd be gone for a while, but he couldn't say for how long. He heard a rumor about a traitor in Faerie."

Ice cascaded down Mal's spine. Steve wouldn't have betrayed him, surely. Not with the first task safely completed. But Rodric had seen Mal, recognized him—with a foothold in Faerie, even in the Unseelie sphere, who knew what kind of havoc the vengeful bastard could wreak? "Rumor? Where?"

"From one of the supe councils. The vampires, I think. They keep pretty close tabs on one another, from what I gather."

"You got that right."

"Anyway, Alun had to go roaring off to investigate. I think he's in Faerie, but I don't have any way to tell now that . . ." David shrugged. "Now that I'm exiled, since Gareth refuses to set foot in the place unless he's forced."

David smiled apologetically. "It's not your fault and not your issue. But I can't help but worry, so if you should hear anything, you'll tell me?"

Assuming he didn't hear it from Steve—or assuming Steve wasn't the traitor in question. "Of course."

"Good. I'll go now and call Aunt Cassie. I can't guarantee she won't show up here later anyway, to check on Bryce's homework, but—"

"If she can fix this fecking bond, she can move in for all I care."

He grinned. "I'll tell her."

"Don't you dare."

David stood on tiptoe and kissed Mal's cheek. "Serve you right if I did. I know you're hiding something from me, but I'll bide my time. I'll get it out of you eventually. I always do."

Bryce tried to ignore the murmur of voices in the other room as he squinted at the crabbed writing in the journal. He supposed he should call it a grimoire, since it held spells, potions, and incantations. How old was it? He ran a finger across one of the water-stained pages. The paper was heavy, with high rag content, in contrast to the modern pages, which had clearly been produced with a color laser printer.

He shook his head and studied the instructions for his first official act as a druid. Christ, even *thinking* that sounded nuts. But, then, everything about the last couple of days was nuts, so why should this be any different?

Potion to ward off evil. Will also adversely affect creatures whose nature or intent is evil. Weapon grade 10.

Hmmm. Maybe the original authors of *Dungeons and Dragons* had a bit more official knowledge than one might expect.

Bryce started on the spell, measuring the ingredients meticulously, because who knew what might happen if he added too much St. John's wort or not enough rue? The whole thing might backfire.

If, as the notes in the grimoire hinted, every supernatural creature had its vulnerabilities that could be exploited, did that mean druids did too? What about greater fae, like Mal? Obviously something could harm him or he wouldn't be cursed. It stood to reason, though, that if you had a giant Achilles' heel, you wouldn't want to spread it around on whatever the Faerie equivalent of social media was.

Was the inverse also true? If every creature had its vulnerabilities, did they also have their advantages? Mal had hinted about his position in Faerie, his magic—or lack of it. What would it be like to be nearly invincible one day, and stripped of every defense and weapon the next? No wonder Mal was so ill-tempered most of the time. He must feel completely exposed.

An unexpected surge of protectiveness caught Bryce unawares. Suddenly, he didn't care what else was in Cassie's notes, what else she wanted him to accomplish before she arrived at her own convenience. He wanted— No, he *needed* to give Mal something back. Something that would counteract the disadvantages of his exile and his curse.

He needs a weapon. One he could wield one-handed, that didn't depend on magic, and that would be easy to master without a lot of practice, but that would nevertheless deal enough damage to his enemies to deter them.

Bryce drew the line at truly lethal weapons, but surely he could come up with something that would do the trick. His gaze strayed to the lesson printout. *Potion to ward off evil.*

That's it. All he needed was the proper delivery system—and he had just the thing in mind. Next time something breached the threshold, they'd be ready for it, and not only because he wanted Mal protected. This time, he intended to get some answers about who was screwing with the wetlands.

And who was causing the trees in Faerie to weep.

CHAPTER ✤ 14

Mal shut the door behind David, cursing his brother under his breath. How many times had Alun taken the piss out of him for the way he chose to live? Too many times to count over the millennia they'd been alive. Still, he knew Alun had only their best interests at heart, would always have his brothers' backs, even if Gareth still had a stick up his arse about Faerie, and even if Mal hadn't ever needed to ask for help before.

This time, when he could have used Alun's advice, the bloody bastard was MIA. He might not have been able to discuss Steve overtly, but maybe in the guise of Alun's psychology practice, he could've snuck some information out. *So much for that notion.*

At least the second task was out of the way. He walked across the room to the fireplace, at the very edge of his invisible leash, and opened the box David had brought.

The scale glowed, pulsing with its own inner light, an ombré that morphed from scarlet to indigo. A scale from the dragon queen. If this didn't pay off Steve's debt, whoever held his IOU was either a moron or had more power than Mal wanted to think about.

He flipped the lid on Steve's casket—and since the bloody thing opened with barely a flick of his finger, it must have recognized the scale for a task completed. *For a treasure like this, the bloody thing should have sprung open on its own.*

As he lifted the scale from its nest of silk, it quivered in his hand as if it were alive. It was beautiful just as it was, although someday it would evolve into an equally beautiful jewel. He cradled it next to his chest, and its pulse aligned with his heartbeat. What would that jewel look like? A ruby red as blood? A sapphire dark as twilight? A—

"Shite." He dropped the thing in Steve's box and slapped the lid closed. No wonder dragons didn't part with their scales willingly. If the hoarding instinct was that ingrained in the things, strong enough to affect anyone who held it? Teresa Tomlinson, queen of all the dragon shifters on the whole fecking planet, must really, really like David.

"Mal? Is David gone?"

Mal whirled at Bryce's voice, lifting his arms as if to hide Steve's casket and its seductive contents from Bryce. How stupid was that? The bloody mantel was as high as Mal's shoulders, and the box was clearly visible next to his head.

What was he protecting though? The scale from Bryce—or Bryce from the scale?

Damn the elder gods to hells of their own making. He'd never again know whether his thoughts were his own or the result of a spell older than Faerie itself.

Countless students had tried to snow Bryce about why they couldn't get a paper in on time, or why they couldn't possibly make the mandatory Saturday morning work crew. None of them had ever seemed as obviously guilty as Mal Kendrick at this moment.

"So . . . David?"

"Right. He had to leave. He's got a class."

"A class? I thought he was a nurse?"

"Studying to be one. He's not there yet."

"Tell me—" Bryce stopped himself before he flat out demanded the truth. *If you phrase the question right, make your voice sound just so, he'll tell you anything.*

You could make him do *anything.*

No. So wrong. He stomped on the temptation, running his hands through his hair. Christ, he really needed a shower.

You could take one with Mal. He'd do it if you told him to.

Where the hell were these ideas coming from? Had he always had a streak of cruelty in him? He didn't remember ever having these kinds of impulses before. He was a caretaker, damn it. His whole life had been about caring for the plants, the earth, its inhabitants. Why did this particular inhabitant make him want to ignore all of that and turn into an asshole?

Mal was watching him, unmoving, as if the beginning of Bryce's demand had put him on hold. Bryce cleared his throat and tried again—without the dictator imperative. "He's a student, then? That's surprising. He seemed fully capable of handling your injuries."

"He's an *achubydd*, so he can heal supes through his own magic. But the boyo wants to do the same thing the mundane way, and for humans too, so he's going to school to become a psychiatric nurse practitioner. Wants to help my brother in his practice. Did I mention that Alun is a psychologist for the supernatural communities?"

"Once or twice."

"It's a royal pain in the arse sometimes. He's always trying to counsel me and Gareth—although that might come from being the eldest."

"You have another brother? Is he a warrior too?"

"Nah. He's a rock star."

Bryce grinned. "Get out. A fae rock star."

"Gareth is the last true bard in Faerie. He has a band. Hunter's Moon. He—"

"Hold it." Bryce frowned. Mal had never had this kind of verbal diarrhea before. And the sheen of sweat on his forehead was a definite tell as well. What was he trying to hide? Why had he suddenly decided to spill family secrets? What had he been doing to prompt these extreme evasive maneuvers? "You don't have to go into detail."

Mal took a shaky breath and wiped the sweat off his forehead with the back of his right wrist. "Thank you, my—" He clenched his teeth. "Thank. You."

Okay. This was getting more peculiar by the minute. But Bryce had learned from years in faculty meetings how to be patient. Or at least how to endure.

"Come with me. I need to get something out of my garage."

Shit. He hadn't meant to be so peremptory. Even when he supervised work crews, he requested rather than demanded. "I mean, can we go next door? There's something I'd like to show you."

Mal nodded, the muscles in his jaw tight. "Right. Lead the way."

Bryce walked out the doors onto the patio. Mal followed, but when they were on the grass between the houses and Bryce expected Mal to pull up even or slightly ahead as he'd always done before, he hung back, just behind Bryce's shoulder.

It was freaking weird. It should have been annoying. Instead, he found it inexplicably arousing.

God, this has to stop. Ignore the hot man at your heels. The one whose ass you plowed not twelve hours ago. His cock popped under his sweatpants, a highly inconvenient tent. *Focus. Think about other things.* Such as what would happen to the wetlands if the two of them couldn't find out who was poisoning the water, and fix it.

That took care of the semi. He keyed in the code for his garage door and resolutely watched it slide up rather than feast on Mal's profile.

"Flaming abyss. I've never seen a garage this neat. You sort your underwear by color too?"

Heat swept up Bryce's neck. All his clothes, including his underwear, were sorted by color and function. How else could he find what he needed when he needed it? "You should be grateful. It means I know exactly where to look for what I want."

He edged past the LEAF, and sure enough, on the shelf over his potting bench was the box he needed, just beyond his reach. He looked around for his step stool, but before he could grab it, Mal dropped to one knee.

"What?"

"Stand on my knee. You can reach it then."

"Won't that hurt?"

Mal shrugged, but didn't offer further explanation. *Fine.* Bryce boosted himself up, snagging the box without putting all his weight on Mal's knee. He managed not to drop it when he jumped back down.

Mal was slow to stand up. Had it hurt him after all? It hadn't been that long since he'd been brained by those redcaps, although that was a head injury, not leg. Could Mal's odd behavior be an aftereffect? Maybe Bryce should make him call David—

Ask him. *Ask* him to call David. Shit.

He plopped the box onto his potting workbench and opened one end. "I had an idea. Take a look."

Mal steadied the box with his right forearm and stuck his left hand inside. "What is this?"

"A tagger, otherwise known as a paintball gun."

"A what?"

"It's from a game. You'd probably like it, since it's violent. These guns shoot round gelatin capsules filled with paint, half an inch or so an inch in diameter. In a game, you try to tag your opponents with the paintballs. He who sports the least paint at the end wins."

Mal turned the gun over, studying its design. "A tree hugger like you, I'd think you'd object to littering the landscape with shite like this."

"It's all biodegradable, even the paint."

"Never had much use for guns." He laid it down on the bench. "In Faerie, metal and explosives don't always combine in the way you'd expect."

"This is plastic. Gravity-loaded. Hold out your hand." Mal complied immediately, although he swore under his breath. Bryce wrapped Mal's hand around the grip. "See how you can hold it with one hand? Brace it with your other arm?"

"So?"

"My first druid homework was an anti-evil potion and a spell for sympathetic magic. I can use the spell to transform the paint inside the balls into the potion. Then, with the gun as the delivery system, you'll have a weapon to use against the Unseelie."

Mal lifted his gaze from the gun, a look on his face as if he'd just witnessed a miracle. "You did this? For me?"

The intensity of Mal's gaze caused the usual effect below Bryce's waist. "Anyone could have done the same." He smiled and shrugged. "If, you know, he was a druid and had a spare paintball gun lying around."

"You're wrong. You're the only one who's—" He took a deep breath. "Gareth thinks I ought to be overjoyed to be shut out of Faerie. Alun and David only try to make me *feel* okay about being useless. But you—you found a way for me to *do* again."

Mal tossed the gun onto the workbench with a clatter and flung himself at Bryce, threading his fingers through Bryce's hair and looping his right arm around Bryce's neck. For a moment, the two of them locked gazes, and Bryce couldn't breathe. Something sparked: a connection that shot like lightning down his spine, pooled in his belly like liquid fire, went to his head like vintage wine.

"Fuck the elder gods. You're the one. The only one." Mal kissed him, devouring him, inhaling him as if Bryce's breath were the only thing keeping him alive.

CHAPTER ❈ 15

Goddess, this kiss—the velvet thrust and parry, chase and retreat, lock and caress. Mal didn't care whether the feelings that lit up every nerve in his body were nothing but a biological booby trap. It was fecking perfect.

Bryce's hands gripped Mal's hips hard enough to leave bruises. Mal moaned. *Goddess, yes.* He craved them. Craved being marked by this brilliant man who'd found a way for Mal to keep his identity—to resume the fight against the enemy that had defined his whole life. Who cared whether he wanted nothing but to feel this man's foot on his neck as he worshipped at his feet? Bryce deserved that and more.

But not from anyone but Mal. Mal growled into Bryce's mouth at the idea of anyone else being allowed that honor—the honor of kneeling and taking whatever Bryce chose to give.

He tore his mouth away, although his instincts screamed at him to stay, to submit, to beg.

He'd beg all right. But he'd demand too.

"No one else, yeah? Anything you want, you get from me."

"Anything?" Bryce's voice vibrated with druid power, and Mal's knees nearly melted.

"Anything. *Everything.* Only me." He sank down onto his knees and pressed his face into the soft fleece over Bryce's groin, feeling the heat and hardness of that glorious cock against his cheek. "Goddess, I want to taste you." He looked up to see Bryce's eyes gone black with lust and power. "May I?"

Bryce stroked his hair, and Mal's eyes fluttered closed. "Yes."

Mal whimpered and jerked the waistband of the sweatpants down below Bryce's bollocks. He licked the sack, teasing the tender skin with his tongue, and then sucked one into his mouth, his own cock hard to the point of pain at Bryce's moan. He lapped at the other, then all the way up the shaft, where a single crystal drop glittered at the slit, beckoning him, tantalizing him. Dragon scales and jewels be damned—those were nothing when he could have this.

He sucked just the tip of Bryce's cock into his mouth, tongue working the slit, the salty taste of Bryce like water and air to him, so necessary, something he'd looked for all his life, for millennia, never finding anything remotely close.

He wrapped both arms around Bryce's thighs and took Bryce's cock all the way down his throat, swallowing against the head again and again until Bryce cried out, his hands clutching Mal's hair to the point of exquisite pain, and emptied himself down Mal's throat.

Filling him. Completing him. Owning him.

Mal groaned and came in his pants.

Bryce's vision took at least a minute to return after he collapsed on the hood of the LEAF with Mal trembling at his feet. God, what the man could do with his mouth. Although it wasn't that so much as the way he'd surrendered control. Bryce would never have believed that would affect him so profoundly.

But something stirred in his chest, urging him to take care of Mal, see to his needs. He knew so little about this kind of sexual play. Wasn't there some kind of aftercare?

And what about that declaration? Had he just committed to an exclusive relationship with Mal Kendrick, the ill-tempered knight of the Seelie Court? Yet since they'd returned from Faerie, Mal hadn't been the same brash, curmudgeonly asshole he'd been before. Instead of angry and aggressive, he'd turned achingly vulnerable. And while part of Bryce wanted to see how far he could push before Mal said no more (and where had *that* thought come from?), another part wanted nothing more than to see him well and happy.

"Hey." He slid down until he landed on his ass with Mal between his legs. Mal's head was hanging forward, his shoulders shaking, chest heaving. Bryce slid his fingers under Mal's chin and nudged it up, but Mal jerked away before their gazes could meet.

Bryce was not having that. No freaking way.

"Mal. Look at me." Something—was it because the car was behind him?—made his voice echo strangely in the garage. Whatever it was, it worked: Mal looked. The expression on his face was half-agonized, half-blissed-out. Bryce hadn't missed the giant wet spot on the front of Mal's sweatpants. He felt bad for not reciprocating, not giving touch for touch, stroke for stroke, during the most amazing blowjob on the planet. But for some reason, simply holding Mal's head, restraining him, had felt so *right*.

Now, though, he needed something else—they both did. Bryce leaned forward and kissed him softly, then rested their foreheads together. "Do you have any notion of how incredible you are? How you make me feel?"

"Bloody hells." Mal pulled away. "I can't— This is shite. I'm—"

"Hey, hey, hey." Bryce grabbed Mal's shoulders. "Nothing to be ashamed of. We agreed. We only do this with each other. Nobody else needs to know, right?"

Mal took a deep breath. "Right. Nobody."

"Good." Bryce kissed him again. "Now, what do you say to a shower and a little target practice?"

Mal's smile bloomed. "I'd say bloody brilliant."

Bryce stood and offered Mal a hand up, which, for a wonder, he took without arguing. "I've got a spare pair of tactical pants and a vest you can wear. Easier to pack the paintball charges when you've got plenty of pockets."

"Oi. I'll look like a wanker in those."

"Are you saying I look like a wanker?"

Mal grinned. "Yeah, but on you, it's a good look."

CHAPTER ✤ 16

Only the promise of target practice with his new weapon—Goddess, to be armed again!— kept Mal from begging Bryce to fuck him in the shower. Afterward, he helped Bryce set up a straw bale as a target midway down the hill, with their backs to the wetlands.

"These charges are only filled with water. We don't want to waste the potion until we actually expect to encounter something with evil intent."

"Evil intent is everywhere, mate." Mal patted the pockets of his ridiculous tactical pants. "I should carry live ammo with me at all times so I'm prepared to meet it."

"Listen to you. Talking about ammo like a card-carrying NRA member." Bryce grinned, and Mal practically wagged his nonexistent tail at the praise. Gwydion's bollocks, Cassie better have a cure for this shite, because it was fecking humiliating.

Then he remembered the golden contentment that had nearly swamped him after he'd submitted to Bryce. *Maybe potential humiliation is worth it—especially if nobody else ever finds out.*

Bryce, though . . . Clearly the man hadn't a cruel bone in his long, elegant body. Plus he'd come up with this way for Mal to be less bloody useless. For that, he'd blow him whenever and wherever the mood struck.

But, now, they had a mission. After half an hour of steady practice, Mal had the hang of the paintball gun. He tucked it under his right arm and patted it affectionately. "It may not have the elegance of a broadsword, but it does have a certain style. Don't suppose you've got a scabbard for it?"

Chuckling, Bryce dropped a kiss on Mal's nape as he passed by on his way to the target. "You don't have to haul it around with you 24/7, you know."

"Oi. Remember the Unseelie who showed up in your slough? We're under siege, mate, and enemies aren't in the habit of scheduling their ambushes in advance."

"So you wore your sword all the time?"

Mal frowned. "All the time in Faerie. Come to think of it, Unseelie have never shown in the Outer World before."

"That you know of."

Mal's eyebrows shot up. "Shite. You're right. After the Unification treaty, Unseelie weren't under the jurisdiction of either the Queen or the supe councils, so any incursion would take careful diplomacy to sort out—Alun's brand of fancy-worded, psychological diplomacy. They wouldn't want to send their proxy executioner to crash around like a berserker, endangering their hard-won peace."

Bryce stopped adjusting the target and strode over to Mal. "Whatever your job used to be, you're more than that. More than your function. You know that, right?"

"*You* might be." But Mal was less and less sure that he could say the same for himself. What had he ever done with his life besides brawl, kill, and fuck any man he could beguile into bed with his *glamourie*? Pretty fecking ironic that he was on the receiving end of the beguilement now. He leaned into Bryce, nuzzling his neck, breathing in the scent of grass and earth. *But what a way to go.*

Bryce chuckled. "Careful. We pushed our luck with the open garage door. We're lucky we're at the end of the road here, and the homeowner's association didn't decide to send an inspector by."

"Why? Is garage sex against the covenants?" Mal murmured against Bryce's jaw.

"If it wasn't before, it might be if they catch us at it. You ready to be done with practice?" Bryce's voice deepened, quivering with the edge of druid power, and Mal was instantly hard again.

"I—"

"Well, well, well. What have we here?"

At the sound of that voice, Mal reared back, thrusting Bryce behind him as Rodric Luchullain sauntered out of the trees at the edge of the slough, his hands clasped behind his back. "What the bloody hells are you doing here, Rodric?"

"Tracking you, of course."

Bryce moved to stand next to Mal. "Why wait until now to follow us?"

Rodric's brow knotted in confusion. "This is now."

"Obviously. But we saw you yesterday. If pursuit was so critical—"

Mal gripped Bryce's elbow before he could go off on a professorial rant that Rodric could never comprehend. "Time moves differently in Faerie. He probably followed as soon as he picked up the trail, but he still has no business in the Outer World."

"I could say the same for you, *Lord* Maldwyn." The big blond bastard bared his teeth in what could pass for a smile, assuming the others in the room were sharks. "Dallying here with your pet?" He clucked his tongue. "Whatever would your dear brother Gareth say? As I understand it, he takes a dim view of fae consorting with humans."

"Leave my brother out of this. You need to go. Now."

"Not very hospitable, are you?" Rodric stood next to a stand of cattails, rocking back and forth on his heels as if he hadn't a care in any world. "Won't you give me a tour of your oh-so-charming—what do you call it? A cottage? A cabin? Perhaps a hovel? How far you've fallen."

"I could say the same for you. Not so mighty now, skulking around in the Unseelie sphere like the traitor you are." Mal squinted against the light reflecting off the water, trying to see if any Unseelie soldiers were lurking under the trees.

"Interesting thing, that. Because I seem to recall seeing you in Unseelie lands as well. Curious, isn't it, since if I recall . . . what was it again?" He pursed his lips and gazed at the sky for a moment. "Oh yes. You were exiled from Faerie for violating the consort laws."

Bryce edged closer, his arm brushing Mal's. "Is there anything we can do to him?" he murmured.

Mal glanced at him. Bryce's eyes had gone black again, his expression grim. *Of course.* Rodric was threatening his precious slough. *Even my tree hugger would turn warrior for that.* "Not unless he makes a move first. As long as he doesn't interfere with the Outer World, we can't lawfully touch him."

"What is that, some kind of fae Prime Directive?"

"What?"

"Never mind. But when we get rid of this joker, I'm introducing you to *Star Trek*."

"Tell me, *Lord* Maldwyn, how does it feel to know the only way you'll ever regain your so-exalted position at court is to restore me to power first?"

"That's not what the curse is about."

"Isn't it? Make whole what you took that night. Isn't that the way the Bitch Queen worded it? How do you plan to do that when I've taken care of it myself?"

Rodric thrust his hands out, and shite, he had two of them, encased in leather gauntlets with jewel-studded cuffs. How in all the hells had the man regrown his bloody hand? And if he had, maybe the bastard was right. If he'd already magicked a hand onto his arm, how was Mal supposed to make him whole?

"What exactly are the terms of your curse?" Bryce whispered. "You never said."

"Now is not the time," Mal said through clenched teeth.

"But it might be, don't you see? From what I read in that grimoire, the exact words matter enormously. If the exact wording—"

"Silence!" Rodric barked. "This doesn't concern you. Stand aside and leave this to your betters."

Bryce straightened, his eyes narrowing. "You're in my world now. My home. My work. I'd say it concerns me entirely."

Rodric threw his head back and laughed. "Do you imagine your fleeting life matters, human? Not one of you, not a dozen, not a hundred have half the worth of a single Daoine Sidhe."

"Shut it, Luchullain," Mal growled.

"Oh, that's right. You're not Daoine Sidhe, are you? You're nothing more than a jumped up *bwci*, really. *Y Tylwyth Teg* are meant to be lesser fae. You should kneel at my feet and beg me not to kill you out of hand."

"Not bloody likely." Mal had made a vow, hadn't he? He only kneeled for Bryce. "Besides, last I heard, no Daoine Sidhe could be Unseelie. If you've forsaken the Seelie Court, you've lost your rank."

"Enough! Being Daoine Sidhe isn't a rank—it's not even our true name. Do you forget that we were once the Tuath Dé?"

"The who?" Bryce murmured.

"Tell you later. Bugger's not done mouthing off yet, and we have to get him out of here."

"And you." Rodric sneered, ignoring both their comments. "With all your powers stripped from you, unable to even swing your sword— you're no better than the human. In fact . . ." He advanced, treading on the delicate blue flowers that edged the water. "You should kiss my feet. Now. Before I lose patience."

Bryce lurched forward, but Mal caught his arm and hauled him back to relative safety. "Compensating, are you, Rodric? Striking out at me because I was the vehicle for your disgrace?"

Rodric bared his teeth again. "You think me angry with you? Hardly. I'd thank you if you weren't nearly as sanctimonious a git as your elder brother, or as self-righteous a bastard as the younger. I was stifled, tied to that cold bitch for all the best centuries of my life. The presumption of her—*deigning* to grant me consort status. Her unmitigated gall in declaring the likes of you *my* equal. Now that I'm shed of all her rules and trappings, I'm free to claim my destiny, my birthright. With *this*." He drew the glove off his right hand. Instead of flesh and bone, the hand glinted in the sunlight like molten silver.

Flaming abyss. Mal couldn't suppress a shiver. Between Rodric's talk of the Tuath Dé and his shiny new silver hand . . . Gwydion's bollocks, did the deluded arsehole actually believe himself to be the second coming of Nuada Airgetlám? *Not good.* But Mal snorted, refusing to let on how much it alarmed him.

Bryce slanted a glance at Mal. "Does this guy always talk like a refugee from a bad period drama?" He brushed his fingers against Mal's hand, and the accompanying jolt of comfort and support bolstered Mal's courage.

"Sometimes he's worse. You should hear him whine when someone has a fancier suit than his. Or when someone's bested him in sword practice—as Alun did every time they sparred."

Rodric's face suffused with red. "Swordplay? For children. You asked why I came here? I came to kill you, and I now I have the means."

He raised his silver hand over his shoulder, cupped as if he were about to hurl an invisible stone.

"No!" Bryce pushed Mal aside just as Rodric followed through, a blast of crackling blue lightning flying from his hand to hit Bryce square in the chest, sending him flying back to sprawl on the ground like a broken puppet.

Mal scrambled over to him, sparing only enough attention for Rodric to make sure he wasn't readying another attack. "Bryce! Goddess. Bryce?" Mal felt frantically for a pulse. *There.* A heartbeat, although it tripped unevenly.

Chuckling, Rodric strolled forward. "As satisfying as killing you will be, it's almost more amusing to watch you suffer."

Shooting a furious glare over his shoulder, Mal shielded Bryce with his body. "Do you forget, Rodric, you wanker? Spill Seelie blood in the Outer World without the Queen's permission, and you've signed your own death warrant."

"Nonsense," Rodric growled. "The laws don't apply. You're an exile."

"A *temporary* exile. I'm still fae, still Seelie. Kill me and you're fair game for the Queen's Champion, whose magic safeguards are proof against your little fireball trick. And *that* honor is currently held by my brother Alun."

Rodric blanched, his gaze darting around the lawn as if Alun were hiding under a convenient stone. *Good. He's still a coward at his core, no matter what he thinks is due him.*

"I see you remember that you never beat him in the ring. Not once. Not even when he hadn't wielded a blade for two hundred years. He's that good." He jerked his chin at Rodric's hand. "Your new toy might sparkle prettily in the sun, but don't think I didn't notice you can barely move its fingers. I'll wager you're incapable of holding a sword, let alone wielding it with any skill." *Any more than I can.* In fact, if he ignored the obvious difference in composition, Rodric's hand looked exactly like Mal's.

Regaining his color, Rodric sauntered forward. "Perhaps I can't kill *you*, although you're a miserable excuse for a fae, Seelie or not, but I don't need the Queen's permission to spill *human* blood. I'll finish your little pet while you watch."

His gaze locked with Rodric's, Mal lay down, face up, on top of Bryce. The position left him open and vulnerable, but his life—and the threat of retribution—was the only weapon he had. "You'll have to go through me to do it."

Rodric barked a laugh. "So fucking noble. But what's the point? Humans are so short-lived that he won't last long anyway. Move aside."

"No."

"Cynwrig . . ."

The menace in Rodric's tone, the speculative look in his eyes—shite, was he actually crazy enough to think he could get away killing them both?

"Do you really want to take the risk, Rodric? You know Alun. You've known him for centuries. If you hurt me, he will hunt you down. He won't stop until he ends you." Mal threaded just enough mockery into his tone. "So tell me—are you feeling lucky?"

For an instant, Rodric appeared to waver, and Mal braced himself for the blow, praying to the Goddess that the bastard would be satisfied with Mal's life and leave Bryce alone. But then he yanked his glove back onto his silver hand. "This isn't over. You can't hide behind your brother's coattails and the Queen's skirts forever. I'll kill you yet." He stalked off, muttering to himself as he disappeared into the trees.

"You're damned right it's not over." *You have a lot to answer for, and somehow I'll see you pay for it. In full.* Although how he'd do that, dodge Rodric's murder attempts, and still fulfill the terms of his curse, Mal couldn't say. Maybe Steve would come through for him yet.

Mal wrestled Bryce's inert body up the hill and into his living room. Once he arranged him on the sofa, he checked his heartbeat again. It seemed stronger, no more erratic than Mal's own.

Shite. He had no clue what to do. He wasn't the medic—but he had a brother-in-law who could heal damn near everything.

"Where the fuck is my cell phone?" He'd stuck it in the pocket of these thrice-damned tactical pants. What good were they if they didn't hold the weapons he needed? He was never going unarmed again, not when Bryce's life depended on it.

He found the phone and speed-dialed David. Who didn't pick up. Shite. Was he in a class? He called Alun's office but got voice mail,

David's mellow tenor informing him that the office was closed while Dr. Kendrick was out of town.

Brilliant. Alun was still missing and Rodric Luchullain was on the loose with a bloody Taser hand.

He texted David instead: *Emergency. Bryce injured by Rodric Luchullain. Need you now.*

He barely had time to hit Send before his front door burst open and Cassie strode in, no hint of a limp in her gait and her eyes black as midnight on the winter solstice. She didn't spare Mal a glance, just went directly to Bryce's side.

"Make yourself useful, Maldwyn Cynwrig, and bring me that poof."

Poof? Oh. The footstool. He dropped it next to the sofa. "How did you get here so fast? I'd only just texted David."

"He's my apprentice, you stupid man. I felt him fall." She roosted on the footstool next to Bryce's head. "What happened?"

"Rodric bloody Luchullain. Bastard showed up in the wetlands. He's found someone to replace his hand with a prosthesis that shoots fecking lightning bolts, which seems to make him think his ego-driven treason was a divine mandate or some shite. How in the hells can that be right?"

"It's not," she said, smoothing Bryce's hair back from his forehead. "Where are his glasses?"

"I think the jolt knocked them off. They're probably on the lawn somewhere."

"Go get them."

"No." He wasn't budging. Not until he knew Bryce was all right.

She glared at him. "Lord Maldwyn. I said *go get them*." Her druid power voice rattled his gods-be-damned triple-glazed windows, but for a wonder, he didn't give a shite.

"And I said no. I'm not leaving him."

She stilled, her hand on Bryce's chest, over his heart. "What have you done?" she whispered.

Panic shot through him. "I brought him in here. Shouldn't I have moved him? Called 911 instead? But I didn't want to chance Rodric coming back, and David can do—"

"Be still. That's not what I meant." She grabbed his wrist, her fingers over his pulse point. "Your hearts. They beat as one."

He frowned at her. "That sounds like some bloody pop song. Save it for later and help him."

"Hush, you foolish man. Bryce will be well. Partly because of you."

"You mean because I called David? But you said you already felt—"

"No. Because *you* are well. Somehow, you've activated the ancient bond between fae and druid. Although I must admit . . ." She glanced back at Bryce, who was breathing as erratically as Mal. "To my knowledge, no druid ever aspired to bond one of the greater fae, let alone a Sidhe lord."

"Don't forget I'm only Sidhe by decree. According to Rodric, I wear *y Tylwyth Teg* roots like a brand across my bloody forehead."

"I hadn't thought of that. The genetic markers for servitude are still there. And I've looked into it—for all that Bryce denied it, he's of the line of Robert the Bruce, although on the distaff side. The magic is quite potent in that line."

"He's potent in more ways than one," Mal muttered.

"How far has this gone? Have you exchanged essence?"

Shite. Now he had to go into details? "We've kissed. A lot. So there's that exchange."

She waved a hand. "Yes, yes. That primes the pump, so to speak. Gives the druid the notion of compatibility, whether the bond will take and if you're both likely to benefit from the association. What else?"

Mal squinted at her. "You really want to know how two men have sex? These specific two men?"

She poked his chest with one twig-like finger. "You forget my Davey is married to your brother. There is little you can say that would shock me."

He ran his good hand through his hair and looked at the ceiling, the floor, his feet, anything to avoid looking at her face while he confessed. Not shocking her was one thing. But this whole story still shocked *him*. "He, ah, fucked me. And I sucked him off."

Her brows, finally growing back after her illness caused by hiding David's *achubydd* nature from everyone—including David himself—drew together. "His essence into you both times?"

"Yeah."

"No return?"

"Well, not really. Maybe sort of. Most of my . . . er . . . essence was on me. He might have gotten some on his skin by proximity, but nothing direct, if you get my meaning."

She frowned. "Interesting."

"'Interesting' as in 'I know to fix this' or 'Interesting' as in 'Holy shite, the world is about to end'?"

"I suppose it could be down to Mr. MacLeod not knowing the meaning of the compulsion, but normally, in the first two exchanges, one goes one way, and the next the other. Sharing, you see. Establishing parity."

"What if—" He cleared his throat. "What if I didn't want parity? What if I wanted him to . . . be on top?"

"Are you saying that being the receiver in both cases was your idea?"

"Not just my idea. I begged him. Shite, Cassie, I would have let him take me dry in the middle of the road if he wanted. It was as if the only way I could get off, the only thing that mattered, was his pleasure. I've never done that before, never felt that before, not with anyone."

"You felt compelled?"

He nodded miserably. "Like another person entirely. Afterward, I couldn't understand why I'd do anything like that. Allow someone so obviously, well, weaker than me to *own* me that way."

"Weakness is not always of the body, Lord Maldwyn. And if I judge right, Mr. MacLeod has a strength even he has yet to comprehend."

"I heard that there are ways, druid spells or potions or something, to . . . to block the bond. So I don't feel the urge to throw myself at his feet every minute and beg him to fuck me."

"Yes. There are. But there are consequences. And there are other things you should know first. If—"

The door flew open again, and David ran in, breathless, his hair in disarray as if he'd spent the night in a wind tunnel. "Sorry, sorry, sorry. I came as soon as I got your text." He rushed over to the sofa and dropped to his knees next to Bryce. "He's holding his own?"

"Yes, Davey."

David took Bryce's hands and peered at his face for several moments. Then he sat back on his haunches, heaving an enormous sigh. "Yes. I think he'll be fine. I'll take it from here."

Cassie rapped her cane on the floor. "Then walk with me, Lord Maldwyn. We have more to discuss."

CHAPTER ❖ 17

B ryce tried to keep his breathing steady, but he couldn't.
He couldn't believe what he'd just heard. Something in him, the equivalent of a druid roofie, had made it possible for him to ensorcell Mal without even knowing it.

Christ. His heart lurched and a lump formed in his throat. He'd essentially raped Mal. Twice. He should have known that someone as beautiful, as confident, as arrogant as Mal Kendrick would never have willingly submitted to gawky Bryce MacLeod without a mind-altering intervention.

And what about what he'd felt himself? He'd *gloried* in that feeling of holding Mal's will in his hand. Was this druid crap going to change him? Turn him into a sociopath like that bastard Rodric, who saw everyone as incidental to his own desires?

"You can stop pretending," David said, a thread of humor in his voice. "I know you're awake."

Bryce opened his eyes. David smiled down at him, his eyes the color of the slough at sunset. "I . . . Sorry. I'm not feeling so great."

"I know. I'll take care of that in just a minute."

David grasped both of Bryce's hands, and a tingling warmth spread from the man's fingers up Bryce's arms.

Bryce snatched his hands away. "Don't."

David blinked at him. "It's okay. This is kind of what I do, and it doesn't hurt."

"Could you maybe make it hurt? I think I deserve it."

David laughed. "I mean it doesn't hurt *me*. Alun is always in a tizzy because of the way fae used *achubyddion* in the past, and no matter how often I tell him that aid freely given is its own reward and doesn't drain me in the least, he won't listen."

"Alun. Your husband. Mal's brother, right?"

A flicker of worry crossed David's face. "Yes. And if the big doofus doesn't contact me very, *very* soon, I will have some words for him that he won't want to hear."

Bryce smiled in spite of himself. David looked as fierce as the world's cutest twink could look, but kittens were probably more intimidating. "If Alun is Mal's size, I doubt words would make much of a dent." Although . . . The grimoire had stressed the importance of the right words in conjunction with the right ingredients. Had something he'd said been the catalyst that had ignited the change in him and Mal?

"If the words are 'No sex until you clean up your act,' believe me, they'll leave a huge dent."

The mention of sex drained all desire for laughter out of Bryce. He zeroed in on something David said. "You said fae used the *achubyddion*. Do you mean like servants?"

David shook his head as the warmth emanating from his hands curled around Mal's heart. "Worse. Kind of like disposable battery packs. Apparently none of the idiots ever *asked* the *achubyddion* how their powers worked." He patted Bryce's shoulder. "If you spend much time around Mal, you'll find that's a fae occupational hazard. They never ask. They simply do."

Bryce swallowed. Mal had asked. No, Mal had *begged*. If that was aberrant behavior in fae, then Bryce had definitely done something to subvert Mal's will. "What did they do to the *achubyddion*?"

"Slaughtered them, mostly. Or took without consent, which is just as deadly. Now take this, right here—I love helping people feel better. It's why I've always wanted to be a nurse." He wrinkled his nose. "Although I may have wanted to be a nurse because I was *achubydd* and never knew it." He laughed and shook his shaggy hair off his forehead. "That's what's such a pisser about this supernatural crap. You never know whether you're doing something because you *want* to do it, or because some deep, dark, extra-twisted part of your DNA is playing king of the hill with your inclinations."

"How do you . . ." Bryce shifted on the couch. "I mean, how can you tell for sure?"

David shrugged. "Just go with it, I guess. I mean, does it really matter *why* I want to be a nurse? It makes me happy to help people, which creates a feedback loop that replenishes any energy I use to heal them. Although . . ." He released Bryce's hands, a frown pleating his forehead. "I can't do anything really extraordinary with human patients. No curing cancer or anything like that. Just palliative care, helping them feel better. Supes, though, have this extra *thing*. Auntie always called it a 'center,' so I thought it was just a woo-woo meditation concept, but it's an actual gland or organ or something. My *achubydd* mojo interfaces with it and voilà—anything goes."

The center. Gran had referred to the *wee center* too. "What do you think would happen if you decided not to be *achubydd*? Not to use your power?"

"I'm not sure I could resist, now that I know the truth. I didn't find out about it myself until June. Before that, Auntie had tried to protect me from discovery by loading me down with a boatload of spells, but all they ended up doing was making everybody around me crazy. She turned me into a kind of anti-*achubydd*—instead of making everyone feel better, I caused everything from mild discomfort to borderline homicidal mania."

Despite himself, Bryce chuckled.

"You laugh, but the altercations in clubs? The near riots in all the jobs before I started temping for Alun? Not. Funny. It was *such* a relief to find out none of it had been my fault!"

"I'll bet." Bryce sighed, and David peered at him anxiously.

"You're not worrying about apprenticing with Auntie, are you? Just between you and me—" He leaned forward, lowering his voice to a conspiratorial whisper. "I just happened to overhear her telling my Aunt Regan that you had the potential to be the most powerful druid in at least a century, including all of them."

"There are more druids?"

"Oh my goodness, yes. They work in groups, usually. Circles. Aunt Cassie's circle has six other women in it—my honorary aunts, although if you want to get technical, Cassie's honorary too. No relation at all, but she rescued me out of foster care when she found out I was *achubydd*."

"So there are other circles?"

"Sure. All over the place, although most of them are in the UK or the non-Bible-belt parts of the US."

Good. I've got options. As much as he loved his job, his house, the work he'd done with the wetlands, if staying meant victimizing Mal, he'd leave it all behind. If Cassie didn't give him an acceptable answer, he'd ask another circle to take him in.

Although the thought of never seeing Mal again—

"Hey. What's going on?" David scooted the footstool closer. "You were fine, and now you've got a giant red blob of negative energy swirling around in your chest. Let me—"

"No!" Bryce knocked his hands away. "I don't deserve any more of your help."

"Everyone deserves to be healthy and pain-free, Bryce."

"Not me," he whispered. "Not after what I've done." *What I still want to do.*

David tucked his hands between his knees, clearly respecting Bryce's wishes. *If he can control his biological imperative, maybe I can too.* But David was *achubydd*, not druid. He healed. He didn't hurt. Didn't destroy. Didn't manipulate.

"You know what I've found out since being with Alun? Everyone makes mistakes. Everyone does things they regret, and sometimes the perceived guilt is so huge, at least in our own minds, that we think we'll never get past it."

"Tell that to your garden-variety sociopath." He crossed his arms, tucking his hands against his sides. "Tell that to Rodric Luchullain."

David's eyes darkened and his mouth thinned. "Rodric," he said, as if the name tasted foul and he couldn't spit it out fast enough. "As far as I'm concerned, *everything* is his fault."

No. Not everything. Some of it's on me.

As they stepped off the patio, Mal offered Cassie his arm to support her on the uneven ground. After a few more steps down the hill, he stopped abruptly, measuring the distance from the house—and Bryce.

"Why can I be this far away from him without your damned leash pulling my guts out?"

She waved a hand. "I've loosened it for a time so we may speak privately. It is not," she pierced him with a fierce glare, "loosened for good."

For some reason, that filled him with relief. He didn't stop to think what that meant.

They found Bryce's glasses halfway down the slope, twenty feet or more from where he'd fallen. Mal folded them carefully and tucked them into a vest pocket, belly clenched in fear. David had said Bryce would be all right, but what could he know about the long-term effects of this kind of attack?

"Cassie, without this connection between Bryce and me—not your wee tether, but the new one—do you think he'd have survived Rodric's blast?"

She leaned on her cane, her gaze fixed on the edge of the woods. "Truthfully? No. He's come into his power too recently to know how to protect himself." She cut a glance at him. "Or you."

"I don't need protection." But on the other hand, *refuge*—as he'd felt in Bryce's arms? Goddess, yes.

She sighed. "You claim these feelings, these actions, are things you have never felt or done before. But tell me, Lord Maldwyn, are they things you have *wanted*, yet hadn't the courage to pursue?"

Mal clenched his fist. "Of course not."

"Think carefully. Not all who submit are weak, although in Faerie, where your roles are bred into your very bones, this might be a hard concept to grasp. Think of your struggle—the struggle of the Welsh fae to fit in after Arawn abandoned you to the Queen's unification plans. How could you ever show weakness then? To do so would mean not only your own dishonor, perhaps your death, but that of your brothers, and all other *y Tylwyth Teg* who craved a place at this new table."

She had a point. The Unification hadn't been easy for the branches without strong leaders. As the highest ranking Welsh fae, he and his brothers had taken responsibility for the other Welsh refugees.

Mal had to admit that the Queen had dealt with them graciously, granting the high fae rank equal to their Irish or Scottish counterparts, allowing the lesser fae to choose who and how to serve. But the duty was always there. And two hundred years ago, after Alun had been cursed and exiled, with Gareth still shunning Faerie in his anger and grief, it had been left to Mal to be their champion.

He didn't begrudge the duty. Far from it. He was proud to be the standard bearer and advocate for *y Tylwyth Teg*. But, Goddess, sometimes he just wanted a rest. Was that what he'd been searching for all these years? Someone to take the burden off his shoulders, at least for a little while? Someone he could trust to carry *him* for a change?

"So tell me more about this familiar shite."

She leaned on her cane, peering up at him out of bird-bright eyes. "If the druid council found out that Mr. MacLeod had purposely initiated an unsanctioned bond—and in this age, any bond not pre-authorized by the council is unsanctioned by definition—he would be punished to the full extent of druid law."

Mal's fight reflex fired at the idea of Bryce being punished. Even when druids were being helpful, it usually involved intense pain for the supplicant—they didn't believe that anyone should get something for nothing. "There's no free lunch" was probably coined by a druid priest. Hells, it was probably carved in runes on every bloody oak in the British Isles. He didn't want to think what they'd do if they *intended* to penalize someone.

"No. I won't have it."

Cassie tilted her head. "That notion bothers you?"

"Yeah. He *didn't* do it purposely. In fact, he still doesn't know he did it at all."

"You think not? Perhaps. But ignorance has never been an acceptable excuse among our kind. Knowledge is the coin in which we trade, but instinct is our black market."

"Is giving a straight answer to a question a punishable offense too?"

She chuckled, like the rattling of dry twigs. "No. But I'm not certain you truly wish to know the answer. Or else, you know already, but don't wish to accept it."

"Just tell me."

"The bond could not form if both did not desire it. And the bond itself takes the shape that druid and familiar wish it to be."

"That's—" He wanted to say it was ridiculous, but deep down, he wasn't so sure. Hadn't he noticed Bryce's arse from the first? Noticed the way he charged about the bloody wetlands as if he'd subdue it all by the force of his will alone? And what about in the Unseelie sphere, when he'd called the attention of Rodric's goons with a reckless disregard for his own skin, simply to spare the trees?

He'd supported Mal too, refusing to leave him behind although it would have made his own escape easier. If that courage and determination, that honor, wasn't something to trust, what was?

She held up a hand. "Think before you speak. Remember, words have power. The ones we speak to others, yes, but the lies we tell to ourselves as well. In the past, the bond was always between druid and lesser fae. Lesser fae desire nothing more than honorable service, and druids of old required loyal servants. When a pair found one another well-suited, the bond benefited them both."

"Why outlaw it, then?"

"Because sometimes an unscrupulous druid used . . . dishonorable measures to make the fae believe the bond was acceptable. And once the bond is established, it cannot be broken outside of death."

"Comforting."

She shrugged. "It is not intended to be something to enter into lightly, as you apparently did."

"Oi. I didn't know anything about it."

"Ignorance is no—"

"No excuse, yeah. But why keep this information so bloody secret?"

"The supernatural world has changed in the last centuries, Lord Maldwyn. You know it yourself. Our relationship with the Outer World is uneasy at best, destructive at worst. The fae especially seek to find a way to fit, to prove they're not obsolete even in their own realm. How would they feel to know that their original purpose was to serve as handmaidens to druids, who themselves have diminished in importance?"

"Doesn't hiding the information increase the likelihood of unwilling victims?" He'd called Bryce a tree hugger—druids were the originals of that lot. Had he reacted to that deeper knowledge from the first? Had he *let* himself get caught?

"As I said, we police our own these days, and the traditional mistrust of druids has been your royals' effort to lessen the risk."

"Never thought the royals gave a rat's arse about us," Mal grumbled.

"Their care is perhaps not for your welfare, but for their own."

"Shite, woman. Just tell me without the mystic mumbo-jumbo."

"Faerie's equilibrium is more fragile than you've been led to believe, which is one of the reasons fae such as yourself are constitutionally resistant to change. Imagine the havoc that could result from a disgruntled lesser fae backed by druid magic."

Mal remembered the revolutionary murals in the hallway of the Unseelie Keep. "I'll wager that would curl their Majesties' perfect hair all right."

"A true bond between a druid with Mr. MacLeod's prospects and a highborn fae with your experience and influence?" She chuckled. "Oh, my dear. If they knew, they'd tremble in their slippers at this very moment."

"You sound like you'd be glad of that."

She shrugged again, a tiny lift of her frail shoulders. "Druids embrace change more than others in the supe communities. We must. Our entire lives are bounded by our relationship with nature, and what is nature but constant change? The seasons, the weather, the ebb and flow of the tides. We have long believed that a canker eats at the heart of Faerie. That something must happen if the fae are not to vanish from all the worlds."

"That might not be a bad thing," Mal muttered, thinking of Rodric.

"You forget that the fulcrum of the world includes Faerie. If it were to vanish, the balance would tip too far toward the humans and their destructive habits. Faerie needs to survive, but it must evolve to fit the times."

"Easier said than done."

"Yet your Queen took the first step when she unified all the Celtic fae under a single umbrella."

"You mean two umbrellas. The Seelie-Unseelie split is still bloody wide."

"As you say. And perhaps that is something that should be healed as well."

"Are you saying we should merge all Fae, Seelie and Unseelie?"

"They are not as different as you suppose, Lord Maldwyn. Think on it, if you doubt me."

"Later. Right now I need to know what to do about this bond." It was easier to breathe out here, farther away from Bryce and his scent and the hypnotic spell of his eyes when they turned black with desire and, bloody hells, he couldn't think about that now or he'd lose his resolve.

"As you've taken his essence only twice, you can still halt it. After the third time, it can't be broken outside of the grave."

Mal swallowed. Could he handle not having sex with Bryce again? It had been fecking incredible. Better than anything he'd had in . . . well . . . ever. Was that because he'd wanted—*needed*—that kind of mastery and never found it? "Now that I know about it, I can avoid it." He hoped.

"I can give you an herbal tea that you drink twice a day to nullify the effects."

"Nasty?"

"If it wasn't, you wouldn't believe it was doing you any good."

"Do I take it alone, or do we have to convince Bryce to take it too?"

"It should be both of you to deliver the full benefit. After all, the bond is a partnership. In your ignorance, you and Mr. MacLeod have already stepped outside the accepted rituals, and while that might not be disastrous, ensuring balance in all else is critical."

"Always about balance with you lot, isn't it?"

"Everything is about balance, Lord Maldwyn, as well you know. The bond strengthens that which we already desire, but the tea will allow you to reflect without its magnifying effects. You'll be able to objectively consider whether having those desires fulfilled offsets the fact that you and Mr. MacLeod will be effectively joined for eternity."

"You mean like with your invisible chain?"

"Much more effective. This chain will be of the mind—and of your own making."

CHAPTER ❈ 18

Bryce plucked at the blanket over his knees. "Can I ask you something, David?"

"Of course."

"You're studying to be a psychiatric nurse practitioner." David nodded. "Does that mean you know something about . . . well . . . aberrant psychology?"

"Some. But I know more from working at Alun's practice. Why?" He grinned. "Are you feeling the urge to commit delicious, wicked acts with Mal?"

Heat rushed up Bryce's neck, and he buried his face in his hands.

"Oh my God. You *are*." David scrambled off the footstool and dropped on the sofa next to Bryce, placing a comforting arm across his shoulders. And considering David's nature, the comfort was probably literal. "Sweetie, it's okay. Mal provokes that kind of reaction in every guy he ever meets. They fling themselves at him. It's really kind of remarkable."

"You mean, he's a top."

"Thousands of club boys can't be wrong." David's eyes clouded at Bryce's no-doubt guilty expression. "Or can they?"

"Regardless, I've never been that kind of guy. You know. Dominant. Masterful."

"Tell me another one, honey. I looked you up."

"You what? I don't—"

"You single-handedly pushed the reclamation proposal through the Metro Council. Then you browbeat every contractor who worked on the project. They're terrified of you."

"That's ridiculous. We all worked *together* because we were committed to seeing everything done right."

"No, baby. *You* were committed. They just jumped when you said 'frog,' for fear you'd have their 'nads for breakfast if they didn't come through. Know what your students call you?"

Bryce screwed up his face. "Dorky Professor MacLeod?"

"Nope." David leaned closer. "The *Environator*."

"They don't. They couldn't."

"They can and do, because you never give up. You've so got a dominant personality, but my guess is you've never tried it out on a boyfriend."

"A boyfriend?" Bryce scoffed. "I can barely get a date that doesn't want to—"

"To what? Alpha you to death? Believe me, I know *all* about it. I mean, look at me. I'm the poster child for twinkhood. Luckily, my husband knows from experience that appearances can be deceiving."

"But even if I've got the . . . the inclination, Mal doesn't have the reciprocal need. Does he? I mean, you said yourself that he attracts guys who want to be topped."

"And he never stays with any of them." David tapped his chin with one long finger. "Hmmm. Maybe there's a reason for that. Between you and me, I think Mal has classic middle-child syndrome. Because, let's face it, when your big brother is, you know, *Alun*, and your little brother is the last freaking true bard in Faerie, you might have a slight inferiority complex."

"He's not inferior. He's brave and strong and—"

"Oh, honey." David squeezed Bryce's shoulder, and Bryce had the uncomfortable feeling that the contact allowed David to read every shameful thought in his head. "You've got it bad for him, don't you?"

Bryce shrugged out from under David's hand and sat up, his head swimming a bit from the sudden change in altitude. "I know it's stupid." And now he knew it wasn't just stupid—it was dishonorable, if not borderline illegal. "I'll get over it." Maybe.

"Don't be too hasty. He's never been happy with any of those other men, so he's obviously been searching for something."

"I'm pretty sure what he found was not what he was looking for." *Biologically induced sexual submission. Every alpha male's dream.*

"Sometimes they have no clue *what* they're looking for. They're all ancient. I mean like beginning-of-time ancient."

"Hard to compete with that."

"That's not what I mean. Because their traditions are so old, so ingrained, they have a hard time thinking outside their particular box, no matter how sparkly or filled with jewels it is. They *assume*, because they never had to question before. Their lives had certain . . . well . . . I won't call them rules, because they're not that immutable, no matter what the stubborn idiots may think."

Bryce couldn't help but smile at the exasperation in David's voice. "I take it you're speaking with personal knowledge of one stubborn idiot in particular."

He grinned. "Maybe. But Alun isn't the only one. Mal is just as bad. Even Gareth, for all he lives in the Outer World and interacts with humans more than supes. Although," David leaned forward, glancing around as if to make sure they weren't overheard, "did you know that the rest of his band are all shifters?"

"That's— That's—" Bryce shook his head. No matter what the consequences of his heritage, or of his meeting with Mal, he couldn't deny that this stuff was seriously cool. Finding out that a lot of the stories he'd loved as a child, when Gran had spun tales for him at bedtime, were actually based in truth? *Awesome.* Come to think of it, maybe that was why she'd told them, to educate him for his eventual induction into druidry. "Wow."

"I know, right? But Gareth is the *worst* when it comes to biases. I mean, don't even start with him on romantic interactions between the fae and other species."

Bryce glanced out the window. "So does that mean he'd object if—"

"If you and Mal got together? Maybe. But Alun and I didn't let it stop *us*, and given that Mal is just as stubborn as his brothers, he probably wouldn't either. That is, if it's real and not just something . . ." he waved a long-fingered hand, his nose squinched up in thought, "casual and convenient."

Bryce remembered the look in Mal's eyes when Bryce had pushed inside him. The way he'd moaned and begged. *Nope. Not casual. But maybe not consensual either.*

"So. You were saying. Stubborn idiots."

"The thing is, they're not built to look for solutions that might not have existed at the dawn of time. The Outer World has changed pretty rapidly, just in the last fifty years. The supes don't move that fast. They can't. It's not in their nature. So the fact that both of us were raised as humans gives us a perspective that they lack." David's eyes grew clouded—as in seriously, as if clouds were rolling in his irises. "Fae politics are twisted beyond belief. One-upmanship, struggles along nationality lines between the Irish and the Scots and the Welsh, with everybody *terrified* to display the slightest weakness for fear it'll knock them down in status. Their problem is that they don't have anything to *do* anymore, so they act like a bunch of teenage girls, although that may be doing teenage girls everywhere a mega-disservice."

"Sounds like the same problem King Arthur had. That's why he came up with the Grail quest."

David's eyebrows shot up. "You know, that's a very interesting point. The fae could probably do with a good quest of their own these days."

Speaking of quests, Bryce suddenly had an overwhelming craving for salt. He stood up and wobbled a bit.

David steadied him with a hand on his elbow. "Whoa there. You should rest for a while longer. You took quite a jolt."

"I'll be okay." *Yeah, and isn't that a load of crock?* "I just need a quick snack."

David snorted. "We're in Mal's house, and I didn't bring any takeout. What kind of quick snack do you think we can find?"

"Can't hurt to look." He hobbled into the kitchen, not as steady on his feet as he'd like. Cassie and Mal were still in earnest conversation, halfway down the slope. *Wait a minute.* "How can Mal be so far away?" *And why does that feel so wrong?* "Did Cassie do something?"

"She always does something, this time probably so you could rest while she puts the fear of the gods in Mal."

Bryce frowned. "She doesn't need to do that. He didn't do anything wrong."

"You don't know Mal. I'm sure he did any number of wicked things. With him, it's all a matter of degree."

Bryce opened the pantry. It was worse than the refrigerator, with a lone jar of pickles standing in a solitary state. Christ. If Cassie didn't relent and unfetter them, he'd have to drag Mal to the grocery store. He grabbed the pickles, opened them with a pop, and offered them to David.

"Pickle?"

David shook his head and grinned. "I only eat phallic food in front of Alun. Otherwise, it's just a wasted opportunity."

Bryce's cheeks heated. He'd never considered pickles *suggestive*, but now all he could picture was Mal, moaning with Bryce's cock in his mouth, his eyes pleading for more. *Stop it, MacLeod. Just eat the damn pickle.* He fished one out just as Mal and Cassie walked in the back door.

Mal stopped stock-still in the doorway. "You opened the pickles."

Bryce froze with the pickle halfway to his mouth. "Sorry. Were you saving them? I just needed something salty and this was all you had."

Mal's eyes darkened, and he stalked across the dining room. "You're free to devour anything you find here, including pickles." He stopped just far enough inside Bryce's personal space to make it obvious his closeness was intentional. With his gaze fixed on Bryce's face, he drew a large pickle out of the jar and sucked half of it into his mouth, his cheeks hollowing.

Bryce's mouth dried, and he forgot about the dill in his own hand. He leaned forward, but the sound of David clearing his throat brought him back to his senses.

Christ. He couldn't do this. Mal wasn't in full possession of his faculties, and Cassie's tether made it impossible for him to escape. Was he even capable of making his own choices anymore? Bryce needed more information, and he needed it now.

"Cassie. Can we talk, please?"

"It will have to wait." She set a neat packet of herbs on the counter, "This is for you, to counteract the effects of Rodric's attack. Use enough leaves to cover your palm, steep for five minutes, and drink every drop. It will make you sleepy, but it will restore your vitality."

"Okay, but I really—"

"Now, regarding your ill-considered bond with Lord Maldwyn."

"You—you know about that?"

"You are my apprentice. Of course I know. Although it's scarcely the secret you believe." Holding out a scrap of paper filled with crabbed writing, she directed a keen glance at the pickle jar still in his hand. He hastily set it down and accepted the paper. "This recipe is for another tisane. You have all the ingredients in the supplies I sent you earlier. Follow it exactly. You and Lord Maldwyn must both consume exactly one cup this evening, and one each following morning and evening until I tell you otherwise. It will allow you to manage the bond's effects."

"It will?" That was a relief—maybe. But *manage* was as far a cry from *eliminate* as it was from *irreversible*—and Bryce still wasn't sure which direction he wanted to go. "About that—"

"Anything else can wait until tomorrow. Or . . ." She tilted her head—was that the beginning of a smile? "You could always question Lord Maldwyn. He is, after all, your tutor."

The ping of David's cell phone interrupted before Bryce could demand a better answer. "It's a text from Alun. He's home, but he has to leave again soon. He says they've found the traitor." He looked up at Cassie. "May we go, please, Auntie? I want to see him before he disappears again."

"What does Alun have to say about the traitor, then?" Mal asked. "Is it Rodric?"

David keyed in a message and frowned when a beep signaled a return. His smile wavered, and he cast a furtive glance at Mal from under his lashes. "He doesn't say. But I really need to get home. Auntie, I don't mean to hurry you, but—"

"Calm yourself, Davey. We can go."

Bryce reached out, but let his hand drop at Cassie's stern glance. "I really need to talk to you."

"Consider this another apprentice assignment, Mr. MacLeod. A lesson in self-reliance and problem-solving. We need to discuss nothing that can't wait."

David hurried her out the door, a hand under her elbow, although considering the staccato cadence of her cane, she didn't need much help.

Bryce stared at Mal. Alone again. Still tethered, which meant they'd be sharing a bed again. Could Bryce restrain himself? Keep himself from testing whether Mal would do again what he'd done before? From perhaps trying to push it further, to see if he could demand it of Mal before Mal begged?

Or demand that Mal beg.

No. No, that was wrong. Everything he'd ever done, everything he'd ever believed about personal liberty, said it was wrong to hold that kind of power over another human being.

But he's not human, an insidious voice whispered. *And neither are you.*

But, no matter what, he refused to turn into a monster.

Despite Mal's difficult conversation with Cassie, despite her warnings about the permanence of the bond if he and Bryce had sex again, he wanted nothing more than to drag the man to bed.

No. Strike that. He wanted Bryce to drag *him*, so he steeled himself to stay away from Bryce, to resist the compulsion.

But, as it turned out, he didn't have to make any effort at all because Bryce never got close enough to test his damnably weak resolve.

Bryce busied himself following Cassie's orders, brewing up three cups of tea. He pushed a steaming cup across the breakfast bar. "Here. Sorry you have to suffer through this too—the stuff smells foul."

"Druid concoctions always do. But they work—although sometimes the side effects are worse than the ailment."

When Mal collected his cup, Bryce backed away, keeping a minimum five feet of airspace between them. In one way, Mal was grateful. He'd given over thinking he had any willpower whatsoever where Bryce was concerned. In another way, he felt strangely hurt, as if he were reliving the first days after Unification, when he and his brothers had discovered how many ways the Daoine Sidhe could find to shut them out of court life.

He swirled the tea in the cup. Part of him didn't want to drink it, wanted to see how things progressed. What if Bryce could fill the void in Mal's soul that he hadn't realized was there until the first time he'd kneeled at Bryce's feet?

The other part, the sane part, told him to drink the swill and be done with this. Return to his old personality. Finish Steve's bloody tasks, lift his curse, and go back to his life as he knew it.

But what did that really offer him? Yeah, he'd prefer to have two functioning hands because managing with one was fecking inconvenient. But the Enforcer's job? Even if he were whole again, the job wasn't his, not with Alun back in the picture. Alun would never relinquish his position as Queen's Champion, not because he relished it—he fecking hated it. But he never shirked a responsibility. He'd taken the job, and he'd do it to the best of his ability and according to his code of ethics, which were sometimes damned annoying.

Bryce was still hovering at the other side of the kitchen. Judging from the way his mouth was pinched and his eyes were squinted, he'd already drunk his tea.

So. One half the spell was already in motion. "Cheers, mate. Here's to managing the bond." Mal clenched his eyes shut and gulped the stuff down. "Gah! That is revolting."

"You're lucky. You only had to drink one potion. The other one was even worse. I—" Bryce blinked at him. "I think I'm going to . . ." He listed to one side—and kept on going, his eyes rolling back in his head.

"Shite!" Mal leaped up and caught Bryce against his chest before he could hit the floor. "Nice work, Cassie," he muttered. "'It will make you sleepy' indeed. Why not say the thrice-damned stuff will knock you out cold?" He hauled Bryce to the sofa and laid him down, arranging his arms and legs carefully. He couldn't resist brushing his hair off his forehead, stroking his lean face. Maybe the antifamiliar tea didn't take immediate effect, because he didn't feel any lessening of his attraction, even with Bryce unconscious.

A blast of air fluttered Bryce's hair, and Mal whirled, instinctively shielding his body.

Steve was looming by the fireplace, the open box in his hand.

Mal snorted in disgust. "Oh. It's you."

"You've done well, Lord Maldwyn—better than I could have hoped." Steve snapped the box closed and tucked it under his cloak. "Tomorrow at dusk we make our final move."

Mal glanced down at Bryce, whose breathing was mostly regular. This time he'd at least already been lying down when Steve's arrival knocked him out. "Bryce isn't exactly in prime twig. We may need to wait."

"We cannot. It must be now or you default on the bargain, and you know what will happen then."

Mal's temper rose. "Listen, you bloody bastard, you've given me nothing but half-truths and mystic warnings. If you expect me to dance to your piping, you need a better bloody tune."

"A metaphor I'd expect more from your brother." Steve laced his fingers together, leather gauntlets creaking. "Perhaps I should approach him after all. I thought you had the most to gain from the bargain, but Gareth has remarkable potential as well."

Mal lurched forward. "You stay away from him. He'd never agree to help with anything that smacked of Unseelie interest."

"Even if I threatened what he loves most?"

"He's already lost what he loved most. Now he's making do with what he's got left, so you leave him the bloody hells alone."

Mal glanced back at Bryce, tried to imagine what Gareth had gone through when his lover was kidnapped. If Bryce were taken away, if Rodric had succeeded in killing him . . . Mal's belly clenched, and pain lanced through his chest. *Goddess, I couldn't bear it.* Was this the bond talking, or had Mal actually found someone who completed him the way Niall had completed Gareth?

Could he take that risk? Take the chance on that kind of deep connection when the other half could be torn away anytime? Niall had been human. His time with Gareth would have been short in any case. *But that doesn't mean Gareth has nothing left to lose.*

"Leave my brother out of it and I'll do whatever you want." He'd find a way to convince Bryce—if worse came to worst, he'd let Bryce fuck him from here to Aberystwyth if it kept Gareth safe, familiar bond be damned. *After all, it's not like I've got a brilliant life awaiting me anyway.* "So what's your last bloody task?"

"A night for me in the Queen's bed."

CHAPTER ❈ 19

"**A**re you out of your bloody mind?" Mal shouted, then glanced over at Bryce, who stirred restlessly before settling back to regular breathing. "Come here." He jerked his head toward the kitchen. Might as well get as far away as possible before he tore Steve a new one—assuming the bastard didn't already have several. Who knew what kind of fae was lurking under that hood?

He stalked through the darkening dining room and into the kitchen, as far as his tether to Bryce would allow. At least the wall between the rooms would block the sound of their conversation, although given the anger boiling in his chest, he doubted his ability to keep to what David called his "inside voice."

Inside voice be damned. If this idiot expected Mal to put his skin on the line, he'd better come through with a few more fecking details. This time, Mal was sober enough to demand more information. This time, he had more than his own worthless life at stake, since any foray into Faerie would have to include Bryce.

But if he refused, would Steve make good on his threat to approach Gareth? Gareth might actually be able to pull it off—the combined power of his voice and Gwydion's harp was enough to convince the trees to sing and the hills to dance.

Gareth has been through enough. I can handle this. One-handed. With a druid sidecar. *Who I apparently want to shag me every time I look at him.*

Shite. He was fucked. Upside down, backward, and sideways.

Steve took up a position in front of the sink, and in the twilight, his silhouette against the window looked even larger. Mal flipped on the lights to tone down the effect.

He realized this was the first time he'd seen Steve in good light when he wasn't three-quarters pissed. His cloak was embroidered with tiny gold leaves—and given that Faerie thread was actual gold, Steve was clearly of high rank. *So he should bloody well know better.*

"You realize that's an impossible task, right?"

"If curses were easy to break, there would be no point in them, for how would a victim learn to respect the power of a caster?" Steve's sepulchral voice, normally so deadpan, took on a definite sarcastic tone.

"Who are you really?"

"I cannot say."

"If you expect me to—"

"You misunderstand. I *cannot* say."

Oh. *So I'm not the only one with a magical muzzle.* "Your curse. That's part of it, isn't it?" Steve inclined his head. "Can you tell me whether I've met you before?"

"No."

"No, you can't tell me, or no, we haven't met."

"The latter."

"Why is that? I've been at court since the Unification."

"I was never at your court."

If he wasn't at the Seelie Court, that meant— "You're Unseelie. Shite, *of course* you're Unseelie. How else would you get me a talisman to get me through the gates? Goddess, I've tied myself to an Unseelie swine as well as to a druid!"

Could my life get any more fucked?

"Accepting the geas was your choice. Accepting this task is your choice as well."

Some choice. If he refused, he'd lose his other hand and risk condemning Gareth.

"You realize I can't set foot in the Seelie sphere without calling down a death sentence." And, shite, the executioner would be Alun. He wasn't sure who would be more devastated—Alun, at having to execute him, or himself, when he realized Alun would actually do it because his damned code of ethics would demand he do his duty, no matter who the criminal was.

And if Mal went through with this, he'd be a criminal then, no question—a traitor to Queen and court. He couldn't justify his actions even to himself.

"How do you propose we avoid that little complication? I don't suppose you've got a cloak of invisibility up your endless sleeve."

"No."

"A royal pardon?"

"No."

Mal lifted his hands in a there-you-go shrug. "Can't see how I'll be much use to you, then."

"You needn't venture into Seelie territory. Only the common ground. The Stone Circle."

Just fecking grand. The Stone Circle, the site of his last act as the Queen's Enforcer. The night he'd made the huge mistake of taking only Rodric Luchullain's hand instead of his head.

"Even the common areas—I'm not sure that's not a violation too."

"If you don't want to lose the use of your other hand, you must at least hazard an attempt."

"You mean, if I try and fail, I won't be in default of the bargain?" He'd be no worse off than he was now. Not that he was thrilled with that idea, but one hand beat none, hands—as it were—down.

"No. But if you don't try, you will definitely fail. At least in this, you have a chance."

"Lovely."

"This will ease your way." Steve held out another coin. "To open a gate closer to the Stone Circle. You needn't traverse Unseelie lands."

"Small favors."

Steve rumbled. "You would prefer to locate the gate yourself? No doubt your druid paramour could manage it."

What a bloody horrid word. *Paramour*. It made their connection sound so . . . sordid. "I'd say leave him out of this, but I can't."

"Indeed. He must attend you, whether he wills it or not."

"Say we locate the gate. Enter the circle. Then what? It's not as if the Queen holds court there."

"Take this." Steve held out a jeweled dagger, a Celtic knot worked into its hilt. "Strike the ground at the foot of the altar stone, and the Queen will be summoned."

Mal took the dagger. It was a piss-poor weapon, the heavy ornate hilt making it uncomfortable to hold. It would probably do as much damage to the wielder as the victim. Just as well the ground was the target—at least it didn't fight back. Much. "What the hells should I say to her? 'Cheers, Your Majesty, I've set up a booty call for you with this fine Unseelie gentleman.'"

"'Booty call'? What means this?"

"It means you want me to convince the Queen to let you shag her. What possible reason could I give her to listen to that kind of shite?"

"You could tell her that the fate of Faerie itself hangs on her answer. If she refuses, the Seelie Court could fall. Indeed, Faerie itself could cease to be."

"And she should believe this, why?"

Steve rumbled. "I cannot force her to believe. But this might make her more agreeable to my suit."

Steve pulled a delicate wooden box out of his sleeve, this one barely half the size of his palm, its top and sides carved with exquisite tiny birds. Mal took it, but when he would have flipped the lid on its silver hinges, Steve threw up a hand, and Mal found himself frozen in place. "Don't open it."

"Why? Is it bespelled? Because if you've got some double game up your cloak, you can forget it."

"The contents are fragile. Exposing them to air not of Faerie will destroy them."

"Seems what my brother-in-law would call 'sketchy.'"

"Nevertheless, if you intend to keep your bargain, you must do as I say." He lowered his hand, and Mal could move again. "You must arrive at the circle no later than dusk tomorrow. If the Queen agrees, you must await us in the circle until dawn breaks."

"Keeping a human inside Faerie for more than a night—"

"He is not human. He is druid. He will be well."

So you say, but how can I be sure? Mal found he was less willing to take chances with Bryce's safety than he was with the Queen's. After all, she could take care of herself. And if she couldn't, her guards could.

Shite, her guards. Was he likely to be able to get two words in before they arrested him and tossed his arse into prison for the next millennium?

"It seems to me that all the risk is on my side. If I'm doing this—"

"You're doing it to lift your curse. To restore yourself to the honors and privileges due you as a high lord of the fae. What more do you want?"

"I want a gesture of good faith on your part."

"I have not killed you or your paramour, nor reduced your domicile to a cinder. Surely that is good will enough."

"That's just good business. How can I do your dirty work if I'm dead?"

"What then?"

"Uncloak. I need to know what I've got to deal with. Exactly how persuasive I need to be to get the Queen to lift her skirts for you."

Steve rumbled. "You should show more respect."

"Why? Isn't that what you're asking? Don't cloak it in flowery medieval poetry. Say what it is. You want the Queen to let you fuck her."

"No!" Steve seemed to grow another foot in height and three in girth as a frigid wind swept through the room, rattling the blinds and blowing Mal's hair off his face. "Do not speak of her with such disrespect!"

The Queen *is the chink in Steve's armor? A weakness vast enough to make him lose control?* "Don't lie to yourself. It's what you're asking." Maybe at least one of them could manage to own up to his desires. "It's only fair that I know how *persuasive* I need to be. Uncloak, before Bryce wakes up and starts asking questions."

"Very well. But remember, this is your request." And he pushed back his hood.

"Gwydion's bloody bollocks," Mal muttered.

When Alun had been afflicted with his beast curse, he could at least have passed on the street as human, albeit horribly disfigured. But this—this blue-skinned, boar-tusked, serpent-haired horror couldn't pass for anything but what it was: a monster. A monster even among a race that counted web-footed bean nighe, spike-tailed fuath, and one-eyed, skinless nuckelavee as normal.

"As you say." Steve's eyes burned like embers, focused on Mal as if he'd prefer to incinerate him with a glare—which might be one of his superpowers for all Mal knew. "Now, a night for me in the Queen's bed, and you'll be rewarded. Will you complete your side of the bargain or no?"

"You know I will." Whether he'd succeed in this last task was anybody's guess, but he'd at least have to try, if only to keep Steve away from Gareth. Yes, it meant choosing between sparing Alun or sparing Gareth, but Alun had David. Gareth had nobody. And a skittish, out-of-control, monstrous magic-user was a danger to everyone, even the last true bard of Faerie.

The low, furious conversation between Mal and a stranger finally resolved into intelligible words in Bryce's muzzy brain. What kind of an unholy bargain had Mal struck? It sounded as if he were in league to somehow compromise the Queen of Faerie. With whom? He opened his eyes, then clapped a hand over his mouth to keep from crying out. The shadow thrown on the wall by Mal's mysterious visitor was huge and misshapen and utterly inhuman. Was he agreeing to coerce the Queen into a liaison with a monster?

To judge by Mal's muttered expletive, even he was shocked. Yet he still agreed, despite the potential harm to his Queen. *This can't be right—he wouldn't sacrifice another for his own benefit.* Surely Bryce hadn't been so mistaken about Mal's character.

Would he lie again to coerce Bryce into unwitting complicity?

I could keep him here. If I refuse to go, he can't cross. But would that be enough? *I could order him to stay, and he would.*

No. That would make him the same kind of monster as the creature in the kitchen, who wanted to force a sexual encounter on the Queen by conspiracy and subterfuge.

He'd think of something. He had to. If only to keep Mal from damaging himself so much in the eyes of the Queen that he'd never get his position at court back.

Wouldn't that be better, though? If he couldn't go back, he could stay here. With me. But would he stay if he had a true choice? If he hadn't been roofied by fae biology?

Bryce's ears popped as all the blinds flattened against the windows. The shadow disappeared, and Mal muttered a few more words in an unfamiliar language. Welsh? Gaelic? Would Mal tell him what it meant if Bryce asked? But to ask would be to reveal he'd been eavesdropping. *And to ask might* compel *him to answer.* Better to give Mal a chance to explain on his own, without coercion. *Because it would be too easy for me slide down that slippery slope.* He muffled a sigh. *If only slippery slopes weren't so freaking exciting.*

Quickly rearranging himself on the sofa, Bryce pretended to be asleep. He heard Mal's footsteps approach, could detect his shape just by the way the air moved across his own skin. Was this . . . this *awareness* a part of the bond Cassie had spoken of? On some instinctive level, Bryce *knew* that he could do something to deepen the bond. With the right combination of actions and words, he wouldn't simply *feel* Mal—he would *be* a part of Mal, linked in a way that incorporated the physical as much as it transcended it.

Bryce concentrated, and without any effort at all, he aligned his breathing with Mal's, settled his heartbeat into the same rhythm. When they were in complete synchronization, Mal heaved a shaky breath, a near moan.

One finger skated along Bryce's cheekbone. "*Cariad.*"

Bryce opened his eyes, and Mal snatched his hand away.

"Sorry, mate. Didn't mean to wake you."

"It's all right. What time is it?"

"About eight. You're going to have trouble sleeping tonight with a nap that long so late in the day."

"Maybe." Bryce stretched and noticed that Mal was watching him, his gaze flicking from Bryce's chest to his groin and back again. As if responding to Mal's attention, Bryce's dick decided to wake up and say hello.

No. No way in hell. He couldn't manipulate Mal like that, force him into unwilling sex. No matter how good it felt.

A wicked grin grew on Mal's face. "Look you, someone wants to come out and play."

"No. That's just . . . morning wood."

"It's evening, mate."

"But I just woke up." Bryce rolled to a sitting position and scooted down the sofa away from Mal's unsettling gaze. "I need to use the bathroom."

"Need any help?"

He stood up, giving Mal a sardonic glance. "I think I can manage, thanks." He scuttled down the hallway, but Mal followed close behind. "Really. You don't have to help."

"I know. But in case you've forgotten . . ." Mal gestured between them. "Still attached at the mystical hip. If you want, I'll stand at the end of the hallway, but the sofa is out of range."

"Right. Sorry."

He escaped into the bathroom and leaned against the door. Christ. Talk about torture. He didn't feel an irresistible urge to throw Mal up against the wall and fuck him senseless . . . precisely. Although that notion held a definite appeal, he could still *resist* it. Nevertheless, he craved Mal's presence, his closeness.

When he got out of the bathroom, Mal was still lounging against the wall, but he sprang to attention as soon as Bryce appeared. "So. Rodric's attack made you a bit peckish even before Cassie's brew knocked you for a loop. Fancy some dinner? I could call for a takeaway."

Bryce crossed his arms. "Really? That's all you have to say? That we can order a flipping pizza?"

Mal's eyebrows quirked. "Well, I was thinking more along the lines of Thai curry, but pizza's okay with me if you'd rather."

"That's not what I mean, Mal, and you know it."

Mal huffed out a breath. "I don't know shite, mate, unless you tell me."

"We need to talk about what happened today."

"Which part? Rodric? Cassie? The weather?"

"Try what happened between us earlier."

Mal's eyelids drooped and his mouth softened. "Talk, is it? I'd far rather *do*. If you're up for a repeat, I—" He turned away. "Ah, shite. Never mind. Come on, then. Pizza and beer and we'll bloody well talk."

CHAPTER ❧ 20

Unable to pay the delivery guy and accept the pizza hand-off at the same time, Mal had to let Bryce take the box. Shite, his life had turned into a bloody three-legged race—or rather three-handed. With Steve's latest impossible demand, coupled with his threat to Gareth, Mal was beginning to think he'd be limping along like this forever. And to a fae, "forever" wasn't just some meaningless hyperbole.

Bryce hesitated in the middle of the kitchen, glancing at the bare table. "Shall I set out plates?"

"Suit yourself."

"I suppose, given your preference, you'd simply stand over the box and shove it in."

How can I resist a lead-in like that? Mal donned his old cocky attitude. Although it felt as uncomfortable now as a suit of ill-fitting chain mail, it might still offer protection against Bryce's inconvenient curiosity. "It's not pizza I've been wanting shoved into me, in case you hadn't noticed."

Bryce fumbled the box, and Mal's left hand shot out to steady it. *Ha! Left hand—I'm learning.* "Careful there. I don't fancy scraping our dinner off the floor."

"Right. Sorry." He slid the box onto the counter. "Look, Mal—"

"Maybe plates would be a good idea. You know where they are by now."

"Of course." Bryce opened the cabinet like a good little soldier. "But—"

"Want a beer? I've got more of that Double Mountain IRA."

"Sure. However—"

"Grab some paper towels too." Mal brandished his unresponsive hand. "Not exactly tidy at the table these days."

Bryce glared at him. "In case you weren't aware, those are made from *trees.*" He jerked open a drawer and pulled out a stack of folded cloth napkins that Mal hadn't known he had.

"Imagine that. Those come with the house, do they? Present from the homeowners' association?"

"Of course not. I'm sure your brother-in-law—" Bryce clenched his eyes shut for an instant, his chest lifting with a huge breath. "Mal. Stop trying to divert me. We need to talk. We can do it while we dance around your kitchen getting ready to eat. We can do it *while* we eat. We can do it—"

"Can we do it while we fuck?"

Mal immediately wanted to take the brazen response back. He might have meant it—in fact, he was sure he did—but not in the way it sounded, as if it were something offhand and trivial. However, Bryce's tendency to analyze everything down to its bloody bones was far too dangerous, and Mal needed to put him off the scent. *Otherwise, I might learn something about myself I'd rather not know.* Or worse, *Bryce* might learn something about Mal that would drive him away.

"Christ Almighty." Bryce flung the napkins onto the counter and carded his fingers through his hair, giving himself that fetching mad-scientist do. "Will you please, please be serious?"

"You think I'm not serious?" Mal stepped forward until he could feel the heat of Bryce's body against his own. "Think again."

"Mal."

At Bryce's tone of exasperated command, Mal shivered, the shield of his bravado melting away. He closed his eyes, hands hanging limp at his sides, waiting for whatever Bryce ordered him to do next. Craving it. If Bryce would just—

"Shite," Mal muttered, at the same time Bryce said, "Crap."

Mal chuckled. "Amounts to the same stinking mess, eh, no matter how it's translated?"

Bryce sighed heavily. "Clearly the tisane isn't doing much in the way of bond management yet."

"You think?"

"On the other hand, everything I've read so far indicates that individual will is a critical component of any spell. If we expect this one to work, we'd better do our part and . . . well . . . resist."

"Resist." Mal tried the word out, turning it over in his mind. Did he want to resist? *Could* he resist? Furthermore, did he want *Bryce* to resist? "Is that what you want to do?"

"It hardly matters. This *connection* between us is something neither of us intended. So don't you think a little distance"—he flicked his fingers at Mal's middle, where the tether was quiescent, as close as they were standing—"figurative if not literal, would be best while we sort this out?"

Distance? A pit opened in Mal's belly at the very notion. *Hells* no. Bryce couldn't be serious. Could he? Since Mal wasn't sure he'd like the answer, he wasn't about to test his luck by asking the question. "If you ask me, 'best' would be getting something else inside us besides that bloody druid brew. I think it's putting both of us off our games."

Bryce pressed his lips together and nodded, taking the plates and napkins to the table. Mal joined him, where they made it through two slices of pizza and a beer and a half in total silence. Well, Mal ate and drank; Bryce just picked at the sausage and took one or two half-hearted pulls on his bottle.

Shite. If this was what Bryce meant by "distance," Mal wanted none of it. His skin fairly crawled with the need for Bryce's touch. *Guess my will isn't as thrice-blasted powerful as his.* Or maybe . . . Could the residual effects of Rodric's attack be putting Bryce off his feed, despite Cassie's soporific vitality potion?

Rodric. His silver hand. His delusions of godhood. Mal doubted the blighter would be colluding with Steve—and Steve didn't seem the type to resort to arming psychopaths with built-in flamethrowers anyway. But Rodric's plans, whatever they were, could definitely complicate Mal's own mission.

If I'm not prevented from telling Bryce about Rodric, that should prove he's not part of Steve's plot, right? Might as well give it a shot— Bryce deserved to know more about the arsehole who'd tried to kill him.

"Listen, mate. I know you said distance, but we need to chat. We've got bigger problems than our bond."

A relieved smile spread across Bryce's face. "Thank God. Let's get to it, then."

"Here now, really? I never took you for one of those blokes who thrives on a rumpus." Gareth's first—and only—lover had been like that: forever stirring the pot, glorying in the resulting chaos and commotion. Mal had been half-relieved when an Unseelie noble had spirited the blighter away, if only so he wouldn't keep leading Gareth into scrapes. Mal would never have figured Bryce for the same sort.

"No. Of course not. I just mean— Never mind. Go on." He reached across the table and laid his hand on Mal's forearm. "Tell me." Then he snatched his hand away. "Scratch that. I didn't mean—" He took a breath. "If you want, I'd love to hear any concerns you choose to share."

The sudden release from the compulsion to tell made Mal a bit dizzy—and disappointed, if he wanted to be honest. *Damned PC tree hugger.* He tried to reorganize his scattered thoughts, wishing Bryce would touch him again, help him focus.

"Right, then. What do you know about the Irish?"

"The *Irish*? But—" Bryce's eyebrows drew together. "Okay, I'll bite. I assume you're not referring to the current inhabitants of the country."

Mal barked out a laugh. "Hardly. Ever hear of the Tuath Dé or the Fir Bolg?" Bryce shook his head. "The Fomorians?" Another shake. "Guess I'm utter shite as a tutor, eh? The Tuath Dé lived in the land—Ireland that is—in the time of the elder gods. In fact, some say that they were gods themselves, but that's revisionist propaganda put about by the Daoine Sidhe, if you ask me."

"Why would they care?"

"Because the Daoine Sidhe are what the Tuath Dé became after they got swindled out of their kingdom in the Outer World."

"Swindled?"

"Aye. When they were dividing up Ireland after one of their shiteload of battles, the fools let a poet from the other side call the terms. And he, being a clever sort, picked *everything above ground.*

So off toddled the Tuath Dé, into the sidhe mounds and straight on to Faerie."

Bryce raised an eyebrow. "I take it the Tuath Dé weren't happy about this."

"You got that right. That's one of the reasons the Daoine Sidhe are such a bloody pain in the arse. The thing is, the Tuath Dé stole the place themselves first from the Fir Bolg and the Fomorians, who were rumored to be a bit on the dodgy side in both appearance and behavior."

"Ah. So *that's* the kind of being he—" Bryce shook his head, and this time his smile was nigh on nuclear. *What was that about?* Whatever it was, that smile turned Mal's insides to jelly. If he were to *encourage* Bryce to do it again, maybe from on his knees? Mal licked his lips, tempted to give it a go, but Bryce made a get-on-with-it gesture, then sat forward, his eyes bright. "Sorry. Dodgy. Got it. Go on— I mean, you were saying?"

"Right." Mal swallowed his disappointment. *This is important. To be safe, he needs to know.* "In the first battle, Nuada, the Tuath Dé king, faced an opponent who cut off his right hand with a single sword sweep." Mal raised his own. "Sound like anyone you know?"

"Wait." The elation drained from Bryce's face, leaving him austere—*and fecking hot.* "This isn't about— You're referring to *Rodric*?"

"Of course. Who did you think I was talking about?"

Bryce's eyes darkened, and for a moment, Mal feared—hoped?— that a druid command would be forthcoming. But instead, Bryce balled up his napkin and tossed it on the table. "Never mind. I suppose it was too much to hope for."

"What was?"

"That you would trust me enough to tell me the truth."

Mal's heart stuttered, then took off at a gallop as anger and hurt warred in his chest. "Oi. Everything I just told you is absolutely true." *Although I left out the part about wanting to do you under the table.* "You Outer World yobboes might dismiss it as myth—"

"'Us' yobboes? So I'm still on the other side, am I?" Bryce pushed back from the table and stood, looming over Mal. "Is that why you refuse to tell me about—"

"That's not what I meant." Mal scrambled to his feet, heart sinking at the expression on Bryce's face. *Talk about distance.* "You know it's not."

"I thought I did. Now I'm not so sure." He stacked their plates on top of the pizza box, then stalked into the kitchen. His movements were jerky as he stored the leftover pizza in the refrigerator and loaded the dishes in the dishwasher's energy-efficient maw.

Mal couldn't think of a thing to say, but his druid had always been more about action anyway. So Mal strolled into the kitchen to collect the empty pizza box. After he tucked it under his right elbow, he cut a highly inefficient path back to the dining room so Bryce couldn't miss him. Capturing the necks of their empty bottles between his fingers, he circled the table to stand by the back door.

Bryce didn't glance up from wiping down the counter. Mal cleared his throat. *Nothing.*

"Could I get a hand here, mate? Can't open the bloody door with my arms full of recycling now, can I?"

With a snort, Bryce finally looked at him. "At least you're separating glass from cardboard."

Mal offered a grin, but got nothing in return. *Damn it.* "What can I say? I can be taught, given the right professor."

Bryce's cold glare wasn't promising, but he crossed the room and opened the door, then accompanied Mal to the side of the house. *If only I could believe that he wanted to do more than make sure I put this shite in the right bins, and that he wanted to be with me for any other reason than that gods-be-damned tether.*

"Bryce—"

"Look, today was a little eventful, and I'm ready to pack it in." His glasses glinted in the wan light of the solar-powered streetlights as he turned away. "If you don't mind."

Clearly Bryce hadn't forgiven him for that stupid slip. "Nah. Suits me."

Bryce nodded jerkily, then led the way inside, *resistance* evident in the stiff set of his shoulders.

Goddess, tomorrow would be a pisser. Yeah, Mal had to persuade the Queen to bed a monster, but at this rate, it would be a walk in the park, a day at the beach, a blooming *picnic* compared to convincing Bryce to take another hike across the threshold into Faerie.

Before he could do that, though, he had to get Bryce to talk to him again—or rather listen, since Bryce didn't seem at all inclined to allow Mal to explain himself. *Bloody stubborn druid.*

Then there was the coming night to endure: hours in bed next to Bryce, resisting the desperate urge to touch, to kiss, to beg.

I'm doomed.

Even Mal's lie about the reason for their first foray into Faerie hadn't ticked Bryce off this much, probably because of tonight's massive crash of disappointment. For all of five minutes, he'd truly believed that Mal would open up to him about the secret visitor. Perhaps go so far as to ask for Bryce's help in escaping a bargain with stakes so monumental that Mal considered them a fair trade for treason.

But then Mal had offered nothing but a damned history lesson, which might have been appropriate for a supernatural tutor, but sucked big time for a trusted partner in . . . in . . . whatever it was they were doing.

As they got ready for bed, Mal attempted to start a conversation several times. Bryce ignored him, and stubbornly left his briefs and T-shirt on, although Mal stripped down to mouth-watering nakedness before climbing between the sheets.

Resist, damn it. You've got willpower, so use it.

Bryce lay down on the edge of the mattress, staring up at the ceiling in the near-darkness. When Mal edged closer, Bryce rolled over to face the wall. "Don't."

Mal didn't move away, but he didn't get closer either. "You know I don't think of you that way, *cariad*. As an outsider. As *other*."

"Really? You don't still label me as a 'bloody druid' in your thoughts?"

He chuckled, a rather strained sound that vibrated the mattress, with a predictable effect on Bryce's dick. "Yes, but not in a *bad* way. And I wouldn't lie to you. Not anymore. I don't think I could."

"Because of the bond."

"What? Shite, no. Because—"

Bryce sighed and tugged the sheets up over his shoulder. "Go to sleep, Mal."

"Easy for you to say," he muttered, and flopped onto his back.

It might have been easy to say, but it wasn't easy for Bryce to do. He lay awake for hours—and from the tension in Mal's back when Bryce was weak enough to look—Mal did the same. He must have dozed off finally, because when he jerked awake, his hand was gripping Mal's hip and his nose was pressed to Mal's nape, with Mal moaning encouragement.

Shit. He scrambled back to his side of the bed and tried not to hyperventilate. He didn't drop off again until just before dawn—and then woke with his hips pumping, his dick nestled tight between Mal's ass cheeks.

He rolled away, pressing the heel of his hand *hard* against his misbehaving dick. "This isn't working."

"Only because you stopped."

"I told you. We need to resist."

"Yeah, because that's working so well." Mal's tone revealed he was just as out of temper as Bryce.

"Let's get up. I've got work to do. You can piss first."

"Fine." Mal disappeared into the bathroom, and somehow, even the toilet flush sounded irritated. Clearly the miserable night was about to give way to an equally unpleasant day.

They continued to snipe at one another while Bryce prepped their next dose of the "management" tea. *Gah*, that stuff was foul— it turned Bryce's stomach so much that it nearly made an immediate return appearance.

Mal had snickered at his reaction, which didn't help his mood. So for the rest of the morning, he ignored Mal as much as possible given their enforced proximity, and managed to get a fair bit of work done in the wetlands. The results didn't improve his temper.

Now, as Bryce waded along the edge of the slough in the early afternoon light, he tried to rein in his annoyance and alarm so he wouldn't damage the plants. Mal was brooding on the bank, as he'd done all day, adjusting his position when their tether pulled too tight.

The blight had spread, its virulent yellow-green tentacles snaking through the water. That . . . that *poison* didn't belong anywhere in nature—and definitely not here in his wetlands. A new coil split off and drifted toward a stand of cattails, making his stomach roil. *I have to stop this, no matter what—and if the problem is rooted in Faerie, that's where we'll need to go to solve it.*

Mal was his only means to gain entrance, but Bryce still wasn't sure of the man's motives.

Ankle-deep in water, a dead trout bumping forlornly against his boot top, Bryce turned to face Mal, who was yanking up fescue and piling it by his feet.

"Stop depilating the lawn, Mal. You're worse than an herbicide."

"Never killed an herb in my life," Mal muttered, and scattered the fescue shreds with a swipe of his hand.

"Could we put aside our personal grievances, please? What's at stake here is bigger. The blight is worse. If we don't find a way to fix it, the entire site could be contaminated beyond recovery. This was supposed to be a model project, the template for others all along the West Coast. If I can't even prove this one out, how likely is it that I'll be able to get funding for another?"

"Looking to expand your empire, are you?" Mal stood, slapping irritably at his pants with his good hand. "Become Bryce MacLeod, king of the West Coast swamps?"

Bryce ran a hand through his hair. "Christ Almighty, *no*. The important thing is the work. The plants. The animals." He gestured to the poor belly-up fish. "You really think I'm in this to stroke my fucking *ego*?"

"Why not?" Mal's eyes flashed, and he took a step forward. "People hide their true desires all the time. It always seems to come back to power, though, in the end. Sometimes"—he gestured to the pond, the surrounding trees, the dead fish—"the cause is just the excuse."

Bryce waded out of the water. "This is not. About." He poked Mal in the chest with one finger. "Me."

"That's what you say, but what do I really know about you?"

Bryce snorted. "Ask your brother-in-law. He's the expert."

Mal frowned and advanced on Bryce. "David? What do you mean? Did you know David before? Shite, have you *fucked* David?"

"Of course not, you idiot. He *researched* me. I only met him face-to-face the day before yesterday."

"You'd have had time. When I was outside with Cassie."

"Do you hear yourself? Is that what you think of me? That I'll screw anything that moves? And David—do you really think he'd betray your brother? He's obviously insanely in love with him."

"I trust David. But you . . . you could talk him into it. You could make him do it. The druid power voice can make anybody do anything."

"'Power voice'? What the hell is that?"

Mal snorted. "Just another wee trick in your druid arsenal."

"You mean the control, the . . . the dominance, it's not just our—" he gestured between the two of them, his blood turning to ice, "—our connection? I could affect anybody? Coerce them accidentally?"

"'Accidentally'? Not likely. You're the one who's been on about exercising our wills."

"Mal, please. This is important. Could I do that?"

"Maybe not to humans so much. But supes? Definitely."

Frowning, Bryce tried to think past the panic sparking in his brain. "David said supes have an extra physiological component—"

"You've got it too. Why do you think Cassie was able to sucker you into apprenticeship? Gentle persuasion? The logic of her arguments?"

"You mean, she—" Bryce swallowed convulsively. "Could I have refused? If I'd wanted to?"

Mal shrugged. "Couldn't say. Although as far as I know, it's never been done."

"So an irresistible force. If I have the same power, that means I— That you—" No matter how he looked at it, how he tried to deny it, the truth was inescapable. "This wasn't your choice, was it? I've as good as raped you."

"What?" Mal's face pinched with confusion. "Don't be daft."

"But—"

"Our bond is different. You've never used the power voice on me, and trust me, I'd know. Maybe you have to pass your druid O levels before you qualify, or some shite."

"Are you positive? Have you behaved that way before? Begged someone to *allow* you to blow him? Begged to get fucked? Promised a guy anything? Everything?"

Mal wouldn't meet his eyes, and if that didn't tell Bryce what he needed to know about consent, then none of Mal's glib words would hide the truth. "No," he muttered. "You're the first."

"A first time for me too." Bryce was suddenly too hot in the sun, despite the cool breeze on his back. He ripped his hat off and threw it on the grass. "Aren't we just so fricking *special*?"

"You'll not convince me you're a virgin."

"Hardly. But I've never—" Why was this so hard to admit? "I've never topped anyone before."

Mal's mouth fell open. "You're joking. Nobody can aim like that. Not their first time."

Bryce sat down on the grass, facing the slough. "Guess I'm a fucking prodigy." He let his arms flop over his knees. "What the hell are we doing, Mal? I'm so turned around and irritable this morning, it's as if my clothes are lined with sandpaper."

"You are a wee bit fractious."

"Yeah, well you accused me of seducing David. *David*, of all people, so I'd say you're not much better." Was this the result of the potion, of trying to withstand Mal's pull? If this was Cassie's notion of "managing," he definitely preferred the unmanaged state.

Of course you do. Unmanaged gets you Mal, on his knees.

Mal chuckled, a low, seductive burr. "Maybe not. But you could *make* me better. So. Much. Better."

That does it. Screw resistance. "Really?" Bryce rolled to his knees and faced Mal, creeping forward until a bare half inch separated their mouths. "Are you ready to *beg* me for it?"

Bryce's belly knotted. *What the* fuck *am I doing?* He tried to back away, but Mal clutched his vest, holding him in place.

This close, Mal's eyes were impossibly blue, bluer than the lupines nodding in the grass along the shore. He licked his lips, and the edge of his tongue touched Bryce's mouth, igniting the fires that had lain banked since he'd woken from the tea-induced stupor yesterday to hear Mal conspiring with a monster.

From the way Mal's pupils dilated, swallowing the blue in a sea of black, he felt it too. *I could take him now and he wouldn't resist. Right here on the grass, the sun on our skin and the water murmuring at our feet.*

The water. The blighted water. Full of dead fish.

Yeah, that was a mood-killer. Bryce disengaged Mal's hand to retreat and sprawl on his back. "God damn it, anyway. What the hell is the matter with me?"

"Listen, mate." Mal scooted over to sit tailor-fashion next to Bryce's hip. "We have to talk."

"You think?" Bryce threw his arm over his eyes, both to shade them from the sun and to block the sight of Mal's too-beautiful face.

"I need you to do me a favor."

"At least you're asking, not begging," he muttered.

"Not that kind of favor, you twit. I need to get back into Faerie. Tonight."

Bryce lowered his arm. This was it. The chance for him to find out whether Mal would come clean at last, to prove there was something in this relationship beyond enforced fae subservience coupled with his own awakening desire to be a controlling asshole.

"Why?" *Please, Mal. Please tell me the truth.*

"I—" Mal's breath caught, and Bryce could swear he felt his own throat closing, pain lancing from the base of his spine through the top of his skull, fire burning in the palm of his hand. "To— Shite. " Mal hunched forward, his good hand in his hair.

Is he experiencing this same pain? More? And what the hell is causing it? Bryce laid his hand on the back of Mal's neck. "Shh. Take it easy. Breathe."

For a moment, Bryce thought their heart and lungs would synchronize again, but the alignment stopped just short of perfect harmony. *Damn it.*

Mal's breath evened out, though, and he raised his head to meet Bryce's gaze. "Can't you just take it on faith?"

"Considering you lied to me about our last Faerie excursion, I'm not sure why I should."

"Please, Bryce." Mal sat up straight, his expression earnest. Political candidates would give a kidney and their first born to project the same honesty, but Bryce wasn't buying it. Not yet. Not without a good-faith token. "You may think I've hidden things from you. And . . . well . . . you'd be right. But there are reasons for that. Good reasons."

"*Your* reasons?"

"Not only mine."

Finally, a truth. Not the entire truth, but given the weird sympathetic pain when Mal had obviously—though unsuccessfully—tried to divulge information, Bryce was willing to grant that other supernatural agencies might be at work here. "Go on. I'm listening."

Mal glanced at his hands once, then back at Bryce's face. "You have to believe me when I tell you that if we don't get into Faerie now, tonight, bad things will happen. You can take the mickey out of me all you want; I'll tell you anything, spill my guts, tell you the story of my life—"

Bryce closed his fingers on Mal's nape, just a tiny squeeze, because—*at last*—he saw a way out of this tangle of recrimination. "All right."

Mal blinked. "All right?"

"Yes. Tell me the story of your life."

"Shite, Bryce, we don't have time—"

"Not all of it. One thing. One thing you've never told anyone else. One thing you can offer me in exchange for my trust." Bryce held his breath as emotions chased across Mal's face: denial, resignation, and maybe—if Bryce wasn't projecting—a little bit of hope. "Just one thing, Mal. How hard can it be?"

CHAPTER ❦ 21

How hard could it be, he asks. Mal eyed Bryce, sitting next to him with that earnest tree-hugger expression on his face, no hint of druid black in his eyes. If Mal was going to do this, he had to do it on his own, of his own free will.

Fecking free will. What's it ever gotten me?

Briefly, he considered tossing some tale of one of his club escapades, but he doubted Bryce would count that as acceptable payment for something as valuable as his trust—and for risking his life again in Faerie. Because Mal had no illusions. Between Steve's demands, the Queen's undoubted ire, his own exile status, and Rodric as the loose cannon out to get them all, the danger was very real.

Mal glanced at the sun. His window of opportunity was shrinking rapidly. If he wasn't inside the Stone Circle at twilight to summon the Queen, there'd be no stopping that maniac Steve from hauling Gareth in.

The sad thing was, Gareth would probably jump at the chance. Mal hadn't been kidding when he'd told Bryce that fae could hold a grudge, and nobody held a greater grudge against the Queen than Gareth. He wouldn't care what he forced her to do—and he might actually be able to force her. If he brought Gwydion's harp with him, his song would hold more power inside the Stone Circle than she did.

But if Gareth took that step in anger, in grief, in vengeance, he'd be exiled from Faerie permanently as an oath-breaker. Gareth might spend all his time in the Outer World now, but he had a *choice*. Mal knew what it was like to be stripped of choice, and he didn't want that for his brother, no matter what the cost.

Gareth.

That was the one thing that would satisfy Mal's own sense of what was due to Bryce and what they might have together someday—assuming they lived.

"I betrayed my brother."

Bryce's eyes widened, his brows climbing halfway up his forehead. "Alun?"

Mal almost laughed—almost. "As if anyone could betray Alun. He never does anything wrong. No. Gareth."

"Tell me."

"This was years ago. Millennia, if you want to get particular. Back when Annwn was still the Welsh underworld, with Arawn its king, and three wet-behind-the-ears *y Tylwyth Teg* brothers were trying to make their place at court."

"Before the Unification, then."

"Aye. Alun and I, we spent our days training for combat. Wars were expected back then, even common, and Arawn needed soldiers. We were good at it, meatheads that we are—that is, Alun was bloody brilliant, and I worked my arse off to try to be half as good."

"Surely you're selling yourself short." Bryce's hand on the small of his back warmed Mal, enabling him to go on with the story he'd never even told Alun—and he'd never dream of telling Gareth.

"You've never seen Alun fight. It's like poetry." He drew his knees up and wrapped his arms around them. "Gareth is the youngest of us. Alun and I were already striplings by the time he came along, so he was always a bit isolated. We tried to take care of him, protect him, but to be honest, he always mystified us a bit. He went to the same training rounds as we did, but he never relished it. Then one day, he hesitated in a bout, and his opponent landed a blow that broke his hand."

Bryce winced. "Not good for a musician."

"Thing was, he wasn't a musician then—or at least we didn't know he was. He disappeared from the ring after the injury. Alun assumed he was off to the healers, but I followed him. I found him in the stables, huddled in an empty stall, singing to his hand. He healed himself. With a song. I knew then that he was a bard."

"You mean nobody had a clue before that?"

Mal huffed out a half laugh. "He hid it well. He was afraid of what would happen if anyone found out. Once Arawn knew there was a potential bard in Annwn? He'd order Gareth into apprenticeship before you could say Llanfairpwllgwyngyll."

Smiling, Bryce scooted closer until their sides were touching. "I'm not sure I could ever say that, no matter how long you gave me. But why would that be a bad thing? Apprenticeships were the accepted way to learn a trade, after all. You and Alun were doing the same with your sword training."

"He didn't want to leave us. Like I said, he was a bit of a loner. Not interested in dalliances with male or female partners, nor anyone in between. When he wasn't with us, he kept to himself." Mal took a deep breath. "But there was a war coming, a bad one. I didn't want Gareth to ride into battle, because I was afraid for him. So I told Arawn his secret."

"That he was a bard?"

"Yes, and what Gareth feared actually happened—Arawn sent him away to train. But since there were no living bards left to train him, Arawn had to recruit one from among the nonliving."

Bryce's hand stilled on Mal's back. "He was taught by someone dead?"

"It's debatable."

"Mal, you're either dead or you're not."

"Remind me to introduce you to the vampire council, if that's what you think."

Bryce chuckled, shaking his head. "I keep forgetting I'm not in Kansas anymore."

"Were you ever? I thought you were from Connecticut."

"Never mind. Please." He gestured with an open palm, very careful not to order Mal to continue. *Thank you, mate.*

"The tutor he found was Gwydion ap Dôn himself—a bard who could charm the dead back into their bodies, a mage who could convince the very trees to go to war for him. A man who plunged two kingdoms into war so his worthless arse of a brother could commit a rape."

"Shit," Bryce muttered.

"Aye. Stellar role model, our Gwydion. He'd retired to his caer years before—Caer Gwydion, what you lot call the Milky Way. But he came back to train Gareth."

"I can see how that would be unsettling to a sensitive soul, but—"

"That's not all. Gwydion could only be called to a place bounded by death—Caer Ochren, the citadel of bones—and once called, the doors couldn't be breached or he'd retreat to the stars again."

"So—"

"So I condemned my brother to a century of captivity with nobody but a legendary warmongering opportunist and the voices of the dead whose bones made up the prison walls. Nothing I could ever do for him would make up for that."

"But you kept him alive. He didn't die in battle."

Mal attempted a smile. "I'm not sure he wouldn't have preferred that." He gazed into Bryce's eyes and didn't detect anything but concern—no judgment or revulsion. "Promise me you'll never tell Gareth."

"Of course. I would never betray your trust."

"I know. That's why I told you."

Bryce stroked Mal's cheek once, a feather touch, before drawing away with a wry smile. "And that's why I'll go with you to Faerie."

Mal's heart threatened to burst out of his chest. If this was what it meant to be a fae familiar—acceptance, a true exchange, the symbiotic bond Cassie had nattered on about—why in the flaming abyss would Mal want to deny it? "And *that* is why I'm taking you to bed. Now."

Bryce's first reaction to Mal's offer was *Oh hell yes* as his dick took definite interest. But then he nearly drowned in a wave of self-loathing. *Is this how you repay his trust?* He scooted across the lawn on his ass, putting more distance between them.

"If this is quid pro quo for agreeing to go into Faerie, you don't have to bother. I . . . I want to go anyway."

Mal prowled after him on his knees, making Bryce's mouth go dry with desire. "Believe me, it's no bother."

Scrambling to his feet, Bryce backed away. After that weird attack Mal had suffered (which was probably magic; everything else certainly was), he could accept that there were details Mal wouldn't—or couldn't—divulge. Yet Bryce desperately wanted to believe that when Mal had the choice, he'd do the right thing, make the right choice.

Just as I have to do. No more giving in to his temper or his passions or his desires. He knew how to control himself—he'd had his entire life to learn how.

"We agreed to keep our distance."

"That was your idea. Know what I think? Distance sucks." Mal stood up and stalked toward Bryce, eyes dark with desire. He grabbed Bryce's vest and pulled him close, nuzzling the angle between his jaw and neck. "This is much better."

Bryce shivered. *So much better.* He was tempted—God, so tempted. And for that reason alone, he had to resist. "Please. Don't."

Lifting his mouth from Bryce's skin, Mal murmured, "If you don't want me—"

"Want you?" He barked out a strangled laugh. "Good Christ, Mal, what do you think? You took care of me. You took me on an adventure that I'd never have found on my own. You saw me for what I was when I didn't even know. You're ill-tempered and hotheaded and foulmouthed and—"

"Don't hold back, mate. You're making me blush."

Bryce laughed. "And as snarky a son of a bitch as I've ever met. But you're strong—strong enough to survive losing everything you ever had and not give up. You're also the most beautiful man I've ever met, so yes, I want you. I want everything you've got to give." He gripped Mal's wrist. "But, in return, I'd give you everything I've got too. Not that it's much."

"Not much? Are you crazy? No, I take that back. You're definitely crazy, but you're also an untrained druid with more power than Cassie's seen in a couple of centuries."

Bryce stroked Mal's hair. "But, see, that's why I can't take the offer. You're not making it because you want me. You're making it because you're under the influence of the fae-druid biological imperative."

"That's a load of—"

"David told me you never bottom. You never beg. Men beg *you.*"

"Yeah, but—"

"So when I . . . when you let me fuck you, when you blew me in the garage, it wasn't your choice, don't you see? I *made* you do that, because of some genetic modifications that your elder gods forced on the fae at the beginning of time."

"Bollocks to that. You didn't."

"You can't deny you've never done anything like that before. And lord knows I never have. I've never felt that way. That need to possess, to . . . to . . ."

"Master?"

"Yes," Bryce said miserably. "It's so fucking wrong."

Mal laced his fingers with Bryce's. "What if it's fucking right?"

"You can't know that. Not for sure. You're under the spell or suffering from a supernatural instinct or whatever the hell it is."

"Who cares what it is?" Mal grinned and tugged on his hand. "Stop beating yourself up."

"It must be affecting you. God knows *I* still feel it—this need to . . . to . . ."

"To what? To have me under you? To pound my arse until I scream and come all over your belly?"

"Shit." His cock responded to the suggestive burr in Mal's voice and popped to hard attention in his briefs.

"Or maybe to fuck my face, push your cock so far down my throat that you stop my breath. Is that what you want?"

"Augh! Don't." But he sounded feeble even to himself.

Mal moved closer. "If we have to fight so hard against it, if it makes us into the surly arseholes we've been all day when we deny it, maybe that means it's the right thing for both of us. I mean, I know what I'd rather have in my mouth, and it isn't that damn tea of Cassie's."

Bryce remembered how perfect it had been with Mal—the exact opposite of the discontent that had plagued him all day. "So you think the way we feel, what I'm dying to do to you, with you—"

"True desires laid bare." Mal smiled wryly. "Pisser, isn't it?"

Could it be that simple? Long-buried complementary yearnings that had finally found their match?

Bryce glanced down at Mal's groin, and even in the ill-fitting tactical pants on loan from Bryce's closet, his erection was clear and present.

Danger. But to whom? "If you're sure—"

"You know, mate, I don't think it's me that's unsure here." Mal nudged Bryce's chin with his knuckles. "And I . . . well . . ." He looked down for an instant, a flush blooming along his cheekbones. "Ah, sod it," he whispered, then met Bryce's gaze squarely. "I want someone to take the weight of responsibility off me, at least for a little while. To make the choices *for* me for a change. You can do it. Will you?"

When Mal put it like that, it changed the narrative completely, because if Bryce knew anything, it was how to care for those who needed him—from Gran's garden, to the wetlands, to a student wrestling with a difficult concept. Caring for Mal, giving him what he needed, especially when they both craved it? *Oh yes.* That he could most definitely do, with no guilt whatsoever. In fact, *not* complying would be more hurtful than refusing out of misplaced self-recrimination.

A fire lit in his middle, and Mal must have seen it reflected on his face, because those blue eyes flared with unmistakable hunger. Bryce grasped the back of Mal's neck, pressing their foreheads together. "Get inside. We haven't got long before we leave for Faerie, and I plan to fuck you twice."

CHAPTER ✦ 22

When Bryce kicked the bedroom door closed behind him, Mal's knees buckled, and he collapsed onto the edge of the mattress. *I want this. I need this. And he's just the bloke to do it—to take the burden off my shoulders and onto his own.*

He started to slip to his knees as Bryce advanced across the room. "Stop."

Mal froze at the command, chills skating across his skin. His cock was hard as granite, the brush of the head against the fly of his ridiculous tactical pants enough to send him through the roof.

Mal gazed into Bryce's eyes, black as midwinter night. "Where do you want me? How do you want me?"

"What I want," Bryce murmured, running the backs of his fingers over Mal's cheekbones, "is to make love to you. Think you can handle that?"

"But I thought—"

"Trust me, we'll get to that too." He twined his fingers in Mal's hair and tugged. "We both like it too much to resist."

Mal closed his eyes, reveling in the scent of Bryce's skin, like forest and lake and earth. "Thank the Goddess for that."

"But, first, I want something different. I want to look into your eyes when I push inside you. I want to *taste* you, because if you taste anything like you smell . . . Christ. Have I ever told you how intoxicating that is?"

Mal turned his head to nuzzle Bryce's wrist, and that small movement tweaked his hair again. *So good.* To be held. To be safe. *To be loved.*

Bryce loomed over him, the intensity in his eyes magnified ever so slightly by his completely unfashionable glasses. "This isn't all we have, you know. It's not all we are. You're more than your job, just as I hope I'm more than the nerdy professor who'd never have stood a chance with you if we'd met in one of your clubs."

"If you'd looked at me like that," he whispered, "I would have followed you wherever you asked."

Bryce's smile was rueful. "Even to the recycling center?"

"Even there." He laced his left hand in Bryce's hair—crushed and rumpled from his hat, as usual—and drew him down for a kiss, a press of lips softened by a smile.

"Just so you know, there are some places I would never take you."

"Ashamed of me?"

"No. Because I know you would hate it. You've had to do too many things you hate, Mal. I won't add another."

Mal's chest rose in a surprised breath. No one—not the Queen, not Gareth, not even Alun—had ever considered what the choices they'd forced on him had done to his soul.

Because Alun was stoic, able to withstand any storm but his own guilt, he expected Mal to be the same. And Gareth was free to act out as he liked, his exalted bard status granting him privileges he didn't even comprehend.

Mal had had to muddle through as best he could, relying on bravado and charm to mask his vulnerability. With Bryce, though—

"I don't have to pretend with you, do I? That I can handle it all? That no assignment is too horrible, too overwhelming?"

"Of course not." Bryce lifted Mal's right hand and planted a kiss in the palm.

"*Oh*." And Mal could *feel* it—more than the twitch of his fingers and the tingle of returning sensation that had teased him since Steve had recovered the dragon scale.

Bryce raised his head, his attention snapping to Mal's face. "What is it? Have I hurt you?"

"No." Strangely—and most wonderfully—Mal could still feel that shape, that warmth, that comfort of Bryce's lips, the inverse of the geas brand in his other palm. "Never."

"Good. Because I won't ever do that." Bryce grinned down at him, a little bit sly and a whole lot wicked. "Unless you beg for it."

He lifted the hem of Mal's shirt and eased it over Mal's head. "Raise your arms."

When Bryce would have slipped the shirt over his wrists, though, Mal said, "Leave it."

Bryce's grin was incandescent. "Well. This raises some very interesting options for later."

He leaned down and pressed his open mouth to the spot below Mal's ear, whispering against his skin, "I want to give you everything you need. Because you are more than I ever hoped for." He kissed his way down Mal's throat with beautifully agonizing slowness.

"Bloody tease."

"Yes. Don't you love it?"

Mal's cock tried to punch through his pants. "Goddess, yes."

"The thing is, I'm a scientist. Curious by nature." He licked a circle around one of Mal's nipples and blew on it. "I've never had the opportunity to thoroughly explore the strange new world of Mal Kendrick. I intend to make the most of it." He licked again and then opened his mouth over the nipple and sucked.

Mal nearly came. He arched his back, needing more, needing everything. "Please . . ."

Bryce disengaged, and Mal wanted to weep or curse, he wasn't sure which. Shite, if he could nearly come by the man's mouth on his nipple, what would it be like with that same mouth on his cock? He whimpered.

"Hmmm. I must make a note of that." He peered up at Mal from his position at Mal's chest. "Purely in the interest of science, you understand."

"I never knew—" Mal sucked in a breath, his arms trembling, when Bryce trailed his tongue down Mal's abdomen "—you were so . . . so . . ."

"So dedicated? Oh yes. Why do you— Hunh." Bryce stared at Mal's belly. "You don't have a navel."

"No umbilical cord. We're not born as humans are. Shouldn't be a surprise—we were naked together once before."

"Yes, but clearly I missed several salient features. I need to do more research. Lots more research."

"Works for me."

"Excellent. Let's start here." Bryce popped the button on the tactical pants. Mal raised his hips in mute appeal. Bryce eased the zipper down—and nearly got punched in the mouth when Mal's cock sprang free. "No wonder you scorn underwear. Commando saves so much time."

Mal quivered with need, anticipation, lust. Bryce's mouth was *right there*, a breath away from his cockhead, but the infuriating druid didn't so much as glance at it. Instead, he pulled the pants down all the way to Mal's ankles.

Bryce snorted in disgust. "Boots again. Why don't we ever think of those before we start on the pants?" He tugged Mal's left boot off. "Definitely need more experimentation. It may take us years to get this right."

He made quick work of the other boot, tossing both over his shoulder, heedless of where they landed. The pants were next. Then Bryce stood at the foot of the bed, and Mal felt the heat of his gaze, as palpable as if it were his fingers.

Not enough. Mal wanted the real thing: Bryce's hands. His mouth. His spend. *Everything.*

"Christ Almighty," Bryce whispered, and it truly sounded like a prayer. "You are the most extraordinary thing I've ever seen."

A chill chased down Mal's spine. "'Thing'?"

Bryce caressed his ankle. "We're all things, aren't we? But if you're asking if I think of you as less than a man, less than me, then no. You're a freaking miracle, Mal. Never let anyone tell you otherwise."

"As long as you tell me, I don't give a shite what anyone else says."

Bryce's smile turned predatory, possessive, sending a jolt from the base of Mal's skull to his bollocks. "In that case," he said, his voice like sandpaper and velvet as he trailed his fingers up Mal's thighs to grip his hips, "I'll say it often. Especially when you're naked under me like you are now."

"I—" Bryce dove down and engulfed Mal's cock in his mouth. "Shiiite."

Mal tasted freaking *amazing*. The taste was . . . complete, as if whatever factor in human semen made it bitter had been engineered out. Was it intended to be a way to lure in humans, give them something extra that made the fae more desirable as lovers?

Bryce couldn't imagine anything that would make Mal more desirable or increase Mal's effect on him. When he'd tasted Mal's kiss, that soft, tentative offering, something had snapped, and the self-consciousness that normally overcame him during the peculiar, awkward dance of copulation had fallen away.

He sucked Mal's cock to the back of his throat, and where in the past he'd never been able to escape his gag reflex, this time he was able to swallow around the head, reveling in the way Mal whimpered and squirmed. He hollowed his cheeks as Mal had done, varying the suction as he pulled up the shaft to see what made Mal moan the loudest.

Yes. More research in the future. He needed to know exactly which parts of Mal's body produced that needy sound, breathy and desperate, because it made his own dick ache and throb.

"Bryce. No. About to come."

Bryce released him, but couldn't resist one more lick across the slit. "Isn't that the idea?"

Mal stretched his left hand toward Bryce, his fingers spread, and Bryce answered the unspoken plea, lacing their fingers together. "Not without you in me."

"You sure? I'm happy enough like this." He licked again and was rewarded with several crystal drops, welling like a spring at first thaw.

Mal's fingers tightened on his. "Yes. I choose this. Willingly." Something in the intensity of Mal's voice, the look in his eyes, the way his mouth firmed in a determined line, convinced Bryce that he was dead serious.

"All right." He kissed Mal's cock, smiling at the resultant whimper, and stood up to get the lube.

"Naked. You need to be naked too. Otherwise . . ."

Bryce paused with one hand on the drawer. "Otherwise what?"

Mal shut his eyes, his dark lashes a fan against his cheek. "Just . . . please."

"Since you begged so sweetly." Besides, how could he deny the man something he wanted so much himself?

Bryce tossed the lube on the bed and stripped, remembering to take his boots off first this time—*Yes, I can be taught*. When he finished and stood at the foot of the bed, Mal's hungry gaze chased away any doubts about being too thin, not broad enough through the chest, too narrow at the hips. He finally felt like *enough*. Like he might actually be worthy of someone so extraordinary.

"Raise your knees," he murmured. Mal did, his breath catching in a way that mirrored Bryce's own. "Let them fall open." Mal did that too, and the pulse beating in his throat matched Bryce's own thundering heart.

While he drizzled lube on his fingers and stroked Mal's cleft, circled his hole, pierced him with one finger, two fingers, three, Mal's gaze never left Bryce's, his teeth clamped to his lower lip, and Bryce couldn't have looked away on pain of death.

"Now you," Mal whispered.

"Yes." Bryce slicked himself up and hooked Mal's legs over his shoulders. Cradled his hips and lifted. But as he pressed the head of his cock against Mal's hole, something gathered in his chest, like a storm about to break. Somehow, this was different from the other times they'd joined. Important. Momentous, as if the instant he breached Mal, they would both change in some fundamental way. He tensed, ready to pull back, but Mal reached up and stroked his face.

"Bryce. It's all right, love. *This* is right for us. Take me."

Ah. Permission. The invitation he'd been waiting for. "*Yes*," he whispered, and pushed home.

Mal was right. God, was he ever right. Whereas before, joining with Mal had been incredible, this time, it transcended perfection. Mal's channel hugged his cock in heat and velvet and a sensation that was almost electric but not quite. Something he couldn't describe because he'd never felt it on his skin before.

"Goddess, Bryce." Mal's voice was rough, almost broken. "You— I've never—"

"Shhh." Bryce leaned down and stopped Mal's mouth with a kiss. Hot and wet and possessive. Then soft and sweet and inviting.

"You'll never be empty because you fill me. Feel me here." Bryce thrust into Mal, his rhythm matching the beat of blood in his ears. "The way I feel you here." He brought Mal's right hand to his chest and trapped it there.

Mal's eyes widened. "I— You— I can feel your heart," he whispered.

"That's because it beats for you."

Mal's neck arched, and he cried out as he came, ropes of semen shooting across his chest and Bryce's arm. Bryce leaned down and licked a trail of it off Mal's chest, and at the bloom of it on his tongue, he gasped and came too, his cock pulsing inside Mal, his vision whiting out.

Never. I'll never be the same again.

CHAPTER ❈ 23

Considering how devastating the sex had been, Mal was surprised that Bryce remembered they had a deadline to meet. But after a bare five minutes of cuddling—following the promised *second* fuck—he crawled out of bed and retrieved a cloth to clean Mal off, his smile altogether too smug when he removed the shirt still tangling Mal's wrists. "We should get moving. Assuming you're able to move."

"Shut it, druid. I can take anything you can dish out." And, amazingly enough, it was true. Normally after sex like that, Mal would need at least a short nap to recover and recharge, but now? It was as if he boasted another layer of skin below his own, this one forged of captive stars. He snatched the cloth out of Bryce's hand to draw him in for a kiss, and under his fingers, Bryce's neck thrummed as if he had the same energy-skin.

If this was what it felt like to be a druid familiar? Hells, he had no regrets, barring a tiny niggle of guilt. Maybe he should have come clean with Bryce about the permanence of the bond before he'd asked—all right, *begged*—to be fucked again.

Too late now—it was done, and other than this weird subdermal buzz, he didn't feel that different. For instance, he didn't feel the urge to drop to his knees in front of Bryce again once they were out of bed, which was a damned good thing. If he intended to talk the Queen into bedding Steve, he couldn't afford the distraction.

If he failed in that little task, who knew what else the curse might do? At the very least, he'd have two useless hands or get slapped into slavery at Govannan's forge for the rest of eternity—assuming the Queen didn't finish him off first.

One thing he'd make damned sure of, though. No matter what might happen to him, he'd amassed enough favors in his time as the Queen's Enforcer to strike a bargain for Bryce's safety.

Mal lifted the blinds and peered outside. Twilight was still far enough off that they had time for a more thorough cleanup. Although smelling of earthy sex probably wouldn't bar the gates of Faerie to them, they were about to face the Queen, and she had standards. If he wanted to turn her up sweet, he'd be wise not to purposely piss her off.

"I've been thinking," Bryce said, not meeting Mal's eyes. "About Cassie's bond-management tea."

Mal winced. "Gah. I'd as soon never think about that shite again."

"Well, that's kind of where I'm going. If our willing resistance is part of the spell—well, I don't want to resist anymore, so there's no point in choking the stuff down, is there?"

Now. Tell him now. But Bryce was right—there was no point anymore since their link was irreversible, and Mal suspected no druid potion, no matter how foul, would make any difference. "I'm always happy to forgo druid swill." Besides, worrying about the consequences now was foolish. *First survive the night, then deal with the fallout, including telling Bryce the truth.* "Listen, though. We'll be going to a different place tonight. We need to . . . prepare."

Bryce studied him warily. His eyes were brown again, no hint of druid black, as he wiped his chest down with the towel. *That should be my duty. My privilege.*

Flaming abyss! *Stop it. No distractions.*

"Okay. Like what?"

"Shower, for one thing. We ought to wear only natural fibers or skins. No base metals."

"What about zippers? They weren't a problem last time."

Mal frowned. "Maybe the rules are different for you."

"Or maybe you never tried."

Mal's eyebrows popped up. "You have a point."

"I think we both need the tactical pants. And vests. Because after our last visit, not to mention Rodric's little adventure in the wetlands, I don't want to go unarmed. And no offense, but you can't exactly carry a sword anymore."

Mal ducked his head to hide his face so Bryce wouldn't see the relief that flooded him at the perfect excuse to hide Steve's dagger. "I don't think the paintball gun will pass muster with the Faerie gate."

Bryce's brows drew together. "What about this? We take the paintball charges, but not the gun. I've already got a half dozen or so loaded with the anti-evil potion. We can carry those in our pockets—the skins are biodegradable, and if the spell works, they'll dissolve on contact with the ill-intentioned. Since you've already proved how deadly your aim can be with thrown projectiles . . ." Bryce wadded the towel up and tossed it across the room.

Mal caught it easily, grinning. "Too right, mate."

"Anything else you can tell me?" Bryce's voice held a hesitant note. Not *will you* but *can you*, acknowledging that there were some things Mal *couldn't* reveal. Yes, he was sharp, all right, his druid. *And thank the Goddess for that.*

"We'll be going to one of the spots in Faerie that's common ground for both Seelie and Unseelie. The Stone Circle."

Bryce's eyes lit up. "Like Stonehenge?"

"Quite a bit, only it's intact. All its menhirs are still upright, the capstones in place."

"Does it have an altar?"

Mal swallowed, remembering some of the things that had happened near or on that altar, like the murder of Alun's first love. "It does. If we're fortunate, though, it won't see any use."

"And if we're not fortunate?"

"We likely won't care anymore, will we?"

Bryce shook his head and walked toward the bathroom. "Damn. You take me to the best places."

Mal laughed and followed him. No matter what awaited them in the circle, whether he talked the Queen into whoring herself for the good of Faerie, whether he made it past dawn alive and whole—he'd at least had the chance to laugh again.

In the woods beyond the wetlands, with the low sunlight filtering through the trees, Bryce gaped at Mal, completely at a loss. "I'm supposed to what?"

"Find the gate."

"But I can't do that."

"You did before."

"Not on this side of the threshold. That was you." Besides, they'd followed the bauchan until it'd vanished, so at least they'd known where to start looking. Now, with the whole of the woods and wetlands spread out before them? "I don't know what to do." He felt panic rising in his chest, the same kind that used to hit him when he was unprepared for a critical exam or a crucial funding meeting.

Mal stepped up close behind him and wrapped his good arm around Bryce's waist, hand squeezing his hip. "No worries, mate. You've got this."

Bryce took a breath, and against all odds, the panic faded, as if Mal's hand on his hip had banished it. He might not know precisely *how*, but he had the confidence that he could do *something*. He took another deep breath and leaned into that certainty.

"When we were in Faerie before, it was like a game of hot-cold. I thought about what we needed and—" *There.* Warmth bathed the left side of his face, as if he were standing next to a crackling fire. "This way."

Mal patted his ass. "That's my boyo. Lead on, Macduff."

"I said that already."

"Guess it's my turn, isn't it? And at least you're a bloody Scot."

"If I'm all that bloody, maybe you should call me Macbeth."

Mal's expression turned serious, and he caught Bryce by one shoulder. "Don't even joke about that. No matter what happens tonight, you'll be safe. I may not have the influence I once had in Faerie, but I have that much."

"Hey." He kissed Mal lightly, just for comfort. "We'll both be okay. Unless . . . ." He peered into Mal's face in the fading light. "Is there something else? A greater danger?"

Mal shrugged, and his gaze slid away. *Still hiding things from me, damn it.* "Much the same. We won't be in the middle of the Unseelie throne room." He hitched his vest—which was a little too small—further onto his shoulders. "Although I'm not sure this isn't worse."

"Why? What's the significance of this place?"

"Well, it's a place of power, so everyone's a bit tetchy about it. As for me, I don't have the fondest of memories—last time I was there, I cut off Rodric Luchullain's hand and got myself cursed and exiled from Faerie."

"Mal—" *Tell me. Tell me what you're about to do so I can help you. So I can save you from yourself.*

But Mal simply shrugged again. "Never mind that. Let's get on with it, eh?"

Bryce squinted at Mal, who avoided his gaze. *Fine. I'll bide my time.* But he vowed to get Mal to confess. *Even if I have to order him to do it.*

He led the way between the fir boles and past a lichen-encrusted boulder with Mal sticking close to his heels, until they reached the spot where the stream that fed the wetlands burbled over a knee-high fall of rocks. On the opposite bank, two birch trees leaned toward each other, their branches entwined.

The warmth pulsed against his face. "That's it. Across the stream and between those trees."

Mal patted his pockets, where the paintball charges created lumps like oversized grapes. "Then let's go. Our timing is fecking perfect."

CHAPTER ❧ 24

When Mal followed Bryce through the birch tree arch, the power of the One Tree welled all around him, but faint, untouchable—as if he were encased in invisible armor. Apparently, even in Seelie-accessible lands, he was still cut off from his fae abilities. *Shite.*

Ah well. Maybe it was for the best—if he couldn't touch the One Tree, perhaps the One Tree couldn't detect him, and they wouldn't be overrun by a cadre of guards who'd slash first and ask questions after.

He could always hope.

Bryce's face held the same look of wonder that he'd worn the last time they'd crossed into Faerie. "I still can't believe it. It's a different world. The twilight—the sky is lavender, and not just at the horizon."

"Don't let anyone hear you say 'lavender,' boyo, or they'll know for sure you're gay."

"Is that a problem in Faerie? I mean, is homosexuality as great a potential stigma here as it is at home?"

"The Outer World is *your* home. My home is here." Or it used to be. Considering he felt as if he'd been excised from the realm as surely as if he'd been cut out of it with a dagger, he wasn't sure he had a home anymore.

"You know what I mean. Is sexual orientation and gender identity important?"

"It's important, but it's not an issue. In Faerie, gender is optional."

"Even for procreation?"

"Procreation is different here. Like I told you, we aren't born as humans are. There hasn't been a high fae spawned since the last war before Unification. I think the elder gods must have gotten fed up and decided to let attrition take care of us."

"But the elder gods—you said they'd vanished."

"Vanished from our ken. Doesn't mean they're not still out there. Best to live as if they're still watching, if you get my drift."

"Got it."

Mal glanced around, attempting to orient himself. He hadn't realized before how much the One Tree controlled Faerie and shaped his own sense of direction. "It's like the bloody cell tower is down and I can't access the map app."

Bryce stopped gawking long enough to give him a puzzled look. "What?"

"I have no fecking notion where we are."

"Seriously? Didn't you live here for a couple thousand years?"

"Yeah, but put it this way—how well would your compass work if suddenly the north pole decided to go on holiday?"

"Oh." Bryce grasped his right wrist, and warmth flared in his palm. "You're still an exile, even though you're physically here. Is that it?"

Mal blinked against the prickle in his eyes. Trust his tree hugger to get it. To get *him*. He tore his gaze away from Bryce's concerned face and—*there*. The shape of that rock. He'd only ever seen it from the other side, but it was distinctive enough—like a brownie's profile, all hooked nose and potbelly.

"I've got it now. We're at the base of the tor where the Stone Circle lies."

Bryce turned and started down the obvious path, but Mal grabbed his arm. "Not that way. That leads into Seelie lands. I can't go there. If we're not to bring a kennel full of the *Cwn Annwn* down on our arses, we need to keep to neutral ground. That way."

Bryce nodded and followed Mal down the other path—the one full of brambles and stones the size of a troll's head. Of course this couldn't be an easy trek, now could it?

"What are the—the coon anoon? You mentioned them once before."

"Bloody great hell hounds. Ever heard of the Wild Hunt? Herne the Horned Huntsman?"

"Those are real? Gran used to tell me stories about Herne, but she didn't call his dogs that."

"She was a Scot, mate. Probably couldn't pronounce it." Thorns caught in the fabric of his borrowed pants, and Mal wished mightily for his leathers. "Your damn tactical trousers are for shite in brambles."

"Let me go first. I've got the pruners."

Right. Trust a druid. Always prepared.

When they emerged from the thicket, the path to the top of the tor loomed above them—long and rocky and steep. Bloody marvelous. *It'll be a treat to climb that one-handed.*

Bryce stood shoulder to shoulder with Mal, tucking the pruners back into one of his many pockets. "I take it that's the way up."

"You'd take it right." Mal looked at the sky. The lavender Bryce had so admired was deepening to violet. "Best get on with it. Our time's running short."

He started up the hillside, but didn't get ten feet before a rock turned under his foot. "Shite!"

Before he could fall, Bryce caught him under the elbow. "Easy. Take your time. You lead, since you know where you're going, but I'm right behind. I won't let you fall."

"Thanks, mate."

Mal had never fallen before; he'd always been sure-footed and quick. Had that been part of his connection to the One Tree? Goddess, this bloody quest had to succeed. He couldn't go through the rest of his life as a broken man. Bryce deserved more.

Bryce. If he survived this night, whether his curse was lifted or not, he'd bound himself to Bryce. If Cassie could be believed, that was a permanent condition, and one of which Bryce was unaware. If he survived, he'd have to come clean with Bryce.

Death might be the easier road.

They made it to the top of the tor, chests heaving from the climb. Bryce gaped, stumbling forward onto the plateau.

"Holy freaking shit. I mean, you told me it was intact, but I never imagined it would be so . . . so . . ."

"So bloody pretentious?"

"So impressive." He placed one hand on his chest as if he were trying to hold something inside. "I mean, there have been places I've seen that affected me. Places I could tell held their own intrinsic power. But this . . ." He paced forward as if he couldn't help himself.

"It's calling to your blood, mate." Mal pointed to the altar stone at the spot he knew to be true north. "Your ancestors probably sacrificed the odd goat or villager on a stone just like that one yonder."

"Very funny."

"Not joking." Mal set off toward the circle, tempted to run to beat the steady darkening of the sky. "Some places in Faerie are anchored to similar places in the Outer World."

"Like the gates. Or the wetlands."

"Right. This might be anchored at Stonehenge, or at another site in Brittany or Cornwall or Wales." He shrugged. "Or all of them, for that matter."

"How can that be?"

Mal grinned. "Magic." And because he wasn't sure he'd have another chance once they stepped inside the Circle and he set this whole bloody disaster in motion, he grabbed Bryce around the waist, turning him into an embrace that pressed them together from chest to groin. "But no more magic than this." He kissed his man, his druid, his partner, with the passion and desperation that had pooled in his chest all day.

Because if things went straight to the hells, it might very well be the last time.

Bryce, although he grunted in surprise, didn't hold back, lacing his fingers in Mal's hair with the masterful control that Mal had come to crave like he craved air.

They disengaged, both of them breathing hard as if they'd scaled that bloody hill for a second time.

Bryce smiled at him, swiping his thumbs along Mal's cheekbones. "What was that for?"

"Luck," Mal said, stepping away and turning toward the dolmen. "Because we'll bloody well need all we can get."

When Mal strode into the Circle, Bryce stumbled to follow. He still couldn't quite wrap his head around the fact that he was in an actual intact Stonehenge analog. Its proportions disturbed him on some deep level. He'd never realized how ingrained certain conventions were to the human eye and brain.

He'd seen the pyramids, and they were damned impressive. So was the Sphinx. The Parthenon. But although those were incredible feats of engineering, they were constructed of materials that were proportional to the humans who'd built them.

But these massive stones, raw and rough and primitive, were not sized for the convenience of any man. He could almost believe Mal's tales of the elder gods, because it would take someone of titanic size, power, and, yes, ego, to construct something like this.

He caught up with Mal, who'd stopped directly in front of the altar and reached into the pocket of his tactical pants. Bryce frowned. Nothing was threatening them. Why would Mal need one of the altered paintballs here? Bryce's stomach clenched at the notion of paint splattering these ancient stones—*sacrilege*.

He reached out, ready to block Mal's throw, but the object he drew out of his pocket wasn't a paintball.

It was a dagger—a dagger that pulsed with the beat of its own malevolent heart.

Bryce nearly gagged. "What the hell is that?"

"It's what we're here for." Mal peered at the sky, which had darkened to deep purple above them, only a narrow band of lavender on the horizon.

"That's not—" He swallowed against nausea. "I don't think that thing should be here. It's got its own . . . I don't know . . . agenda."

Mal snorted. "Who doesn't?" And he dropped to one knee and plunged the dagger into the ground at the foot of the altar stone.

A force slammed into Bryce and knocked him flat on his back. Momentarily breathless, he lay gasping like one of the poor dying fish in the slough, blinking up at the purple sky.

Mal's face appeared above him, his brows drawn together in concern. But by the way his gaze kept shifting from Bryce to different points around the circumference of the circle, the concern might not be for Bryce personally.

"You all right, then?" Mal put his hand on Bryce's chest, but Bryce knocked it away and sat up.

"What have you done?"

"What I had to do."

"Really? Somehow I doubt it's benign. Certainly not on me."

"It's nothing."

"Nothing? It knocked me on my freaking ass. And do you see that?" He pointed to the altar, which had taken on a sullen glow, chips of reflective stone sparking red on its surface.

"See what? The altar? It's bloody huge, but it's always on its back like that. Not as if I knocked it over."

"No. It's like someone's trained a failing spotlight on it."

"Sure you didn't hit your head, mate? Because it looks like it always does to me." Mal reached out and felt the back of Bryce's head, but Bryce jerked away and stood up, weaving a little, still a bit breathless.

"My head is fine, but this—whatever you did—it's not good. And you know it's not good. I can see it."

Mal lowered his chin and pushed himself up with his left hand. "Don't know what you're on about," he mumbled.

"Yes, you do. You knew it was wrong and that I'd want no part of it. I *trusted* you to do the right thing."

Mal flinched. "How in all the bloody hells can you know what's right or wrong for Faerie? For me? You'd never heard of either of us before last week."

"True, but I can tell you feel guilty about it. You practically reek of remorse."

"Now what do you suppose might cause that, eh? Can *you* think of anything that's happened in the last few days that I might regret?"

Bryce ignored the sneer in Mal's voice, because it was clear from the way his gaze darted away, from the flicker of despair across his face, that Mal was in full denial mode again. "This is the real reason we're here. The one you couldn't tell me about. For God's sake, Mal, if it hurt you so freaking much to even *try* to talk about it, how could you think it would be a good thing? You know better than that. You *are* better than that."

Mal wrapped his right arm across his body, tucking his paralyzed hand under his left elbow. "You're a fine one to talk. You'll do anything for your precious wetlands, so you know everyone has his price. Well, this is about my price, my—my life. *Mine.*"

"You said . . . you *implied* that this was *our* life. Our true desires."

"And you—you, who's supposed to be so fecking smart. You swallowed it like a spoonful of cream." Mal bared his teeth in a travesty of his smile. "Or should I say a spoonful of come?"

Bryce recoiled as if Mal had knifed him in the gut, the pain so real that when he pressed his hand against his belly, he expected it to come away wet with blood. "But . . . you wanted me to . . . What about taking your responsibilities? Making choices for you?"

"Seems like everybody does that, whether I ask for it or not. Why shouldn't you get in on the party? First it was Cassie and her bloody magical chains. Then it was—" He turned his back, but it didn't mask the way shame fairly vibrated under his skin.

"What? The sex? Is this what it's about? You had a choice the last time. Maybe not before—" He still felt sick to think he'd coerced Mal into those first two times. "But the last one? *You* seduced *me.*"

"Didn't fight against it, though, did you?"

"But . . . but you said it was right for us. If we both wanted it so much—"

"We wanted it because it's in our fecking nature. And if it's in our nature, none of us have any bloody choice."

"I don't buy any of that predestination crap. Once you have all the data, you can make an informed decision. It's when you don't know the alternatives that you screw things up."

"I thought ignorance was no excuse."

"I never said that."

"Mal." The voice booming across the circle wasn't one that Bryce recognized, but it caused Mal to whirl, his eyes wide in his pale face.

"Alun?" Mal closed his eyes and took a huge breath as if a weight had lifted off his shoulders. "Thank the Goddess, you're all right."

Although Bryce had never met Mal's brother in the flesh, the implacable man standing under the capstone opposite the altar didn't look at all like he'd expected. For one thing, he didn't look at all like someone who was happy to see his brother.

Alun unsheathed the sword strapped to his back. "Maldwyn Cynwrig, in the name of the Queen, I arrest you for high treason against the Seelie Court of Faerie."

CHAPTER 25

"You're joking, right?" Mal stared at Alun, waiting for him to give over, but his face might as well have been carved from the same stone as the altar. *Right. This is Alun. He doesn't do jokes.*

"Come with me now. If you cooperate, perhaps the Queen will show you mercy."

"Mercy? She's never shown mercy to anyone in her life." Mal waved his right hand—no longer quite as crabbed, but not fully functional either.

"You violated the consort law, one of the lynchpins of Faerie. The judgment was none of her doing."

"Bullshite. She's the one who added that lovely little twist, that I can't be whole until Rodric Luchullain is too. I think I'd rather cut my hand off and be done with it than give him the satisfaction."

Alun took a step forward, but he didn't relax—or lower his sword. "Did you stop to think that maybe that was all she could give you? I've consulted with Cassie and her circle. According to them, without the Queen's intervention, you would have died here that night."

"So instead I'll die here tonight? Is that what this is about?"

"If you have anything to say in your own defense, say it now." Alun's mouth trembled in the moonlight for just an instant. "Please, Mal. Give me a reason not to think you guilty. A reason not to imprison my brother for something of which I'd have sworn him incapable."

Bryce stepped forward, shoulder to shoulder with Mal. "Wait just a damn minute. Don't you think he deserves to hear the charges first?"

Alun scowled, but his gaze never wavered, as if he were afraid Mal would make a break for it. *Not bloody likely.* As long as Bryce was standing like a stubborn boulder, he couldn't go more than a dozen feet away.

Did Alun know that charming little detail? For that matter, what would happen if Mal got hauled off to the underworld, or chained to a rock like that poor bastard Prometheus? Would Bryce be dragged along, forced to endure the same punishment? Surely Cassie's shackles could be severed then. But who knew? With druids, there was always a catch—maybe even for one of their own kind.

"Who are you?" Alun growled. "You're not fae. You shouldn't be here."

Bryce glanced at Mal, and Mal could tell he was still pissed as all the hells. "I'm beginning to think none of us should be. But since we are, give us the reason for the arrest."

"For conspiring with the Unseelie Court to overthrow the Seelie Queen."

"What? That's a load of shite, brother, and you know it. I would never—"

"Mal." Bryce's voice was low, but the damn Stone Circle had better acoustics than a Greek amphitheater. No doubt Alun could hear every word. "Be careful. Don't compound the charges by lying."

"I'm not. I—" The familiar constriction of his throat stopped his voice and his breath. Bryce grabbed for his own throat as well, his eyes widening, mouth open as if to try to pull in air where there was none. The pair of them looked like dying fish.

Gwydion's bollocks, the geas still gagged him. He wasn't conspiring against the Queen, was he? He was only here to try to persuade, not to overthrow, not to kill, not to usurp. But Bryce was right about one thing: Mal should never have invoked the dagger spell without knowing for sure what it would do. *Because I still have no bloody notion about Steve's end game.*

But if he couldn't talk about it, maybe he could talk around it. That's why Steve had chosen him, wasn't it? Because of his legendary powers of persuading anyone into his bed. He cut a glance at Bryce. Somehow, he doubted he'd be able to work that magic anymore. It had apparently deserted him along with the use of his hand and his connection to the One Tree.

"Out with it, then. Details. Tell me what you think I've done."

"We have evidence that you've consorted with Unseelie minions."

"'Consort'? What's that supposed to mean? I'd never kneel for Unseelie scum."

"That's right. He only kneels for me."

Ah—he's done it, my bloke—the power voice. It echoed across the hilltop, shivering up Mal's spine and causing a below-the-belt reaction totally inappropriate to the setting.

Alun's eyes narrowed. "Druid. I knew you didn't belong, but not how out of place you truly are. No druid has set foot in this circle since—"

"Never."

At the sound of that rumbling voice, Mal whirled. Steve was standing at the foot of the altar, his cloak billowing in his personal localized wind. He crouched unhurriedly, retrieved the dagger, and wrapped it in a blindingly white cloth that he tucked away under the cloak. "No druid has ever stood inside this circle. The ones in the Outer World, yes. But not here. It is a first."

Alun tensed, shifting his stance to divide his attention between Mal and Steve. "Who in Arawn's hells are you?"

"Clearly someone *not* in Arawn's hells." Steve's rumble echoed weirdly in the circle, pinging off the stones in the same way that Bryce's power voice had done.

Alun strode forward, his sword raised as if he were ready to strike first and question later, like any meatheaded guard.

"Alun." Mal moved into his path, trusting Alun not to take his head for interfering. "Stop. I know why he's here."

Alun's headlong rush across the circle slowed to a halt. "You know him?"

"Yeah. I do."

"You brought him here?"

"I think he brought himself." Mal eyed Steve, wishing for a bit of help, but Steve had apparently decided to impersonate one of the standing stones, the arsewipe. "Although I probably opened the door, which would have been bloody nice to know about beforehand."

Steve inclined his head, but didn't speak.

"And you claim not to kneel for Unseelie scum." Gareth stepped out from behind the stone where Alun had appeared.

Mal whirled on Steve, wishing for nothing more than to crush that gargantuan windpipe with his one remaining hand. "You bloody bastard! I did what you asked. You didn't need to bring him. You promised you wouldn't."

"He didn't," Alun said, still standing on the balls of his feet as if he were about to launch himself into battle. "I did."

"Why?"

"If you had been wrongly accused, who better to defend you than a bard?"

"I hear a 'but' in that sentence," Mal growled.

"But if the allegations are true, if you're guilty, this is the last chance he'll have to see you alive." Alun's voice wobbled for a moment. "Would you rob him of that?"

Mal clenched his fist, his belly roiling. After everything he'd done to try to keep Gareth out of this mess, why did Alun have to stomp in and ruin it? "I'd have spared him the pain—as you should have done. He's had enough of that."

"Both of you stop talking about me as if I'm not here." Gareth's velvet voice was broken by fury. "As if I'm not capable of making my own choices or fighting my own battles." He glared at Bryce. "Or seeing what all of you are too blind to see."

Gareth. When Bryce had pleaded with Mal to give him something, some token of trust, the story he'd related hadn't been as random as Bryce had thought. *"Nothing I could ever do for him would make up for that."* While Mal might have other reasons for his actions, clearly he was still trying to protect his brother, to atone for that long-ago betrayal.

Although from Gareth's attitude, Bryce wasn't sure he deserved Mal's devotion—and certainly not his guilt.

"Gareth?" Alun didn't take his gaze off Steve and Mal. "Explain, if you please."

"First, can't you see that our brother is bound to this druid?"

"Cassie's the one who put the tether on us," Bryce said. "She did it for my benefit, because I needed a tutor."

"I'm not talking about that bond. I'm talking about the one you forced on him when you fucked him."

The blood drained from Bryce's face. "That was— I didn't know it was a . . . a biological imperative. Once I found out, though, I wouldn't have. Only if he wanted it. Only if wanted *me*."

Gareth's eyes blazed with anger. Bryce had never realized that could literally occur, but then he'd never believed that he could be Tasered by an arrogant asshole with a silver hand, either. "You think he had a choice? Once the witch shackled you together, how was he to resist? She probably did it on purpose. In fact, you probably plotted together."

Bryce tore his gaze away from Gareth, whose long curly hair fairly writhed in the wind. What the hell was it about wind in Faerie? It didn't obey any natural laws.

Right. Because Faerie wasn't natural. It was a construct, a supernatural biodome, like an experiment the elder gods had spun up and then abandoned.

Mal's arms hung loose from slumped shoulders, head bowed, as if he were willing to take whatever abuse his brothers chose to fling at him.

Well, fuck that.

Bryce closed the distance between them and grasped Mal's left biceps. Christ, he was vibrating with distress, and Bryce's temper rose in direct proportion. "You two need to back the fuck off." He was astonished when his voice rang like a gong in the circle, creating its own unnatural wind that forced both Alun and Gareth to back up a step, blinking as if they didn't know why they'd moved.

Mal turned to him, face strained, eyes haunted. "It's all right, Bryce."

"No, it's not. I don't care if these bastards are you brothers—"

Mal's smile was wry. "That'd make us all bastards, yeah?"

"No." Bryce's fingers tightened on Mal's arm, and Mal let out a shaky breath. "They need to slow down. Listen to what you have to say." He glared across the grass at Mal's brothers. "With an open fucking mind, damn it."

"Resorting to strong language now?" Mal's joke sounded feeble. "I like it. It's hot."

"You're the one who told me fae are resistant to change. Maybe this is why. They never bother to fucking listen."

"Yeah, well, thing is . . ." Mal swallowed and pulled away. "This time, they're right."

"What? You mean—" His mouth dried, and he reached for Mal but let his hand drop, because if it was true, if he'd forced Mal *again* . . . God, he really was a monster, wasn't he?

"I mean we're bonded by more than Cassie's wee tether. The third time we . . . when we made love. That was the clincher. Before then, it was just potential. But now . . ." He grinned, a death's-head grimace. "Congratulations, mate. You've got yourself a fae familiar."

Bryce stared, open-mouthed. "I—"

"So tell me, Mal," Gareth said, sarcasm dripping from his tone, "who needs to back off now? Sure, he's a druid, not human, but if you hid the truth about sealing the bond, if you knew the consequences and carried on regardless? You've forced an unwanted partnership on him, like any other renegade fae."

"Mal?" Even to himself, Bryce sounded pathetic.

"Stow it." Gareth strode forward to stand at Alun's shoulder. "You can save the hand-wringing for later. There's a more serious accusation on the table." He pointed at Mal. "Did you conspire with the Unseelie scum?"

Bryce could feel Mal trembling next to him, the constriction in his own throat, the stop of his own breath mirrored in Mal's panic-stricken face. *I feel what he feels.* But was this nothing but a spell? The synchronization of their breaths, their pulses when they'd made love; the way he'd imagined he was attuned to Mal's feelings; the connection he'd believed they'd established—

Bryce nearly doubled over with revulsion. They had a connection, all right, but it wasn't real. Or, at least, not the kind of "real" he craved—forged of love, not magic; choice, not coercion.

But one thing he'd learned from that damned grimoire: any spell could be broken with the right tools, in the right time, and with the right will.

Bryce's will had never felt so strong. He intended to break this infernal bond and free Mal. Free himself. He ignored the inner voice hinting that he didn't want to be free, that this was what he'd always wanted, what he'd been missing all his life.

Because just like Mal, his inner voice fucking lied.

"You can't say, can you, Mal?" Gareth taunted. "Oh yes. I can tell a *tynged* when I see one too."

The constriction in Bryce's throat eased, and he and Mal sucked in identical breaths. Mal coughed, rubbing his throat. "Shite. You can see that? I never knew—"

"I'm a bard and we're in the Stone Circle. Of course I can." He glared at Mal. "But I never thought I'd see my brother stoop to consorting with the Unseelie."

"Gareth—"

"I'm done here. You made your bed, brother. One that holds a druid. May you have all the joy in it that you deserve."

He turned and strode for the edge of the circle.

"Gareth! No. Wait!" Mal took off toward his brother at a run, but after ten feet, the tether binding them tore at Bryce's belly, pulling him forward and onto his knees. Judging by the way Mal stumbled, his arms wrapped across his stomach, he felt the same.

Or else his bastard of a brother had just cut out his heart.

CHAPTER ✤ 26

M al huddled on the ground, arms around his knees. He barely registered the soft tread of Alun's boots until his brother was next to him.

"Get up, Mal. Time to go." Alun held out his hand as if Mal were unable to stand on his own. Maybe he wasn't.

How could he have been so bloody stupid? Of course it was obvious now. Only someone with a deep connection to the One Tree and the power of a highborn could have done what Steve had. Only someone with a higher rank than Mal could bind him with a geas. But he'd never stopped to think, had he? He'd been so concerned with the *what*—the chance to regain the use of his hand, to lift his curse, to return home—that he'd completely ignored the *how*.

Not to mention the *why*.

Mal stood without the benefit of Alun's assistance. Once in his brother's custody, he had no illusions he'd be able to escape. Alun was too good at his job and too devoted to duty and honor. He faced "Steve" and posed the questions he should have asked to begin with.

"Why? Why are you doing this?"

"You know why. To lift my curse."

Bryce stepped forward. "Are you the cause of the blight? The one we saw in Unseelie lands? The one in the slough behind my house?" Bryce held one of the charmed paintballs in his hand. A fat lot of good that would do here, against someone with Steve's obvious power.

"I am not."

"How do I know you're telling the truth? It's easy to lie."

"Perhaps. But it is easy for you to see the truth, if you but look."

Despite a situation that was growing more desperate by the moment, despite one brother who loathed him and another who was about to throw his arse in prison to rot or execute him on command, Mal was tempted to roll his eyes. Trust Steve never to give a straight answer.

But, then, Mal had never given Bryce a straight answer himself, had he?

Bryce didn't look perturbed by the statement, nor irritated like Mal, nor poised to attack like Alun. His eyes widened, and his right hand crept to the same spot on his belly where Mal always felt the pull of the tether. "You mean, all along, the only thing I had to do was *try* and I could have detected . . . That I didn't need to even ask . . ." He swallowed, his Adam's apple sliding beneath his two-day stubble, then squared his shoulders and squinted at Steve, the light of the rising moon glinting off his glasses. "No. You're not lying. Exactly. The blight—it affects you too, doesn't it?"

Steve inclined his head but didn't say anything.

"Then why the subterfuge? You should have known we'd help. Why all the drama?"

"An excellent question." The coiled power and buried anger in the Queen's voice lifted the hair on Mal's neck. He and Alun dropped to one knee at once as the she glided across the grass toward their pathetic little band. "One of many we would be pleased to have answers for."

Bryce gawked at the Queen, mouth agape. In a way, Mal could understand the effect she must have the first time someone saw her. She was beautiful—that went without saying since all Seelie fae were beautiful. But with her long red hair, eyes the green of new leaves, and skin that glowed like moonlight, she'd give anybody reason for a second look. Not to mention she was over six feet tall and wore her power like a visible cloak. No one could ever mistake her for anything but a queen, just as no one could ever mistake her for human.

He managed to catch Bryce's eye and jerk his chin down. Bryce got the message and dropped to his knees. Mal frowned. *That's wrong. He shouldn't be on his knees, not for anyone.*

Steve didn't kneel, but he bowed his head, his hands clasped in front of him.

She stopped two paces in front of Alun. "What is the meaning of this gathering?"

"You," Bryce whispered, still goggling at the Queen.

She shifted her gaze to Bryce. Shite. You never spoke in the Queen's presence unless invited to do so. Mal tensed, ready to launch himself between them. Bryce might have survived Rodric's attack—barely—but if the Queen decided to blast him for impertinence, neither one of them stood a chance.

Bryce couldn't tear his gaze away from the woman—no, she wasn't a woman. Female, yes, as the earth was female, or the moon, although the idea of assigning that kind of label to her was almost laughable. Mal was nearly right. Gender in Faerie was not so much optional as inconsequential—a convenience for a language that didn't have a word for what she was.

But the way she held herself—her spine as straight as a birch sapling, her hair the color of maple leaves in October, her eyes the green of the first unfurling shoots of spring. His druid sight showed him the way she connected to the ground. *No, that's not quite right.* The ground reached up *to* her, as if to beg for her touch, for her footfall. And with each step she set down a new root, renewing their bond.

"You're the woman on the tapestry. The one in the Unseelie throne room."

"We have given you no leave to speak, druid, nor any right to be in our lands."

Maybe he should worry about the warning in her tone, but he needed to know. This was important. This was *vital.* "That's not the royal we, is it? You really are more than one person. You're the One Tree. You're Faerie."

"What?" Mal burst out.

Seriously? Hadn't he known? Couldn't he tell by looking that she was part of the center, the fulcrum, the heart around which Faerie turned?

"You see too much for your own good, druid. Do you think such knowledge can be permitted to spread like a canker on a fruit?"

"Don't threaten him," Mal said. "He didn't have a choice. He had to come because of—"

Mal stopped speaking as if she'd cut off his words with an ax. "You think that an excuse, Lord Maldwyn? Or even a reason? You should not be here yourself." Her gaze flicked between him and Bryce, as if following an unseen line in the air. Hell, maybe she could see Cassie's invisible chain too. It wouldn't surprise him. She looked as if she could see anything, through anything and anyone.

Mal had called her merciless, but Bryce saw it differently. Could you ascribe intent, good or bad, to the turn of the seasons? Winter was as necessary for growth as spring. She wasn't merciless—she was inevitable.

"This is neutral territory." The cloaked figure's voice, like the rumble of distant thunder, held no heat or accusation. *I really need to get a name for that guy.*

The Queen allowed her attention to drift to him. "Just so. Yet you corrupted one of our subjects to gain entry. You have no place here either."

She raised one moon-white hand, and Bryce felt the gathering of energy, of potential, like electricity on his skin.

"Wait!" Mal stumbled to his feet and dropped to his knees again between her and Bryce. "Hear him out. You can do this much for me after my years as your hunting dog."

"You are not entitled to special consideration for doing no more than your duty."

"What can it hurt? If you don't like what he has to say, you can blast me to all the hells afterward. But—" He glanced at Bryce, and despite the anger Bryce still felt over Mal's lies, the despair in his eyes cut all the way to Bryce's heart. "One way or another, let Bryce go. Please."

"Do you forget, Majesty?" the cloaked guy asked. "Once inside the circle, however we came here, we have the right to stay."

She regarded him, unmoving. "Few know of that law."

"Does that give you the right to gainsay it?"

She lowered her hand and tucked it into the sleeve of her gown. "Only the bold, foolhardy, or desperate would dare accuse us of an unlawful act."

"Just so."

She inclined her head. "Continue."

Bryce glanced from Mal to Cloaked Guy. Which of them was supposed to continue? Mal looked totally wrecked, his brother looming over him like the Grim Reaper. Bryce tried to catch his eye, to will him to take heart, but it was as if he'd given up.

Fine. He'd lectured to auditoriums full of sullen, sleep-deprived students at 8 a.m. classes. He could do this, at least until Mal recovered enough, or Cloaked Guy worked up the balls to tell them why they were all here.

"Your—Your Majesty, I can see that you're like the avatar of this place. It needs you to keep it going. But the reverse is also true: you need Faerie to keep yourself going. It's a closed ecosystem and you're the engine. Am I right?"

"In a way, although we wouldn't put it so bluntly, or with such a lack of poetry."

"But something's wrong. When you walked across the circle, the grass nearly cried for your touch, but it wasn't enough. Look." He pointed to where her footsteps still showed. Even in the Outer World, healthy grass should have sprung up by now. "The blight, it's not just localized, is it? The heart of Faerie, the One Tree is infected. It's dying." The bleak look in her eyes told him he'd gotten it right. "*You're* dying."

"No." Alun's voice was broken, and he dropped his sword at his feet. "It can't be true. The druid lies."

"Peace, Lord Cynwrig." The Queen raised her chin, and in the light of the moon—full and huge and way too close—Bryce could see what the softer light of the stones had hidden before: the web of lines at the corners of her eyes. "We do not punish those who tell the truth, no matter how inconvenient it might be."

"Lord Maldwyn," Cloaked Guy rumbled, "please offer Her Majesty the token I trusted you with."

"The what? Oh. Right." Mal fumbled in his pocket and drew out a tiny wooden box. He held it up on the palm of his hand so the Queen could take it or refuse it if she wanted. "I—I can't open it. Not with one hand."

Bryce stood and walked slowly to Mal's side, keeping an eye on Alun in case he decided to retrieve his big-ass sword. "Allow me."

When no one objected—not the Queen nor Cloaked Guy, nor Alun and his sword—Bryce placed one hand on Mal's shoulder and took the box from his hand. He squeezed Mal's shoulder once, then released it to open the tiny box.

Inside, a single fragile blossom glowed upon a cushion of moss. Its ivory petals were the color of the Queen's skin, but their outer edges held a rusty stain, as if they had been dipped in blood.

The Queen inhaled on a gasp, and somehow that sound was as shocking as if the moon itself had screamed. "It's begun."

"It has," Cloaked Guy said.

The Queen stared down at Mal, her eyes cold and hard. "We hold you to blame for this, Lord Maldwyn. If you had not deprived us of our Consort—"

"Blame not the messenger, my lady." Cloaked Guy's tone was sharp. "The blight began far earlier than that night, and indeed, your former Consort was part of it. Lord Maldwyn did you a favor, will you but acknowledge it."

She looked as if she were about to wring her hands, like a heroine in a melodrama. "I suspected. But the traditions, the laws. I could not be without a Consort or—"

"Or this would happen." Cloaked Guy finally moved, gesturing to the blood-edged flower with one leather-gauntleted hand. "Our world out of balance. The end of Faerie."

"Yes."

"Yet to be with a Consort who was not your equal, who craved your power for his own—the balance had tipped long before Lord Maldwyn separated the traitor's hand from his arm and freed you from his evil influence."

"What do you know of such things?" Her chin was up again, and if ever Bryce needed an illustration of the word *haughty*, she was the epitome of it. "You speak as if you have experience of such evil."

"I do. If you permit?" He raised his hands, hesitantly, almost apologetically.

Bryce held his breath. He was about to see what had cast that monstrous shadow, and he was torn between his avid scholar's curiosity and his primitive flight reflex. But as long as Mal was hunkered in front of the Queen, he couldn't stray more than a dozen feet away; his curiosity won by default.

Cloaked Guy lowered his hood. Bryce sucked in a breath. As much as he was expecting something on the upper scale of horrifying, he was unprepared for the reality of a giant blue-skinned cross between Medusa and a Tellarite from *Star Trek: TOS*.

Alun snatched up his sword and moved between the guy and the Queen. Mal clenched his eyes shut and bowed his head.

And the Queen—she merely looked at him, calmly, as if she saw such horrors every day, or the years had worn away her ability to be shocked by them.

"Neither you nor the Unseelie King, were he inclined to do anything other than grasp for more power, can halt the decay alone. It requires sacrifices on both sides, sacrifices the King is not prepared to make. He seeks always for an easy path, or one that others will clear for him. But his actions, his ill-advised alliances, tip the scales ever further, allowing the poison to leach into the Outer World. I've done what I could to thwart him, but thus far have been unsuccessful. Indeed, I was exiled for my pains."

"Yet you have come here as if you have a solution."

"Not a solution. But perhaps an opportunity."

CHAPTER ❈ 27

Steve stared at Mal, his eyes aflame in his blue-skinned face, the serpents that passed for his hair writhing and hissing in apparent agitation. *What . . .?* Oh. Right, then. Mal had to be the one to do the persuading. Perhaps Steve's own geas made it impossible for him to ask for what he needed. One thing Mal had learned in his days trolling the Outer World clubs: if you can't ask for what you want, chances are you'll never get it.

He glanced at Bryce, who scowled at Steve and pushed his glasses up his nose with one knuckle. *He gave me what I wanted when I didn't even know I had a question.*

Mal cleared his throat, and everyone's attention snapped to him. "Your Majesty, I would never have come here tonight except we . . ." Mal waited for the familiar crush of his windpipe whenever he tried to speak of the bargain, but it didn't come. "That is, Steve—"

"'Steve'? Seriously?" Bryce muttered. "If you believed *that*—"

Mal glared at him. *You're not making this easier, mate.* "Steve craves a . . . a boon." *Shite, that's one fragging huge understatement.* "An indulgence from you."

"Indeed?" Her chilly Majesty wasn't giving him much to work with either.

"He requests . . ." *Goddess grant me strength*, "a night. In your bed."

If Steve uncloaking got everyone's attention, that little bomb blew the top off the hill. Alun growled, his attention split between Mal and Steve as if he didn't know whom to behead first. Bryce's mouth fell open, and the look on his face was something Mal would have paid anything never to see: disappointment, hurt, betrayal.

The Queen looked as remote as the moon. No change there.

"Can you give us a single reason why we would countenance such a request, Lord Maldwyn?" Her voice could have carved diamonds. "A single reason why we shouldn't punish you for daring to suggest it?"

"Ah. Well. If you— I mean . . ." How in all the bloody hells was he supposed to persuade her to do something he didn't understand himself? *Steve could have prepared me a little better for this.* He sighed. "Not a bloody one."

"You hold the reason in your hand, my lady." Steve's voice, in comparison to the Queen's, was as near to gentle as he'd ever gotten.

She looked down at the sad little flower, already wilting in the night air. "A return to balance."

"Wait a minute." Bryce strode forward until he was in direct line of sight between the Queen and Steve, and within reach of Alun's sword. "You can't do this." He rounded on Mal. "Coercive sex is no better than rape. How can she refuse? If she wants to save her world, all her subjects, she has no choice but to agree."

"There is always a choice," Steve rumbled, "and every choice has its own consequences. Choosing the good of others above our own comfort and desires is the nature of sacrifice."

"How do we know it'll even work? Maybe this is all part of the Unseelie King's plot. You said he wanted power. What better way to get it than to steal it from her?"

"How do you imagine I could do that?"

"How the hell should I know? You've clearly got the power to teleport yourself up here when you're supposedly banished. Plus, you're packing a dagger—we saw you tuck it away just now."

"If that is your only objection . . ." He removed his leather gauntlets, revealing scaled skin and talons like an eagle's, and drew the dagger from under his cloak. He offered it to her on his plate-sized palm. "It must be near if I'm to remain undetected, but you're welcome to keep it close, my lady."

"Forget that. You're like twice her size. You could overpower her—"

"You underestimate her abilities, druid. She is the Seelie Queen. The heart of Faerie, as you have so astutely observed. But the One Tree cannot stand if its roots wither and rot."

"But—"

"We grant you your boon."

"What?" Bryce and Alun shouted in unison.

She looked down at Mal. "We all make the choices we must, do we not? Our reasons may not be evident to others, perhaps least so to ourselves, but they are valid nonetheless." She inclined her head again, but it had nothing to do with surrender or supplication. "You may keep your dagger, my lord. It matters not to us."

"Your Majesty," Alun stepped forward. "You can't mean to go through with this. We have no notion what his motives might be."

"His motives are likely the same as ours for agreeing. The role granted us by the elder gods is not one we take lightly. Your honor and duty demand that you serve your realm to the best of your ability. How can we offer any less?"

Alun bowed. "As you wish. But I cannot let you go unaccompanied."

"Your authority does not extend into our bower." When Alun would have protested, she held up one white hand. "You may guard the door, if you wish. But you may not interfere, no matter what you hear." She raised her chin, tilted her head, her hair sweeping across shoulders bared by the neckline of her gown. "Shall we retire?"

Steve took three measured strides toward her, ignoring Alun's sword, and dropped to one knee at her feet. "You do me great honor."

"It is not you we honor, sirrah, but Faerie."

He pressed one scaled fist against his chest in salute, bowing his head. Thank the elder gods the snakes had gone quiescent. "As you say." He stood, graceful despite his monstrous form, and offered her his arm.

Bryce turned to Mal, unable to watch the Queen pace across the circle, her hand on the monster's forearm, Alun dogging their heels. "Stop them."

"What do you imagine I can do?" Mal rose heavily to his feet. "She owned me when I thought she was only the Queen, but now you tell me she's bleeding Faerie itself."

"Relative power is immaterial, don't you get it?" He grabbed Mal's shoulders, barely resisting the urge to shake. "It's still wrong to deprive someone of choice."

Mal jerked out of Bryce's hold. "You ought to know about that, eh? Seeing how much practice you've had with choice deprivation lately."

A scalding geyser of anger shot from Bryce's chest to the roots his hair—but not at Mal. No, he knew exactly who to blame. "This is all Gareth doing, isn't it? No matter what you feel like you owe him, you don't have to listen to everything he says."

"That's what you think. He's always been smarter than me, plus he's a bard. They . . . they know things. If he thinks the druid bond is shameful, then—"

"Stop it. He can't know what's right for us. Only *we* can know that. Besides, when we drank the management tea, we bypassed the compulsion."

Mal's face twisted in a sneer. "If it was so fecking *bypassed*, then why did I still want you?"

Bryce's breath stalled. "But . . . why? Why go through with it? If you thought what you felt wasn't real, then . . ." *Why invite me in?*

"Why not?" Mal stared down at his hands, flexing one while the other stayed still, fingers half curled into his palm. "Why the bloody hells not?"

So I was nothing more than a distraction. He doesn't want me. He never did. Not really. How could he? He was *Lord* Maldwyn, for God's sake. Practically immortal and more beautiful than the day. How could he ever want an awkward science nerd with one foot in the swamp and the other squarely in his mouth?

The lump in Bryce's throat threatened to choke him. "Very well. After tonight, I'll tell Cassie my supernatural indoctrination is complete. Get her to release us." Why did that feel as if he were cutting his own heart out with his fucking pruners? Would Mal still live in Hillsboro now, in their laughably modest houses that Bryce had once been so proud of because they had a zero carbon footprint? After what he'd seen here, his pride seemed pathetic. "You'll never have to talk to me again."

"Not bloody likely, mate. Remember? Thanks to that last shag, we're connected until one of us dies. If you're lucky, maybe Alun will do you the favor of killing me before the night is over, and you can go home."

"Now you're being an asshole. What's the point of giving up? You know there's a problem here. You've seen it."

"No, mate. *You've* seen it, and clearly a bunch of other shite as well, which you didn't see fit to share with the class."

"What are you talking about?"

"Your fecking druid sight! If you could tell when bloody Steve was lying, why didn't you tell me when he first showed up?"

"Oh come on, Mal. Be fair. Even if I'd known I could do it, I didn't get a good look at him in the kitchen, and tonight—"

"Hold on." Mal grabbed his arm, this time in a grip hard enough to bruise. "You saw him in my house?"

"Just his shadow."

"Why didn't you say anything?"

Bryce dropped his gaze, ashamed of decisions that were rooted in his own self-doubt and unfounded suspicions. "Because the two of you were talking about some kind of . . . of conspiracy."

"So you thought I was the traitor too? Why bed me, then? Get off on a bit of rough, do you?"

"No. Of course not. But—"

"Gwydion's bloody bollocks. You and David, you're always on about how fae take too much for granted, assume too much, when all we need is to ask. So why didn't you, Bryce? Why not ask the fecking question?"

Bryce threw up his hands in disgust. "Because I didn't know what the fucking question was!"

"So you settled for fucking, and hang the question?"

"You think that's what I wanted?"

Mal shoved Bryce away. "*I* did, more fool me, and now we're stuck with it."

"If you're so unhappy about it, what do you think the Queen is going to feel like if she sacrifices herself on our say-so, only to find out she's stuck with whatever the consequences are. You don't even *know* what the consequences are. Nobody does. Why doesn't anybody think about this shit?"

"Because we're bloody fae, you sodding druid!" Mal roared. "The elder gods did our thinking for us. Talk about consequences—we've been dealing with those since time began."

"If you don't like it," Bryce roared back, "then *do* something about it!"

"What do you—"

"Gentlemen." The Queen's voice wasn't loud, but it bisected their argument like a scalpel. She was standing at the far side of the circle, Steve looming next to her. She didn't say any more, but the order—and it was a command, Bryce had no illusions about that—was clear.

Shut the fuck up.

He compressed his lips and strode toward the Queen's group, putting on enough speed to strain the tether—enough to inconvenience Mal but not hurt him. Bryce's desires didn't lead him *that* far into uncharted waters. In fact, he sheared away from them as if they were marked on an ancient map. *Here be monsters.* He didn't want to be one of them.

The Queen reached the tree line as Bryce cleared the ring of stones, Mal still stomping along behind him and cursing under his breath. Apparently he had no wish to close the distance either, keeping them just on the edge of discomfort.

She turned and raised her hand. "Lord Maldwyn. Your transgressions have not yet been forgiven. You will await our judgment here."

All of Bryce's nerves sparked as if he'd just stuck his pruners into a light socket. Mal echoed his own cry of pain and surprise. *What the hell?*

He rubbed his chest as the Queen's group disappeared down a path lined with flowering trees, their branches laced together to form a living tunnel. Bryce imagined that in better times, it would have been . . . well . . . magical. But now, he could see the dark threads running through the heart of each branch and twig, the curl of each blossom. Something was definitely rotten in Faerie.

He waited until the trio had disappeared around a curve in the tunnel, and then strode forward to investigate. He'd never seen trees like this before. If he could touch them, feel them, would they speak to him the way the trees in the Unseelie sphere had? Would they cry? Would they beg him for help?

But he never got there. The tether wrenched him to a halt five feet from the outer edge of the Stone Circle.

He sighed. "Look, Mal. I know you hate this"—*hate me*—"but could you at least cooperate while we wait? Please."

When he got no response, he turned around. Mal was standing between a pair of menhirs in the outer ring, his feet braced wide, his shoulders tense. Bryce took a couple of steps toward him, and the set of Mal's jaw eased.

"Mal, I get that you want nothing to do with me. But—"

"It's not that. She told me to wait."

"I know. But maybe we can do something more interesting than stare at each other. I'd like to take a look at those trees."

Mal sank down with his back against one stone, stretching his legs out toward its neighbor. "Sorry, mate."

Bryce's temper boiled up again. "So that's it? You've decided to do nothing, so you'll prevent me from helping too?"

"You don't get it. She told me to *wait*."

"So?"

Mal extended his hand until it reached a spot in roughly the center of the short side of the megalith. Light flared, green and yellow, like a force field with the stones as its power poles. Mal flinched and so did Bryce as an echoing spark lit up his nerves. "So she made sure of it. And with you on the outside of her magical prison and me on the inside . . ." He shrugged.

Ah, crap. "So we wait here? All night?"

"Looks like it." Mal patted the ground next to him. "It's the bloody equinox, so the night won't be the longest it could be, but it won't be the shortest either. May as well get as comfortable as possible."

CHAPTER ✤ 28

Mal stared up at the slice of sky visible beyond the capstone overhead. When he hadn't been trolling for sex in the Outer World, he'd always loved the nights in Faerie, where the moon seemed close enough to touch if only he could find a tree tall enough. He'd always imagined that the One Tree stretched all the way to the moon. Now it turned out it didn't even reach beyond the throne room.

He ignored Bryce's exasperated muttering as he settled against the same stone on the other side of the barrier. At first, Mal thought Bryce intended to give him the silent treatment all night. No such luck.

"How could you not know that guy had ulterior motives?"

"Everyone has ulterior motives." He'd had several himself, chiefly to get his hand and his life back without giving Rodric Luchullain a damned thing. Without restoring Rodric, though, could Steve deliver on what he'd promised? Maybe that was the plan—Steve would restore Rodric, which would break Mal's curse. But if that was the case, when and where would the alleged delivery occur? Shite, Mal should have gotten a few more details at some point along the line. "Besides, I was drunk at the time. Thanks to you."

"Now it's my fault you can't hold your liquor?"

"I wouldn't have downed so much if I hadn't suddenly become shackled to a bloody druid."

"Which wouldn't have happened if you hadn't tattled to your brother-in-law."

"'Tattled'?" Mal picked up a pebble and threw it at the barrier. It passed through, of course—the Queen hadn't told *it* to wait—and narrowly missed Bryce's boots. "Gwydion's bollocks, man, I'm not a toddler—I've been out of short coats for millennia."

"Really? You threw a beer bottle"—he nudged the lucky escaped pebble as if to say *among other things*—"at a coyote."

"That wasn't a coyote. It was an Unseelie redcap."

"Really?" Bryce drew out the word until it had triple its usual number of syllables. "Are they particularly susceptible to beer bottles, then?"

"No," Mal growled. "But it was the only thing I had to hand."

"And it got you nowhere except facedown in the slough."

"That wasn't until later. They'd have come after me anyway, so can we give it a fecking rest?"

For a wonder, Bryce shut up. But after a handful of minutes, Mal broke the silence himself. "It's not necessarily rape, you know."

Bryce scowled at the next stone over, as if he could break it with his gaze. "It's a coercive sexual relationship. That's the definition of nonconsensual, and nonconsensual equals rape."

"No. I mean they don't have to have sex to meet the terms of Steve's request."

"But he said—"

"A night in the Queen's bed. Those were the exact words, and in the elder times, they were a euphemism that everybody understood with a wink and a nudge. But nowadays, if you want to shag someone, you wouldn't just ask for a night in their bed. Hells, from the wording, the Queen doesn't even need to *be* in the bed. Only Steve."

"You mean—"

"Yeah. The Queen is nobody's fool, and she can best ninety-eight out of a hundred Sidhe in hand-to-hand combat, so she's got resources. But I don't think Steve would force her even so. He seemed almost . . . apologetic about it."

"You think he was faking?"

"You tell me, Mr. Druid-Sight."

Bryce leaned his head against the stone, gazing up at the stars for so long that Mal thought he'd finally stepped over the line and offended him for good. "He's definitely hiding something."

Mal snorted. "No news there. Can you really see it?"

"In a way. It's hard to explain. But there's a place in his chest where the flow of energy stops. Like a locked room in his mind."

"Is it his mind or his chest? There's a bit of a difference there. His chest doesn't have snakes sprouting from it, for one thing."

"I told you it was hard to explain. That's as close as I can get. Sorry."

"Your inner eye needs spectacles, mate."

"Maybe." Bryce sighed and lapsed into silence. Mal thought he might have even dozed for a few minutes, but then he spoke up again. "So why'd you do it?"

"Told you. Too many beers."

"I don't mean your conspiracy with . . . Steve? God, really? I mean signing on to be my . . . my familiar. How does that work?"

"I asked Cassie for details about that and got nowhere. Why do you bloody druids have to be so gods-be-damned cryptic all the time? At least in a sword fight, you don't have to figure out the deep dark meaning of the blade sweeping toward your neck. Simple and uncomplicated, that's what I like."

"See? That's the problem with the fae mindset. It's too binary. Seelie, Unseelie." Bryce held his hands out flat, as if he were weighing his words in each palm. "Greater fae, lesser fae. Faerie, Outer World. But if you look at it more closely"—he laced his fingers together— "none of those are separate at all."

"Getting right philosophical, aren't you? If you intend to go on like this all night long, I may throw myself against the Queen's wee barrier just to end my misery."

"Would it really kill you?"

Mal rolled his head so he could see Bryce's face, the rough stone catching in his hair. He had a brief memory of Bryce restraining him, fingers threaded through his hair, and a wave of heat crested in his chest. *Shite.*

This was why he'd never taken a lover, had never wanted to chain himself to that kind of anchor. He'd had his brothers as cautionary object lessons: Alun, who'd guilted himself into exile when he thought he'd been responsible for his first lover's death; Gareth, who was so devastated after the Unseelie abducted his human lover that he'd become the first voluntary fae ex-patriot.

The problem with anchors was that you could lose them. Be cast adrift, as Alun had been, as Gareth was. And as Mal would be when he was locked away from Bryce.

"Death would be easier," he murmured.

Bryce's eyebrows snapped together. "What?"

Flaming abyss, he hadn't meant to admit that aloud. "Nothing."

"Don't try to bullshit me, Mal. I can tell when you're lying. In fact, I can feel it. The way your skin prickles and the way your dick shrinks."

Mal covered his groin with one hand. "It does not."

Bryce grinned wolfishly. "It does. You know how I know? Because mine reflects it. It's like that sympathetic magic spell I did on the paintballs. By changing the nature of the potion in the mirror cup, the paintball changed too. I think we're like that now."

"You think it's part of the familiar bond?"

"That's my guess, although without anybody who's experienced it to tell us what to expect, who's to know?"

"Shite. Any road, I want to say—" He swallowed. No point in lying now, was there? "I'm sorry. I should have given you the whole story before. Given *you* a choice."

"Yes. You should have. And, in future, you always will, right?"

Mal scrubbed a hand through his hair. "Bryce. We don't *have* a future. Or at least I don't."

"Bullshit. You've learned things tonight, we all have, that are game-changers. So don't go fatalistic on me. Fight. Work with me. Because I'm not giving you up."

Mal's eyes gleamed in the soft light. "Truly? Even after my little deception?"

"Not so little. But I doubt I could have given you up even if we weren't permanently attached at the hip."

"It's just that I needed to get in here. Steve threatened Gareth. Said if I didn't fulfill my part of the bargain, he'd force Gareth to do it instead."

"Based on Gareth's little tantrum tonight, he'd probably have jumped at the chance if he thought it would piss off Alun, or screw you over, or stick it to the Queen."

"He's not— You can't judge him that way. Yeah, he might have done it, but if he had, there'd be no coming back from that. It would have been a point of no return."

"So why would it be a bad thing for him, but okay for you?"

Mal chuckled, low and mirthless. "I'm already beyond the pale, mate. No great loss if I fuck my future."

"Don't say that."

"Why not? It's a pretty much done deal that when Alun escorts Her possibly debauched Majesty back at dawn, he'll be escorting me away with rather less ceremony and more chains." He leaned his head against the stone. "I just wish the whole thing hadn't been such a bloody waste. This was supposed to lift both our curses, but so far, mine is still firmly intact. My memory of that first encounter is cloaked in a beer haze, but I seem to remember Steve saying he had to be fully restored—whatever that entails—before he could flick his magic fingers at me and make good on his end of the deal. I should have asked to see the fine print, since I don't even know what Steve's curse might be." He snorted. "Maybe it's having to be called Steve."

"Seriously? He looks like a blue-skinned cross between a gorgon, Lord Voldemort, and a wild boar, and you wonder what his curse is?"

"For all we know, that's what he looks like normally. The elder gods had some pretty rubbish ideas about bioengineering, our own situation being a case in point."

Bryce gazed at Mal's perfect profile. "I don't know about that. Other than the familiar time-bomb, they did a pretty spectacular job with you."

"Don't be daft." Mal ducked his head, red washing his cheeks.

Bryce chuckled and leaned against the stone, facing Mal, to enjoy the view. "You had that same look—kind of a gobsmacked wonder—during paintball target practice."

"Don't remind me. We got sideswiped by Rodric afterward and he nearly—" Mal clenched his eyes shut. "Goddess, if I didn't hate the bastard's guts already, when I thought he'd killed you?"

Bryce shuddered at the memory. But . . . "Why would he attack us in our own backyards anyway? Did he still consider you a threat?"

"I have a theory about that—and it's not one that makes me happy. Remember later that night at dinner, when I started to tell you about Nuada?"

"Yeah. I thought you were ready to spill about Steve's visit. Imagine my disappointment."

Mal's eyes widened. "So *that's* why you were so pissy."

"You weren't much better. Go on."

"Is that an order?" Mal purred.

"You know it's not."

"All right. So Nuada lost his hand in battle, much like our dear Rodric. Well, the Tuath Dé had some funky rules about the qualifications for kingship. One of them was that the king had to be 'perfect'—that is, whole. Since an imperfect king wasn't qualified to rule, he stepped down in favor of a half-Fomorian bloke who was a bloody nightmare. Later, two others, a physician and a craftsman, created a hand for him made of silver—and that allowed him to retake his throne as Nuada Airgetlám—Nuada Silverhand."

Bryce's eyes widened. "That's a pretty disturbing parallel."

"Exactly. If Rodric imagines himself as the second coming of Nuada Airgetlám, he'd see me as the avatar of Sreng, the bloke who bested him."

"So you think he's got some kind of obsession about you, then?"

"Aye. He always was an overly dramatic sort." Mal snorted. "You should see his court wardrobe. But aside from that, if he's got it into his head that he's Nuada nouveau, and failed to grab the Seelie crown? If I were the Unseelie King, I'd be watching my back, that's all."

Bryce peered beyond Mal's shoulder at the altar stone, which was still winking with baleful red sparks. "If he's as entitled as you say, why would he stop at one realm?"

"Shite," Mal muttered. "You think he's aiming for all of Faerie."

"Why would he stop there?"

Mal's mouth dropped open. "Gwydion's bloody bollocks." He shook his head and turned away. "No. Not even Rodric would be insane enough to think the Tuath Dé could rule in the Outer World again. Things have changed too much."

Bryce remembered the blight spreading through the wetlands, its mirror in the Unseelie woods. "What if he's trying to change them back?"

For an instant, Mal simply stared at him, then smacked his fist into the ground. "Flaming abyss. We've got to tell the Queen. It may not mean anything—Rodric would need the gods' own power to do anything close to that—but she should know." Red washed Mal's cheeks. And his forehead. And his . . . hair?

"Mal, is the sky turning red? That can't be good. Can it?"

He cast a distracted glance at the sky. "Never mind that. Color spectrum sky. Yellow at noon, violet at night. Red means it's almost dawn."

"Does that mean they'll return soon? Is the night technically over?"

"Could be. This is one of the shadow times between night and day, so it could go either way. Fae love this shite. It's their favorite time for magic to go down."

There had been something in the grimoire about this—something about the awakening of power, if only he could remember. "It's important, isn't it, this time between? It's the point where the ancients, who didn't understand how day and night worked, would start to hope the light would come again."

"Deep, mate. Very deep."

"Shut up." The energy surging in Bryce's veins had changed. His chest felt tight, as if it were suddenly too small to contain whatever was about to crest in his blood. "Something's happening."

Mal rolled to his knees, his nose almost at the point where a faint gleam marked the barrier. "Goddess strike me down, Bryce, you shouldn't have spent the night here. Sometimes in the old days, humans got trapped in Faerie with the dawn."

"I'm not human, remember?" And that made all the difference, but how? The knowledge, the answer, the *key*—it hovered at the edge of his consciousness as if it were behind a barrier of its own, shimmering just outside the reach of his fingers. *If I could only touch it, harness it, I'll understand. Everything.*

Which was nuts. It wasn't as if he'd be able to jack several millennia's worth of data into his brain in an instant, but instincts were awakening in him, their velocity increasing since he'd made love to Mal that third time.

From down the hillside to his left, Bryce heard the rustle of leaves and the subtle tramp of at least one pair of feet.

"Someone's coming." Bryce scrambled to his feet, aware without looking that Mal did the same. "But I don't think it's the Queen's party. They're coming from the wrong direction and there aren't enough of them."

"We're bloody sitting ducks if the Unseelie show up to stage one of their little shows." As Mal searched the far side of the circle, he shuffled a little closer to where Bryce was standing, his right hand trembling against his thigh, and Bryce had the sudden impulse—no, the absolute need—to comfort him. To touch him. To hold him.

Slowly—*it's all about the will, and fuck anyone or anything who keeps me away from him*—he reached out, past the barrier that registered as barely a tickle on his skin, and took Mal's trembling right hand in his own left.

Mal's head snapped around, his eyes wide and startled, the worry knotting his brow replaced by wonder. "How did you—"

"Shhh." Instead of stepping through the barrier, Bryce drew Mal toward him. Mal swallowed, his Adam's apple bobbing, but he kept his gaze fixed on Bryce and took a step.

The tightness in his chest erupted, expanding like a supernova. *Trust.* Mal was willing to take the chance, risk the pain of the barrier crossing, because Bryce had asked him to. *This. I want this.* But he'd think about it later. Right now, the true danger was approaching from the other side of the circle, and they needed to get under cover. The Queen had constructed this magical cage to keep Mal in, but there was no guarantee it would keep everyone else *out*. Bryce had just proved he could bypass it; the new arrivals might very well be able to do the same.

As Mal inched toward him, Bryce focused every ounce of his will into getting this right. Mal fed into it too, his jaw tight in concentration, and something—energy, etheric force, whatever— flowed through their joined hands.

Mal's hand hit the barrier and he gasped. Bryce stopped, afraid he'd gone too far, but instead, Mal practically leaped forward into his arms. "Your hand," he whispered into Bryce's ear, his breath raising the hair along Bryce's hairline. "I felt it. I—"

"Save it for later," Bryce murmured. "Right now we've got to hide."

CHAPTER ⚮ 29

Although he was still distracted by the sensation in his right hand, Mal agreed wholeheartedly with Bryce's plan. If the fae approaching like a herd of bloody swine were Unseelie, the situation would be dire enough. If they were Seelie, it could be worse.

He tugged Bryce toward the trees next to the path the Queen and her entourage had taken. Bryce didn't release his hand—*thank the Goddess*—creeping behind him, silent despite his ridiculous heavy-soled boots.

They made it inside the tree cover, still hand in hand, just as a tall blond fae burst into the circle, driving a cowering Unseelie bauchan before him.

"Is that—" Bryce whispered.

"Aye. Rodric fecking Luchullain, in the fallen Sidhe flesh."

"I know that. But the other—isn't that the same one we saw near the Unseelie Keep? The one who'd been injured?"

"Hard to tell. They all look alike to me."

Bryce shot him a disgusted look. "Seriously?"

Mal shrugged and jerked his head at the two figures in the circle.

As they neared the altar stone, Rodric planted one foot on the bauchan's back and shoved. The creature stumbled and sprawled on the ground, whimpering. In the reddish light of near-dawn, it was hard to tell if its back was welling with fresh blood or not.

"You failed me."

The bauchan scrambled to its knees. "Sorry, master. So sorry."

Rodric kicked it in its side, and it squealed. Bryce tensed, and anger not Mal's own roiled in his chest like a gathering storm. *Bryce's reaction; Bryce's anger.* Shite. Is this what the familiar bond meant?

That they'd never be able to hide their feelings from one another again? Mal tucked that away for later study, not sure if it was a good thing or a bad thing.

"Your miserable life has but one purpose." Rodric strutted around the bauchan like a dunghill cock. "One." He kicked it again, and Bryce growled. "Single." *Kick.* "Purpose." *Kick.*

Bryce actually lurched forward, rustling the leaves of their hiding place, before Mal hauled him back with their still-joined hands— *my right hand, Goddess be praised.* Mal wasn't entirely sure *why* he'd regained some functionality—he hadn't felt the energy wave, Faerie's reaction to a curse being broken—for either himself or for Steve.

Rodric cast a single irritated glance at where they were hiding before returning his attention to the bauchan. "I ordered you to meet me at the Well at midnight, not dawn. Are you too stupid to tell night from day?"

Bryce leaned close and murmured into Mal's ear. "What well is he talking about?"

Mal didn't need Bryce to feed him anger anymore; his vision began to narrow, the precursor of battle trance. "There's only one that matters—the wellspring of all water in Faerie."

"The King, master. He—"

"I don't give a shite about the King. He doesn't appreciate the true grandeur of my vision. He's as useless as you. Although he does show a certain creativity in torture. He might be quite inventive when he learns you were willing to aid me in betraying him."

The bauchan threw itself on its face at Rodric's feet. "Please, master. I will do better, I swear."

Rodric looked down his nose and planted his foot on the bauchan's back as he stripped the leather gauntlet off his silver hand. "Why should I give you another chance, you who are incapable of the simplest task? Perhaps I'll award the assignment to a troll and reward him with your puling spawn. I understand its kind consider them a delicacy."

The bauchan wailed, scrabbling at the ground in an effort to escape from Rodric's boot. "No, master. Not the little ones. Please."

"Hand over the *Gloine nan Druidh* and I might be persuaded to spare one or two."

Mal sucked in a sharp breath. "Shite. The bastard has a Druid's Glass?"

"A what?" Bryce whispered.

"Adder stone, serpent's egg—whatever you call it, it's a bloody powerful charm. If he's about to drop it in the Well—"

"The blight. He *is* trying to change the world back." Bryce's eyes darkened. *He's sharp, my druid.* "He's trying to poison all of it. All the water."

"I gave you an order." Rodric's voice echoed in the circle. "Hand it over."

"I— I—" The bauchan wheezed as Rodric shifted more weight onto the foot pinning it down. "I left…behind. King…summoned—"

"Where is it? Answer me or the spawn die tonight."

"Throne room. Please, master—"

"This has gone far enough." Bryce shifted, legs bunching under him as if to stand, but Mal tightened his grip on his hand.

"Hold up, mate. What are you about?"

"I'm about to beat the ever-loving shit out of that asshole before he hurts anybody else."

"I'm with you there, but shouldn't we—"

"The paintballs. Can you hit him?"

"I'll bloody well try." He pulled his paintballs out of his pocket. The three of them fit easily in his left hand.

Bryce nodded, releasing his hold on Mal to dig in his vest pocket. Immediately, the feeling in Mal's right hand began to fade. *What the—* Startled, he fumbled his paintballs, and they disappeared into the underbrush.

"Fuck. I dropped them."

"Here." Bryce slapped two paintballs into Mal's hand and displayed the two he'd kept. "I wish I could have made more, but I ran out of St. John's wort. These are all we've got left, so make them count. Skin if you can manage it. Otherwise the chest."

"Got it."

Bryce burst out of their cover and took off, forcing Mal to run after him before he reached the end of the tether. Rodric noticed them as they breached the ring of megaliths—no surprise, since they weren't exactly stealthy in their approach. The bastard didn't remove his foot from the bauchan's back, a smug grin splitting his face. He raised his silver hand with a flourish, like some charlatan Outer World magician.

"Now!" Bryce shouted.

They skidded to a halt, took aim, and each threw a ball. Shite, Bryce had an arm on him, but his aim was faulty. His first ball hit Rodric's shoulder, spattering paint across his velvet doublet and spraying across his cheek. His second one missed entirely.

Mal's first shot landed square on the throat, the second on his chin. Damn. He'd wanted to land a hit flush in the bastard's eyes, but apparently this was close enough, because Rodric staggered back, his hands—both flesh and metal—clawing at his face and throat.

The bauchan scrambled away, and as Bryce made a beeline for it, Rodric pointed a metal finger their way. Mal's insides turned to ice— *Too far, I'm too far away, damn it to all the hells*. He launched himself into the line of fire anyway, clenching his eyes shut and bracing himself for the blast.

But nothing happened other than a frizzle accompanied by a faint smell of burnt flesh—and judging by Rodric's pained cry, the flesh was his.

Anti-evil potion indeed. Well done, druid. Mal lunged for Rodric, but got pulled up short by the wrench in his gut when he reached the end of the tether.

"Augh!" Damn it. This shite was beyond old. Bryce was still hunkered down next to the bauchan, speaking earnestly. Meanwhile Rodric had recovered enough to stagger out of the circle. "Bryce! He's getting away."

"Just a minute."

Mal quivered at the end of the invisible leash like a dog ready to course, but Rodric reached the tree line and disappeared down the hill before Bryce so much as budged.

Mal kicked the altar stone and got a stubbed toe for his pains. "Gods damn it to all the bloody fecking hells!"

At Bryce's hand on his shoulder, Mal was startled into taking a swing at the man. Bryce blocked his flailing fist. "What's wrong?"

"He got away."

Bryce's hand tightened. "No worries there. We know where he went."

"We do?"

"The throne room in the Unseelie Keep."

"Shite." Mal gripped his hair with his good hand. "If he's crossed into the Unseelie sphere, we can't follow."

"Why not? We did before."

"That was because of Steve's token. It granted us access. Masked our presence."

"So it was like an escort."

"Yeah, fat lot of good it does us now. He took it back."

"We don't need it. We have our own escort." Bryce nodded at the bauchan, who was huddled next to the altar stone. It nodded to Mal, tugging its forelock.

"It'll not be able to mask our presence, though. Every fae, Seelie and Unseelie, will know we've breached the barrier. They'll catch us before we've gone twenty yards."

"If you please, masters, I—I know a way."

Bryce turned to the creature, an altogether too sympathetic smile on his face. *He's mine. He doesn't need another familiar.* "Thank you, Heilyn. We'd appreciate it. But we're not your masters."

Heilyn? It has a name? "Speak for yourself," Mal muttered.

Bryce shot him a pointed look. "I do. Let's go."

Heilyn, no higher than Bryce's waist, still had the divots of its prior open wounds on its back. It seemed far too fragile to have withstood Rodric's beating, but it scurried to the edge of the stone circle faster than Bryce expected. He grabbed a surly Mal by the hand and pulled him along in its wake. Mal might be annoyed at Rodric's escape, but in Bryce's mind, Heilyn was the higher priority, and not just from a humanitarian perspective.

Bryce hadn't forgotten those murals in the corridor behind the Unseelie throne room. The servant classes were anything but complacent, and if history taught anything, it was that oppressors frequently lived to regret their cruelty, once their victims found their own agency.

They'd made it nearly to the trailhead where Rodric had disappeared when a shout rang out across the hilltop.

"Mal!"

"Shite. It's Alun. We're out of time."

Bryce glanced over his shoulder. Sure enough, Alun was advancing across the circle at a run, his sword in his hand. Neither Steve nor the Queen were with him, but that could mean a number of things. Bryce chose not to think about any of those at the moment.

"Then let's run."

They took off, crashing down the path in Heilyn's wake. Bryce couldn't believe the squat little body with its paddle-like feet could move so quickly through the underbrush, like a fish through a coral reef. But, then, perhaps the underbrush was its natural habitat.

"This way. This way," it chattered. "No time to lose."

Bryce felt it when they crossed into the Unseelie sphere, like passing too close to a fire. Beside him, Mal cursed louder.

"You okay?"

"I'll live. Go faster."

Since Alun was still thundering down the hillside behind them, Mal had a point. "Can he cross over?"

"Don't know," Mal panted. "Ordinarily, no, but his role as the Queen's Enforcer grants certain privileges."

As they ducked under a withering oak branch, a nearby flutter of yellow caught Bryce's attention—the flag he'd used to mark their path on their last trip. "I think I know where we are."

"Glad to hear it, but it's where everyone else is that concerns me. Like— Ah, shite."

CHAPTER ✤ 30

Alun stepped out of the trees on the path directly in front of them. "Hold."

Perfect timing, brother, as usual. Mal shouldered his way in front of Bryce, noting absently that the bauchan—Heilyn—had vanished into the trees. So much for their escort. "Look, I know I was supposed to stay in the circle."

"I'm less interested in the fact of your escape—since you never do what you're told—than in *how* you managed to do it. And why you sought Unseelie lands."

"It looks bad, but—"

"Now isn't the time . . . Alun, is it?" Bryce took hold of Mal's elbow and drew him closer to his side. Just that contact was enough to calm his jangling nerves. "I've met your husband."

"Leave my David out of this. You—"

"No. I don't believe I can. David said you were stubborn—" Alun scowled, and Mal nudged Bryce.

"Not the way to turn him up sweet, mate."

Bryce shot him a fleeting smile. "But he also said you were one of the only fae who was able to change, who accepted the necessity for change."

Goddess, did Alun just *blush*? "Sometimes it's obvious. And unavoidable."

"Well, this is one of those times. Rodric Luchullain is about to—"

"Luchullain?" Alun crouched in a battle stance and scanned the surroundings. "Where?"

"We're on our way there now."

"*Where?*" Alun's demand was perilously close to a battle roar. Mal took a moment to be thankful it wasn't aimed at him.

"That's not your concern," Bryce said, cool as you please, though his hand on Mal's elbow vibrated like a leaf in the breeze. "We have a more urgent task for you."

"My business is with the traitor Luchullain."

"No, Alun. I have to do it." Mal knew this as well as he knew his own name. "My curse. My responsibility."

Alun opened his mouth, no doubt to argue, but Bryce cut him off with a raised palm.

"There's someone else who needs your help."

"*You* need my help. How can you best Luchullain? Neither of you can wield a sword."

"But neither can Rodric." Heat rushed through Mal's chest. *And I never will again, unless Steve finally comes through—or I find a way to make fecking Luchullain whole tonight before I end him for good.* Of course, Steve had never told Mal exactly how he intended to break the curse. Maybe delivering Rodric to him was his arse-backwards way of meeting the conditions. "One way or another, Alun, you have to let me try. If I fail, you can back me up." He smiled crookedly. "Just like I backed you up the night I took Rodric's hand and got myself into this mess."

Alun's hard gaze softened at the reminder, and he gripped Mal's shoulder. "You saved me that night, Mal—but more importantly, you saved David. As far as I'm able within my duty, I'll grant you your request."

"Thank you," Mal whispered, throat tight.

Bryce beckoned to a spot beyond Alun's shoulder, and Heilyn crept onto the path, cutting a wide berth around Alun until it could shelter behind Bryce's legs, one paw clutching the pocket of his tactical pants. "This is Heilyn, whose children are being held hostage by several of Luchullain's thugs. You are their only hope of rescue."

Alun gazed down at Heilyn, who huddled closer to Bryce. "Do you know where your little ones are being held?"

It nodded. "At the Keep. King's men all gone after feast-day. Only guards are with the little ones."

Mal nudged Alun. "That's where Luchullain's headed. Come on. An empty Keep is a bit of luck we can't expect to last forever."

Alun nodded, lips compressed into a firm line. "Very well."

Mal heaved a sigh of relief, followed by an upsurge of urgency until he was vibrating at the same frequency as Bryce's hand.

"We haven't much time. Heilyn will see us into the Keep. We'll pursue Luchullain to the throne room while you rescue the babies."

Babies. Goddess, he'd never thought of them that way. Well, he'd never seen any to speak of. A bauchan with young was sequestered until the young were able to hop off and fend for themselves, but yes, he supposed they were babies.

"As you wish." Alun lowered his sword. "But there are developments you should be aware of. The Queen—"

A faint wail echoed in the woods, causing Heilyn to whimper and dart away down the path. Since Bryce followed, Mal had no choice but to stumble along at the rear.

"Mal, come back!"

"Later, Alun," he called over his shoulder. "Arrest me, imprison me, behead me, whatever your duty commands. But, for now, move your bloody arse!"

Heilyn scuttled along the path, which grew increasingly familiar, so Bryce wasn't the least surprised when they drew to a halt outside a rough wooden door.

"These are the kitchens, right?" Heilyn nodded. "Are there others of your kind inside?" At the second nod, Bryce turned to face the Kendrick brothers, Alun in particular. "We're entering through halls that are only travelled by lesser fae. Do you understand the implications?"

The brothers glanced at each other and shrugged. Bryce glared at Mal. "Do you remember anything about the last time we were here, Mal?"

"The last time?" His eyes widened and his mouth lifted in a smirk as he cut a glance at his brother. "Right." He turned to Alun. "Don't be shocked, brother, but the lesser fae may not worship us as we might wish."

"I never—"

"Alun." Urgency grew in Bryce's chest, the certainty that speed was of the essence. "These are Unseelie fae. Servants of the King, yes, but they have little choice and shouldn't be terrorized."

Alun blinked. "Why would I—" Bryce raised an eyebrow and jerked his chin at the sword, longer than Heilyn was tall. "Ah." He sheathed the sword in the scabbard strapped to his back.

"Draw it after we get through the kitchens, so you're ready for Rodric's thugs, but we need to look as nonthreatening as possible now."

Heilyn tugged on Bryce's pant leg. "Lord Cynwrig is fair. Won't punish servant for ill-seasoned soup."

"Of course not. I— Wait. The King does that?"

Heilyn bobbed his head. "More of late. Since the beast."

Bryce met Mal's gaze uneasily. "The beast. Could he mean Steve?"

"The beast who stole my young. That beast."

"Rodric bloody Luchullain," Mal growled. "What are we waiting for?" He pulled at the door handle. The door didn't budge. He pulled harder.

"Mal. Remember, this isn't your realm."

"Shite." He stood aside and allowed Heilyn to open the door—with only two of the six fingers on one hand. Bryce might have imagined it, but he thought it gave him a sly wink. Bryce chuckled. *Can't blame the downtrodden for rubbing it in a bit when they've got the advantage—even an advantage as small as opening the door to their own house.*

They ducked through the door and followed Heilyn through the scullery into the kitchen. As opposed to their last visit, the big room was redolent of scents both savory and sweet. It also wasn't empty.

Two creatures similar to Heilyn, who had been turning a haunch of some large animal on a spit in the wide hearth, shrieked and abandoned their post. One leaped for a swag of onions and scrambled up into the rafters. The other scuttled into the corner and hid behind a butter churn.

Three others, who'd been icing tiny cakes, dropped their pastry bags and dove under the table.

Heilyn said something in a language Bryce couldn't follow, and the two from the hearth crept back to attend the spit. The others didn't come out of hiding, but considering how much real estate the Kendrick brothers occupied, Bryce wasn't sure he blamed them.

He nodded an apology to each frightened face as they threaded their way through the room and out the other side. Once into the hallway, Bryce touched Heilyn on the shoulder.

"We know the way to the throne room from here. Take Alun . . . er . . . Lord Cynwrig to where your children are being held."

When Heilyn pointed to a narrow stairway that spiraled out of sight, Alun unsheathed his sword again. "I'll dispatch these fellows as fast as I'm able, and join you in the throne room."

A pitiful wail, weak and heartbroken, echoed in the stairwell, and Heilyn trembled in distress. It tugged on Alun's shirt tail. "Please. Even if the beast's men do not hurt them, without me, they die."

Alun cast one more glance at Mal and ducked through the doorway, disappearing up the stairs at a run with Heilyn at his heels.

"Come on." Bryce squeezed Mal's hand. "That's our cue."

They raced down the hallway to the throne room door, the bloodthirsty murals more lurid in the light of the rising sun. Bryce paused in front of the door and met Mal's determined gaze.

"How reliable is Heilyn's intel likely to be? Could the throne room be full to bursting of Unseelie warriors? Or, you know, the King?"

"He seemed certain. Besides, it's barely dawn. If the Unseelie are anything like the Seelie Court after a party, no one's recovered from their carousing yet."

"Would they have done that? Caroused, I mean?"

"Any chance they get, and the equinox is one of the quarter-day feasts."

"Let's hope Heilyn's right and all the warriors are still in a food coma, then." He leaned forward and pressed a quick kiss to Mal's lips. "For luck." He grabbed the door handle.

"Wait." Mal's hand landed on his arm. "You do have a plan, right?"

He flashed a grin. "Don't worry about me—I'm a druid."

"Bryce—"

Dropping the attitude, Bryce cupped Mal's jaw. "We'll do what we have to, right? You've got the training and the drive to handle the fisticuffs with Rodric; I've got the druid sight and the incentive to keep the stone out of the Wellspring. But we've got each other, and we've got your brother for backup, right?"

Mal's brow wrinkled with uncertainty, but then he nodded. "Right."

"Good. Now let's toast this bastard."

He eased the door open and peered inside. Despite Bryce's misgivings, the room was empty.

Almost.

At the far side of the room, opposite the throne, Rodric Luchullain was upending copper bowls and bronze urns, ripping tapestries off the wall, smashing vases on the floor and pawing through the shards. *Heilyn didn't tell him* where *in the throne room to find the stone.* Paint splattered the front of his gold velvet doublet, and angry red welts marred his throat and cheek.

Excellent.

Bryce burst out of the door and powered across the room, an undervoiced curse from Mal the only indication that he'd taken the man by surprise.

Rodric's head snapped up at the pounding of their feet on the flagstones. He bared his teeth in a feral grimace and pointed his metal hand at them. A weak wave of energy lapped against Bryce's chest. It was no worse than a static discharge at the moment, but it meant that the potion's effects weren't permanent. *Damn it.* They needed to finish this before he regained full use of his Taser hand.

Rodric cursed and heaved a jagged, head-sized chunk of porcelain at Bryce. Mal shoved him out of the way, but took the blow on his own temple instead, staggering against Bryce's shoulder.

When Bryce felt the bright star of sympathetic pain in his own head, the potential that had been building in his chest since before dawn crested and broke, lighting him up with druid-augmented senses. Lines of force swirled around the flagstones, the wooden tables, the throne with its jewels—everything that was born of nature. The tapestry glowed brighter than anything, as if it were made of the earth itself. *Or maybe of Faerie itself.*

The energy flowed over his hands like water, twining around his fingers like tender vines. He closed his fists and the power nestled there, awaiting his will.

I could do it. He could close off Rodric's windpipe. Stop his heart. Fry every synapse in his brain. All it would take was one . . . little . . . push.

"Bryce." Mal's hand on his arm startled him, and he wrenched his gaze from Rodric's twisted features. "Don't. Remember the plan."

Luchullain looked up at them, his eyes reddened under a smear of paint, but Bryce could see the fear there. "What, the druid allows his lapdog to give him orders?"

Bryce tensed, the desire to strike out nearly overwhelming. This was the man who'd tortured Heilyn, who had no compunction about killing helpless children, who'd attack an unarmed stranger for no reason other than spite. He was prepared, moreover, to cripple Faerie and destroy the wetlands and possibly more in a self-centered quest for power.

And he wants to kill Mal.

He didn't deserve to live. Bryce would be doing Faerie and his own world a favor if he ended this right fucking now.

"Mind how you go, Luchullain," Mal said, his grip tightening on Bryce's arm. "You're playing with fire."

"Him? He won't even take advantage of what he's got. He won't step up and own you as is his right. He ought to have you on a leash, like the dog you are. Or locked in a kennel where he can drain your power at will."

"Is that what you would do?" Bryce asked.

"No. I'd kill him first. He's not worth the trouble."

Bryce lunged, but Mal was quicker, blocking him, chest to chest. "Easy, mate. Take this step and you'll regret it."

"Regret killing him? Not likely."

"Maybe not tonight, but tomorrow or the next day." Mal's gaze locked with his. "This isn't you, my tree hugger. You're the clever one, remember? The compassionate one."

"Pathetic," Rodric said. "And to think I equated you with Sreng."

Mal didn't bother to glance at Rodric. He grinned wolfishly, eyes blazing neon-bright in Bryce's enhanced vision as he squeezed Bryce's arm again. "It's not you, love, but it's bloody well me."

He let go of Bryce and launched himself at Rodric. The two of them rolled halfway across the floor, until the tether that still bound him to Mal pulled Bryce to his knees. The kneepads in his tactical pants prevented him from breaking his kneecaps, but his palms landed on a scatter of pottery shards in a burst of pain. When he sat back, his hands left several bright blots of blood on the floor.

Mal grappled Rodric with his good hand, struggling to press his right elbow against Rodric's throat. Rodric struck Mal's chest with his Taser hand, and when Mal jerked, Bryce gasped, an echo of the shock jolting his own chest. *The hand may not be fully powered, but if Mal takes too many hits over his heart . . .*

He took a step forward.

"Keep back, Bryce," Mal barked. "This is *my* battle. *My* responsibility."

"Your doom," Rodric growled and hit him with another shock.

"Not on your bloody arse," Mal said, and cracked Rodric's jaw with a left uppercut.

Bryce wanted to interfere, wanted to unleash that alien, seductive power and end this now, end Rodric, before Mal got hurt. But he had no idea of the mechanics of lifting Mal's curse. The curse itself was a knot that bound both Mal and Rodric, and his druid studies had told him enough to know that severing it with brute force might as easily backfire and make the effects permanent. Steve might have other resources—although even Mal didn't seem to know what those might be. If it came to a choice, however—Mal's life or Mal's curse—he'd choose Mal's life.

For now, though, he forced himself to look away, wincing at the sound of blows against flesh, at the echoes of those blows on his own body. He had another task here: find the adder stone before Rodric did. *Stupid—I should have asked Heilyn where it was.* Might as well start where Rodric left off. Unfortunately, that was at a long refectory table across the room from where Mal and Rodric were grappling on the floor.

He eased toward it, but at the end of the invisible cable, he felt the pull in his gut and Mal faltered, allowing Rodric to score another hit with the Taser hand.

God damn it. *This is a druid spell, and I'm a fricking druid.* There must be some way to loosen the metaphysical chain. After all, it had happened before, the first time they'd entered Faerie, and Cassie had done it herself so she could enjoy a private chat with Mal.

Bryce resolutely ignored the fight and concentrated on the energy connecting him to Mal. Odd—there appeared to be two bonds: one with hooks in their bellies, and another, brighter one that wound around their hearts.

Tentatively, so as not to distract Mal, he reached out and closed his hands around the belly-to-belly cord. With the power twining around his hands like an affectionate cat, he pulled, stretching the magical rope like taffy. When he released it, it stayed stretched.

Elation flared in his chest. He grabbed another section. Stretched. Another. And another. He was worried that the other link, the one between their hearts, would stop him too, but it seemed much more elastic. *I'll worry about that when the time comes.*

Although he'd increased its reach by five feet or more, the litter of smashed porcelain was still just out of reach beyond the tips of his fingers. *If only Mal and Rodric would grapple a* little *closer.*

Although the tether was dangerously thin now, it had lost none of its strength, impervious to Bryce's attempts to break it or stretch it further. He was torn between admiration for Cassie's abilities and a futile wish for a less competent mentor.

He laid down on the floor and stretched out his full length. *My ridiculously long arms have to be good for something.* One more inch. Just one more. *If I can—*

A booted foot came down on his wrist. Pain shot up his arm and he cried out at the same time that a sickening crunch sounded from across the room. Someone moaned. Was it Mal? Rodric?

Bryce looked up into a gaunt face under an ornate crown.

"You trespass in my realm and defile my throne room. The penalty for that is death."

CHAPTER ✦ 31

The satisfying crunch of Rodric's nose under his fist lit up Mal's chest like a *Calan Mai* bonfire, although it sent a wave of pain up his arm too. *Damn. I'm out of practice.* The bastard hunched into a ball, his fleshly hand attempting unsuccessfully to stem blood streaming from his nose.

Mal grinned, stressing his split lip, but bugger that. *I've still got it.* He could hold his own, even if the other blighter had a magical electrocution hand.

With one knee pinning the wrist of said magical hand to the ground, Mal gripped Rodric's hair and yanked his head up, pressing his right arm across the bastard's throat. "I don't need two hands to choke the worthless breath out of you."

Rodric gagged, his chest shaking, and for a moment Mal thought he'd already gone too far. But then he realized the sound coming out of Rodric's mouth was laughter. "Your timing, *Lord* Maldwyn," he wheezed, "is impeccable as always."

Mal frowned but followed the direction of Rodric's gaze and froze. A tall, emaciated fae in velvet robes the color of smoke, glinting with red and gold jewels like hidden embers, was standing over Bryce, his foot pinning Bryce's arm, the point of his sword hovering over the back of Bryce's neck.

Mal met Bryce's gaze. His eyes faded from druid black to warm ale-brown, but they held no fear. He lifted an eyebrow as if in apology.

"I take it," Mal tightened his hold until Rodric grunted, "based on the pretentious moth-eaten crown, that you're the Unseelie King."

The King's cadaverous face split in a sneer. "I take it, from your complete incompetence, that you're Lord Maldwyn Cynwrig."

"If you're the King"—Bryce's voice was muffled with the side of his face pressed to the floor—"your tapestry portrait is entirely too flattering."

"Silence, druid." The King's weight shifted, and Bryce winced. Mal could feel the bones shift in his own wrist. "If you do not want the druid to die, release Lord Luchullain." The King's eyes narrowed, and he glanced between Mal and Bryce. "Or perhaps you'd prefer the druid to die after all. There is no other way to release you from his thrall."

"Fuck you."

The King tutted, weaving the tip of his sword in a figure eight over Bryce's back. Mal could see sweat beading on Bryce's forehead, one drop falling to make a dark circle on the flagstones. "Surely that's not the opportunistic Lord Maldwyn who speaks. I have heard tales of your escapades. Always with an eye for the main chance."

"Your hearing must be as decrepit as your face."

The King snagged the tip of the sword in the hem of Bryce's vest and sliced it open up the back. "This druid, your master. He means so little to you? Perhaps he might do for me. I've heard the sacrifice of a druid under the midwinter moon can grant power. Much power."

Mal's belly clenched. *Keep him talking. If he thinks Bryce is a future asset, he won't hurt him.* "I don't know where you get your information—"

"Kill him," Rodric wheezed. "Do it now."

Bryce winced again when the King leaned forward, putting more pressure on his wrist. The flesh on his back crept, expecting to feel the bite of the blade at any moment.

"You do not give the orders here, Lord Luchullain. Despite your valuable assistance, I am still King. And I think perhaps the services of one of the famed Cynwrig brothers might serve me better than a disgraced former Consort, a fallen Daoine Sidhe who can claim no distinction save the dubious honor of swiving the Seelie Queen whenever she chose to allow it. Although . . ." He tapped his sword on Bryce's back, and Bryce held his breath against an accidental slip.

"I understand she allowed it remarkably seldom. Perhaps she found other ways to take her pleasure. Other bedmates to satisfy her."

"Like you did?" The voice that boomed in the vast hall, taunting and confident, was Steve's.

From Bryce's position on the floor, he had a skewed sideways view of the room and of the huge figure standing inside the doors. The boots were Steve's and the cloak was Steve's and the jeweled gauntlets were Steve's. But his headful of snakes had transformed into wavy hair the color of peat, his skin was smooth and golden brown instead of blue and scaled, and his face was the face of a god.

The Unseelie King straightened, his sword dropping from Bryce's neck. "Eamon."

"Father."

Wait. What?

"'Father'?" Mal's tone was half-outraged and half-fearful. "Gwydion's bloody bollocks, you're not just royal, you're the gods-forsaken Unseelie prince?"

Steve—no, Eamon, a much more appropriate name for him— paced forward, his own sword loose at his side. "I was."

"Guards!" the King shouted.

"They'll not answer. I've seen to that."

"Is this some fiendish *glamourie*?" Bryce couldn't see the King's face, but his voice held a sneer. "You cannot have escaped your fate. The unwinding of the curse was impossible."

"Improbable, perhaps. But not impossible." Eamon held out his arms, his sword pointing toward the ceiling. "As you see."

"But— But—"

"It's true, Father. Despite your best efforts to destroy your sons, you've failed."

"My sons." The King spat on the flagstones. "Worthless, both of you. Your brother had one task to prove his loyalty. *One.* An insultingly easy task for a true Unseelie—his target had no battle skills. How hard could it have been to kill that swine? But could he do it?"

"He had his reasons."

"He defied me! As did you. My own sons!" The King retreated as Eamon paced toward him, and Bryce could finally breathe without worrying he'd impale himself. He drew his aching wrist closer to his body and slowly flexed his fingers. Nothing appeared to be broken, but *damn*.

"Did you never consider how your actions appeared to your people? If you could punish your own sons this way, what might you be capable of against those to whom you held no close ties?"

Bryce dared to lift his head to check on the rest of the room. The King was occupied with Eamon, indulging in a little family therapy. Mal was still holding Rodric in a death grip, although they were nearer to Bryce than they had been before the King's arrival. Would it be enough? Bryce had no idea how this drama would play out, but his goal hadn't changed: find the adder stone before it could be used to destroy both this world and his own.

Slowly he raised himself to his hands and knees, trying not to draw anyone's attention. Eamon and the King were focused on each other. Rodric was watching them avidly, almost as if he'd forgotten Mal's restraining hold.

Mal, though, focused on Bryce at his first movement, turning his head slightly so he could keep Bryce in his line of sight while still tracking the discussion between the King and Eamon.

Bryce eased back to a sitting position. *Nothing to see here, folks. Just getting comfortable.* Scooting on his ass, he inched closer to the table, pretending to be absorbed in the family drama. As the King grew increasingly shrill and loquacious, Eamon grew ever more stoic and monosyllabic. *Balance. It's everywhere.*

Mal must have figured out Bryce's target, because he angled his body, leaning toward Bryce without loosing his hold on Rodric. Finally Bryce was next to a half-dozen mounds of broken porcelain, the vases Rodric had been smashing when they arrived. *Now what?* He couldn't dig through it unobtrusively—plus he didn't know if the stone was under any of these piles at all. If only he could see—

Idiot. If he weren't trying to play secret agent, he'd have slapped himself on the forehead. *I don't have to see it to find it.* He'd had contact with the stone's effects in his poor blighted wetlands, so he was far too familiar with its energy signature.

Concentrate on the flow, the lines of power. Where's the disturbance? The wrongness? The thing that doesn't belong?

Tendrils of power curled around him, caressing his skin, inviting him to join in their dance. So beautiful. So harmonious. So— *There*.

It wasn't in the broken crockery at all. It was tucked under the table itself, at the point where a leg met the ornate skirt—eye level for someone, say, the height of a bauchan. *Or for a druid sitting on the floor. Who says there's no such thing as karma?*

He scanned the room. Eamon and the King had moved their argument—which was getting increasingly crazed on the King's part—all the way to the edge of the throne room, in front of the arch that led to the corridor. Rodric's attention was still focused on them. Mal, though—Mal's lips quirked, and he gave an infinitesimal nod before turning to face the royal spat, a tiny encouragement that filled Bryce with more warmth and confidence than any ten professional accolades.

He needed all of it too, because when he reached out and plucked the stone from its hiding place, its malignant essence nearly made him retch. Nevertheless, he forced himself to close his fist around it. For the sake of both worlds, he needed to keep it safe.

CHAPTER ❈ 32

Flaming abyss. *The Unseelie prince.* How had Mal missed the signs? With the power that Steve—no, sod it, *Eamon*—had tossed around so casually, he had to be royal, or at least a highborn who outranked the Sidhe. And if he'd been Seelie, Mal would have heard rumors about a lord who'd gotten himself ensorcelled into a monster. The fae were notorious gossips. What else did they have to do in these latter years? They had no wars to fight. Couldn't abduct the occasional random human for dalliance—although Mal managed his dalliances just fine in the Outer World.

He glanced at Bryce. *No more random dalliances for me. I've found the one I want.* Although his druid didn't look too chipper at the moment, leaning against the heavy leg of a table with his fist clenched in his lap and his face positively green. Poor bloke. This adventure wasn't exactly a skip through the park. When they got home—

Wait a mo. It hadn't fully registered when Mal was adjusting his position to give Bryce more slack, but they were separated by easily half again the length of their tether. *How—*

Rodric struggled a bit in his chokehold. Mal jerked him sideways slightly so he was facing the squabbling Unseelie royals rather than Bryce. "Give over, Luchullain. You're done."

"So why haven't you ended me? Waiting for your druid master to give the order?"

"Shut it, you poncy git."

"Can't do anything without his leave now, can you? Does he reward you well if you follow your orders? Does he pat you on the head and say 'good boy'?"

"You're a fine one to talk about taking orders. Here you are, at the beck and call of His rotting Unseelie Majesty, all to score a bit of power and a fancy-dress hand."

"I take orders from no one," Rodric growled, glaring after Eamon and the King, who'd moved their party into the corridor. "That fool is naught but a puppet. Even now he spares no thought for anyone save himself."

"You mean he's sparing no thought for you. Hurt your feelings, did he, leaving you to get pummeled so he could enjoy a cozy chat with his son?" *His son. I still can't believe it.*

"Neither of them is of any consequence. Soon I'll—"

"Soon you'll have a gag shoved in your gob if I have anything to say about it."

"But you don't. None of you do. Not you. Not that cold bitch of a Queen. Not even your incompetent druid." Rodric jerked his chin at Bryce, who was staring at something in his hand with a look of revulsion. "There he sits, for all the world like a—" Rodric tensed, pulling against Mal's grip.

Shite. The *Gloine nan Druidh.* Bryce must have found it; that's why he looked so ill and why Mal's stomach was roiling in sympathy. "Don't even think—"

A shout and a clash of swords from the corridor startled Mal, and Rodric shoved his elbow into Mal's stomach *hard.* Mal doubled over, trying not to hurl, and Rodric twisted out of his hold to scramble toward Bryce.

"*Shite.*" By the time Mal staggered to his feet, Rodric had made it across the room. He backhanded Bryce with his metal hand, sending Bryce sprawling and the *Gloine nan Druidh* spinning away toward the throne.

Bryce's head rang from Rodric's blow, and he swallowed convulsively against a wave of nausea. *The adder stone. Where is it? Must keep it away from Rodric.*

He staggered to his feet, disoriented. Swords clanged outside in the corridor, followed by a cry and . . . was that a double set of retreating footsteps? Mal was barreling toward him as if their tether had just rebounded.

"You all right, mate?"

"Never mind me. Where's—"

With a shout of triumph, Rodric scrabbled something out from under the throne and clutched it to his chest. From the sick yellow swirl of *wrongness* in his nonmetallic hand, he'd retrieved the adder stone. *Damn it.* Bryce's head was still swimming too much for him to manipulate the energy as he'd done before.

Rodric leaped to his feet and pumped both fists in the air. The anti-evil potion must've still been affecting him slightly, because a frizzling bolt of murky power shot into the rafters, raining dust and cobwebs and splintered wood down on them all.

"Oho. It seems your poison is wearing off." Rodric thrust his metal hand toward Bryce. "Shall my next shot relieve you of your druid master?" He grinned, the smug bastard, and shook the dust out of his hair. "Faugh. The state of this Keep is a disgrace. When I take the throne, any servant who shirks his duty so will be treated to a turn in Govannan's forge."

"You're hallucinating," Mal growled. "You'll never be King."

"Who better? I've the bloodline, and now I have this." He thrust out his silver hand. "Absolute proof that I'm destined to rule—not just the paltry Seelie sphere, or only Faerie, but our true kingdom in the Outer World." He held up the adder stone. "When I toss this little beauty into the Well, I'll usher in a new order."

"The new order of what?" Bryce's head was clear enough to perceive the gaping hole in Rodric's logic. "You'll have nothing to rule over if you poison the water both here and in the Outer World."

Rodric sneered. "The Outer World must be cleansed of its corruption, of the unworthy, of everything not Tuath Dé. I care nothing for its current degenerate state."

"You should." Bryce swayed, and Mal steadied him with an arm around his waist. "Good God, man, Faerie is an artificial construct. It depends on analogs and anchors in the Outer World. If you destroy them, do you imagine there will be anything left?"

"You know nothing about Faerie, druid. A fortnight ago, you had no inkling it even existed."

Mal's warmth, his presence, his touch, was restoring Bryce's strength by the second. "I may not know Faerie, but I know ecosystems, and this one is seriously out of balance. It's at a tipping point, close to the limits of its ability to self-correct."

"Druid nonsense. All will be well."

"No, it won't. That spell—" Bryce pointed to the adder stone, "it's not evolution, not even *revolution*. It's total annihilation."

"Lies!"

Bryce shared an exasperated glance with Mal. "Why do villains always claim that anything inconvenient to them is a pack of lies? This guy belongs in Congress. The opponents of global warming would love him."

"Enough talking." Rodric backed away, his attention swinging from Mal and Bryce to the empty doorway where Eamon and the King had vanished. "I have an appointment with destiny. But, first, perhaps I'll do a bit of housecleaning myself."

He pointed one metal finger at Mal.

"No!" Bryce lunged in front of Mal, bracing for impact, but before Rodric could get off his shot, Alun surged out of the door to the kitchen passageway with a roar and barreled across the room, sword drawn. But then a small figure darted past him and whacked Rodric in the kneecap with a cudgel the size of a four by four.

Rodric bellowed, dropping the adder stone to clutch at his knee, and Heilyn clubbed him on the back, twice, sending him sprawling.

"Well, well, well." Mal strolled over to Rodric and planted his foot on the wrist with the weaponized hand. "I see you've found yourself a sidekick."

Alun planted his feet, glaring down at Rodric. "Heilyn's assistance was of course appreciated, but—"

"I wasn't talking to you, brother." Mal grinned at Heilyn. "Those wee arms are sturdier than they look."

Bryce rather thought the issue was "never underestimate the power of righteous anger," but when Heilyn scooped up the adder stone to offer it to him, he changed his opinion: *never underestimate the power of kindness.*

Unwilling to touch the adder stone with his bare hand again, Bryce stripped off half his bifurcated vest and used it to wrap the stone securely, stowing the bulky bundle in a pants pocket. He might not know what to do with the vile charm, but Cassie probably would. In any case, it would be out of Faerie and nowhere near his wetlands.

"Thank you, Heilyn." Bryce had to raise his voice to be heard over Rodric's curses and moans. "If it weren't for you, we'd have been screwed."

Heilyn tugged on its mossy forelock. "Always that is true—even if the task is preparing luncheon."

"Really?" Bryce cocked an eyebrow at Mal and Alun. "You high fae can't even make your own sandwiches? No wonder your fridge is full of takeout."

Mal shrugged, staggering slightly when Rodric struggled to free his hand. "What can I say, mate? We're creatures of engineered habit." He swore as Rodric bucked again. "Bryce, give me the other half of your vest so I can tie this arsehole up."

"Also . . ." Heilyn collected Bryce's vest and handed it to Mal, then retrieved its club and climbed atop Rodric's back. "We can become quite heavy when we choose."

"You dare," Rodric rasped as if all the air had been squeezed from his lungs, "you dare to raise a hand against your betters. You shall suffer, you and all your—"

"Oh stow it, Luchullain," Mal said as he secured Rodric's hands. "You've got nothing."

He grimaced. "Even now, my loyal guards are putting the bauchan whelps down like the vermin they are."

"Wrong again, Rodric." Alun nudged Rodric's side with his boot—although considering Rodric's grunt, it might have been more than a nudge. "Your loyal guards are . . . shall we say . . . indisposed?"

Mal snorted. "Is that what you're calling it to get around the letter of the Seelie-Unseelie treaty?"

"Terminology is irrelevant." Alun sheathed his sword. "The salient point is that they'll cause no further trouble to us—or to anyone."

"I don't know, brother. It's not like you to exceed your official authority." Mal's expression was troubled as he glanced down at Rodric. "As pathetic an excuse for a fae as Rodric is, he's still technically Seelie. But offing random Unseelie bravos? Not sure the Queen will back a rampaging Champion."

Alun hooked his thumbs in his belt, drumming his fingers on the leather. "I do not rampage. And besides—"

"Our Champion has our full confidence and support." The Queen appeared in the doorway, then glided across the floor as if it were the same grassy hilltop where they'd last seen her, with Eamon behind her, sword in hand, gripping the sullen King by one elbow.

Lovely. The party's complete. Although Bryce would have preferred to strike a few guests off the approved list.

Heilyn immediately hopped off Rodric's back and bowed low. With a glance at Alun, as if checking to make sure he'd take charge of Rodric, Mal strode forward to drop to his knees at the Queen's feet. "Majesty. I realize I should have stayed—"

"You may spare us your excuses, Lord Maldwyn."

At the drop in Bryce's belly—an echo of what Mal must be experiencing—his anger flared, banishing the last of his adder stone–induced nausea. "Just a goddamned minute." Mal shot him a panicked glance and gestured for him to kneel, but screw that. "Did you stop to consider that by imprisoning him like that, you put his life in danger? Rodric could have executed us both. It's not like we could run away."

The Queen regarded him coolly. "And yet you did."

Heat prickled under Bryce's skin. "No thanks to you. I get the whole feudal overlord motif here, but—"

"Peace, druid. There is no need for excuses because our decision has been . . . overtaken by events." She cast a sidelong glance at Eamon, and for just a moment, pink glowed under her moon-pale skin.

Okay, then. So much for a G-rated night for those two.

"You— The two of you?" The King's gaze bounced from Eamon to the Queen. "Impossible!"

"I told you I practiced no deception, Father. My curse is at an end."

"Whore!" Rodric shouted, staggering to his feet, still bound by the remnants of Bryce's vest. Alun clamped a hand on Rodric's shoulder, unsheathing his sword. "You spread your legs for an Unseelie swine but—"

"Enough, Luchullain." Eamon's deep voice rang in the room like the toll of a funeral bell. "I have had my fill of you and more."

Eamon waved his hand in Rodric's general direction, and the silver hand dropped off his wrist, ricocheting off the throne to land on the floor with a clang.

Gwydion's bollocks, what a turn-up. *Court protocol be damned. Nobody's paying attention to me.* Not with Rodric howling over the loss of his hand on one side and the King screeching at Eamon on the other. So Mal stood up and limped over to join Bryce.

Bryce's hair was rumpled and dimmed with dust, his glasses were askew, and he had a scrape along his jaw crusted with dried blood.

Yet he'd never looked more beautiful to Mal. "You all right, mate?"

Bryce smiled tiredly. "I'll be better once I get rid of the adder stone. The damned thing is screwing up the energy patterns in here like you wouldn't believe, not to mention making me want to puke."

"Well, it's druid magic. Doesn't mix well with Faerie." Mal peered around the room. "Where'd your fan club disappear to?"

"Heilyn? I don't know."

"To reunite with its young," Alun said absently, his attention on the King and Eamon. "They'd been separated for almost too long."

"Ah. Right." Mal studied the King, who was holding his crown on his head with both hands as if he were afraid it would fly off. "Does His hysterical Majesty look smaller to you?"

"Pay attention, brother. I think we're about to see something that hasn't happened since the dawn of Faerie: the succession of a new Unseelie King."

"No!" he shrieked. "*I* am King. *I* wear the crown."

"The crown is but a token." Eamon was as unruffled as usual. "Faerie confers its own honors, and you have failed in your covenant with your land, your people."

"You think to usurp the throne, but you can't. Not as long as I hold the Seat of Power."

"But you do not." Eamon reached into the recesses of his cloak and pulled something out. He unfurled his fist to display the little stone Bryce and Mal had recovered the first time they'd ventured into Faerie. "I do."

The King goggled at the rock. "It's a trick."

"Is it?"

"You haven't been in this room since I banished you. You've had no chance—"

Eamon merely smiled, which sent the King over the top. Still bawling curses at the top of his lungs, he staggered to the throne and fell to his knees, scrabbling underneath the seat.

Good luck with that, mate. You'll not find a bloody thing.

Hold on though—if the Seat of Power was so crucial to Unseelie sovereignty, would His paranoid Majesty have risked including it in a spell that could result in its loss?

Steve, you bloody bastard.

Mal stalked across the floor until he could look Eamon in the eyes—much less alarming now that said eyes were the blue of a midsummer day and not glowing like infernal coals. "The Seat of Power. That wasn't one of the tasks you needed to break your curse, was it?"

A slight smile curved Eamon's perfect lips. Mal hadn't missed the surreptitious glances the Queen kept stealing at him either—shite, he was handsomer than Rodric Luchullain could ever hope to be. "It was not."

"Damn it, man. I mean, Your Highness. You had no right to risk Bryce's life just to retrieve some random royal trinket. I may have entered into a bargain with you, but he never did."

"It was necessary."

"So you could stage a coup and overthrow your psycho father?" He jerked his thumb at Rodric, moaning on the floor, handless arm clutched to his chest and Alun looming over him like a well-muscled brick wall. "Not to mention his even more psycho minion?"

"Would you have preferred these two remained in power?"

"Are you mental? Of course not. But I'd have preferred not to have gone unarmed into an enemy court without a damn good reason either."

"The destination was unimportant."

"The hells you say."

"I do. The recovery of the Seat of Power was a bonus. If you had not recovered it in the allotted time, I could have found another way to depose my father. The task, the one you succeeded at far more brilliantly than I had hoped, was in the journey."

"Say what?"

The King stood and faced Eamon, his face a feral mask. "It's gone. You traitorous whoreson. You filthy—"

With a *zhing* of metal, the Queen stepped forward to lay her sword against the King's throat. "Say no words that make me regret not depriving you of your tongue."

Mal blinked and shared a dumbfounded glance with Bryce. "Did she just refer to herself as 'me'?"

"Yeah. Has she ever done that before?"

"No." Mal marveled at the heated glance she exchanged with Eamon. "Maybe this wasn't only politics after all. For the first time, I think she's made a choice just for herself."

CHAPTER ✽ 33

M al glanced between Eamon, who was regarding his father with somber eyes, and the tapestry behind the throne. The fellow standing under the One Tree looked a lot like Eamon. Had there been a family resemblance before the King had disintegrated into the death's-head mockery he was now? Or was this another magical verification of Eamon's right to rule?

"Father, by your actions, by your poor stewardship, and by your cruelty, you have forfeited the right to any mercy. Yet I would not begin my reign with patricide."

The King sneered. "You mean regicide." When the Queen's sword nicked his jaw, he stilled.

"And you, Rodric Luchullain, who aspired to a position far beyond that which your character warranted, do you think you deserve to live?"

"As much as you or that—" Rodric gaped, his remaining hand clutching his throat, his eyes bulging.

Eamon observed him coldly. "Since you are unable to speak civilly, speak not at all."

Rodric tried to lunge at Eamon, but Alun yanked him back.

Bryce turned to Mal, his eyes wide. "Did he just—"

Mal nodded. "Cursed the bugger. Handy fellow with a geas, our man, Steve."

"Does he borrow all his curses from the kindergarten playground?"

Eamon glanced at Bryce, his head tilted to one side. "An interesting notion, Sir Druid. Shall we borrow another?" He faced the King. "Since you consigned your own son to slavery in the underworld forges, you will now take his place. And you, Rodric Luchullain, who snatched at glory by clinging to the coattails of the more powerful, you will share his fate as you would have shared his favor. Indeed, the two of you are well-matched."

"Wait a moment." Bryce nodded at the now-mute Rodric. "You struck off his false hand. Can you give him a flesh and blood one in its place?"

"You refer to the terms Lord Maldwyn's curse, I take it."

"You're damn right I do. He did everything you asked, but it seems you aren't keeping your side of the deal."

"But if I grant Lord Luchullain his hand, how will Lord Maldwyn satisfy the terms of his curse? My promise was for the curse to be lifted—not that I would do it myself. As you well know, Sir Druid, curses are tricky things."

Bryce lifted a skeptical brow. "So, apparently, are Unseelie princes."

Eamon gazed somberly at Mal. "You do not have the authority to execute Lord Luchullain. However, now that I have the full authority of the Unseelie throne, I can grant you the power of Dian Cecht, of Creidhne, and of Miach."

Bryce turned a bewildered gaze on Mal. "Who?"

"The blokes who gave Nuada his silver hand, and the one who later made it flesh." Mal glowered at Eamon. "Was this your plan all along?"

Eamon inclined his head. "It is the best solution." He glanced at the Queen. "Do you agree, my lady?"

She studied first Mal and then Rodric. "It will serve. I commend you."

"Well I don't," Mal said. "You could have told me."

"It would have changed nothing. Do you wish for this? Miach's spell will transform the silver hand to flesh over nine days and nights. As his hand transforms, so will yours recover. The process," Eamon said drily, "will not be painless."

Mal shrugged. "Pain isn't an issue." Rodric whimpered. "Bring it on."

"You should consider this carefully, Lord Maldwyn." Eamon's deep voice echoed in the room. "When Lord Luchullain is again whole, the chances of him doing harm in future would be increased.

Would you take that risk, if it meant being restored to your former estate?"

Ah, shite. A catch worthy of a druid. Mal glanced down at his hand, joined with Bryce's. Considered their neighboring houses next to the wetlands in the Outer World. Swallowed hard at the memory of the connection he'd discovered—no, *reveled* in—with the familiar bond. "No."

"What?" Bryce released his hand and grabbed his shoulders instead. "This is what you've wanted from the first. How can you pass up the chance to do it now?"

Mal shook his head. "The blighter did enough damage with one hand. I can't take the risk."

"Mal—"

"He would have destroyed both our worlds. You want to reward him for that?"

"No, but—"

Mal faced the Queen. "What about you, Your Majesty? Are you inclined to grant your former Consort that much clemency?"

Her gaze, fixed on Rodric, was stony. "No."

"Well, then. The nays have it." He turned to Bryce. "This is what I am, love. What I will be forever. Can you live with a damaged familiar?"

Bryce grasped the back of his neck in a firm hold, and Mal's eyes closed. *This. So right.* "You aren't damaged. One-handed or not, you're perfect. And screw the familiar shit." He looked over Mal's shoulder to where Eamon waited. "If you can do that kind of big magic, can you reverse the familiar bond between druid and fae?"

"I can."

"Then do it."

Mal stomach plummeted. "Hold up. You want to be shed of me now? I thought—"

"Hey. I want to be with you. For us to be together. But I want it to be your choice, not some random act of genetic manipulation."

"My choice, eh? Then why are you deciding to sever the bond unilaterally?"

Bryce frowned. "I just assumed . . . I mean, you hated it so much."

"I didn't. I don't. This connection, this *belonging.* I've never had this with anyone before. Not even—" He cast an apologetic glance at Alun. "Not even with my brothers. If you want me, you've got me, mate."

"I—"

"Perhaps we could table this discussion also until after we've dispatched our villains." Eamon's tone was dry.

Heat rushed up Mal's chest, and judging from the red cresting Bryce's cheeks, he was feeling the pinch of embarrassment too. Shite, what was he thinking? Airing their private affairs in front of anyone, least of all the Queen and—Goddess help him—his *brother.*

"Right, then," Mal said. "Take it away, Your Majesties."

"Yes. That is the issue isn't it?" Eamon studied Mal and Bryce, his eyes narrowing. "Yes, I think it will do." He held out his hand. "My lady, if you would be so kind as to assist?"

"Certainly." The Queen laid her right hand on top of Eamon's left, her palm to the back of his hand. Together, they slowly curled their fingers, forming a double fist. "Now."

They jerked their arms back, and Mal felt a tug in his belly as the hook of Cassie's tether came loose. "What the bloody hells?"

"A druid tether, ready-made to hand. Most expedient." Eamon nodded at the Queen, and they gestured at Rodric and the King with their joined hands. "There. These two are bound together in their punishment as they were in their crimes." His hand sketched a loop between the two prisoners and the throne. "They will remain safely shackled to the throne until I can escort them to their new home in Govannan's forge."

"Do you need to do so personally, my lord?" the Queen murmured. "My champion would be pleased to escort them."

Alun saluted with his right hand on his chest and bowed. "It would be my honor."

"I thank you for the offer, but I have a brother to rescue, and wouldn't yield that duty to another."

Duty to a brother? That, Mal understood perfectly. Maybe he and Eamon were more alike than he knew.

While Eamon and the Queen made sheep's eyes at one another, Bryce decided he wouldn't hold Mal to his decision to retain their bond, regardless of what it did to his own heart. Today was full of drama and excitement and near-death experiences. Mal couldn't be thinking clearly, or surely he'd have jumped at the chance to sever their inconvenient accidental bond. Now that the two of them weren't forced to stay within ten feet of one another, Mal would be free again. *Should* be free. Free to resume his place in Faerie, his old duties, his old life.

But to be completely free, he needed to get rid of his fricking curse.

Bryce took a step closer to Eamon. "Excuse me . . . uh . . ." What was the accepted way to address fae royalty if you still weren't sure if the crown had been passed? Bryce settled for clearing his throat. "Could you have lifted Mal's curse yourself, without the new-silver-hand-regrowing-the-flesh mumbo jumbo?"

"No, I could not."

"Then it seems like you made the deal in bad faith—and you led him to believe you could *help* him."

"Bryce. It's all right, mate."

"No, it's not. You did everything he asked, even when it wasn't necessary for his curse or yours. He should have *told* you. And, speaking of that, what the hell did you mean about the journey being the task?"

A ghost of a smile flitted across Eamon's face. "Ah. I thought we might come back to that."

Bryce folded his arms. "Well?"

"The key to lifting a curse is always contained in its casting. Because my father believed me intractable and disloyal, my curse could only be lifted by three acts of unimaginable cooperation and trust."

"The dragon shifter scale," Mal murmured.

"Just so. A dragon trusts no one with his scales, sometimes not even himself. That he should cooperate so fully with another race as to relinquish one? That is magic indeed. Tell me, how did you manage that?"

Mal shrugged. "That was the easy one. My brother-in-law is friends with the dragon prince."

"Extraordinary. I knew I made the right choice. I nearly chose Lord Cynwrig at first." Alun straightened, his hand going to his sword hilt, and Eamon chuckled. "And that reaction is why I did not."

Of course. "Cooperation between races that have every reason to distrust one another, like fae and druid."

Eamon inclined his head. "As you say. Lord Maldwyn became the perfect choice after you and he became associated. While Lord Cynwrig has the full trust and . . . cooperation . . . of the last-known *achubydd*, his moral center would not have allowed him to negotiate for me in the last task."

"You make me sound like a bloody prig," Alun muttered.

"You are a bloody prig, brother. But you're getting better." Mal cleared his throat, eyebrows raised at the way Eamon and the Queen ducked their heads and peeped at each other from under their lashes. "I take it that the final act of cooperation—"

"Seelie and Unseelie, in the act of ultimate trust. While you gained me the opportunity, only Her Majesty could grant me success." Eamon reached out and took the Queen's hand. For all that the Queen was nearly as tall as Bryce, Eamon's hand dwarfed hers, his brown skin contrasting beautifully with hers, like a yin-yang handclasp. Not that that would be a concept for such relentlessly Celtic sensibilities. "Dare I ask, or am I too forward, that you would allow me to woo you in earnest?" He pressed a kiss to the back of her hand.

"As far as we—as far as *I* am concerned, the wooing occurred in the night." She turned his hand over and kissed the center of his palm.

Immediately, wind swirled through the room, like a miniature cyclone with the two of them at its eye, setting tapestries twisting and detritus flying. Bryce inhaled a lungful of dust and had to release Mal to cough as the wind died.

"Holy shite," Mal whispered. And grabbed Bryce's shoulders. With *both* hands.

CHAPTER ❈ 34

If he hadn't been holding on to Bryce's shoulders, Mal would have fallen on his arse as his link to the One Tree surged into him, the rush nearly buckling his knees.

A grin dawned on Bryce's face. "Your curse. It's gone?"

"Yes. But how—" He smacked his forehead with his palm—his right palm, Goddess be praised. "'Make whole what you cost us this night'—those were the words. But it wasn't Rodric I had to make whole. It was you."

"Not me precisely," the Queen said, her hand still in Eamon's. "But the aspect of me that is Faerie. It relies on balance, and without a helpmeet, the balance cannot be maintained. Although *that* one," she cast a disdainful glance at Rodric, "was a most unsatisfactory Consort. The realm suffered before you and your brother exposed his treachery, and it suffered afterward. It suffers still. I trust that this union will provide a new hope for both Seelie and Unseelie."

"My lady, I am loathe to leave you, but I must convey these two to the forge."

"I will come with you. It is too long since I've greeted Govannan, and if we ask of him this favor, it is only polite to do so in person."

Mal chuckled. "Fine talk, Your Majesty. You just want to see Rodric sweat, don't you?"

A small sly smile tilted her mouth, and Mal realized it was the first he'd ever seen. A miracle indeed.

Alun pulled the King and Rodric to their feet. "Mal. We'll talk later."

"Your threats don't frighten me anymore, brother. Talk we shall."

Alun herded the prisoners out of the throne room, the Queen and Eamon—although he should probably start referring to him as the King—pacing behind in stately procession.

"Gwydion's bollocks," he muttered. "Must be a right pain to be royal."

Bryce moved up next to him. "Why's that?"

"Because you have to be so bloody proper all the time. You'd never be able to do this."

Mal turned and grabbed Bryce's head, launching into a kiss that curled his toes inside his boots and raised his cock to half-mast. Bryce growled into Mal's mouth, his hands cupping Mal's ass as his tongue dove halfway down Mal's throat.

Goddess, yes. I want this. All of it, and more.

Bryce backed him up until Mal's arse hit the edge of the refectory table, his boots crunching in broken porcelain. Then Bryce pulled away, and Mal whimpered. "Come back."

"Much as I'd like to, I'm pretty sure we shouldn't hump each other in the Unseelie throne room."

"Got a better idea?"

"We could go home. I know we're not attached at the hip anymore—"

"No, mate. We're attached at the heart."

Bryce's eyebrows climbed up his forehead. "Mal Kendrick, that is the sappiest thing I have ever heard in my life."

Mal grinned. "Don't care. It's true. Far as I'm concerned, the tether we forged together, that we chose?" He gestured between their chests and then laid his hand over Bryce's heart. "This one is permanent and stronger than anything the elder gods in their infinite busybody wisdom could cook up."

"But the biological imperative . . ."

"You know, funny thing about that. Check this out." Mal drew on the One Tree and nipped the bond as neatly as Bryce with his pruners.

Bryce's eyes flew wide. "Oh." He rubbed his chest. "It's gone."

"Yeah. Cassie was all about 'till death do you part,' but I figure the elder gods never imagined a druid would catch a high fae in his familiar net. My full powers are near equal to yours."

"Balance," Bryce murmured.

"Yeah. So I can neutralize the bond if I want. Thing is . . ." Mal rescinded his command, and the delicious certainty, the trust that Bryce could take him, keep him safe, let him rest, was back. "I *don't* want. I mean, who gives a shite what other people think? If this works for us, it's a bloody miracle. Question is, do *you* choose? I'm a right handful, or so I've been told."

Bryce's eyes turned black, and Mal shivered. "You are. But that's what I love about you. Nothing worthwhile is ever easy."

A tiny noise like a kitten coughing snapped their attention to the side. Heilyn was standing there, a glass bottle stoppered with brass in its paws. It bowed, and where once there had been three bloody divots, now miniature versions of the bauchan nestled, peeping at them with wide golden eyes.

"Your back," Bryce said. "I thought you'd been tortured."

"So I was, separated from my little ones, when they need me to rest and grow."

"Faerie." He lifted an eyebrow at Mal. "Remarkable. A whole new ecosystem."

"Shall I bar the doors, masters?"

Bryce laid a hand on Heilyn's shoulder, much to the interest of the young. "We're not your masters."

"I choose too. Masters." It offered the bottle to Bryce and scuttled out the door to the kitchen.

"Well, mate, your fan club just grew by three. What did the little bugger give you?"

Bryce opened the bottle and sniffed. He tipped a little of the contents into the palm of his hand, then dipped his finger and thumb into it. He started to laugh.

"What's the joke?"

"It's oil. About a quart of it." He sniffed the puddle in his palm, and his eyebrows rose. "Scented."

Mal grinned. "In Faerie, we call that lube, mate. Now . . ." Mal dropped to his knees to finally use both hands on the fly of Bryce's tactical pants. *Let me show you a few tactics of my own.* "What do you say we start using it up?"

Explore more of the *Fae Out of Water* series:
www.riptidepublishing.com/titles/series/fae-out-water

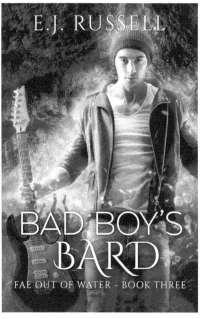

Dear Reader,

Thank you for reading E.J. Russell's *The Druid Next Door*!

We know your time is precious and you have many, many entertainment options, so it means a lot that you've chosen to spend your time reading. We really hope you enjoyed it.

We'd be honored if you'd consider posting a review—good or bad—on sites like **Amazon, Barnes & Noble, Kobo, Goodreads, Twitter, Facebook, Tumblr,** and your blog or website. We'd also be honored if you told your friends and family about this book. Word of mouth is a book's lifeblood!

For more information on upcoming releases, author interviews, blog tours, contests, giveaways, and more, please sign up for our weekly, spam-free newsletter and visit us around the web:

Newsletter: tinyurl.com/RiptideSignup
Twitter: twitter.com/RiptideBooks
Facebook: facebook.com/RiptidePublishing
Goodreads: tinyurl.com/RiptideOnGoodreads
Tumblr: riptidepublishing.tumblr.com

Thank you so much for Reading the Rainbow!

RiptidePublishing.com

ACKNOWLEDGMENTS

Thank you, thank you, thank you to my awesome editor, Rachel Haimowitz. I couldn't have asked for a better partner on this journey.

As ever, my undying gratitude to the wonderful team at Riptide Publishing: Sarah Lyons, Amelia Vaughn, L.C. Chase, Alex Whitehall, May Peterson, Kelly Miller, and Kelly Hidlebaugh (among others). Thank you, Lou Harper, for the fabulous cover art—you're amazing (and incredibly patient)!

And naturally, thank you to the family—Jim, Hana, Ross, and Nick—who don't mind (much) when I vanish into the writing zone. Love you all.

ALSO BY E.J. RUSSELL

Fae Out of Water
Cutie and the Beast
Bad Boy's Bard (coming soon)

Legend Tripping
Stumptown Spirits
Wolf's Clothing

Geeklandia
The Boyfriend Algorithm
Clickbait

For a Good Time, Call . . . with Anne Tenino (a *Bluewater Bay* story)
Shadow Painter

Sun, Moon, and Stars (in *Magic and Mayhem: Fiction and Essays Celebrating LGBTQA Romance*)

ABOUT THE
AUTHOR

E.J. Russell holds a BA and an MFA in theater, so naturally she's spent the last three decades as a financial manager, database designer, and business intelligence consultant. Several years ago, she realized Darling Sons A and B would be heading off to college soon and she'd no longer need to spend half her waking hours ferrying them to dance class.

What to do with all that free time?

A lucky encounter with Jim Butcher's craft blog posts caused her to revisit her childhood dream of writing fiction, and now she wonders why she ever thought an empty nest meant leisure.

Her daily commute consists of walking from one side of her office to the other, from left-brain day job to right-brain writer's cave, where she's learned to type with a dog attached to her hip and a cat draped across her wrists.

E.J. is married to Curmudgeonly Husband, a man who cares even less about sports than she does. Luckily, C.H. also loves to cook, or all three of their children (Lovely Daughter and Darling Sons A and B) would have survived on nothing but Cheerios, beef jerky, and satsuma mandarins (the extent of E.J.'s culinary skill set).

E.J. lives in rural Oregon, enjoys visits from her wonderful adult children, and indulges in good books, red wine, and the occasional hyperbole.

Sign up for E.J.'s newsletter at ejrussell.com/newsletter or find her online at ejrussell.com, on Twitter at twitter.com/ej_russell, and Facebook at facebook.com/E.J.Russell.author.

Enjoy more stories like
The Druid Next Door
at RiptidePublishing.com!

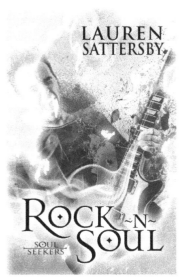 

Rock N Soul
ISBN: 978-1-62649-311-7

Half
ISBN: 978-1-62649-520-3

Earn Bonus Bucks!

Earn 1 Bonus Buck for each dollar you spend. Find out how at
RiptidePublishing.com/news/bonus-bucks.

Win Free Ebooks for a Year!

Pre-order coming soon titles directly through our site and you'll
receive one entry into a drawing for a chance to win free books for
a year! Get the details at RiptidePublishing.com/contests.

CPSIA information can be obtained
at www.ICGtesting.com
Printed in the USA
LVHW052121150921
697893LV00008B/1270